"Rosenberg's talent is amply displayed here as she gives us a sweaty-palm story of evil and betrayal—and a sharp-eyed look at the gritty world of Southern Californian law enforcement. It's guaranteed to keep you turning pages all night long."
   —Jeffery Deaver

"Authentic . . . the author's ability to generate narrative drive holds readers. A dark, perilous, and compelling ride."
   —*Booklist*

"*Sullivan's Justice* is a heart-thumping, pulse-pounding thriller filled with vivid, original players and a plot that grabs hold and sweeps the reader along until the last, breathless twist."
   —Judith Kelman

"Superb . . . plenty of action, the storyline is fast-paced, and readers have a good time wondering who the killer might be. The heroine is a valiant warrior in the fight against crime."
   —*The Midwest Book Review*

"Confidently plotted . . . Thriller enthusiasts will relish the intricate plot, accelerating action and novel climax of this gripping ride."
   —*Publishers Weekly*

"Rosenberg's personal experience in law enforcement brings a chilling reality to this page turner . . . Begins with an eerie leave-the-lights on murder and ends with a high-speed chase. In between are breathtaking action and non-stop suspense."
   —Sandra Brown

Conflict of Interest

"Rosenberg's legal thrillers make the most of breakneck pacing and high-energy plotting."
  —*Booklist*

"Rosenberg, author of six best-selling legal thrillers . . . writes with fast-paced energy."
  —*Library Journal*

"Frighteningly real."
  —*Los Angeles Times*

Buried Evidence

"Nancy Taylor Rosenberg is back with a vengeance, and *Buried Evidence* is the best evidence that she's at the top of her game!"
  —Lisa Scottoline

"Watch your pulse and don't forget to breathe. Nancy Taylor Rosenberg's legal thrillers are a guaranteed adrenaline rush!"
  —Tess Gerritsen

"The plot presents a compelling moral dilemma, the action is fast-paced and the pages turn easily."
  —*Publishers Weekly*

Trial by Fire

"Incredibly fast paced and exciting from page one until the end."
  —James Patterson

"A legal thriller with the works."
  – Nelson DeMille

"Draws us not only into a suspenseful plot, but also into issues of American crime and law, justice, and revenge."
  —*Cleveland Plain Dealer*

Interest of Justice

"Intricate, vivid, thrilling . . . one of the year's ten best."
— *Los Angeles Times*

"A taut thriller, written with authority."
— *New York Times Book Review*

"Arresting and fast-paced."
— *San Francisco Chronicle*

"Moves at the speed of light and keeps readers frantically turning the pages—a thriller with the undeniable air of authenticity."
— *Orlando Sentinel*

Mitigating Circumstances

"A highly entertaining legal thriller. . . . Unflinching . . . compulsively readable, intricate suspense . . . Rosenberg's overwhelming portrait of the incendiary, universal emotions of vengeance and guilt definitely touch a raw nerve."
— *Publishers Weekly*

"A compelling insider's view of the criminal-justice system and a moving portrait of a woman bent on revenge."
— *Library Journal*

"Adrenaline-pumped . . . No woman has ever had a stronger motive for vengeance than Lily Forrester."
— *New York Times Book Review*

"Intricate and satisfying . . . Rosenberg develops a startling premise skillfully . . . [her] familiarity with the police and courts gives the story a strong veneer of reality."
— *Los Angeles Times*

Also by Nancy Taylor Rosenberg

Mitigating Circumstances

Interest of Justice

First Offense

Trial by Fire

California Angel

Abuse of Power

Buried Evidence

Conflict of Interest

Sullivan's Law

Sullivan's Justice

Nancy Taylor Rosenberg

PINNACLE BOOKS
Kensington Publishing Corp.
http://www.kensingtonbooks.com

To Forrest Blake, without you, this book wouldn't have been possible.
In tribute to my beautiful mother, Ethel Laverne Taylor, and my latest grandchild, Elle Laverne Taylor.

Chapter 1

Thursday, December 23—12:30 P.M.

Death was waiting, crouched inside the garage of Suzanne Porter's beautiful home.

Her shoes slapped against the wet pavement only a few blocks away. The sky had been overcast when she'd left on her daily run. Now it was raining and she was soaked. Because her hair was layered, its thick strands stuck to her face and annoyed her. The only way to tame it was to wear a baseball cap. She didn't like to wear hats, though, as they gave her headaches.

Trivial things couldn't upset her today. She loved Ventura when it rained. Crossing to the other side of the street, she glanced through an opening between the houses and caught a glimpse of the Pacific Ocean snaking its way along the shoreline, the whitecaps churning. The surfers must be in heaven, she thought, seeing their heads bobbing in the water as they waited to catch the next wave.

The town had grown around the historic San Buenaventura Mission, founded in 1782. Suzanne was delighted with her husband's hometown, framed on one side by the sea and the other by the mountains. She felt certain they would spend the rest of their lives here. Her parents were dead and she had become very fond of Ted's mother and father. In addition, they had a wide circle of friends, some who had known Ted since childhood.

She was filled with anticipation. Several months back, she'd decided on the perfect Christmas gift for her husband. Actually, it was a combined birthday and Christmas gift, but she was too excited to wait two weeks to give it to him. Her husband restored cars as a way to relax from the stress of his job. Once a car was finished, it could take months to find a buyer. He was always eager to start on another project, but he couldn't, due to lack of space. Three weeks ago, she had secretly sold off some of the stock she'd owned prior to their marriage and hired a contractor to expand their garage so it would hold four cars. She would show him the plans on Christmas Day. Ted would love it.

She had spent the last week preparing for the holiday. This was Suzanne's year to have the family over and she wanted everything to be just right. Her sister-in-law, Janice, was a gourmet cook. Rather than take a chance, she'd arranged to have the meal catered by La Orange, one of the best restaurants in Ventura. She'd threatened to tell Ted's mother that he looked at pictures of naked girls on the Internet if Ted told anyone. So what if she was a lousy cook? She could make salads and spaghetti. Most of the time they ate out.

Before she married, Suzanne had been a bond trader on Wall Street. When, at age twenty-eight, she started seeing her hair turn gray, she knew it was time to shop for a husband. Ted had been in New York on a business trip. He brokered for Merrill Lynch.

During the holidays, Suzanne always lost her willpower and would eat everything in sight. The night before, she'd wolfed down half a box of Godiva chocolates. Since she'd turned thirty-five the month before, she knew her indulgence would show up on her thighs. Her daily workout consisted of lifting weights for an hour in her home gym, followed by a two-mile run. That morning, she'd forced herself to step on the dreaded scale. She'd expected three pounds, maybe four tops. How could she have gained eight pounds in two months? All her clothes were a size six. She decided to extend her run.

Crossing the street again, she picked up the pace. By the time she reached her house, she was exhausted. She'd only added one mile. A few years ago, she could run ten miles and hardly break a sweat. She leaned over and clasped her knees, then started up the sidewalk. The rain had eased up, but the weather report had predicted another front would move in by evening. She missed snow. Suzanne had grown up in Connecticut. She remembered the snowball fights in their front yard on Christmas Day, ice-skating on Whitman Lake, and sledding down Black Canyon with her brothers. Sure, the constantly sunny skies were nice, but when the average temperature ranged in the seventies, she sometimes forgot what month it was. And it didn't seem like Christmas without snow. At least the rain provided some atmosphere. She laughed, thinking she should throw white sheets on the lawn and turn up the air conditioner.

Seeing her neighbor's nineteen-year-old son pull into the driveway, she walked over to speak to him. Rap music blasted through the windows of his black Mustang. His mother had bought it for him on the condition that he only drove his motorcycle on the weekends. Franny was afraid he was going to get killed.

Suzanne waited until he turned off the car's ignition, then approached him. "Is Franny home from work yet? I'm planning a surprise birthday party for my husband and I wanted to invite your parents."

"You have a phone, don't you?" Eric Rittermier said, getting out of the car and slamming the door. He was a tall, brooding young man with pale skin and dark eyes. He had two diamond stud earrings in his left nostril, a blue knit cap pulled down low over his forehead, and he wore a stained gray sweatshirt with low-slung baggy jeans.

She took several steps backward, watching as he disappeared inside the house. Maybe Ted was right about having children. She could certainly live without trying to parent some arrogant, moody teen. Babies were adorable, but they didn't remain that way. You never knew if they were going to become criminals or geniuses.

When she retrieved her mail from the box at the curb, several items fell to the ground. The market was in a slump. That's the way it was in the stock market, feast or famine. Everyone got used to living the high life. They might obsess about their finances, yet they seldom changed their spending habits. If you started cutting back, you felt like a failure. In this profession, confidence was essential.

Reaching her front porch, she bent over and removed her key from underneath the mat. Ted had cautioned her to set the alarm and stop leaving her key where someone could find it. Old habits died hard, though, and she kept forgetting. She'd only been gone a short time. Their former house hadn't had an alarm. The type of security system they had now made it impossible to open a window without setting off the alarm. Every window and door in the house had to be locked before she could arm the system. She refused to be a prisoner in her own home.

When she unlocked the door, she was greeted by her tan basset hound, Freddy. His excitement was underwhelming but cute as he tried to jump, his legs not strong enough to support his body. He ran toward the door leading into the garage, barking.

"What's wrong, Freddy?" Suzanne said, clapping her hands. "Let's go upstairs, boy. Mommy's smelly. She's got to get pretty for Daddy."

She walked over and adjusted one of the animated ornaments on the Christmas tree—a miniature soldier beating a drum. Inhaling the delightful scent of pine, she mentally went through her shopping list, confirming that she didn't have any last-minute gifts to purchase.

She wished they had a view of the ocean instead of the

foothills, but she couldn't complain. The money they'd saved had gone into improvements, like her luxuriously appointed cherry closet and the two-story library where she spent most afternoons, reading and sipping tea with Freddy curled up at her feet. Even her ulcer had finally healed.

Suzanne removed her shorts and T-shirt and draped them over the laundry basket to dry, then stepped onto the cold bathroom floor. Grabbing a plush blue towel with flowers embroidered on the borders, she tossed it over the shower enclosure before she entered. The warm water cascaded over her body, the heat causing the clear glass to fog. Tonight they were going out to dinner with Ted's best friend and his new wife. She hadn't decided what she was going to wear yet, and she wanted to blow-dry her naturally curly hair.

She dried off and opened the shower door. She heard Freddy barking again. Throwing on her robe, she headed downstairs and found him scratching at the door leading to the garage. When she opened it, she heard a noise near Ted's latest project. Under a car cover was a Jaguar XKE. Did they have mice again?

She shrieked when someone came out of nowhere and grabbed her from behind. A forearm pressed against her throat. Struggling, she threw an elbow back in an attempt to get away.

"Calm down or I'll kill you."

Suzanne craned her head around, seeing a towering figure wearing a black motorcycle helmet with a mirrored eye shield. A gun was pressed against her left cheek. The assailant had her in a choke hold, clasping her left arm firmly through his leather gloves. Her heart pumped like a rabbit.

She prayed it was the boy next door. "Eric?"

The intruder remained silent.

It couldn't be Eric, she decided. His voice was different. She couldn't be certain, though, as the person was outfitted with leather clothing.

"Don't kill me," she pleaded, tears pouring out of her

eyes. "I have almost a hundred dollars in my purse. Take it . . . take anything you want. I won't call the police. I swear."

"You think I'm a thief?" he said, pressing his arm even harder against her throat.

Suzanne gasped for breath. The intruder dropped his arm and spun her around. She felt his eyes wash over her. He was going to kill her. She remembered the family that was killed not long ago. The killer was so brutal, he'd murdered a six-month-old baby. The newspaper said he'd also decapitated his own mother. A stream of warm urine ran down her legs.

Looking down at the puddle on the floor, she saw Freddy whimpering at her feet. The intruder kicked him through the open garage door, then closed and locked it. She remembered a self-defense tactic and locked her fingers on his arm, then dropped her body weight to the ground to break his grip. His arm felt like steel. He looked down at her and laughed.

Suzanne's teeth were chattering. She bit the inside of her mouth, tasting the salty blood. "Help me!" she screamed, hoping someone would hear her. "Call the police!"

The assailant used the end of the gun, moving her robe aside in order to expose her naked body. Her stomach muscles twitched as she recoiled in terror. "Take me to your bedroom," he said.

Suzanne climbed the stairs, the gun pressing against her back. Why hadn't she set the alarm? When they reached the master bedroom, her eyes went to the phone on the end table. She had to stall him, find a way to call 911.

"Put on your bra and panties."

He must be a sadistic pervert who got turned on seeing women in their underwear. Maybe that was all he wanted. She yanked open a bureau drawer and pulled out a white push-up bra, snapping it in the front, then turning it around so she could shake her breasts into it. Next she found a pair of lacy T-back panties and quickly stepped into them.

The assailant was standing perfectly still. The gun fell to

his side. She could see his chest rising and falling. She didn't care if he raped her, as long as he didn't kill her. Her mother had taught her to imagine the worst thing that could happen, and then everything else would seem insignificant. She wiped her eyes with her hand, then straightened her back. She had to be strong. He might be one of those men who couldn't get an erection unless the woman was submissive. He couldn't rape her without an erection. If he didn't get what he wanted, though, he might kill her. She made the decision. She'd take an aggressive stance and pray he would back down.

"Why don't you take off your clothes?" she asked, trying to sound seductive. "Then we can party. I bet you're a better lover than my husband." She forced a smile. Rotten bastard, she thought. You're going to burn in hell. "My husband loves pretty underwear, too. I have drawers full of this kind of stuff. I can model it for you if you want." She grabbed a handful and tossed it in his face, then threw herself in the direction of the phone.

The intruder was too fast. She felt him on her back as she slammed face-first onto the floor. "Stupid woman," he snarled, grabbing a handful of her hair and pulling hard until her face was visible. "You should have never opened the door to the garage."

"Jesus, help me!" Suzanne cried, seeing him pull a plastic-wrapped syringe out of his leather jacket. "What are you going to do to me? Oh, God . . . please . . . my husband can get you big money, thousands. . . . Let me go and I'll call him. He can be here in fifteen minutes."

The assailant placed the gun in the waistband of his pants, then used the toe of his boot to roll her onto her back. Bending down, he clasped both of her hands and dragged her to the bathroom. Her fear was so great, her entire body stiffened. Propping her up near the toilet, he grabbed her left arm and then slapped his gloved hand against her forearm.

"I'll do anything," Suzanne pleaded. "I'll suck you off . . . anything." She felt a stick and a stinging sensation.

She saw her husband's face, smiling at her on their wedding day. Then she spun further back in time. She was with her mother at the park down the street from their house. She was swinging. The sky was beautiful, filled with puffy white clouds. She wanted to swing high enough to touch it. The tree beside her was full of birds. Their chirps sounded like a secret language. Her mother was sitting on a bench across from her, wearing a white sundress. The wind whipped through her glossy dark hair and exposed the delicate skin on her neck. The next thing she knew, she had flown off the swing and landed in the dirt, her right arm bent backward. She heard her mother's voice . . . soft and comforting, *"You'll be fine, honey. Be a big girl now and stop crying. After Dr. Lewis fixes your arm, I'll take you for an ice cream."*

Suzanne looked down and saw the needle slide out of her vein, wondering why it didn't hurt. There was a trickle of blood, but her mother dabbed it with cotton. Warmth spread throughout her body. She felt as if she were floating in a sea of pleasure, so intense that she couldn't bear it. Her vision blurred. Her head rolled to one side. Everything was beautiful and peaceful. She wanted to stay in this place forever. Her mother was holding her, stroking her.

Her stomach suddenly rose in her throat. She was choking on her vomit when she felt someone push her head down into the toilet. Her skin felt as if it were on fire. *"It's just the flu, sweetheart,"* her mother's voice said. *"Once your stomach settles down, I'll give you some aspirin for the fever."*

Everything would be fine, Suzanne thought, the warm, comforting sensation washing over her again. She could go to sleep now. Her mother would take care of her.

Chapter 2

Carolyn Sullivan pulled her white Infiniti into an open parking slot at the government center complex, reaching into the backseat for her umbrella and briefcase. It was one of those days. It rained fifteen minutes, then stopped, then a few hours later, started again. Wearing a white shirt, with her trademark silver cuff links, which had been in her family for over a hundred years, a black velvet vest secured around her waist with a patent leather belt, and a black skirt that grazed her knees, she stepped out into a puddle of water. "So much for the shoes," she said, glad they were inexpensive.

A few yards away, she saw a tall, slender man dressed in a dark-colored parka coming from the back area of the jail where they released prisoners. Because his hood was up, she couldn't see his face. When he started walking briskly toward her, she worried he might be someone she'd handled who was bent on revenge. She quickly glanced over her shoulder to see if there was someone behind her. The man raised his head slightly and ran toward her.

Slamming back against the car, Carolyn dropped her briefcase as she reached into her purse for her gun. Before she could get it out, the man seized her by the shoulders. "Damn you, Neil," she shouted at her brother, shoving him in the chest. "What in God's name are you doing? I almost shot you."

The megawatt smile appeared and Carolyn's anger instantly disappeared. "I came to see you," he said. "And this is the treatment I get? Why are you so jumpy?"

Neil was a handsome, successful artist. At six-two, he had dark hair and expressive green eyes, a lanky frame, and strong but classic features. "I'm not jumpy," Carolyn said, retrieving her briefcase. "I work with criminals, in case you've forgotten. You never know when one's going to come after you. I have to be alert. Most of them hate me."

"How could anyone hate you?" he said, draping an arm over her shoulder, then taking the umbrella from her so they could share it. "They've probably got the hots for you, sis. You're a good-looking woman, even if you are past your prime."

Carolyn stomped on his toe, causing him to yelp. "That was a joke, I hope."

"Jesus," he said, walking beside her as she headed toward the building. "Of course it was a joke. First you try to shoot me; then you try to cripple me. Where are we going, by the way? I'm starving. Don't they have a cafeteria or something in this place? I'll buy you breakfast."

She stopped and stared at him. He generally worked all night and slept all day. He hadn't shaved, so she assumed he hadn't been to bed yet. "Is something wrong?"

"Sort of," Neil said. "Nothing major. I mean, I don't have a disease or anything. I wouldn't mind selling a few paintings, but that's not what I came to talk about."

"Where's the new toy?"

He laughed. "The Ferrari? Didn't I tell you? The woman's husband sued me. The car's been locked up in a warehouse for the past month. Her old man was having an affair with a younger woman, so she traded it for spite. The guy screwed himself because he put the car in his wife's name. Just because she traded it for four of my paintings didn't mean it wasn't legal. I was hoping they'd take the car back and give me the cash, but they released it to me yesterday. I didn't want to drive it in the rain. I'm still getting used to the way it handles."

They ducked inside the building and Carolyn folded up her umbrella. "Look, Neil," she said, touching his arm, "I love you, but I don't have time to have breakfast. Traffic was terrible this morning and I'm running late. Can you call me tonight after the kids are in bed?"

"Please, Carolyn," he said, turning serious. "I have to do something about Melody."

People were streaming past them. Carolyn pulled him into a corner. "We talked about this the other day, Neil. I hate to say it, but you created this mess. You should have stopped seeing Melody when you got back together with Laurel."

"I know. I know." He pushed the hood back on his parka and ran his hands through his thick black hair. "I'm in a bind here. I'm in love with Laurel. I've been wild about her since we were in high school. She finally divorced her husband. I'm meeting her for lunch today. I might ask her to marry me. Should I tell Melody the truth or make up some kind of story?"

"Here's the deal," Carolyn said. "Listen closely because I need you to help me. Call John and Rebecca. They should be at the house no later than four. Tell Rebecca you're going to stop by and look at her drawings. You promised to help her if I enrolled her in art school. Since John got his driver's license, he isn't around as much. I should be home by eight. We can talk then."

"I'm always taking care of your kids," he complained. "Can't you give me a few seconds of your time? I drove all the way down here."

"Not now, honey," Carolyn said. "Brad called me at six o'clock this morning. Veronica went into labor last night and I have to finish one of her reports. It's a big case, Neil, that multiple murder, the one where the whole family was killed, including three small children. You must have heard about it."

Neil was brooding. "I don't watch the news."

"Okay, listen," she said, placing her palm in the center of his chest. "I promise I'll call you after my meeting." She looked at her watch, knowing she had to end their conversation. "I'm supposed to be at the jail interviewing the defendant right now. Are you going straight home? Have you slept yet?"

"I'm not planning to go back to bed, if that's what you mean."

Carolyn stood on her tiptoes and kissed him on the cheek. "You could make this decision by yourself, you know. In reality, you probably should."

His eyes were red with exhaustion. "You're my big sister. I never make a decision without you. I'm not a murderer or anything, but this is important. Don't you care? I'm about to ask someone to marry me. Laurel will be a part of our family. All I need is for you to help me figure out how to handle the situation with Melody. What time will you be through with your interview?"

"Before noon," Carolyn told him. "Go home, give this more thought; then when we talk, you'll have a better handle on everything. Once I hear the whole story, I'll give you my opinion. The sooner you let me do my job, the sooner we can talk."

She waited until he walked off, then hurried off toward the entrance to the men's jail.

Punching open the doors, Carolyn stepped up to a glass window. Her shoulder-length dark hair was pushed behind her left ear. The other side swung forward onto her cheek when she moved. Wearing a belt that accentuated her small waistline, she wasn't as thin as one of her brother's models, but she was also the mother of two teenagers. Most people thought she looked younger than her thirty-eight years.

The Ventura County government center complex was similar to a small city. The courts, district attorney's and public defender's offices, as well as the records division, were all housed on the left side of a large, open space. A bubbling fountain stood in the center, surrounded by concrete benches. To the right was the Correction Services Agency, the formal name for the probation department, as well as the sheriff's department, and the women's and men's jails. The general public assumed that the two structures were not connected, yet an underground tunnel was used to transport inmates back and forth to the courthouse.

The jail was actually a pretrial detention facility, and as a result of housing over one thousand inmates with a rated capacity of 412, the fairly new facility had an infrastructure of a thirty-year-old building. Ten years ago, the county had erected another detention center, which was called the Todd Road Jail, and was located in the city of Santa Paula. Todd Road was designed to hold over 750 sentenced male inmates. Only the minor or repeat offenders served their time in jail. Serious offenders were sentenced to prison.

On the other side of the window, a dark-haired deputy named Joe Powell looked shocked when he read the prisoner's name on the inmate visitation request sheet. "You can't see Raphael Moreno. He's in solitary. Only two more days and we get rid of this piece of shit."

Moreno had decapitated his disabled mother and murdered his twelve-year-old sister. Leaving their bodies in the house, he'd gone on a killing spree.

His next victims were a family of five. The father had been a thirty-one-year-old real estate agent. The mother had been a stay-at-home mom who cared for the couple's three children. Moreno had entered through a rear window just after dark, lying in wait inside a closet in the baby's room.

When the mother came in to put the six-month-old boy to bed, Moreno had gunned down her and the child, then shot and killed the father and the couple's other two children. The Ventura police had found all five bodies lined up military-style in the living room.

The case had perplexed the authorities. Nothing was

taken from the residence, and Moreno had as yet to provide them with a motive for the killings.

"I have to see him," Carolyn said into the microphone. "And I have to see him immediately, Joe."

"Listen," he told her, "all you investigators wait until the last minute to finish your work. The captain says we don't have to take it anymore. Besides, there's no way you can interview Moreno in a room. He's one of the most dangerous inmates we've ever had." He turned to a powerfully built black sergeant with a shiny shaved head. "Tell her what our pal Raphael did last night. She wants to play patty-cake with him."

"He tried to kill three inmates," Bobby Kirsh said, leaning over Powell's shoulder. "This is a mean son of a bitch. I know one when I see one. I've been on the job for twenty years. A little over a hundred and thirty pounds and he took down all three in a matter of minutes. No way you gonna get a face-to-face." He turned away, then tossed something into the bin. "Take a look at what he did before you end up like this guy."

She picked up the photograph, horrified at what she saw—the bloodied face of a black man with his left eye missing from the socket. "What happened to his eye?"

"Moreno snatched it out. Since we didn't find it, we assume he ate it."

Maybe Bobby was right and Moreno was too dangerous. Collecting herself, she mustered up a stoic look, determined not to back down.

The sergeant continued his litany, "We found the second guy with a shattered hand stuffed in his ass, his dislocated shoulder dangling like a dishrag." He grimaced. "I don't even want to tell you what he did to the third guy."

"Put him in a room, Bobby," Carolyn said, scared but challenged. She wanted to break Moreno, now more than ever. "You know our reports are mandated by law. You also know how I work. Moreno has never cracked. He didn't say more than two words to his public defender. The DA negotiated a sentence of seven consecutive counts of second-degree murder. No death penalty. No life without parole. Moreno's only twenty years old. He might live another sixty years and kill dozens of people." She decided to try a personal appeal. "If he'd killed your family, wouldn't you want to know what makes him tick?"

"Not this one," the older officer said. "When Moreno first came in, we placed bets on how long he'd last. I was sure the prisoners would turn him into dog meat within twenty-four hours. Jesus, he sliced off his mother's head and shot a six-month-old baby. Every cop in the county, on the street or inside, would blowtorch Moreno and call it a barbecue if they thought they could get away with it. Even my wife offered to take him out."

"I understand," Carolyn said. "That's just talk, Bobby. Right now, I'm the only one who can do anything."

"The three inmates he tangled with last night are bigger than me. You're good, Carolyn, but you're not going to get inside this maniac's head."

The longer she stood there, the less chance she had of getting the information she needed. The only people who seemed to appreciate the role investigative probation officers played in the criminal justice system were judges. Probation officers did most of their work for them. They pulled the case together from arrest to conviction. Then they applied the laws as directed by the judicial counsel in San Francisco.

Probation officers spent sleepless nights trying to decide what sentence should be administered. When the sentencing judge picked up the case file in the courtroom, his eyes swept over the probation officer who had handled it. Fifty years in prison, sure, no problem. The judge was only following the probation officer's recommendation. No blood on his hands.

"Our reports are reviewed at every parole hearing," Carolyn

reminded the sergeant. "You want this guy back on the street? Put him in a room and I'll destroy him. He'll never taste freedom again."

She heard the buzzer for the door and stepped inside. "How long?" she asked, storing her gun in a locker.

"Give me ten," Bobby said to the other deputy.

"Can't you set him up faster?"

"Are you nuts, woman?" he told her. "I'm talking about ten men." He stared at her briefcase. "What's in there? Open it up."

Carolyn's frustrations escalated. "I don't have to submit to a search. You saw me lock up my weapon." Scowling, she opened the brown leather satchel. "A yellow pad and three file folders. Satisfied?"

Sergeant Kirsh reached into one of the compartments, pulling out a pair of panty hose, then dangling them in front of her face. "Good thing I looked, just for your sake. I thought you were smart, Carolyn," he said. "Moreno could strangle you with these things." He dropped them into her hand. "Put them in a locker or toss them. You're not taking them in with you."

"Thanks, Bobby," she said, depositing the hose in the trash can. "I didn't know I had them. I keep an extra set of nylons in case I get a run."

The sergeant put his meaty hands on his hips, tilting his head to one side. "Sure you still want a face-to-face?"

Carolyn let her eyes answer for her.

Twenty minutes later, Carolyn sat two feet away from a sadistic killer in an eight-by-eight room. Her palms were sweating and her mind was racing. She turned sideways in her seat and read through the incident report from the night before, wanting to give him a chance to get used to her. A pungent scent drifted past her nostrils. She assumed it was his body odor. Masking her true feelings, she kept her expression pleasant and nonjudgmental.

Raphael Moreno sat perfectly still, his head held high, his back straight. Fifteen minutes passed as Carolyn studied him out of the corner of her eye. He might be small, but his body was well developed. His arms were laced with sinewy muscles, the kind you saw on farmworkers. His features were somewhat refined, almost handsome. He looked more like a native of South America than Mexico, possibly Argentina or Colombia. His skin was brown and thick. In several places, it appeared either badly chafed or discolored. He may have gotten the best of three inmates in last night's fight, but he hadn't walked away without injuries. His kidneys had been bruised and he had suffered a concussion. She suspected the three inmates had attempted to sodomize him. They had picked the wrong man. All three had been seriously injured.

Although she was finished reading the report, Carolyn continued as if she were still preoccupied. It wasn't time yet to make eye contact. This was something he would have to earn. And the only way he could score points in the dangerous game she was about to play was to start talking.

Entering into a negotiated disposition must have been a difficult decision for the DA's office, Carolyn thought. All things considered, she would have probably done the same. A diminutive twenty-year-old defendant who had never spoken and was depicted as mentally deficient by his attorney had the potential to generate sympathy in the eyes of the jury. Allowing him to plead guilty to seven counts of second-degree murder had saved the taxpayers a fortune. Even if they'd taken him to trial on first-degree murder charges, getting a conviction would have been difficult. They would have to prove premeditation and explosions of violence; even crimes as heinous as these were hard to portray as carefully planned acts. Other evidence could also surface during the trial. If the DA had taken him to trial and the case had ended in acquittal, Moreno could never be prosecuted again. Even prisoners who couldn't read or write knew what double jeopardy meant.

The DA had additional factors to consider. By refusing to testify or cooperate with his public defender, Moreno would have been declared incompetent to stand trial. When the state shrinks finally cleared him, the law still allowed him to plead not guilty by reason of insanity. The only period of consideration was the time and day the crimes occurred. It was a conundrum. As nonsensical as it sounded, a person had to be sane in order to stand before the court and plead insanity.

Carolyn began to tap her heels on the yellowed linoleum flooring. The direction of his eyes shifted slightly, but he didn't move. With some criminals she could flirt and extract information no one had ever heard. Moreno was not one of them. If she hit the right nerve, he would talk. A study had shown that most violent male criminals had high levels of testosterone that produced uncontrollable sexual desires and murderous levels of anger. This had to be the case with Moreno. Except for the three men from the night before, she knew everyone had approached him in a cautious manner. To get him to talk, she was going to make him mad, cause him to lose control, then pray he didn't kill her. She'd successfully used this tactic with rapists and pedophiles, even ones who had killed their victims. If she could go up against scum like that, she could handle Moreno.

Removing her cell phone from the pocket of her skirt, she called Neil. "I'm sorry I couldn't talk this morning," she said. "Did you get your breakfast?"

"What are you doing?"

"Sitting across from an ugly deaf guy."

Neil gasped, "The man who killed all those people? Should you be talking on the phone? Aren't you afraid he'll hurt you?"

"He's in chains." Carolyn tossed her head back and laughed. "Besides, this guy couldn't find his way out of a paper bag, let alone hurt anyone. He's just a punk-ass kid. They say he's twenty, but he looks fifteen. He's a pretty boy, you know. He was sucking dicks for a living, then went nuts and started killing people. Did I tell you he sliced off his mother's head? He'll be dead twenty-four hours after he hits the joint. Cons hate creeps who kill kids."

Moreno wasn't deaf, Carolyn decided. She could tell when someone was listening. Not only had he blinked several times, one corner of his mouth was curled in contempt. She knew it wasn't a natural expression as the muscles had started to twitch. If he'd defended himself against three larger males in order not to be raped, her comments about him being a male prostitute must be making him furious. He couldn't sit there like a statue forever, and pride was a big thing with Hispanic males. It was one thing to tune out the attorneys, doctors, or other inmates. Having an attractive woman ignore him had to be an insult to his masculinity. And she was ridiculing him to his face. If they'd been on the street, Carolyn was certain he would have either beaten her or killed her.

"You're doing something stupid, aren't you?" Neil said, not accustomed to hearing his sister use such crude language. "Please don't tell me you're baiting a killer? I don't want to be on the phone when some lunatic goes after my sister."

Carolyn said, "When nothing else works, you've got to use your mouth."

Neil rambled on about his problems. Twenty-nine minutes passed. One of the jailers' faces appeared in the window. When Carolyn put her thumb up, he disappeared. Seeing a vein bulge in Moreno's neck, she bent over and pretended she was rummaging in her briefcase so she could peek under the table and verify he was still safely restrained. His hands were tiny, she thought, almost smaller than her own. Satisfied everything was okay, she saw an old package of gum in the side pocket of her briefcase and removed a stick.

She placed it on her tongue, then let it linger before she pulled it into her mouth. Moreno licked his lips. In jail, even a piece of gum was a coveted item. Unlike prison, the jail didn't have a commissary. Unless a relative or friend supplied him, a prisoner had nothing other than what was issued to him when he was booked.

"Look, hon," she said, "I'm going to call you later like I said. I just had some time to kill and wanted to hear your voice. Have you been thinking about—"

The phone suddenly popped out of Carolyn's hands. Moreno had used his feet to lift her chair several inches off the ground. Grabbing onto the edges of the seat to keep from toppling over, she looked for the phone but didn't see it. When she heard a crunching sound, she spun around, but by then, a tangled mess of metal and plastic was lying on the floor and Moreno was sitting exactly as he was before.

His hands and feet were shackled, Carolyn thought, ready to bolt from the room. No one could move that fast, and it would take tremendous strength to crush a cell phone. Carolyn reached over to hit the button to call for help.

No, she thought, pulling her hand back. She refused to give him the satisfaction. "Up against the wall!" she yelled, standing and kicking the table out of the way. "Do it now! Put your palms up where I can see them."

Blood dripped onto his orange jumpsuit. A flap of skin had been torn off on one side of his hand, near his right thumb. Carolyn assumed it was from the handcuffs. His hint of a smile told her he was pleased with himself. Her eyes narrowed in anger. "I'll talk to anyone I want whenever I want, shithead," she snarled at him.

Moreno looked up and smiled. He brushed up against her as he turned to the wall. He smelled clean, like Ivory soap or laundry detergent. The odor she had noticed when she'd first entered the room hadn't been Moreno. The scent that had repelled her earlier had been her own fear. Had Moreno sensed it?

She jerked her head around. He had whispered something in her ear, but his voice had been too low to hear. In an awkward and dangerous way, they had broken the barrier and made a connection.

Having heard the commotion, a blond-haired young jailer flung open the door, his baton out of its sheath. Another deputy was right behind him.

"Get out!" Carolyn shouted, her voice booming out into the quadrant. Seeing the distress on the officers' faces, she said calmly, "I'm in charge here. Everything is fine. The prisoner and I are having a discussion. I accidentally knocked the table over. Leave us alone now, please."

"But he's bleeding," the blond deputy said, pointing to the spots of blood on Moreno's jumpsuit. "What happened? Are you okay? Sergeant Kirsh . . ."

"Tell Bobby not to worry," she said, placing a hand on the man's shoulder to nudge him out of the room. "If I need help, I'll let you know."

The man shook his head and then retreated, locking the door behind him. Moreno was standing against the wall. Carolyn kicked her open briefcase toward him. "Now get on your hands and knees and pick up my damn phone before I make you eat every last piece of it," she said. "Put the pieces in there."

She knew the risk she was taking, but she couldn't turn tail and run. The situation had turned into a battle of wills. If she allowed him to get the best of her, word would get out inside the jail. The next time she came inside to interview an offender, she might be challenged again. The prisoners called her "the Angel of Death." Over the years, she had become something of a folk hero. The rumor was the pretty probation officer came to see you and a week or so later you disappeared. The men were too stupid to realize that the inmates she visited were scheduled to be sentenced, and the only thing that happened to them was they were shipped off to prison.

Moreno scooped up the broken cell phone and dumped the debris in her briefcase. Carolyn picked it up and placed it by the door.

She slid the plastic chair in front of him and righted the table. "Now we're going to sit down and talk like two civilized people. If you don't talk, I'm going to charge you with assaulting a police officer and drag your ass back in court. Then I'm going to tell the judge that you're not deaf, insane, or retarded. They'll revoke your plea agreement and retry you. This time, you'll receive the death penalty."

"You can't throw that shit at me, ho," Moreno said, the voice that no one had heard finally surfacing.

His voice was low and he slurred his words. Carolyn heard a slight Spanish accent. "Your life is a pretty big thing to gamble with, Raphael," she told him, softening her tactics now that he was talking. "All I'm asking you to do is to answer a few questions."

"It's over, man." He smirked. "Where you been? DA too chicken to try and get me killed. They can't change my deal. I ain't no idiot. A deal's a deal."

"Why did you murder those people?" Carolyn asked, thinking round two had gone to Moreno. He was smart. He had called her bluff accurately. Once a plea agreement had been negotiated and accepted, it could not be overturned. No matter what she learned, he could not be sentenced to more time in prison or put to death. "An explanation could go a long way when your case comes up for parole."

"At least I ain't fuckin' my brother," Moreno said, smiling. *"Te bato, que de aquella ramfla traes."*

Carolyn knew what he'd said—that she had a nice car. How did he know what her car looked like?

"I thought some homey was gonna jump you this mornin' in the parkin' lot. Then I seen you rubbin' up against him. Get down and suck my dick, ho. If you suck your brother off, you can suck me. Do that and I tell you anything you want to know."

The color drained from Carolyn's face. How had he known about Neil? His eyes were locked on her and she couldn't look away. His lids were hooded, and his pupils were dark and murky, as if she were staring into a frozen pool of dirty water.

Hold the line, she told herself, pressing her back against the chair. He must have heard the other side of the conversation, then somehow put it together. There were no windows in solitary. Then she remembered that he'd spent the night in the infirmary, which had windows overlooking the parking lot, as did at least 50 percent of the cells. Whoever had designed the complex had never given thought to the safety of the people who worked there. Ever since they had moved from the old courthouse on Poli Street, Carolyn had been expecting something to happen. Now the most vile criminal she had ever met knew what kind of car she drove, and could share that information with his friends on the street or other inmates, both in jail and in prison. Had he memorized her license plate as well? Of course he had. His alertness and attention to detail were remarkable. She would have to get a new plate as soon as possible. He knew her, though, and would find her even if she came to work in a different car. Scores of violent offenders were serving lengthy prison sentences as a result of her investigations and recommendations. Everyone eventually got out. She'd only handled one offender who had been executed.

Her safety and that of her family had been compromised.

If Moreno managed to escape or the jail released him by mistake, which had occurred on numerous occasions, he would come after her. What else had he learned from her call to Neil? She'd once had a probationer who'd trained himself to recognize numbers through the tones in the phone.

Carolyn had finally met a criminal who truly frightened her.

"Shit, man," Moreno said, "everyone wants me dead. Instead, I'm gonna be taking a nap on the state's dime. What's that about, huh?"

This wasn't the kind of comment you'd expect from a man who'd gone crazy and went on a killing spree, Carolyn thought. Was he playing with her, or did he mean it?

"Cops scared of me," he continued, his chains rattling under the table. "Cons scared of me. Everybody 'fraid. Next thing you know, they'll put one of those masks on me like that guy in the movie who ate people."

"Let's talk about the people you murdered," she said. "I'm a probation officer. I'm here to prepare a report for the court."

She exhaled as understanding struck her. Had Moreno slaughtered the Hartfield family to make certain he ended up in prison? She forced herself to detach emotionally and analyze the case with the cool eye of a mathematician.

Raphael Moreno may have traded certain death on the streets in exchange for the sanitized death he might meet after years on death row. Unless a killer was mentally deficient, which Moreno was assuredly not, he would have made some attempt to avoid apprehension. According to the arresting officer, Moreno had locked himself inside the trunk of Darren Hartfield's white Cadillac CTS parked inside the closed garage. An officer found him when he heard him kicking the trunk lid. By the time the other units arrived for backup, Moreno was cuffed and sitting quietly in the backseat of a squad car. The frenzy of violence had occurred only thirty minutes prior to his capture.

"Who are you running from?" Carolyn asked him, forging ahead on her hunch.

His jaw locked in anger. She watched as he contemplated whether to respond to her statement, or simply clam up again. He closed his eyes, but she could see them moving beneath his lids as if he were reading or watching a tennis match.

"Do I look like I'm fuckin' runnin' from someone?"

Carolyn jumped. Moreno's voice seemed several octaves deeper. Her fascination evaporated and her fear intensified.

Something didn't add up. Killers generally followed a pattern, particularly when it came to weapons and manner of death. The pathologist believed the mother had been decapitated with a scalpel, although they had failed to locate it on the property or on Moreno's person at the time he was apprehended.

After murdering his mother, he had bound and gagged his sister, then later returned to crush her skull with a hammer. They believed the sister had been murdered the same day as the Hartfield family, who were killed execution-style with an AR-15 assault rifle on November 18. This weapon, too, had never been located. Rarely did they see a killer use such a diverse set of weapons and modes of death. At the onset of the investigation, the police had assumed there was more than one killer. Outside of the Hartfield family's, the only fingerprints located inside both premises were Moreno's.

Several psychologists had analyzed the facts of the case. Their conclusion was that Moreno's mind had disintegrated after years of caring for his disabled mother and sister. After killing his own family, he had vented his rage at another family, who seemed to be living the American dream. Carolyn was certain they were wrong.

She couldn't begin dictating the interview portion of the report until she forced Moreno to reveal himself. To achieve her goal, she would have to leave and return later.

The one thing a person like Raphael Moreno couldn't stand was being controlled. She hoped what she was about to do next would enrage him. Getting a prisoner to talk was her greatest skill. Moreno had talked, even led her in a new direction, but he had failed to tell her anything about the murders. A question was circling in her mind, one that demanded an answer. She knew the police had agonized over the same thing. The difference was Moreno now knew he had nothing to lose. Carolyn just might walk away with a full confession.

Standing, she pushed the buzzer to be released. She didn't

speak, nor did she look at Moreno. When the door opened, she saw a sea of uniformed officers. Glancing back at Moreno, she saw the look of shock register on his face. He couldn't understand why she was walking out on him. He opened his mouth, then closed it.

"Were there problems?" Bobby Kirsh asked as she strolled into the corridor.

"Raphael and I got along just fine," Carolyn lied, seeing the prisoner straining to hear what she was saying. "Really, Bobby," she continued, "I don't know why everyone's making such a fuss."

"Reynolds told me Moreno had some spots of blood on his clothes," he said. "Were they already there, or did something happen?"

"I think he scraped his wrists on the cuffs," Carolyn said, then recalled that Moreno had an untreated bullet wound on his shoulder when he was arrested. The police had tried to find out who had shot him, but had gotten nowhere. With street thugs, scars from gunshots were like freckles. "It's nothing to be concerned about. I remember seeing him scratching his shoulder wound."

Bobby gave her a suspicious look, but he didn't say anything.

Once they made their way to the locker area, Carolyn faced him. "Leave him in the room. No matter what he does, don't move him. I'll come back after lunch. If anything happens, call me. If I'm not at my desk, tell them to page me."

"Did he talk?" he asked, curious.

"Yes," she answered, removing her gun from the locker and placing it in her purse.

"What did he say? Why did he kill those people? Is he a psycho? Did he talk about what happened last night? Most of the population is scared to death of him." He paused, waiting until Joe Powell turned away. "They're freaked, man. Things like this don't happen. Yeah, guys get jumped every now and then. Not like they do in prison, of course. I mean, the majority of our inmates are serving time for minor offenses . . . tickets, thefts, burglaries, nonpayment of child support. The captain thinks the three men who almost got wiped tried to jump Moreno. The men swear he came after them."

"I'm strapped for time," Carolyn explained. "Moreno didn't talk about the murders, but I think I have a lead on some information. That's more progress than anyone else has made. Let me do my job, Bobby, and I'll let you do yours. As soon as I find out something, you'll be the first to know." She closed her briefcase with a clank.

Bobby gestured toward her bag. "Don't you think you'd be safer if you carried your gun in a place where you could get your hands on it? Most of the people in your department wear shoulder holsters. I know you're going to law school and all. You won't make a very good lawyer if you're dead."

Carolyn gave him a chastising look. "A little melodramatic, don't you think?"

"You're good people, okay?" Bobby said defensively. "Just trying to keep you from getting hurt."

"I normally wear my gun," she told him. "I appreciate your concern. Taking my panty hose in there would have been a mistake." She started to leave, then turned back. "As a precaution, post some of your people outside the interview room. I assume he's as safe in there as where you had him earlier."

"Well," he said, shrugging, "we're not a maximum-security prison. The glass is reinforced and the bars behind it are steel. I guess it won't do any harm to let him stew. He's safely contained."

"Don't let this guy con you," Carolyn said in a hushed voice, wondering if Moreno had stashed some of the metal pieces of the cell phone. Once she was through with him, she'd have him strip-searched. "He may bloody himself up or something to trick you into opening the door. Instruct your men not to go in there under any circumstances or they'll be risking their lives. No food, no water, no bathroom. I don't care what the rules say. Think you can find some officers willing to go the distance?"

"Yeah," he said. "Sounds like you're scared of this one, Carolyn. I told you not to do a face-to-face. Shit, even I wouldn't let someone lock me in there alone with Moreno."

"I haven't finished what I set out to do, Bobby," she told him, her face set with resolve. "I'll try to get back around noon. I might be afraid of him, but I'm not going to give up. Moreno may not be the only killer. He could have an accomplice who's still out there. The Hartfield family was killed with an AR-fifteen assault rifle. When he decapitated his mother, he used a scalpel and he smashed in his sister's head with a hammer. I don't think he would kill with a gun. He has sensitive ears. He wouldn't like the noise."

Bobby gave her a disbelieving look. "And you're going to get him to tell you who his accomplice was?"

Carolyn smiled. "Don't I always?"

Chapter 3

Carolyn was sitting in a chair in her supervisor's office. She was behind on all her reports and Brad Preston knew it. "Veronica wasn't due for another seven weeks," she said, tapping her heels. She stared at Preston with weary brown eyes. Like many single parents, she struggled through each day in a constant state of exhaustion.

How could a man be beautiful and ruggedly masculine at the same time? Carolyn thought. Brad had it all. His blond hair was fashionably cut. He used some type of gel to make the front stand up, making him look like a college student. His skin was burnished by the sun. Unlike other men who indulged in outdoor activities, he had hardly any lines in his face. Her eyes feasted on the muscles straining against his crisp white shirt. She forced herself to look away. She should have transferred out of the unit when Brad became supervisor. Now she had to work with a former lover.

Until someone new had come into Carolyn's life, her past involvement with Brad hadn't been a problem. Her relationship with Paul Leighton, a physics professor and neighbor, had shaken Brad's enormous ego. He pursued her relentlessly. When sending her cards and flowers failed, Brad had switched tactics.

Carolyn was already handling almost twice as many cases as the other investigators in her unit. The only one who came even close to her was Veronica Campbell. The woman had three kids at home and was about to deliver the fourth. She referred to her last child as a goof, so the new baby became a double goof. If she made it to a triple goof, Veronica had jokingly told her a few days ago, duckwalking down the hall to her office, she would fake a nervous breakdown so her husband would get stuck with the kids.

Brad had just told her the Moreno report was due the next day and she was livid. "Investigating a case like this takes weeks."

"Hey," Preston said, tossing his feet on top of his desk, "I'm just the messenger. Wilson specifically wanted you to handle it. The hearing is at ten o'clock in division twenty-four."

"This is insane!" she shouted. "Do you know what tomorrow is?"

"Christmas Eve," he said. "Unless there's a problem, you can take off as soon as it's over. The rest of us are working until five. We haven't been this slammed in years. I had to tell three people to cancel their vacations."

"Get the DA to ask for a continuance," Carolyn argued. "Raphael Moreno decapitated his own mother. How can I possibly submit a report on seven counts of homicide in twenty-four hours? I have to be in court in thirty minutes on Brubaker."

"They've already continued the case three times. Judge O'Brien said the sentencing is set and there's no way in hell he's going to delay it. The jail wants Moreno shipped to prison. The DA's office is under fire because they pleaded the case out and eliminated the death penalty. The victims' families are demanding justice." He paused and flashed a smile, light reflecting off his straight white teeth. "Stop whining and get the job done. You don't have to recommend a prison sentence. It's already been negotiated in the settlement agreement. What's the big deal, for Christ's sake?"

Carolyn walked over and slammed the door to his office. She didn't want Brad's assistant, Rachel Mitchell, to eavesdrop on their conversation. "You're doing this to me intentionally. At first, I didn't mind your games. This time, you've gone too far. Keep pushing me like this and I'm going to file a complaint."

Brad laughed, taking his feet down and placing his palms on top of his desk. "You think I'm scared of you," he said, his blue eyes dancing with mischief. "I may be deputy chief by this time next year. Wilson is considering you as my replacement, but he'll be relying heavily on my recommendation."

"You're being cruel, Brad," Carolyn told him, perspiration dampening the back of her neck.

"I heard you dropped out of law school. Is that true?"

"I didn't drop out for good. I just took a semester off."

"The type of work we do is specific," Brad said, turning his attention back to the matter at hand. "What would you do if you lost this job? I guess you could find some low-level position at the DA's office. I hear they're looking for help at the women's jail."

Carolyn's jaw locked. She took a deep breath and forced herself to relax. She started to tell him that she'd managed to get Moreno to talk, then decided to forget it. Later, she might have something worthwhile to tell him. "Do you have Veronica's file?"

He tapped a thick folder on the edge of his desk, waiting until she walked over. When she turned around, she felt his hand on her buttocks. As of that moment, Carolyn knew she had a legitimate case of sexual harassment. She didn't have time to think about it, though. Her skin was hot, almost as if she'd come down with a fever. Brad knew her. She might complain, but she would never let a less experienced officer handle crimes this serious.

"I'll need a progress report every hour. I'm sending Rogers

to represent you on the Brubaker matter." Brad's phone rang and he answered it, gesturing to Carolyn to wait until he was finished.

"Yeah," he said, "we're taking care of Moreno." Cupping his hand over the phone, he whispered to Carolyn, "It's a girl. The kid was born an hour ago. Six pounds, three ounces."

"Is that Drew?" Carolyn asked, assuming he was speaking to Veronica's husband.

"No," Brad told her, "it's Veronica. She's high as a kite. Maybe that's why she keeps popping out a baby every nine months. She likes the drugs." He hung up and thumbed through some paperwork on his desk.

"Rogers can't represent me with only an hour's notice. Brubaker mowed down eleven people," Carolyn said. "It took us three years to get a conviction."

"Vehicular manslaughter is a long way from murdering an entire family," Brad said, making a paper airplane and sailing it over her head. "You beat me up or I would have never allowed you to recommend a prison sentence for Brubaker. Everyone knows it was an accident. The DA waited so long to file because they thought the old fart would croak and they wouldn't have to deal with it. The city was responsible. There were no official road signs at the street market."

"After he hit the first person, he made no attempt to stop," Carolyn said, shaking her head in disagreement. A strand of hair ended up near her nose and she blew it off. "I talked to Brubaker on four different occasions. He looks like a sweet old man, but he's not. He was terrified of losing his license. What he did falls clearly under the guidelines for vehicular homicide."

Brad sighed, then said loudly, "The guy panicked and stepped on the gas instead of the brake. I'm sick of this case. You've got Moreno. Stop wasting my time."

"Brubaker was negligent," Carolyn said, refusing to weaken. "Eighty-five-year-old people shouldn't drive. I don't care who the signs belonged to, you'd have to be insane to drive through a crowd of people like that without stopping. Bodies were bouncing off his car like basketballs."

"Write a letter to your congressman. Brubaker had a current license issued by the state of California. He generally didn't go out on Wednesdays because that's the day his housekeeper comes and he enjoys her company. He wasn't aware he couldn't use the street. It's open every day except Wednesdays when they have the market." Brad stood and picked up his jacket off the back of his chair. "I'm late to a meeting. You got your ten-year prison sentence. I feel sorry for the guy. Old age is the ultimate humiliation."

Brad slipped his arms into his expensive Italian jacket, then adjusted his tie. Behind his desk were framed photographs of him standing in front of high-powered race cars. Racing was supposed to be his hobby. Carolyn thought it was more than that. He worked to occupy himself between races. His father had left him some money, and Brad had invested it wisely, earning ample funds to pursue his outside interests. A nonstop bundle of energy, he was able to handle twice as much work as the normal individual. Even with the demands of the job, his cars, his women, and his partying, Brad was always looking for something new and exciting. Carolyn recalled the nights she'd spent in his bed. When their bodies had connected, she felt as if she'd plugged herself into a wall outlet.

"How do I look?" he said. "Is my tie crooked?"

Out of habit, Carolyn walked over and redid the knot. She caught a whiff of his aftershave as she looked into his eyes and gathered his tie in her hands. "Continue Brubaker or I'll strangle you."

"Yeah, yeah," Brad told her. "I already did. The hearing is set for January fifth at three o'clock." As Carolyn proceeded to fix his tie, he added, "As for Moreno, I'll get all the trial transcripts and pertinent evidence moved to your office. If you think it's necessary, we'll send it home with you. That way, you can work without interruption until the report is ready to be dictated. The most vital thing was the interview with the defendant and you've already got that in the bag. I thought Veronica had already contacted the victims' relatives. From what she just told me, she didn't get a chance to speak to the mother's sister."

She snapped, "Why weren't you straight with me about Brubaker?"

"Ah," Brad said, smiling again. "Then I wouldn't have been able to enjoy our scintillating conversation. You look great in that suit. New, huh?"

"You're an asshole," Carolyn said, storming out of his office.

Carolyn sat at her desk with her head in her hands. She was so far behind, she would never catch up. The only way a probation officer could stay on top was to forge ahead each day. It was similar to climbing a ladder inside of a house with no ceiling. Every day, new cases were dumped in her basket. Brad Preston sat in his office and assigned them with the speed and efficiency of a Las Vegas dealer.

A clerk appeared in her doorway, pushing a dolly loaded with boxes. "Is that all?" she asked, telling him to stack them in the corner.

"Are you kidding?" the young man said, letting the dolly hit the floor with a thud. "I've got two more loads of this stuff. Preston said if I ran out of room, I could stash the rest in Veronica Campbell's office. I just picked up the same boxes from her yesterday. I've only been working here six weeks," he continued, straining as he lifted the boxes off the dolly. "Is this some kind of a test?"

Veronica worked in the partitioned space next to Carolyn. She'd have to call her friend at the hospital and get the password to her computer so she could retrieve the rest of the work she'd done on the case.

Carolyn's phone rang. She heard the gravelly voice of Detective Hank Sawyer.

"Homicide is throwing a last-minute Christmas party tonight," he said. "Wondered if you wanted to join us?"

"I can't, Hank," Carolyn said. "I caught Moreno this morning. The sentencing hearing is tomorrow."

"You've got to be shitting me."

"No," she said. "I'll probably need to speak to you this afternoon or later this evening. If you go to the party, be sure you don't drink." Before he bit her head off, she added, "This has nothing to do with your history. I would have said the same thing to someone else." Sawyer was a recovering alcoholic and could be touchy about it.

He paused before speaking and she could sense his irritation. "How could that prick, Preston, have dumped Moreno on you? We've been pressured from the beginning because the DA cut him a deal. The guy has only been in custody since November eighteenth. Anyway, I thought Veronica Campbell was handling it."

"She's not handling it now," Carolyn said. "I've got to get going on this thing, Hank. Just make sure you're available if I need to ask you some questions."

"Listen to me!" he shouted. "Moreno attacked three inmates last night. Don't go over there and put on your usual routine. You could get hurt, understand?"

"I've already spoken to him," Carolyn said, searching in her desk for some Tylenol. It wasn't noon yet and her head was already pounding. Veronica swore it was Carolyn's eating habits. She never ate breakfast, and when she was busy, she frequently skipped lunch.

"He talked?"

"Yeah," she said, giving up and shutting her drawer. "I'm sweating him for a few hours, then I'm going back. If my instincts are right, there's more going on than meets the eye. He's nasty, but I'm almost certain he's not crazy. Just the opposite. I think he's smart, really smart."

"You're amazing," the detective said. "I don't know why in the hell you want to stay with the probation department. Come over here and I'll make you a detective." He coughed, then added, "I'm warning you, Carolyn, don't push your luck with this guy."

"I'll do anything in my power to make certain he spends the rest of his life in prison," Carolyn said. "Risking our lives is what we get paid for, in case you've forgotten. Sometimes it's the only way to get the job done."

"We make only a few dollars more than the sanitation workers," Hank argued. "No one cares if you get your head blown off, or some psycho like Moreno cracks your neck like a twig. It isn't worth it, understand?"

"Aren't you the guy who jumped off the top of a moving car onto the back of a junkie with a shotgun?"

"That was different."

"Sure it was," Carolyn said, recalling at least fifteen other instances when Sawyer had done something with a million-to-one chance of succeeding. Even today, being a woman in law enforcement wasn't easy. Most of the younger officers treated women like equals. Old-timers like Hank Sawyer would never come around. All she was to him was a little girl with a dangerous weapon. And it wasn't necessarily a gun.

"Enjoy the party," she said. "Some of us have to work around here."

Chapter 4

Neil Sullivan's home was on top of a hill overlooking the ocean. He unlocked the glove box in his Ferrari and removed a small white envelope. Pulling down the visor, he slipped out the makeup mirror and placed it on the center console. He separated the crystal meth into two thin lines, using the razor blade he kept in the ashtray. Bending down with a rolled-up hundred-dollar bill in his hand, he snorted the white powder up his nostrils. Better, he thought, leaning back in the seat.

He started to put the envelope back in the glove box when he noticed it was empty. How could it be gone? He'd just bought it yesterday. No, he thought, it must have been the day before. Then he remembered that he'd been driving his van, so he knew it had to have been Wednesday. He hadn't picked up the Ferrari until after dinner. Someone had found his stash, maybe the valet at the restaurant he and Laurel had gone to last night.

He didn't use on a regular basis, only when things went wrong. Something had gone terribly wrong today.

Images flashed in his mind. He remembered storming out of the house. Everything before that was muddled and frightening. No one had stolen his stash, he realized. This wasn't the first time he'd snorted today. The ritual was so familiar, he sometimes used it twice without realizing it. He had to stop, but he couldn't stop now. Now was never a good time to give up something you needed.

When he backed out of his driveway, transparent sheets of rain splashed against his windshield. Reaching over, he turned the wipers on high. He hoped the storm would pass soon. The drugs made him jittery, and he had a miserable hour-and-a-half drive ahead of him. He had to see Melody. He couldn't be alone. He was flying far too high. That's why he'd snorted twice in one day. He didn't want to go down that far again. Not today, not tomorrow, not ever.

His eyes filled with tears. He'd planned everything perfectly. He and Laurel had had a lovely dinner at his favorite French restaurant, Le Dome; then he'd surprised her with the Ferrari. They'd been so happy together. Then came today's lunch, and it all changed.

He removed the two-carat diamond engagement ring from his pocket. Raising his hand to throw it out the window, he thought about how much he could get for it at the pawnshop. It wasn't the money, it was the credit. Al's Pawnshop was his drug connection. Not only that, it was on the way to Melody's.

So much for "happily ever after," he thought bitterly, placing the ring back in his pocket. Nothing ever worked out for him. Just when he got a taste of happiness, it was ripped away. God hated him. Everyone hated him. His paintings weren't selling. Laurel was supposed to make everything right. Instead, she made everything wrong.

Neil downshifted as he navigated the winding road. He'd traded four of his best paintings for the red Ferrari. He hadn't sold a painting in six months. His agent, Mark Orlando, had talked him into the deal, telling him that he could always sell the car later if business didn't pick up. He swore only one 550 Barchetta Pininfarina Speciale had been manufactured. According to Mark, the woman who'd made the trade was a fool.

Suffering from a midlife crisis, Lou Rainey had been having an affair with a twenty-three-year-old girl. His wife had caught him and thrown him out a few days after he took possession of the four-hundred-thousand-dollar car. To spite him, Mrs. Rainey got drunk and impulsively traded the car while attending one of Neil's shows. Mark had told him the Ferrari was too valuable to drive all the time. Who wanted a car you couldn't drive?

Beautiful machine, Neil thought, hearing the powerful engine engage as he traveled down a treacherous decline. He wished people could be engineered. Then they might be able to live up to his expectations. He was a disgusting loser. Everyone else was worse, though. Everyone except Carolyn. His sister was an angel. He'd been worried when she had called him from the jail, particularly when the phone had gone dead. Thank God she had called him back later and let him know she was okay. She was tough like his mother, but right, always right, and always there for him. The first memories he had were of Carolyn. She used to stand by his bed at night until he fell asleep. She taught him how to ride a bicycle. She fought his battles for him, read to him, tutored him, nursed him when he was sick. No matter what he did, Carolyn would never abandon him. She was his security blanket.

Laurel Goodwin taught English at Ventura High. He'd bumped into her at Barnes & Noble six months ago. A mutual friend had told him that she was divorced and had moved back in with her family. They began seeing each other every now and then for lunch or a movie. When they'd finally made love, Neil knew that she was the woman he wanted to spend the rest of his life with.

Neil had known Laurel since his teens. He would have married her straight out of high school, had her father not interfered. Even today, the old goat despised him. Stanley Caplin had worked for State Farm Insurance for thirty-five years. He couldn't understand how a man who painted pictures for a living could afford a million-dollar home.

Laurel had laughed when she'd told him that her father thought he was a drug dealer. Neil didn't think it was funny.

Just because he used it occasionally didn't mean he was a dealer. Crystal meth was his drug of choice. They lived in a chemical society. Everyone needed a fix. His friends who abstained from illegal drugs took antidepressants, tranquilizers, muscle relaxants, pain pills, steroids, or they drowned themselves in alcohol. The health nuts were just as bad. They mixed this herb with that and looked down their noses at people who used street drugs, while they ran around in their fancy workout clothes with their spray-on tans and liposuctioned fake abs. The doctors could do that now. Sit-ups weren't necessary. For five grand, a guy could turn a beer gut into a six-pack. A few thousand more and he could have instant biceps.

People were idiots. Where did they think speed came from? What about cocaine? He'd been raised by a chemist. If he wanted to, he could go down in his mother's basement and make his own drugs.

The speed allowed him to work for days on end, filling one canvas after another. Some of his best work had been done on drugs.

Neil had studied at the most renowned art institutes in the world—Rome, Florence, Paris. He'd even restored priceless paintings inside the Vatican. How many artists had had the honor of so much as touching the tip of their brush to a Michelangelo? He laughed, thinking the Sistine Chapel could have been painted in a few months if Michelangelo had cranked himself up with meth.

In contrast to conservative Laurel, Melody Asher was a gorgeous and seductive party girl. An heiress, she bought whatever she wanted. A newspaper story said she'd once paid fifty grand to buy a wedding ring right off a woman's finger. When she walked into a room, everyone stopped and stared. Melody loved attention. She could never be happy with one man.

Neil pulled into the driveway at Melody's tri-level Brentwood home. The rain persisted. Using a newspaper to cover his head, he jogged toward the front of the house. When he knocked, the door swung open. Obviously, she'd been expecting him.

"Melody," he called out, "it's Neil." Stepping into the foyer, he turned to his left and passed through the archway into a long hall. He could hear the water running in the master bathroom. "Melody, I'm here," he said again, glancing at the designer names on the unopened boxes scattered around the room. Melody didn't use narcotics. She told him her scotch was medicinal. A robust girl, she was tall, thin, and blond, the kind of woman who could make a garbage bag look like it came from Saks Fifth Avenue.

Neil had dated models who starved and barfed. He called them stick women. When he had sex with them, their hip bones dug into his stomach. Once they finished, they would smoke ten cigarettes in a row. He had to sleep with some of them in intervals. They either needed a cigarette break or their laxatives kicked in early. Quite a sight to see a girl who made a grand an hour run to the john with her hand over her crack.

He went into the marble-walled bathroom, and Melody waved at him. "Hi, baby."

He turned to leave, saying over his shoulder, "I'll be waiting for you in the living room."

Her voice echoed out of the shower. "No, don't leave. Come in here . . . I have something important to tell you."

When Neil returned to the bathroom, his eyes locked on her naked body behind the opaque shower enclosure. She looked different without makeup, softer and more appealing. He stood silently, gazing at her tall, slender frame as the water cascaded off her white skin. His eyes focused on her genitals. Every month, she had her pubic hair shaped into a heart.

She lathered her pale blond hair, letting the soap slither down onto her perfectly proportioned body. The scent of vanilla permeated the room. He felt a tingling sensation spread throughout his body. The drug made him horny. He was instantly aroused.

"What are you staring at?" Melody asked, putting her knees together and moving her hands down to cover her genitals in mock shyness. "It's not like you haven't seen a woman before."

Neil placed his hand on his head, flustered. "It's just . . . I came here to . . ."

"Get laid," Melody answered for him. "All you have to do is spend less time painting those pictures that nobody seems to want and spend more time with me. Then your dick wouldn't be so lonely, sweetie. You know I'm always ready for you."

"I have to paint," Neil argued, raising his voice in an attempt to prevent what he suspected was inevitable. He was stung by her remarks about his work, but he wouldn't give her the satisfaction of knowing. "I'm an artist, okay? It's what I do for a living."

"Shoot, I forgot to get a washcloth," Melody said, acting as if she hadn't been listening. "Can you get me one?"

Neil sighed, wondering if she turned all of her lovers into errand boys. When he returned, Melody opened the shower door. As he handed her the washcloth, she grabbed his hand, pulling him into the running water.

"Now you're all wet," she said, giggling. "Why don't we have some fun?"

"No, damn it," Neil told her, "I don't have a change of clothes. Besides, I didn't come here to play games. I need to talk to you. It's important."

"Calm down, let me release some tension." Melody dropped to her knees. Unbuttoning the single button, she unzipped him. With both hands latched onto the sides of his jeans, she yanked them hard, exposing his tight-fitting Calvin Klein underwear. His penis was barely contained within the white fabric. A moment later, he felt himself inside her warm mouth. He tried to pull away, but it was too late. He succumbed to the pleasure. Besides, seeing this princess on her knees was emotionally gratifying. Melody Asher didn't get on her knees for just anyone.

She slithered up, rubbing her breasts against him as she looked into his lust-filled eyes. Lifting the bottom of his soggy shirt, she exposed his muscular chest. Neil quickly removed the rest of his clothes and tossed them into the empty Jacuzzi next to the shower.

Their lips met. Melody placed her hands on his buttocks and squeezed. His body was pulsating.

"Why don't we continue this in the bedroom." She reached behind him and pushed the door open. He carefully stepped back onto the plush carpet. He thought it was odd that she'd positioned her right leg behind him until she moved forward, causing him to fall. She caught him with her right hand and they tumbled to the carpet in a collage of flesh.

The next thing Neil remembered, he was fighting Melody for position. A hair under six feet, she made love like a man, forcing him onto his back and riding him like a horse. He'd been surprised that a slender woman could have such strength. Her body was deceptive. Her muscles were lean but incredibly powerful.

Melody's mouth fell open as she reached orgasm.

"I have an idea," she whispered into his ear a few minutes later. "Come with me."

Neil followed her into the bedroom.

"Don't move, I need to position the cameras." She went to the other side of the room and opened a floor-to-ceiling wall unit that housed two JVC digital cameras.

"Melody, I don't "

"Shut up and do me," she said, stretching out on the bed with her legs open.

Neil thought about leaving, but his body wouldn't let him. She'd teased him since he'd walked in the bathroom. The drug was driving him. He was living moment to moment, his mind washed clean of thought. With his back to the camera, he thrust himself inside her. He began perspiring, the beads of moisture reflecting in the lens of the cameras.

Melody cried out, "Harder . . . harder, Richard."

Neil jerked his head up. The day's events resurfaced and he felt a hard ball of rage deep in his stomach. Who in the hell was Richard? He rolled off her, going to the bathroom to retrieve his soggy clothes. When he returned, he shouted, "You're nothing but a slut. You could have all the money in the world and you'd still be trash. I don't know why I didn't see it sooner."

Melody flipped over onto her stomach, bracing her upper body with her elbows. Her lips spread in a broad smile. "Night, night, baby," she said in a breathy little girl's voice. "Oh, I've been meaning to ask you, is your sister still dating that physics professor?"

"None of your business." Neil glared at her for a few more minutes, then spun around and stomped out of the house.

Chapter 5

"Where's Bobby?" Carolyn asked, stepping up to the window at the jail.

"Hold on," Joe Powell said, "I'll go get him."

Veronica had contacted most of the relatives of the Hartfield family, except for Mrs. Hartfield's sister. She had made no attempt, however, to complete the most crucial part of the investigation—the interview with Raphael Moreno. The only explanation Carolyn could think of was that the crime was simply too gruesome for a woman in Veronica's condition.

After filling Brad in on where they stood, Carolyn had dictated the details of the various crimes from Veronica's notes. This portion of the report was compiled from arrest reports, trial transcripts, forensic evidence, and pathology reports. In crimes of this magnitude, a report could run up to fifty pages. Veronica had written four pages. Because the defendant was allowed to plead guilty to seven counts of second-degree murder, there were no trial transcripts. All they had to work with were the police and evidentiary reports. The only way anyone would ever know what really happened was to hear it from the defendant himself.

Carolyn understood Veronica's position, but she felt her friend had been negligent. Her disinterest was disrespectful to the victims. If she had tried to interview Moreno and failed, it would be acceptable. She had never tried. Anyone who was unable to confront criminals and the aftereffects of crime had no business being a probation officer.

She had spoken to Bobby Kirsh after lunch. When she heard what he had to say, she decided to let Moreno stew a few more hours.

"He didn't move?" Carolyn asked when Bobby's shaved head appeared in the window. "All this time and nothing happened? He didn't ask to go to the bathroom or want something to eat? He's been in there over five hours."

"Listen," Bobby told her, "I told you this guy was scary. He didn't so much as blink an eye. He hasn't even changed his position in the chair."

"Humph," Carolyn said, wondering what she should do next. "I want to talk to the men he assaulted."

"No way," he answered, his dark eyes blazing. "A few guys start mixing it up and the whole facility goes crazy. Last night was a disaster. You want to see Moreno again, I can't stop you. But you're not going any further than that, Carolyn. You have no legal right to talk to the inmates he assaulted."

"Keep him on ice, Bobby."

His face became stony. "No!" he said. "What's wrong with you, woman? Do you have a death wish or something? See him now or we're moving him back to solitary."

Carolyn reached out and touched his sleeve. "I've been looking at autopsy reports all day," she said, speaking softly. "Moreno isn't going to spend his life in prison. It's our last chance to document his behavior, find out who his contacts are on the outside. I'm almost positive he murdered the Hartfield family simply to ensure he was safe. Don't you understand? We didn't arrest Moreno, he arrested us."

"Why didn't the homicide guys figure that out?"

"Maybe they were too close to the case."

"Talk about wild speculations," the sergeant told her, letting forth a nervous chuckle.

Carolyn continued undaunted. "He wasn't afraid of the cops, Bobby. Someone was after him. How many mass murderers do you know who lead the police to their hiding place?"

"I don't know any mass murderers."

"You do now."

"You've got an hour."

"Take me back," Carolyn asked him, walking over to the door leading into the jail.

"But I thought you didn't want to see him right now."

"I don't want to interview him," she told him. "That doesn't mean I don't want to see him."

They walked in silence. Several times, the sergeant looked over to say something and then stopped when he realized Carolyn was deep in thought. When they reached the room where Moreno was being held, she tapped on the window with her knuckles. Moreno looked up. A flicker of recognition was followed with a grimace. She smiled brightly, then waved. She could see a puddle of what she assumed was urine under the small table.

Bobby yanked her away. "You're intentionally inciting this man. Don't come back, because I'm not letting you in. It's over, Sullivan."

Carolyn ignored him, her eyes roaming around the quad. "Are all three cells and the interview room on the same air-conditioning and heating system?"

A dark-haired young deputy was standing next to her. "No," Norm Baxter told her. "The interview room runs on the left thermostat. Because it's so small, it's always stifling in there."

"Good," she said. "Turn up the heat."

Before Bobby could react, she headed off down the corridor. When she glanced back over her shoulder, Carolyn saw him shaking his head, while the young deputy unlocked the thermostat box on the wall. "Thanks, Bobby," she yelled. The fact that she would risk her life to get a few more words out of a murderer had finally impressed him.

* * *

Deciding to take an early dinner, Hank Sawyer was chatting up his favorite waitress at Denny's when the dispatcher told him to respond to 1003 Seaport Drive on a report of a homicide. At forty-six, he was slightly under six feet and about twenty pounds overweight, most of it in his midsection. He had thinning brown hair and a ruddy complexion.

The detective was a shrewd and highly esteemed investigator. He'd tracked down and apprehended a murderer several years before. In the process, he'd taken a bullet to the abdomen, one of the most painful places in the body to incur a gunshot wound. He had been back at work in less than three weeks.

By the time Hank reached the address on Seaport, four patrol units were already on the scene. A crowd of onlookers had formed on the sidewalk and adjacent lawns. Trevor White and another officer, Daryl Montgomery, were stretching yellow police tape and attaching it to poles they had placed in the ground.

Spotting Detective Mary Stevens in the kitchen, Hank headed in her direction. At thirty-six, Mary was a striking woman. The only female assigned to homicide, she had ebony hair that hung to her shoulders in tight ringlets. She had a long, elegant neck, gorgeous maple-colored skin, and a dynamite body. She was dressed in jeans and her customary red shirt. She kept it in her car, calling it her "murder shirt." He had to admit it made her easier to find in a crowded scene. "What do we have?"

"The victim's name is Suzanne Porter. White female, thirty-five years old, five-three, a hundred and fifteen pounds. Last seen around one o'clock by the nineteen-year-old boy who lives next door. Husband came home from work and couldn't find his wife in the house." Mary stopped and yelled at one of the crime scene technicians. "Collect all the silverware, dishes, and pots and pans. Oh, and don't forget the dishwasher."

"Neat, huh?" Hank said, taking in the spotless kitchen.

"Extremely." Mary removed a rubber band from her wrist and pulled her hair back in a ponytail. "And I'm talking about the killer, not the victim. No signs of a struggle. No fingerprints. He must have worn gloves and wiped everything down just to be certain. Husband found the body in the backyard when he got home from work at four. One puncture wound in the left arm. Cause of death could be some type of lethal injection. Of course we won't know until the toxicology report comes in. Nude except for a bra and panties."

"Forced entry?"

"Lock picked on the outside door leading into the garage. Smart, really. The garage isn't armed. From what the alarm company told me, most people don't alarm their garages."

"He still had to get into the house," Hank reasoned.

"No problem if she was home. This wasn't a burglar, Sarge. The husband said as far as he could tell, nothing was missing. There's some valuable stuff in here. You know, TVs, computers, jewelry, silver."

"Could it have been a drug overdose?"

"Doubtful," Mary told him, massaging her left shoulder. "When you see her, you'll know what I mean. One puncture wound, remember? It would take a hell of a lot to convince me that this lady woke up one morning and decided to start shooting dope. Husband says she jogs every day. Doesn't smoke, drink, overeat. Look at this place, Hank. She doesn't even have kids to chase around. Handsome, successful husband. Most women would die for a life like this."

"Other witnesses?" he asked.

"We haven't been here that long," she told him. "The woman across the street was doing her dishes in front of the window overlooking the street around eleven. She saw a person on a motorcycle circling the block. Believes the motorcycle was red and black. She doesn't know a lot about cycles, but we showed her some pictures and she picked out a Yamaha."

"Did she get a look at the driver?"

"Dressed in black leather and the helmet had a face guard. No license plate. It could have been someone who lives around here. Won't know until we canvass the neighborhood again. A lot of people weren't home."

"Have you broadcast it?"

"Yeah," Mary said, her face damp with perspiration. "I also made sure Charley Young was notified. Coroner's office says he should be here in thirty minutes. What do you want to do about the press?"

"Stall them as long as possible. Where's the husband?"

"Sitting in Scott Underwood's unit. Do you want him taken to the station for questioning?"

"Not yet." Hank walked outside to take a look at the body. Several officers were positioned around it. He squatted down and removed the canvas tarp. The expression on Suzanne Porter's face was pleasant, almost as if she'd drifted off to sleep. She'd been a pretty lady—dark hair, nice features, clear skin. He could see what Mary was talking about. She seemed to be in excellent physical condition. He put on his reading glasses, picking up her left arm with his gloved hand to check out the puncture wound. It looked so harmless, he thought, like a mosquito bite. The last time he'd had blood drawn, the nurse had stabbed him three times. If the killer had administered a lethal injection as Mary suspected, he must have known what he was doing. He looked for other wounds and bruises. Other than a few scratches on her forehead, there was nothing.

Wandering back into the residence, the detective climbed the stairs to the second floor. The energy inside a house changed after a homicide. Like the victim, it became still and lifeless, regardless of how many law enforcement personnel were searching for evidence. He picked up a coaster in the master bedroom, then let it fall back to the table. It seemed to snap in place as if it were being drawn by a mag-

net. One of the dresser drawers was half open. He looked inside and found it filled with expensive lingerie, the kind she
was wearing when the husband found her. What woman
walked around in the middle of the day in sexy underwear?
Maybe she was having an affair and the hubby came home
and surprised her. Good motive for murder. He would have
to keep an eye on the husband.

The other rooms were sparsely furnished. Big mortgage,
he thought, for such a young couple. The house had to be
worth over a million. He walked over to the window. They
were on the wrong side of the street. Instead of facing the
ocean, they had a view of a lot of other houses and the
foothills. He knocked down the value to eight hundred.

Hank entered the master bathroom. He caught the odor of
either cologne or some other type of beauty product.
Reaching inside the shower, he sniffed a bottle of KMS
Velocity shampoo. The smell matched. This murder was
fresh. Either the victim or the suspect had taken a shower
and washed his hair. He reached in and stuck his fingers in
the drain, pulling up a wad of damp, dark hair.

Moving to the toilet, Hank lifted the lid and stared. The
porcelain smelled like bleach. His eyes went to the chrome
handle. Not even a smudge. Something had happened here.
He could feel it. Practically sticking his head inside the
bowl, he noticed something green in the far left-hand corner.
As he looked closer, he saw that there was also a streak of
red. He darted out in the hallway. "Get in here," he said to
one of the crime scene officers. "I think she vomited in the
toilet. Scrape it off and send it to the lab."

"Looks like the remains of a salad," the man said, produc-
ing a specimen cup.

He went downstairs and stepped out on the patio. It had
an overhang, the kind that generally came with the house.
The boards were open, so the sun and rain would come
through. He saw an object on the ground and bent over to

pick it up. It appeared to be a top to something. "Hey," he said, seizing another tech by the arm, "what do you think this is?"

"Lens cover," he said, extending his hand to take it. "Must have fallen out of someone's bag."

"Book it into evidence," Hank instructed him. "Maybe the killer took pictures as souvenirs."

Mary appeared beside him. "Charley called. He should be here in fifteen minutes." Her dark eyes scanned the interior of the house through the sliding glass window. A patrol sergeant was organizing a team of men to canvass the neighborhood again.

Hank stepped into the shadows at the far side of the house so they weren't constantly interrupted by the other officers. He unwrapped a toothpick and shoved it in his mouth. He hadn't smoked in four years, but he was only a year off what the teenagers called "quit gum." He had trouble concentrating without something in his mouth. Oral fixation. He wouldn't mind keeping his mouth busy on Mary, but she was out of his league.

"Want some?" she said, holding a paper cup filled with coffee. "It's disgusting, but we've got plenty of it."

"Nah," Hank said, placing his hand over his stomach. "Tell Scott to drive the husband to the station. Vernon has seniority, you know. You should have notified him. Captain Holmes will want him to be second lead."

Mary threw her arms out to her side, sidestepping beside him as he made his way back to the house. "Vernon isn't here," she told him. "He turned his pager off. What kind of homicide detective is that? Besides, I heard he was trying to get a position with the FBI. Give Vernon the reins and a caravan of FBI agents will be here by tomorrow morning."

She had a point, Hank thought. He didn't like Vernon Edgewell himself. He had no self-motivation. If someone didn't tell him what to do, he did nothing. Although he had a dozen commendations from his days in patrol, he fell short as a detective. He needed the immediacy of the street. Homicide required patience. Other than a major case like the one they were investigating, most detectives worked alone, plugging away at a case for years until they either solved it or closed it. If a man was so inclined, he could goof off and never get caught. The only reason the captain kept assigning Vernon cases was so he could fire him when he dropped the ball.

Vernon was a pitiful detective, but the FBI had received a glowing recommendation. That's the way it worked in civil service. A superior could transfer an incompetent officer and end up working for him a few years down the line. Passing him off to another agency was faster and less complicated.

Mary, however, had street smarts, an almost photographic memory, and would work a case until she dropped. "You're on," he told her. "I'll tell the captain. We might need a woman on this case."

"How about a good detective?" Mary said, punching him in the shoulder. "One of these days, I'm going to whip your sexist white ass."

"Sure you are," Hank said, elbowing his way out of the house.

Chapter 6

Brad Preston caught Carolyn in the corridor. "In," he said, pointing at the door to his office. "What in the hell is going on? You haven't checked in for hours. I want that report filed by eight o'clock tomorrow morning."

Carolyn sat down in a chair facing his desk. She felt like she'd been called to the principal's office. "I've already dictated most of it. If I have to, I'll type it myself after I go home."

Brad removed his jacket and draped it over the back of his chair. "Someone from the jail said you got Moreno to talk," he said, yanking off his tie. "Is that true?"

"Yes and no," she answered. "He talked, but he didn't crack. Another hour and I might get the goods."

"Christ, woman," he said. "We don't have another hour. You keep trying to find the victim's sister. I'll finish the interview with Moreno."

"Brad, please," Carolyn said. "I'm close, really close. If you go over there, everything I've done today will be worthless. Let me call records and see if they've located the sister. If they haven't, all I have left is Moreno's statement. I told the jail I'd be back before five-thirty. Once I talk to him again, I'll dictate the report."

"Give me the file," Brad said, rolling up his sleeves. "I'm

going to put this baby to bed. You might come down with the flu or something. Ronald Cummings and Patty Trenton went home sick today. I don't want you to be next."

She was tired of fighting everyone just so she could do her job. When Brad set his mind to something, there was no way to stop him. "Be my guest," she said, pulling Moreno's file out of her briefcase. Removing the information she needed, she slapped it down on his desk. "Moreno is violent. He got his hands on my cell phone and crushed it. I had him pick up the pieces, so he may have hidden one to use as a weapon. Don't try a face-to-face."

"Why not?" he said, thrusting his chin forward. "You did, didn't you?"

"That was this morning," Carolyn said, sighing. "I've kept him in an interview room since nine-thirty. He's not going to be a happy camper."

"He's a scrawny piece of dog shit," Brad told her. "He gives me any trouble and I'll mop the floor with him."

Brad walked beside Bobby Kirsh, glancing at the prisoners inside the quad. As far as he was concerned, Raphael Moreno didn't deserve to live. Judges should have shotguns and take down murderers right in the courtroom. Either that, or hang them in the parking lot of Ralph's supermarket. Then murdering thugs like Moreno might think twice before they started robbing and killing people. Right now, the system coddled criminals. Everyone but the victims had rights. The six-month-old baby Moreno killed, what rights had that infant had?

He peered through the window, seeing a small Hispanic male seated at the table. "What's that on the floor?"

"Urine," Bobby said, arching an eyebrow. "Sullivan said to let him stew. Want me to have the room hosed down before you go in?"

"No," he said, deciding he would rather tolerate the stench than drag this on any longer.

In law enforcement circles, Carolyn was famous. For some reason, whenever she appeared, prisoners talked. One inmate had been convicted of armed robbery. Carolyn had managed to get him to confess to killing his wife in Alabama. No one knew exactly how she did it. Brad took a deep breath as if he were about to bench-press two hundred pounds. "Open the damn door."

The smell of human waste was sickening. He checked the chair before he sat down to make certain Moreno hadn't defecated on it, then pulled a silver microrecorder out of his pocket. Placing it in the center of the table, he depressed the record button. "Officer Brad Preston, Ventura County CSA," he said. "Defendant is Raphael Moreno, case number A856392."

He stared at Moreno, waiting to see if he would speak without prompting. When he didn't, he began. "Want to tell me why you killed those people?"

Moreno's eyes narrowed into slits. His face was dripping with perspiration. His shirt was saturated. It had to be a hundred degrees in here, Brad thought, using his hand to wipe the sweat off his forehead.

"You don't have to talk if you don't want to," Brad told the inmate. "You probably think there's no reason to cooperate since your term of imprisonment has already been decided. That might not be true. If you show no remorse for your actions, it's doubtful if you'll ever taste freedom. You're a young man. There's still a chance you might be released in a reasonable amount of time."

He was trying to mimic Carolyn's style—bullshit him until he dropped his guard. He didn't agree with her about all this early-release stuff, that the parole board kicked everyone out as soon as it was legally possible. She was right, though, when it came to truth in sentencing. When the judge had sentenced Moreno to serve eighty-four years, he'd failed to point out that he would be eligible for parole in less than half that time. If the judge had sentenced him concurrently instead of consecutively, Moreno could conceivably be out in six years. Victims should be told the earliest date a criminal would be eligible for release. The courts didn't tell them.

As far as Moreno was concerned, even if he turned out to be a model prisoner, it was doubtful if the parole board would ever release him. If he'd taken out an entire street gang, it might be different. The seriousness of a crime rested not only on how a person was killed but whom they killed. His mother and sister didn't count. Their next of kin were a couple of cousins who resided at an unknown location in Mexico. The Hartfields, however, had been a middle-class family. Their relatives and friends would appear at every parole hearing.

Brad glanced at his watch in frustration. It was almost four-thirty and Moreno hadn't moved or said a word. Carolyn had more patience than he did. "Listen, punk," he said, leaning down so he could look in Moreno's eyes. "You're not worth my time. Besides, you stink. What did you do? Shit your pants like a baby? Guess your mama won't be able to clean you up since you chopped her head off."

When the prisoner didn't react, Brad hurled the plastic chair against the wall. Deciding not to waste any more time, he walked over to press the buzzer for the jailer.

It happened in an instant.

Moreno sprang to his feet. Raising his arm high, he whipped his leg irons with tremendous force and struck the probation officer in the back.

Brad collapsed, his body blocking the door. He had trouble catching his breath. "Help me," he gasped, fearing he might be hit again. "Get me out of here! God, get me out of here!"

He felt something pushing him in the side. The guards were trying to force the door open. Moreno leaped across the room and straddled him.

"No one talks about my mother, *comprende?*" he said, his body trembling with rage. Reaching down, he squeezed Brad's crotch. "If I had a blade, I'd cut your fucking balls off and eat them. But you ain't got balls. All you got is a mouth."

Bobby grabbed Moreno's arm while Norm Baxter shocked him with a stun gun. Moreno's body jerked, then became limp. The two officers pulled Moreno out of the room. The sergeant instructed them to take the inmate back to solitary.

Brad had used his hands to pull himself into the corner. Once the prisoner was removed, Bobby dropped to his knees beside him. "Ambulance is on its way," he said, panting. "Where did he get you?"

"My back," Brad answered, wiggling his toes inside his shoes. He hurt like a bitch, but at least he wasn't paralyzed. "How did he get out of the restraints?"

"The freak must be a contortionist," the sergeant said, glancing up at Baxter. He picked up the handcuffs and leg irons, holding them where Brad and the deputy could see. "The restraints didn't break and they weren't loose. Look how small the openings for his arms and legs were. He must have compressed his hands and slid them right off." One of the deputies began speaking fast, seemingly fascinated. "I've seen things like this on TV. Some of these people can even collapse their bones."

Brad was not amused. "Why didn't you tell me he was a contortionist?"

"We didn't know," Bobby said. "We've never had a prisoner who could do this before. Shit, how can we ever restrain this guy? He can slip out of anything. Inmates don't stay in their cells all the time. We transfer them to court, the infirmary, the visiting area." He stopped and handed the restraints to Baxter. "I guess Carolyn had a point. I was getting fed up with her stunts, but it looks like this one paid off. She swore there was more we needed to know about this guy, and that if she pushed him hard enough, he would show us. She left him in here all day. Even had us turn the heat up. If it weren't for your gal, Preston, this maniac could have escaped and been back on the street killing people. He was probably planning to make his move on the bus to prison. You know the first person he'd look up, don't you?"

"Who?" Brad said, wondering how much longer he'd have to lie there on the floor in pain.

"Carolyn Sullivan."

Chapter 7

The section of Ventura where Neil lived was subject to mud slides. If the storm didn't pass by tomorrow, he might have to evacuate. The previous year, a house on his street and its owners had slid off the cliff.

He should have broken it off with Melody months ago. He'd intended to tell her over the phone, then decided that it was a chickenshit way to handle it. Now he wished he had.

Turning into his driveway and hitting the remote for the garage, Neil parked next to his black paneled van. Carolyn had teased him about the van, telling him it was the vehicle of choice for serial killers. As soon as she'd heard about the Ferrari, she had sworn he would end up with a suspended license.

He opened the glove box and removed the new white envelope he'd purchased on the way to Melody's house. Instead of separating it into lines, he dipped in with his little finger and placed a small quantity of the crystallized powder into his nostrils. He couldn't go on like this—he had to quit before Carolyn found out. If he hadn't been on meth, he wouldn't have gone crazy and hurt Laurel. The drug made him feel good, but it also had the capacity to turn him into a madman.

Getting out of the car, Neil dumped the remaining contents of the envelope onto the wet grass next to the garage.

He walked next door and deposited the envelope in his neighbor's trash can. The house was formerly occupied by a couple, but the husband had croaked last year. The widow played country music at deafening levels all day long, making it impossible for him to sleep after a night of painting. When he needed to dispose of anything related to drugs, it went in Samantha Garner's trash. He never took a chance that his housekeeper, Addy, might stumble across something she wasn't supposed to see. Part of the mystique of using drugs was making certain you didn't get caught.

Neil opened the door leading into the house, his heart pumping like a steam engine. He started to punch in the alarm code when he realized it wasn't activated. He held down the stay button until he heard the series of beeps that confirmed the alarm was set.

His expensive leather shoes squished on the marble entryway. Taking them off, he left them on the mat by the door. They would probably have to be thrown out.

Stopping in the guest bathroom, he relieved himself, stripped off his wet clothes, then rinsed off in the sink. He occasionally slept in the extra room because it was closer to the garage. If he used too much speed, he became paranoid and thought he was having a heart attack. Driving around helped him calm down.

The laundry room was across the hall. He found a plastic bag and placed his clothes inside. The stupid woman could have at least let him undress before she pulled him into the shower. Her wealth had turned her into a first-class bitch.

Melody's family owned APC Pharmaceuticals. He'd read in the *Wall Street Journal* that her net worth was estimated at fifty million. They'd never discussed it, yet he suspected the money was one of the reasons she shied away from permanent relationships. She wasn't only a bitch, she was selfish and greedy, terrified she might have to share her precious money.

Neil passed through the dark house to the master bedroom. After putting on a clean pair of jockey shorts, he went to the kitchen to grab a bottle of water. Seeing a smudge on the refrigerator door, he retrieved a basket of cleaning supplies from under the sink and went to work. When he finally stopped, he was on his hands and knees, wiping down the tile floor.

Before he left the kitchen, he stood in the doorway and stared, making certain he hadn't missed anything. Satisfied the room was clean, he turned off the light, being careful not to touch the switch plate.

Neil walked through the rest of the house, flicking on the lights and checking the rooms. Outside of the bedrooms, kitchen, and bathrooms, the house resembled an art gallery. Large oil paintings were mounted on the walls, Neil's style was that of the old masters. The formal rooms were sparsely furnished. He had cocktail parties on a regular basis, inviting potential buyers as well as established patrons. He seldom used the rooms for anything else. His studio was located in a thousand-square-foot guest house behind the swimming pool.

Satisfied that everything was in place, he went to the master bedroom and collapsed on the bed. He was lucky he'd used most of the meth earlier in the evening. The drug could keep him awake for days. To circumvent his insomnia, he used Depakote, a drug used to control the manic stages of bipolar disorder. The only way he could get the pills was to go to a shrink. Psychiatrists were sadistic freaks. They sat there with smug expressions on their faces, baiting you until you said something they could use to have you committed.

He didn't feel right. He began to panic, wondering if the guy at the pawnshop had sold him heroin instead of meth. The stuff was so pure today, junkies sometimes snorted it instead of shooting up. When he'd stopped off at Al's Pawnshop, Al wasn't there, so he'd dealt with a black guy named Leroy. If not heroin, Leroy could have sold him Ajax or rat poison. His nostrils felt as if they were on fire. He reached up and touched them to make certain they weren't bleeding. He kept a bottle of saline rinse in the guest bathroom, and he usually cleaned out his nose before he went to bed. He wondered if people who fell into drugs were simply bored. The rituals alone were exhausting. At the same time, they were somehow comforting.

Socializing had always been difficult for him. Being an artist allowed him to withdraw into his own world. Over time, however, he had become lonely. In the past, all of his girlfriends had been like Melody—beautiful, independent women he could see whenever he felt like it. The thought of a permanent relationship had always frightened him. He had too much to hide, and not just his involvement with narcotics.

Laurel had been different. Maybe it was because they'd known each other as kids. Back then, everything had been so simple. He had deluded himself. It never would have worked. When she had realized who he really was, she would have left him.

His head relaxed into the pillow. He never went to bed this early, but he felt as if he had lived an entire life in one day. Was Addy coming in tomorrow? He couldn't recall what day of the week it was. She generally came on Fridays, but she occasionally switched days. He turned on his side and gazed out the sliding glass door. His mind was so muddled that he'd forgotten that it was almost Christmas. Addy was on vacation. He couldn't provide her with health insurance, so he gave her two weeks off every year with pay.

A bolt of lightning illuminated the yard. He jumped out of bed when he saw a white object floating in the pool. At first, he thought one of the lawn chairs had blown over. When he saw that all four chairs were still in place, he darted outside into the rain. The shrill of the alarm sounded in the background.

As he came closer to the pool, Neil realized the floating object was a person. Without thinking, he dived in and swam toward the body, grabbing it around the shoulders. He stopped swimming and they sank underneath the water. Gulping air as he surfaced, he swam to the edge and hoisted the person onto the wet concrete. He recognized her face.

Laurel!

With the alarm still blaring, the rain stinging his eyes, Neil desperately attempted to revive her. After twenty minutes, he gave up, certain Laurel had been dead for some time. Kneeling beside her lifeless body, he sobbed in grief and confusion. Distorted images filled his mind. He remembered her crying, the anguished look on her face. She had raced outside to get away from him. She'd never seen him mad before and she was frightened.

Neil was cradling Laurel's head in his lap and tenderly stroking the thick, wet strands of hair from her once-lovely face when he saw a man in a uniform running toward him. From a distance, the body appeared to be nude. Laurel's bra had been pushed up to her armpits. Her white silk panties barely covered her pubic hair.

The officer pointed a gun at him. "Move away or I'll shoot."

Neil ignored him, his eyes scanning the yard for the rest of Laurel's clothing or anything he could use to cover her. He heard the officer speaking, asking his dispatcher to alert the police and paramedics. When he glanced back at the man, he saw 21ST CENTURY SECURITY emblazoned on his white shirt. He gently lowered Laurel's head, then stood and raised his arms. The security officer pushed him aside and began administering CPR.

Neil staggered into the house to call Carolyn. His hands were shaking so badly, he had to enter the alarm code twice to disable the system.

Laurel was gone and it was all his fault.

*   *   *

"Do you know what time it is?" Carolyn said groggily, staring out into the dark room. "You know the rules, Neil. You don't call me after ten unless it's a life-or-death situation. I've already taken my pill. I had an awful day. Now I'll never get back to sleep."

Carolyn was a chronic insomniac. Inability to sleep ran in their family. Even her fifteen-year-old son had trouble quieting his constantly churning mind. Several years ago, she'd given up and gone on medication. She took her Xanax at ten o'clock and became furious if her brother woke her up, which he consistently did.

Afraid his sister was about to hang up on him, Neil blurted, "Laurel's dead. I think she drowned in my pool."

Her younger brother had a dry sense of humor. When he wanted attention, he would say outlandish things. "If this is a joke, Neil," Carolyn told him, "it's in very poor taste."

He began sobbing. "Please, I'm serious. The police will be here any minute."

God, no, Carolyn thought, bolting upright in the bed. "Did you call the paramedics?"

"The security guy did. . . . Why would she go swimming in the rain?" he said, his voice cracking. "Jesus, this can't be happening."

Carolyn pushed the button for the speaker phone so she could continue talking while she dressed. "Were you at home when it happened?"

"No," he said. "At least I don't think I was. I saw her floating in the pool after I went to bed. I could see her through the sliding glass door in the bedroom."

Carolyn would have to get Paul's housekeeper, Isobel, to look after John and Rebecca. She threw on a pair of jeans and a white turtleneck sweater, then shoved her feet into a pair of sneakers. "I'm on my way. Stay calm. Don't do or say anything until I get there."

"I messed up again," Neil said, his voice strangely calm.

"I loved Laurel. I never meant for anything bad to happen to her."

A sense of dread gripped Carolyn. "What are you saying? What did you do, Neil?" When he didn't respond, she shouted, "Holy Mother of God, answer me! What did you do to Laurel?"

When she heard the dial tone, she raced down the hallway and out the front door of her house. She would call Paul from the road. She had to get to her brother before the police did.

Melody Asher sat in the dark, her face lit by the glow of computer monitors, as she plunged her spoon into the quart of Dreyers' Rocky Road ice cream. Her red silk robe slipped off one shoulder, exposing her naked skin. She was naturally slender, one of the reasons modeling agencies had recruited her at the age of fifteen. That, of course, and her height. The ice cream was an indulgence she seldom allowed herself, even though her modeling days were behind her and she was now an actress. She still couldn't afford to gain weight. Chubby actresses weren't in great demand.

Melody felt she deserved to indulge in the thick chocolate, almonds, and light mini marshmallows that were melting in her warm mouth. Tonight, she'd given Neil something to remember. Now she owned him, like she'd owned all the other men who had passed through her life. Her philosophy regarding men was simple—give them something shocking to think about and they'd keep coming back for more. It was all part of her game plan, total control or nothing.

How could Neil have called her a slut? He'd had the time of his life. Just because she'd turned on the video camera and called him another man's name. She'd filmed him before and he had never complained.

A month after Melody started dating Neil, she had tapped into his home security system. To protect his artwork, he had multiple cameras installed in every room of his house, as well as the front and rear exteriors. Without his knowledge, she'd attached a wireless transponder to the main system with an off-site receiver. This made it possible for her to receive and store movie files on her home computer.

After engaging in sex with Neil, Melody could experience the evening again. Her best orgasms came from watching. Even after she broke up with a man, she could revisit their sexual episodes whenever she wanted.

Melody watched all of her lovers.

Technology had brought voyeurism to an entirely different level. As far as she was concerned, every woman should keep tabs on her man. The head of her security company had warned her never to give anyone a key to her house. She chuckled as she recalled her reply. "Oh, I see, Keith," she'd said, leaning forward so he could see her breasts. "Are you saying it's all right if I give them access to my body as long as I don't give them a key to my house? Does that mean my house has more value than my vagina?" She had watched as the man's face turned beet red. Wearing a dress and no panties, she'd circled around to the back of his desk. "Maybe you could figure out a way to secure this?" she said, raising her skirt. "Then every time I want to have sex, you'll have to come to my house." The poor man had become so flustered, she was afraid he was going to have a heart attack. Dropping her skirt, she'd told him, "Why don't I just change my locks—I don't think your wife would want you coming over three or four times a day."

Men were scum. They thought with their dicks. She had a right to know if they were cheating on her. She didn't want to contract AIDS or some other sexually transmitted disease. Watching them was her insurance policy.

Technology was a cinch for her. Most people who came into contact with Melody thought she'd have trouble plugging in a blender. Playing dumb had been her first starring role. She'd always been a good actress, even as a child.

Deceiving those around her was entertaining. That's what life boiled down to, she thought, just passing time until you croaked.

She didn't believe in God. When you died, your body rotted. She'd never once seen a dead body come back to life. Right and wrong only mattered if you got caught. Most religious people were weak-minded individuals who could only exist if their lives were guided by someone else. They were puppets on a string. The Bible was nothing more than a bestselling, poorly written work of fiction. She'd like to own the rights to that baby, she thought.

Part of the reason men became so infatuated with her was her feminine facade of helplessness. Because Melody asked them to set her clocks or figure out how to operate a new cell phone, they classified her as the stereotypical dumb blonde. Suckers, she thought. It wasn't that she couldn't do menial tasks, she didn't want to. Why waste time when she could get someone else to do it for her?

Even her female friends were shocked when she lied and told them she didn't know how to operate a computer. Her town house had what the realtor had touted as a penthouse. In reality, it was a room about the size of an average bedroom. The door was secured with Medeco locks, the key next to impossible to duplicate. In this room alone, she had three 50-inch plasma monitors, three Dell computers, an Atlas 8 EQ Reflector telescope with photo capability, numerous digital film cameras, and an Avid editing bay, similar to the kind used by film production companies. This was her viewing room.

While her girlfriends wasted hours shopping, chatting, playing kiddie games, and surfing the Web, Melody was either spying on someone or expanding her knowledge base. She spent hours reading about the criminal justice system. Crime and criminals were fascinating. She'd even studied briefly at the John Jay College of Criminal Justice in Manhattan, and had completed most of the agent training program at the FBI Academy before they discovered a discrepancy in her background investigation. Melody had threatened to file a lawsuit to get them to reinstate her, but her attorney told her it wasn't worth it.

She had a myriad of intellectual interests. She loved technology, although she held a degree in both mathematics and psychology. A few years ago, she'd enrolled in Caltech, wanting to become proficient in physics. The other students had been astonished when the leggy blonde with the designer clothes and dynamite body had risen to the top of the class. Knowledge was her secret weapon.

Several months back, Melody was surprised when she saw a woman who appeared to be in her midthirties frequenting Neil's place. Not only had he cheated on her, he'd looked her straight in the eye and denied it. Typical.

Men should be treated like dogs, taught to obey their masters. Sit when they were told to sit and fetch on command. If they got out of line, they would be swatted with a rolled-up newspaper or thrown out in the cold for the night. If they got sick or stopped being loyal, they were put to sleep. During her life, she'd put down a string of man's best friends. Who wanted to be a damn dog, anyway? Maybe they'd be reincarnated as a woman.

Melody had watched Neil and the other woman jumping nude into the outdoor Jacuzzi. When they'd had sex, she was reminded of the nights she and Neil had spent together at his home in his backyard.

Opening one of her stored files, Melody's hand drifted between her legs and her head fell back as she watched herself and Neil in the throes of ecstasy. She smelled the aroma of the Glenlivet scotch and heard the sound of the ice cubes tinging in the glass. Imagining Neil's face between her legs as the action played out on the monitor, she became intensely aroused.

Melody suspected Neil had intended to break it off with her tonight. She could tell by the way he touched the other woman that he was in love with her. Mousy little thing, she thought. What in hell did he see in her? Her clothes looked like they came from Target. Even her maid had better taste.

Their affair would end when and how she wanted it to end. No one walked away from Melody Asher.

Turning to another monitor, she saw people moving around in Neil's backyard. Her ice-cream spoon tumbled out of her hands onto the expensive carpet. The flashing lights of the emergency vehicles reflected off the wet pavement. Her eyes jumped to another monitor. She spotted Neil's panicked face among the police officers in his backyard.

Her lower lip protruded as she spoke out loud, "You won't be cheating on me now, Neil, not after I bail you out of jail."

Melody was ripe for a little action. The news was more fun if you knew the players. She picked her spoon off the floor and finished savoring her ice cream.

Chapter 8

By the time Carolyn arrived, Neil's house was swarming with police and emergency personnel. She'd rushed out without remembering to bring an umbrella. At the time, it had only been sprinkling. Now it was pouring again and she was drenched. A dark-haired officer in his early twenties stopped her. His ID badge read DANIEL CUTTER. "This is a crime scene, lady."

Carolyn fished her county ID out of her purse, holding it in front of his face.

"Was the man who owned this place your probationer?"

"No," she said, never liking it when she found herself on the opposite side of the fence. "He's my brother."

"I'll have to check with my sergeant."

A middle-aged woman in a white flannel bathrobe pushed through the onlookers, taking a position next to Carolyn. "Do you know what happened here?" she asked, peering out from under her umbrella. "They said a girl was raped."

Carolyn's stomach rose in her throat. "Where did you hear that?"

"A guy over there told me," she said, gesturing toward the crowd of spectators. "I'm not surprised, you know. The man who lives here is weird. He stays up all night and sleeps all day. My daughter thinks he's a vampire. She went to his house selling Girl Scout cookies and he bit her head off. It was three o'clock in the afternoon and he was furious that she woke him. Can you believe it? I'll never let her go there again, that's for sure." She stopped and extended her hand. "I'm Joyce Elliot, by the way. I live in the house on the corner."

"Excuse me, I have to check on something." Carolyn moved a few feet away. Might as well get used to it, she told herself, knowing Neil had a rough time ahead of him. People loved excitement. If the truth wasn't that interesting, they embellished, blending fact with fiction.

Her thoughts turned to Neil. He had been hysterical, she told herself. He didn't know what he was saying. He would have never done anything to hurt Laurel. It had been a long day, and she had overreacted, let her imagination run wild. The woman's death was a tragedy, but her brother had not done anything wrong. Maybe Laurel had got drunk and had accidentally fallen into the swimming pool. She might not have been able to swim. People drowned every day. Backyard swimming pools had always frightened her.

Laurel Goodwin was six years younger than Carolyn, but she had known her fairly well. She'd seen a lot of her back when Laurel and Neil had first started dating. Carolyn had also seen Laurel around town during her marriage, and assumed she was happy. It was emotionally wrenching to know she was dead. But it was Neil she was worried about. He appeared confident, but underneath, he was emotionally fragile. Because his income had substantially diminished during the past six months, he had begun making drastic changes in his life. He'd only resumed dating Laurel a short time ago. Carolyn had told him how foolish it was to ask Laurel to marry him. Neil could also be stubborn. He'd refused to listen to her. She shouldn't have called him from the jail yesterday. When she'd called him back around noon to tell him she was all right, he'd been rushing out to pick up Laurel.

Hank Sawyer placed his hand on Carolyn's shoulder and

she jumped. "Guess you were right about not drinking tonight. How's Preston? I heard our boy Raphael did a number on him."

"He has a few broken vertebrae," she told him, wincing. "I warned him. Moreno is a scary character. Brad's lucky to be alive."

Carolyn and Sawyer were close friends. He was not only a detective, but a sergeant over at the homicide division. "What are you doing here, Hank?" she asked, trying to appear nonchalant. "The poor woman drowned. I need to talk to my brother. He was terribly upset when he called me."

"Looks like we've got ourselves a homicide," he said, chomping on a toothpick.

Carolyn felt her blood pressure shoot up twenty points. She knew now was the time to keep her mouth shut. Hank was here in an official capacity. Pushing past him into the house, she saw Neil seated at the kitchen table. His dark hair was wet, his eyes red and puffy, and he had one of the gray blankets used by the paramedics tossed over his shoulders. She pulled up a chair beside him. "What did you mean on the phone? Did something happen between you and Laurel?"

"I don't know what you're talking about," he said. "I came home and found her. . . . She was . . . she was floating in the pool." He stopped and wiped the tears from his eyes. "I tried to save her. She was . . . gone. Why would she go swimming at night during a rainstorm? It doesn't make sense. All she had on was her underwear. I looked for the rest of her clothes, but I couldn't find them."

"Were you alone when you found her?"

"Yes," Neil said. "It was late . . . after eleven. I'd already taken my medicine to help me sleep and gone to bed, then I saw . . ."

Carolyn looked up. Hank was conversing with a black detective named Mary Stevens.

She leaned over and whispered in her brother's ear. "Don't

talk right now. The police are handling this as a homicide. You may be a suspect."

Neil's eyelids flickered in fear. He grabbed hold of his sister's forearm. "That's ridiculous," he said. "I didn't kill her. Besides, I'm certain she's been dead a long time. Her body was stiff and cold . . . so cold." He placed his palms over his face, then slapped them down on the top of the table. "I was in LA most of the day. I wasn't even here. How could the police accuse me of killing her?"

"Stay calm," Carolyn told him. "We'll get to the bottom of this. You have to do exactly what I say, though. Don't answer any questions or make any spontaneous statements."

They linked eyes; then Carolyn went to speak to Hank. Mary had gone outside where the coroner, Charley Young, was examining the body. "Tell me what you have, Hank."

He held up a plastic evidence bag containing the syringe. "We found this in the master-bathroom sink. Is your brother a diabetic?"

"No," Carolyn answered, wrapping her arms around her chest. "Is there anything in there?"

"Looks like it," Hank told her, pointing at a small amount of yellowish liquid located at the bottom of the syringe. "Won't know what it is, of course, until the lab processes it."

"What about time of death?"

"Charley's pretty sure the victim's been in the water for at least four hours. Your brother claims he was in love with the woman. Is that true?"

Carolyn felt bad. Neil had been calling her a lot lately. Because of her work, she'd been lucky to exchange a few words with him. When she'd come home that evening around eight, John and Rebecca said they hadn't seen or heard from him. He'd promised to stop by and look at Rebecca's drawings. He was flaky, but he seldom went back on his word.

She looked up at the detective. "They only recently started seeing each other. Neil cared a great deal for her, though. Have you notified her family?"

He skipped over her question. "Charley found only one injection site on her left arm. We'll know more when he gets the body to the morgue. The rain isn't helping us much. Whatever evidence there is outside will more than likely be worthless."

"Did you find any signs of a forced entry?"

"Not yet," he said, pausing and staring at her. "Are you sick or something? You're really pale."

Damn men, Carolyn thought, how did he expect her to look under the circumstances? "I didn't have time to put on my makeup. You want to talk about my appearance or the crime? Were there any prints on the doors or windows?"

"Nope," Hank said. "Whoever did this is a tidy person. Most of the prints we lifted, outside of the victim's, are probably your brother's. I don't know any killer in the world who would leave that many fingerprints. Did he have a housekeeper?"

"Yes," Carolyn said. "I'm not sure which day she works. Can I have a few minutes alone with him?"

Hank frowned, moving his feet around on the marble entry. "The victim's father, Stanley Caplin, thinks your brother's a drug dealer. He claims he personally witnessed him using narcotics. The narcs say there's some potent smack floating around. Two junkies have overdosed in the past week. Maybe he gave his girlfriend some killer heroin."

Hank looked as if he were about to collapse. The stress must be getting to him, she thought, or he would never have made such an inflammatory statement about Neil. He might have been teasing, though. Individuals who dealt with death on a regular basis frequently used humor as a way to cope. Either that, or he was trying to test her reaction.

Carolyn knew Laurel's parents. Ventura wasn't that big and they'd all gone to the same schools. "The man's lying," she snapped. "Neil doesn't use drugs, let alone sell them. He's a successful artist." She raised her arm toward the row of large canvases mounted on the walls. She could understand why some people didn't appreciate contemporary art. Her brother, however, had been trained in the classical style of painting and his work was renowned. "His paintings usually sell for between ten and twenty thousand. A few years ago, one of them went for fifty."

"I thought those were prints like they sell at those museum stores." Hank gazed at the lifelike physiques, the exquisite draping in the folds of fabric, the detailed backgrounds.

"When did Caplin say he saw Neil using drugs?"

"I didn't ask," the detective told her. "The guy just learned that his daughter was dead." He sucked in a deep breath before continuing. "I'll give you ten minutes, Carolyn. I need to get your brother out of here, one way or the other. I just sent one of my men over to pick up the parents so they can identify the body."

"Why put them through that?" she asked, running her hands through her wet hair. "Neil has already identified her. I know Laurel, if you need a second ID. Anyway, this is supposed to be a crime scene."

"Don't you have any sympathy for these people?"

"Of course I do," she answered, a chastised expression on her face. "I'll talk to Neil in the garage." She started to walk away, then stopped. "Whatever happens, try to remember that this is my brother."

"If he's innocent, he's got nothing to worry about."

"Cut the crap, okay?" Carolyn shot back. "I know how the system works. Neil was in the wrong place at the wrong time. He's not your murderer."

Chapter 9

Neil was leaning against the wall in the open garage. One of the officers had brought him a pair of jeans and a white sweatshirt they'd found in the laundry room.

While the crime scene technicians went about their job of collecting evidence inside the residence, Carolyn drilled Neil. She asked him if he'd seen Laurel earlier.

"That's what I'm concerned about," he said, lowering his head. "She came here and we had lunch. I asked her to marry me."

"Did she accept?"

He swallowed hard. "No."

"For your own good, don't ever repeat that," his sister said in a hushed voice. "If you do, you'll give the police a motive."

"I understand," Neil said, sniffing. "We got into a big fight. You know how I hate rejection. She said she could explain everything, but I was too bent out of shape to listen. Th-that . . . was the last time I saw her alive."

Now she understood his comment about messing up. Although he kept it under control most of the time, Neil had a temper and had been known to fly off the handle. They'd had a fight, that's all. He'd probably said things he regretted, things he didn't really mean. "You left her in the house? Alone?"

"I didn't think she would kill herself."

"Where did you go?"

"I drove around for about an hour, then I decided to go to Melody's. I didn't expect Laurel to be here when I got home. I thought she'd call a friend to come and get her."

Carolyn stared at his eyes. His pupils were dilated and his movements were jerky, almost manic. "Are you taking your medicine?"

"I don't need lithium," Neil said, slapping his arms against his thighs. "You know I can't paint when I take that shit. How many sleeping pills are *you* taking? Are you going to accidentally overdose again, like you did last summer? Stop trying to run my life, Carolyn. You've got enough problems with your own."

She started to react, then stopped herself. When the criticism was deserved, she had no right to protest. She'd once walked in on a probationer in the middle of a cocaine buy and ended up wrenching her neck trying to arrest him. The doctor had prescribed a muscle relaxant called Soma. She had mistakenly thought the drug was nothing more than a big aspirin. Unable to lift her head one morning, she'd popped a handful of the pills in her mouth. Within fifteen minutes, she was out cold on the living-room floor. Her son, John, had called an ambulance. Fifteen minutes later, she was in cardiac arrest. If her heart had stopped anywhere outside of the emergency room, she would have been dead.

Neil's chest was expanding and contracting. Carolyn moved closer, placing her hand in the center of his back. "Try to relax," she said. "Everything's going to be all right. All you have to do is help me figure out what happened. Why did you go to Melody's? I thought you were going to break it off with her."

"Laurel didn't want me. You're too busy to talk to me. I thought driving a few hours in a rainstorm to break up with Melody would be the perfect ending to my miserable day." He saw the look on her face. "Don't worry, it's over. All she wanted me for was sex. I'm never going to see her again."

"Did you sleep with her?"

Neil's eyes glistened with tears. "Laurel's dead. Why do you keep talking about Melody?"

"Nothing you or I can do will bring Laurel back, Neil," Carolyn told him. "Whether you realize it or not, the police may charge you with murder. How long were you with Melody? Did you go out somewhere? Were the two of you with other people? We need to establish your whereabouts at the time of the crime."

Neil turned toward the door leading into the house. He hated confrontations. In most instances, he simply walked away. That's probably what he'd done to Laurel, Carolyn thought. "Listen to me!" she shouted, a line of perspiration breaking out on her forehead. "You're going to be questioned. I need to know where we stand. We have to decide whether we should hire an attorney."

Neil returned to where she was standing. "I left for LA around three this afternoon."

Carolyn placed her hands on her hips. "I'm trying to find out if anyone other than Melody can substantiate your alibi. Did you go out to dinner?"

"No," he said. "We stayed at her place in Brentwood. I left around nine or a few minutes earlier."

Carolyn had seen Melody Asher on numerous occasions. The woman had even spent Thanksgiving with them. Neil had been crazy about her in the beginning, boasting that she had the face and body of an angel. Although she was somewhat flashy for Ventura, with her blond hair, designer clothes, and fancy Porsche, Melody had come across as a nice young woman who genuinely cared about her brother. Until a month ago, Carolyn had thought she was a former fashion model trying to break into acting. When Neil informed her that his girlfriend was worth over fifty million, she had been flabbergasted. From that point on, she felt uncomfortable around Melody. Their lifestyles were dramatically different. Melody was only twenty-seven. Carolyn couldn't fathom what it would be like to be young, beautiful, and outrageously wealthy.

Women had always flocked to her brother. At thirty-two, Neil was a handsome and enthralling man. In many ways, Melody and Neil had made a good pair. Her brother was talented and charming. He was also playful and boyish. Things had changed recently. The art market had grown stale, causing Neil to experience a bout of insecurity. The typical artist, he knew nothing about money, other than how to spend it. She had a feeling that before everything was over, the Ferrari parked next to them in the garage would be history.

Carolyn was afraid for him. She didn't like the way things were shaping up. "Did Melody know you were seeing Laurel?"

"No," he said, tilting his head. "Why would I tell her something like that?"

Hank Sawyer and Officer Cutter entered the garage. "We need to talk to him, Carolyn," the detective said, a solemn look on his face. "We can either do it here or at the station."

"Give us five more minutes, Hank." She took a deep breath. She was used to dealing with criminals. The idea that her brother might one day be a suspect in a homicide had never crossed her mind. Because of Christmas, the case would be in limbo for several days. They had to use the time to their advantage. The jilted lover would make a viable suspect, but from what Neil had said, Melody knew nothing about his relationship with Laurel.

Now that she knew he had proposed to Laurel and she'd refused him, her brother fell into the same category. The other possibility might hurt him more than being charged with murder. Laurel could have found out about Melody. That could be the reason she turned down his marriage proposal. She might have done the same thing, though, even if she hadn't known. It was too soon in their relationship and Laurel may not have recovered from her divorce. She turned to Hank. "You have to rule out suicide."

"It's impossible to kill yourself, then dive into a swimming pool."

Carolyn felt the hairs prick on the back of her neck. Stay calm, she told herself. Think rationally. "You found a syringe, right? Maybe Laurel overdosed on narcotics and someone dumped her in the pool to make it look like a drowning."

"Depends on what's in the syringe," Hank told her, his eyes fixed on Neil.

He was trying to get inside Neil's head, Carolyn realized. She'd been surprised when he hadn't tossed both of them out rather than take a chance they might contaminate the crime scene. He'd gone even further by discussing the circumstances of a murder with a person who could turn out to be a suspect. He was shrewd and Neil was naive. Sawyer wanted to watch Neil, hear him talk, see how he responded. Two could play the same game. She needed to find out if Hank thought they had a case against her brother.

"Laurel wasn't on drugs," Neil said, his face flushing. "She was a schoolteacher, for Christ's sake. Don't ruin her reputation."

"People aren't always who you think they are, know what I mean?"

"What about her ex-husband?" Neil suggested. "He was a marine or something."

"Navy," Hank said. "He's a lieutenant commander. Mr. Caplin said he was on a ship somewhere in the Atlantic."

Carolyn opened her mouth to say something.

Hank cut her off. "Don't worry, we'll verify his whereabouts through the proper channels."

"Neil has security cameras in every room," she said excitedly. "You may have the murderer on tape."

"We checked," the detective said. "Nothing there but a vacant house." He turned to Neil. "Was something wrong with the security system?"

"Yeah," he answered. "The tape recorder started making this weird sound, so I turned it off."

"How long ago?" the detective asked.

"Maybe three months."

They returned to the house. To keep from getting in the way of the crime scene technicians, Hank told Officer Cutter to wait with Neil in the guest bedroom.

Carolyn followed Hank back to the kitchen. Through the window, she saw the coroner still bending over the body. The rain hadn't let up and the white carpet was covered with muddy footprints. The officers were wearing raincoats with VENTURA POLICE DEPARTMENT on the back in fluorescent yellow. "I'd like to see the body," she said. "Maybe it's someone who resembles Laurel. It's pretty dark out there, even with the lights on."

Hank opened the door in the kitchen and walked outside with Carolyn. The damp, cold air caused her to shiver. "Here," he said, removing his jacket and handing it to her.

"Thanks," she said, tossing it over her shoulders.

Charley Young was one of the top forensic pathologists in the county. A short man in his late thirties, he had a sprinkling of gray in his hair. He peered out at her from behind thick glasses. Carolyn had worked with him on a homicide several years ago. He spoke with a slight Korean accent. "I hear this is your brother's house. Did he know the victim?"

"Yes," Carolyn said, staring into the face of Laurel Goodwin. Her eyes moistened. She'd seen her share of dead bodies, but most of them she didn't know. She remembered what a pretty teenager Laurel had been, always a smile on her face, bubbly and cheerful. She wasn't pretty now.

Other memories passed through Carolyn's mind. She recalled waking up late one night and catching Neil and Laurel necking on the living-room sofa. Laurel didn't get along with her parents, so she spent a lot of time at the Sullivans' house. When she stayed for dinner, she always insisted on cleaning up the kitchen.

"It's her," Carolyn said, unable to avert her eyes. A large umbrella had been placed over the body. Portable lights allowed her to see the deceased woman fairly clearly. Her skin had a bluish cast and her limbs were awkwardly positioned.

Her face was twisted. Carolyn wasn't an expert, but she'd seen scores of autopsy pictures. What they referred to as a death mask was not a pleasant sight. Laurel's soggy bra was ripped from the paramedics' attempts to resuscitate her and the electrodes from the EKG machine were still attached to her unmoving chest. Her cotton panties had slipped down her hips, exposing a portion of her pubic hair. Even though the person who'd killed her didn't appear to have tortured her, Laurel Goodwin did not die with dignity.

"Hank said you only found one puncture wound," Carolyn said, turning to the coroner.

"When I get the body to the lab," Charley Young told her, "I may find more puncture wounds. See this contusion on her forehead? I suspect she may have fallen forward onto a solid surface, perhaps a table of some sort. She could have passed out after the contents of the syringe entered her body, or the assailant may have knocked her unconscious prior to the injection."

Carolyn returned to the house while the detective lingered. The killer could be Neil's rich girlfriend. She asked the officer to give them some privacy and sat down on the bed across from her brother in the guest bedroom. "Did Melody have a key?"

"No," Neil said. "No one has a key but you and Addy."

Since Melody had spent time there, Carolyn knew she could have taken Neil's keys and made a duplicate while he was either sleeping or engrossed in his painting. She didn't ask about the security code, as anyone who came in and out with her brother could have seen which numbers he punched into the alarm pad.

The fact that Laurel was a teacher didn't mean she lived a pristine life. And Neil had only recently started seeing her again. They would have to rule out the chance that her ex-husband or a former lover might have found out about Neil and had become enraged enough to kill her, then staged it so it looked as if her brother was responsible.

At the moment, they didn't even know what type of drug had been ingested, or whether it was the cause of death. For all they knew, Laurel could have had blood drawn for medical reasons.

When Hank stepped back into the room, Carolyn told Neil to give him Melody's phone number and address, as well as inform him that he'd been with her for most of the afternoon and evening.

"How many times did you go in the pool today?"

"Only once," Neil said, a blank look on his face.

"And you were wearing your jockey shorts, right? You were in bed when you saw the object floating in the pool."

"Yeah," he answered. "I told you all that before. What's the problem?"

Carolyn stopped the detective before he asked more questions. He was fishing, but she didn't know why Neil's clothing was an issue. Regardless, it was time to shut him down. "I'm sorry, Hank," she said. "You'll have to question Neil in the presence of an attorney."

He was quiet for some time. She could tell that he wasn't prepared to make an arrest. She understood his position. He needed information. Refusing to cooperate with the police was also viewed as a sign of guilt. Carolyn recognized several reporters waiting on the front lawn behind the evidence tape.

"Excuse us," Hank said, guiding Carolyn into the bathroom, then kicking the door shut behind him. "We had another homicide this afternoon . . . three blocks away."

"Christ, Hank," Carolyn exclaimed, "why didn't you tell me?"

"I haven't exactly had time," he tossed back. "Besides, we're trying to keep the press at bay for as long as possible. Don't repeat anything I tell you, understand?" He paused, then said, "There's a strong chance the two murders are related."

Her jaw thrust forward. She started to yell at him again,

but she didn't want Neil to overhear. "Then why are you treating my brother like a suspect?"

The detective shook his head, refusing to answer.

Carolyn erupted, stomping her feet like a child. "Don't you dare pull that shit on me. You may have a serial killer on your hands. Why put Neil through the wringer? He might have information that could help you put these two cases together. Besides, I thought we were friends. Do you think I'd treat you like this if *your* brother found his girlfriend dead in his swimming pool? Neil is distraught enough as it is. Level with me, damn it."

Hank turned to the sink and splashed water on his face. "You think I'm not under stress," he told her. "Raphael Moreno killed seven people last month. Now I've got two homicides in one day."

"That's not the point," Carolyn said, closing the lid on the toilet and sitting down. It was hard to think when she was surrounded by her brother's Fendi cologne, a rich mixture of leather, citrus, and musk. She knew it well since she'd bought him a bottle for his birthday. They were in the guest bathroom near the garage. Neil probably stopped in here to check his appearance before he went out. She stared at the gold fixtures, the lion's head ornament on the spigot. His talent had provided him with a rich life, far better than hers when it came to material possessions. She'd never begrudged him his success, though, and he had always been generous. "Maybe I'll forget about the attorney if you tell me what's going on," she said. "I'm not trying to conceal anything, Hank. I just don't want my brother railroaded for a crime he didn't commit."

"I won't deny the cases have similarities," Hank told her, wiping his hands on a brown-and-gold-striped towel. He braced himself against the wall, focused at a spot over Carolyn's head, then began an unemotional recitation of the facts. "The other victim was named Suzanne Porter. We think she may have died from a lethal injection. Charley said there was no other apparent cause of death. Few contusions on her forehead, but not as severe as what we found on Laurel Goodwin. The murders occurred in the same geographical area. Both women were found in their bras and panties. The crime scenes were wiped clean, no evidence whatsoever. This isn't your garden-variety killer. He's ritualistic, methodical, and neat. There was no indication either of the victims was raped. Odd, considering the suggestive clothing. Mary Stevens thinks he may have had them model for him before he killed them."

"I was right, then," Carolyn said, flicking the ends of her fingernails. "There *is* a possibility it's a serial killer. Jesus, Hank, at the rate this maniac's going, he could kill five more women by tomorrow morning. You need to warn people, get help from other agencies."

"This is one of the reasons I didn't tell you sooner," he said, sucking in a deep breath. "We can't jump the gun and throw the city into a panic right before Christmas. The chief wants us to keep a lid on this until we know exactly what we're dealing with. It may not be the same killer. Don't you see? We're looking for similarities. All murders are similar in one way or the other."

"What doesn't make sense," Carolyn said, "is why the killer left a syringe in Neil's bathroom."

"You know what frightens me the most?"

A muscle in Carolyn's face twitched.

"I feel like I'm in the murderer's house," Hank continued. "Both the victims could have stepped out of one of your brother's paintings. Same bone structure, same body conformation. This house is too neat, too sterile. It reminds me of an operating room. It's awfully strange that your brother claims he knew nothing about the syringe. Murderer or not, he had to have seen it. Doesn't he brush his teeth before he goes to bed? Doesn't he take a piss? Our guys claim the prints on the syringe appear to be the same as all the other prints we've lifted in here." He stopped and locked eyes with her. "For all we know, your brother killed both of these women."

"There's got to be an explanation," she said, feeling herself trembling. "He has a housekeeper. Being neat doesn't mean you're a murderer."

"This isn't merely the work of a housekeeper," he insisted. "Even his studio gives me the creeps. Tubes of paints are lined up perfectly. Brushes are sorted as to size. The maid only comes in one day a week. Your brother showers and dresses on her off days, doesn't he? Why aren't there any towels on the floor, coffee cups in the sink, newspapers and mail thrown around? Don't bullshit me, Carolyn. You know he's a perfectionist and so was the murderer in these two crimes."

Neil had a touch of obsessive-compulsive disorder. Today, Carolyn thought, they had a fancy name for everything. In the past, her brother's tidiness would have been viewed as an attribute instead of an illness. So what if he liked things in order? Because of her children, her house was always a disaster. This could be one of the reasons why Neil had never married. Her father had been the same way. Once, she left a speck of ice cream on the kitchen counter and when her father came home and saw it, he flew into a rage and tossed all the silverware on the floor.

There were far more serious things that could come out about Neil. Could she keep the police from finding out? Not if they pursued him for the deaths of two women. The room seemed to be closing in on her. When she tried to swallow, she felt like something was lodged in her throat. "I—I need air."

Hank placed his hands on her shoulder and turned her around. "When something goes wrong with a perfectionist, they come unglued. That's what happened with your brother. He tried to control it, but he couldn't. After he killed her, he went into a meltdown and started making mistakes. Even if he was a heroin addict, a guy this neat would have never left a syringe in his bathroom sink."

"Let me go, Hank," she said, pulling away from him. "The murderer left the syringe and that's not my brother. You'll know when the lab report comes back. Neil never touched it."

"He lied to us, Carolyn."

She placed a hand over her chest, slumping against the bathroom door, feeling as if he had slugged her. "What . . . what do you mean?"

"He told us he'd only been in the pool one time that day. You were there when I asked him. He was wearing a pair of jockey shorts when the security guard got here. We found a complete set of clothing in the laundry room, all of it soaking wet. And don't tell me he washed them. We're talking a silk shirt and expensive slacks. They were tied up inside a garbage bag. He must have intended to get rid of them, then forgot. When he set off the alarm, he messed up his plan. Maybe he was going to put the wet clothes in the trunk of his car with the body. After he set off the alarm, he decided to dump Goodwin in the pool."

"This is insane," Carolyn said, shaking her head in disbelief. "When you set off the alarm, the company calls you before they send someone out. All Neil had to do was give them the password."

"How would he explain the alarm going off? He knew we'd contact the alarm company. There's a dead body floating in his pool and he calmly tells the alarm company that everything is okay. They keep recordings of those calls."

"You're grasping at straws!" she shouted. "I told you to stop, Hank."

"He didn't call the paramedics, Carolyn; the security guard did. He could have killed Goodwin earlier in the day, either before or after he killed the Porter woman. Then he thought he could dump her in the pool and make it look like a suicide."

"As to the clothes," Carolyn said, ignoring his suppositions, "he was out in the rain. My clothes are wet, too. Just because you found some wet clothes doesn't mean Neil lied."

Hank reached in his pocket and pulled out his wallet. Then he slipped off one of his shoes. Handing them both to her, he continued speaking. "I've been walking around in the rain all night. Is my wallet wet? Are my shoes ruined? We found your brother's wallet in the bathroom, only a few feet from the syringe. We also found a pair of fancy leather shoes that look like they've been in the washing machine. Leather is a fairly good water repellent."

"Why is this important?" Carolyn and the detective were face-to-face. His breath reeked of garlic. She felt nauseous. Knowing Hank, he was mad that he'd allowed her to speak with the coroner, now that she was preventing him from questioning her brother. He wouldn't let her leave until he planted seeds of doubt. Sadly, he'd already accomplished his goal.

"Your brother could have injected Goodwin, then struggled with her, causing them both to fall into the pool. Afterward, he went to the bathroom, where he neatly laid out his wallet to dry, then accidentally knocked the syringe into the sink. He stripped off his wet clothes, placed them in a plastic bag, then went outside in his jockey shorts. He might have thought it was too risky to dispose of the body. Besides, how could he get rid of Suzanne Porter's remains? Two bodies is one too many, especially in an eight-hour period. So he intentionally set off the alarm, knowing the company would dispatch an officer. Now he'd have a witness who saw him sobbing over the body, and we'd assume a maniac was running loose in the neighborhood killing women."

The maniac he was referring to was her baby brother. Carolyn felt as if she were about to break apart. She had loved and protected Neil since infancy. Her parents hadn't planned on having more children after her. They were studious people who wanted their time to themselves. But she had pleaded for a sister or brother. When her mother came home from the hospital with Neil, she had placed him in six-year-old Carolyn's arms. Other girls had dolls; Carolyn had little Neil. He grew into an adorable, chubby little boy, hanging onto the legs of his big sister and following her around the house like a puppy.

She pushed the past aside and looked up at the detective. "Let's forget that Neil's my brother. Why would a killer this methodical, as you described him, leave a syringe behind? Even if he knocked it into the sink by mistake, he would have checked the house before he staged the scene by the pool."

"He forgot," Hank said, shrugging. "By the time he set off the alarm, he had murdered another woman. This wasn't the same as the first murder. Suzanne Porter was a stranger, or at least that's what we're assuming. Killing a stranger isn't the same as killing someone you know, particularly a girlfriend. He was rattled, so he missed things. He had too much to do, and the clock was ticking. I'm fairly certain the Goodwin murder was impulsive. She did something to make him angry. He could have struck her and she fell, causing the injury on her forehead. That's when he panicked and shot her up with drugs." He stopped, rubbing his chin as he thought. "There's another more sinister scenario. What if your brother started seeing Laurel to prime her as a future victim? Insignificant schoolteacher. Who would make a fuss if she disappeared?"

Carolyn blinked back tears, her struggle to remain rational disintegrating. "Next time you want a sounding board for your outlandish speculations, find someone else."

Officer Cutter knocked on the door. "The coroner wants your permission to transport the body."

The detective ignored him. "You know I'm not supposed

to discuss the case outside of the department. Whether you realize it or not, I'm trying to prepare you."

"Right," Carolyn said facetiously.

"Hire an attorney," Hank told her, his eyes as cold as marble. "Your brother's going to need one. And if you have even an iota of concern for the women who lost their lives today, keep an eye on him. Trust me, if he kills again, you're going to regret it."

Before they left, Neil gave Detective Stevens the contact information for his housekeeper, Addy Marshall. He wanted to call Melody himself, but his sister talked him out of it. Under the circumstances, she thought it was better if the police handled it.

Carolyn asked Hank if they could leave through the backyard to avoid the reporters. The small house behind the swimming pool was also cordoned with police evidence tape.

As soon as they opened the gate leading to the alley, a female reporter for the *Ventura Star* shoved a microphone in Neil's face. A man with a Minicam perched on his shoulder began filming. Neil instinctively threw his hands up. "Did you know the victim? Was she your girlfriend? How long have you been dating?"

"He has nothing to say to you," Carolyn said, positioning herself in front of Neil.

Her car was parked on the street in front. She motioned for her brother to follow her and darted through a side yard, then dropped down behind two large trash containers. Once the reporters had passed, they waited, then finally made it to her white Infiniti and ducked inside, speeding off down the street.

By tomorrow morning, Neil Sullivan would be famous for more than his artwork.

Chapter 10

Carolyn lived in a modest one-story house near Ventura College, a far cry from her brother's sprawling house in Ocean View Estates. The exterior was painted white with blue shutters, and the walkway to the door was lined with blooming rosebushes. Her sixteen-year-old son, John, took care of the yard in exchange for gas and car insurance money.

When Carolyn arrived with Neil, she found her boyfriend, Paul Leighton, snoring softly on the sofa. At five-ten, he wasn't muscular like Brad. His clothes hung nicely on his body, though. He was wearing a white Polo shirt and jeans, and his salt-and-pepper hair was pushed back behind his ears. He blow-dried it straight every morning, but when there was moisture in the air, ringlets formed on his neck and forehead. Since he didn't spend much time in the sunshine, his skin was chalky white. Paul jokingly said it made him look like a ghoul. She thought it provided an interesting contrast against his mostly dark hair. His eyes were such a pale shade of blue, they looked gray except when they caught the light.

Leaning down, she shook his shoulder to wake him. "Why didn't you send Isobel over, Paul?"

"I didn't want to bother her," he said, yawning. "What time is it?"

"Almost three," she answered. "Did John or Rebecca wake up?"

"No," he said, glancing over at Neil. "I guess I'll head home. I'm sure you two need to talk. If there's anything I can do to help, you know how to find me."

Every day, Carolyn became more attached to him. In addition to being her lover, Paul was the type of person who was always willing to lend a hand. Maybe that was the reason he'd become a teacher instead of taking a high-paid position in the private sector. One of his fellow professors at Caltech said he wasn't self-absorbed like many people in his field, and Paul appeared to have dedicated himself to shaping young physicists' lives and careers. He'd taken a sabbatical to write a book. His goal was to demystify physics for the general population. In order to distance himself from the university, he'd left his home in Pasadena and rented a house three doors down from Carolyn's.

"I'll meet you in the kitchen in five minutes," she told her brother, stopping to turn off the Christmas-tree lights. "Have some cookies and milk. It might make you feel better."

Stepping outside with Paul, Carolyn filled him in on the evening's events. The rain had stopped, but the night air was damp and frigid. She rubbed her hands together to warm them. He removed his jacket and draped it over her shoulders. Placing a finger under her chin, he tilted her head up and kissed her.

"Sounds like you went for a walk in hell," he said, his hands encircling her waist. "I've had a few of those days myself. Don't worry, they'll catch the bastard who did this. You know your brother wasn't involved."

His comments didn't settle her nerves. What Paul and Hank didn't know was that Neil had suffered a nervous breakdown five years ago. He'd been dating a high-spirited Irish girl who could drink most men under the table. After a night at the pub, they had argued. Neil had become enraged and slugged her, knocking out three of her teeth. Megan O'Connor had agreed not to press charges if Neil underwent treatment at a psychiatric hospital. When he was released, he'd put his life back together. As long as he focused on his painting, he was fine. But in stressful situations, he had a tendency to unravel.

Setting thoughts of Neil aside, Carolyn remembered that they were celebrating Christmas at Paul's house. His daughter, Lucy, was the same age as Rebecca. John wanted to go to MIT and major in physics. He loved spending time with Paul. The man had become a father figure to both her children. Frank, her former husband, was finally in rehab. A talented writer, he had turned to drugs when his first novel was rejected. A man who wrote technical books like Paul was a world apart from a novelist, or she would have never entered into a relationship with him. Handling one artist was enough.

"Since it's morning," Carolyn said, glancing back at the door, "I guess it's officially Christmas Eve. Are you sure you still want us to come over tonight? We may not be very cheerful."

Paul clasped both of her hands. "Bring Neil, of course. As for the kids, they can come over as soon as they wake up. Isobel will make them waffles. I know you have to work, so I won't expect you until later."

"Merry Christmas," Carolyn said, waving as he took off down the sidewalk. She didn't want to spoil things, but if Neil refused to come along, she would have no choice but to stay with him. Recently she'd seen the same frenzied look in his eyes that she saw at the time of his breakdown. The psychiatrist had diagnosed him as manic-depressive and prescribed lithium. Although she thought it was safer if Neil took the medication, she personally thought the doctor was wrong. No one simply had a breakdown anymore, a low spot in their life where they did something they wouldn't normally do. It seemed that anyone who spent time in a mental hospital was diagnosed as either manic-depressive or schizophrenic. The fact that the experts had so few labels for their diagnoses made her doubt their credibility. It would be similar to having only two crimes. Multiple personalities had almost disappeared, seemingly more fitting for the movies than reality. Oh, she'd almost forgotten. He wasn't simply neat. Neil had been diagnosed with another label—obsessive-compulsive disorder, or OCD. A lot of bachelors in his age bracket were neat. She thought their desire to have everything in order was one of the reasons they remained single.

Regardless of how she felt, Carolyn had to ask herself the question: could Laurel's refusal to marry Neil have caused him to spin out of control enough to kill her? Banish the thought, she decided, entering the house and locking the door. She felt guilty for even thinking that her brother could be a murderer. As Paul had said, they'd find the killer and everything would be fine.

Even on the day before Christmas, she couldn't set aside her work, especially now that Brad was in the hospital and several of their top investigators were out sick. The report on Raphael Moreno had to be finished before the hearing that morning. Carolyn needed to be up in just over three hours. Sleep wasn't going to be a luxury she would have this night.

After the hearing, she would stop by the hospital and see Brad. When she'd spoken to the emergency room physician, he'd told her that it might be six weeks before Brad could return to work. Why had he insisted on interviewing Moreno? Jealousy, she decided. He might be her supervisor, but his reputation as an interviewer was not anywhere as strong as hers. Brad was also hardheaded. When he was working with criminals, Brad's attitude frequently led to trouble.

Carolyn felt responsible for what had occurred. She had pushed Moreno to the breaking point. Her plan had been to return and fake outrage that he'd been left in the room so long, maybe even bring him some cigarettes, candy, and gum, hoping he might soften and open up. Now they would never know what had caused him to commit the crimes, or more important, whether or not he'd had an accomplice.

When she entered the kitchen, she found Neil sitting at the table in the dark. "What sounds good?" she asked, turning on the lights. "I can make you a sandwich. How about some eggs and bacon?"

Neil snapped at her, "How could I eat at a time like this?"

Carolyn busied herself loading the dishwasher, telling herself that Neil's edginess was understandable. Rebecca was thirteen now and was supposed to help with the chores. She'd have to talk to her. This was the third day she'd come home to a sink full of dirty dishes. "I may have to take over Brad's job while he's out on leave," she said, opening the refrigerator and grabbing a soda.

"When will I be able to go back to my house?" he said, ignoring her comments.

"I don't know," Carolyn told him, popping the cap on her diet Coke. Since his recovery, Neil had done exceptionally well. While she juggled her kids, a demanding job, and law school, all he'd had to worry about was what he was going to paint and which woman he was going to sleep with. She remembered the reed-thin boy who'd been bullied by his classmates. Before he'd started dating Laurel in high school, rumors had spread that her brother was gay. Neil had no interest in sports or other so-called masculine interests. All he'd ever wanted to do was paint and draw.

The tragedy had struck at the worst possible moment. Neil had already been tipping into depression because of his finances. Resuming his relationship with Laurel, according to her brother, was the only good thing in his life. She didn't understand why he'd been so down. The house alone was worth almost a million, and Neil had paid off his mortgage several years back. When her brother had asked if he had enough money to support a family, Carolyn had laughed, telling him he could support a wife and a dozen kids. Neil also had his stock portfolio, the paintings he had in storage, and the flashy new Ferrari. Her brother had more money than the average person earned in a lifetime. In one night, though, everything had changed. If the DA prosecuted him for murder, his assets would begin to disappear.

"You can stay here as long as you want," Carolyn said. "Why don't you try and get some sleep. The bed in the guest room is made up. The TV you gave to John is in there if you want to watch it. Since he got his license, he's not around enough to use it."

"Thanks," Neil said, his voice picking up for the first time tonight. "I doubt if I can sleep."

"You need to rest," she told him. "Hank Sawyer wants you to come down to the station as soon as we hire an attorney."

"Carolyn," Neil said, a strange look in his eyes, "the answer is yes."

"Yes, what?"

"I did sleep with Melody tonight."

Her brother must think his statement would clear him. Instead, it added another level of complexity. While he was having sex with one lover, the other lover was floating dead in his pool. He certainly wouldn't make a sympathetic defendant. The women would hate him and the men would be envious. "The police have to consider you a suspect, Neil, at least for the moment."

"But I just told you I was with Melody," Neil said, a confused look on his face. "I have an airtight alibi."

"Wrong," she said, crushing the soda can with her hand. "Once they bring Melody in for questioning, she's going to tell them that you were lovers. Then your alibi won't mean much."

"I don't understand."

"How can they be certain Melody is telling the truth? You could have coaxed her into lying. The police might think she did it because she loves you."

"I'm innocent," Neil proclaimed, turning sideways in his seat so he didn't have to look at her. "I didn't kill Laurel."

"We're talking about a court of law." Carolyn knew she had to be forthright with him. The situation was too serious for false optimism. "Your innocence must be substantiated with facts. How do you think a jury will perceive you when they find out that you've been sleeping with two women at the same time? The only way out of this is to flush out the real killer. Did Laurel have any enemies?"

"She's a teacher," he said, tipping his chin up. "She was the nicest person I've ever met. Everyone loves . . . loved her. I can't imagine anyone wanting to hurt her."

"Except Melody."

"Don't be ridiculous, Carolyn," Neil argued, spinning back around. "Melody didn't know Laurel. Why would she kill someone she doesn't even know? Anyway, like you said earlier, Melody was with me when Laurel died."

"We won't know the time of death until the coroner completes his report," Carolyn explained. "You said you drove around before you headed toward Brentwood. Melody could have committed the crime and had plenty of time to make it back to her house before you arrived."

"She was in the shower when I got there," Neil argued. "She must have been shopping. I saw sacks from different stores and all kinds of clothes with the tags still on them. I went there to end it. Things got out of hand."

"In the shower, huh?" Carolyn said, tapping her fingernails on the table. "If you'd just killed someone, what would be the first thing you'd do? Think about it, Neil." When her brother just stared at her, she continued her explanation, "Wash off the evidence, maybe?"

"Laurel drowned," he said. "What kind of evidence would she have on her body? There wasn't any blood or anything. Melody would never kill anyone. Even if she found out about Laurel, she wouldn't care. In the circles she travels in, the only thing I was good for was a few laughs and recreational sex. For all I know, she was sleeping with dozens of guys. She even slipped tonight and called me Richard."

God, Carolyn thought, he was even more naive than she thought. "Just because Laurel's body was found in the pool doesn't mean the killer dived in with her. There was probably a struggle. Laurel could have scratched whoever killed her. All the lab needs is a few hairs, a drop of blood, or a piece of skin under the fingernails. Melody could have arrived at her house only a few minutes before you. Did you stop for something?"

Neil became agitated, gesturing with his hands. "I stopped for gas, okay? There's no way she could have made it back before me. I was driving the Ferrari."

"And she drives a Porsche," Carolyn pointed out, taking a sip of her soda. "Did you exceed the speed limit?"

He looked down at the table. "I didn't speed because I don't want to get a ticket. Besides, it was raining and the roads were slick. I wasn't going to drive it, but the battery was dead on the van and I didn't want to take the time to jump it."

"Melody might not have been as cautious. Besides, there's also the possibility that she hired someone. With her kind of money, she could hire an army of assassins. How often did you see her?"

"Once a week," Neil said, fidgeting. "It wasn't exactly easy for us to get together. It's a long drive to Brentwood."

"You may have meant more to her than you realized," Carolyn said, locking eyes with him. "Neil, this girl may have been in love with you and you didn't even know it."

"I don't think so, especially after tonight. I called her a slutty bitch. Like I told you, she blurted out another man's name while we were having sex. She wasn't serious about me. You think she was at my house earlier today. She was more than likely bouncing around in her bed with this Richard guy."

Was he telling the truth? His body language suggested he was lying. Perhaps he was just upset. She still had to confront him. "You said you got mad when Laurel refused to marry you. Did you hit her? Did she strike her head against a table or something and you panicked, then tried to make it look like someone else had murdered her?"

Neil stood, slamming the chair against the table. "You're not my sister," he shouted, furious. "How can you accuse your own brother? Other than Megan, I've never hit anyone in my life. Christ, she came at me with a butcher knife. No one believed me. I had to spend six weeks in the nuthouse or the DA would have prosecuted me. Like then, you don't believe me. I'm the one who always takes the beating. Remember when I was a kid? Chad and Bolly Cummings beat me to a pulp. I just laid there and took it."

"I'm trying to prepare you," Carolyn replied. "These are the type of questions the police are going to ask."

"Don't prepare me, okay?" Neil said, removing his shirt and throwing it at her. "If you wanted to make me sweat, you succeeded. Now I don't have anything to wear."

She walked over to him. "I'm on your side, Neil. Clothes are the last thing we need to worry about right now, don't you think? Anyway, you can borrow some things from John." When he started to leave the room, she circled around and grabbed him by the shoulders. "Stay away from Melody. She's trouble. You have to do what I say, understand? This girl may be a murderer. If she thinks you're trying to shift the blame on her, you might be her next victim."

Chapter 11

Outrageously handsome, John Sullivan stood six-one and had thick dark hair and luminous green eyes. His body was tan and muscular. When Carolyn had divorced his father, she'd taken back her maiden name. John and Rebecca had later become unhappy because they didn't have the same name as their mother, which sometimes confused people. Because Frank, her former husband, had failed to pay child support, Carolyn felt justified in changing their children's names to Sullivan as well.

The teenager opened the door to his mother's bedroom and found her asleep in her clothes, a stack of papers on the floor beside her. "Mom," he yelled, "it's after seven! Aren't you going to be late for work?"

"What?" Carolyn said in a groggy voice. "I . . . I . . . forgot to set the alarm. Where's Rebecca?"

"She's getting ready," the boy said. "Don't you remember? You told me to drive Rebecca to Grandma's today. I'm going to the beach with Turner. Why is Neil here?"

"He's having his house fumigated," Carolyn lied, sitting up and rubbing her eyes. She'd have to tell them the truth, but she didn't have time to do it now. "Did you talk to him?"

"No," John told her. "He's asleep. Did you ask him why he didn't come over and look at Rebecca's drawings?"

Ignoring him, Carolyn jumped out of bed and rushed to

the bathroom. How could she have overslept? If John hadn't mentioned her mother, she would have thought the night before was a bad dream. What was she going to tell her? Merry Christmas, Mom, your precious son may end up in prison.

Throwing on a black suit and a white shirt, Carolyn stepped into her shoes and headed to her daughter's bedroom. Rebecca was thirteen going on twenty. John had warned her that his sister would be trouble. With long brown hair and fair skin, Rebecca had grown into a lovely young woman. The current fashion trends had turned teenage girls into provocative sex objects. Just last week, Rebecca had shown up at the breakfast table wearing a cropped top and low-rider jeans that exposed the waistband of her underwear. Carolyn thought the stores who catered to young girls today looked as if they were selling costumes for exotic dancers.

Rebecca had her hair tied in a ponytail on top of her head. At least none of her body parts were showing. She was dressed all in black, though, with her feet clad in patent leather military boots she'd bought at a secondhand store. "Hi, sweetie," Carolyn said, walking over and kissing her on the cheek. "It's Christmas, not Halloween. See if you can find something a tad more cheerful."

"We've had this discussion a dozen times," Rebecca said, holding a pocket mirror as she applied her lipstick. "Don't bother me about my clothes."

"Fine," Carolyn said, not wanting to argue. She rushed down the hall to the kitchen, grabbing a handful of Balance bars, a bottle of water, and an apple, dumping them in a large canvas tote. John was outside hosing down his 1992 red Honda Civic.

"What time are we supposed to be at Paul's tonight?"

"I forgot," Carolyn said, her mind going in a dozen directions. "It's dinner. Call Paul and then catch up with me later this afternoon with the time. He invited you and your sister for breakfast as well. Oh," she added, pressing the button for the alarm on her Infiniti, "don't speed with your sister in the car. Next year you're going to be paying the insurance."

Her domestic duties fulfilled, Carolyn took off for work. Her personal cell phone rang just as she turned onto the ramp for the 101 Freeway. She took a deep breath, seeing her mother's phone number on the caller ID. "Mother," she said to Marie Sullivan.

"Did you see today's paper?"

"Not yet," Carolyn said, "but I know what it says. Don't get all worked up and make yourself sick, Mother. I've got everything under control." If only that were true, she thought. "Neil is staying with me right now. There's going to be an investigation."

"Is he unstable again?" Mrs. Sullivan asked. "I've been worried. He didn't look good the last time I saw him. He kept rattling on about some woman. Was she the one who was killed?"

"Her name is Laurel Goodwin. Remember her? Neil dated her in high school. This is going to be hard on him, Mother. To be honest, it's not going to be easy on any of us."

"She was a pretty girl." Mrs. Sullivan fell silent for several moments. "Did he do it, Carolyn? Please tell me he isn't responsible for this poor girl's death."

Carolyn swallowed hard. If her mother felt strongly enough to voice her suspicions, her own fears were certainly warranted. "I don't think so," she answered honestly. "Or at least, that's what Neil told me."

"If he didn't kill her, then who did?"

"That's the big question," Carolyn said, steering into the parking lot of the government center. "Please don't say anything to the kids. I haven't had a chance to tell them yet. We'll talk more tomorrow when I come over to take you out for Christmas dinner."

* * *

Carolyn ran into Agency Chief Robert Wilson in the corridor leading to her office. She'd already noticed the furtive glances from her fellow probation officers, followed by the strange buzz when several people started whispering at the same time.

After Neil had gone to bed, she'd finished the report on Raphael Moreno, then dictated it by phone. The word-processing pool had promised to have it completed by nine forty-five, giving her fifteen minutes to get to the courtroom. The report was supposed to be dispersed to the various parties at least a week prior to the sentencing hearing. Because Veronica's baby had arrived seven weeks early, the judge had waived the time requirement. Moreno wouldn't be on the bus to prison, however, as he was now facing additional charges of aggravated assault on a police officer.

Wilson fell in step beside her. "I saw the paper," he said, steering her by the elbow into his office.

"Who didn't?" Carolyn said, taking a seat across from his desk. She waited as he poured them both a cup of coffee.

Being the chief certainly had its perks, she thought, blowing on her coffee to cool it. Wilson's office was the size of her living room. A conference table was located on the left side of the room. On the right was a miniature putting green. His chairs were real leather, and the office had wall-to-wall bookcases. Instead of looking out over the parking lot, Wilson had a view of the foothills. His desk wasn't cluttered with files. The only things on it were a yellow pad, a pen holder, a stapler, and a neatly folded newspaper. His computer was located on a credenza behind him. The screen saver showed a man swinging a golf club. Other than practice his putting, she wondered what he did all day. She thought of study hall, where a teacher did nothing but sit there and occasionally answer a question.

Wilson was in his late fifties, stood five-ten, and, except for a bulge around his middle, appeared to be in good shape.

A dapper dresser, he was wearing a pale blue shirt with a white collar, a red power tie, and a navy blue suit with faint red stripes. His dark hair was neatly trimmed and his skin was tan from the sun. He had a penchant for practical jokes, and he was often mistaken for the actor Gene Hackman. Instead of telling people the truth, he soaked up the attention, even going so far as signing autographs.

As he leaned back in his chair, he tossed the paper in front of her. "What's this thing with your brother all about? I'd planned on spending the day with my family."

"Why did they put my picture on the front page?" Carolyn exploded. Her eyes were so tired she was having trouble focusing on the lines below. "The woman was found in my brother's pool, not mine."

"News," Wilson said, cracking his knuckles. "Everyone loves it when the good guys get mixed up with the bad. When you stick an heiress in the middle, you've got yourself a whopper of a story."

"There were two homicides, remember? From what Detective Sawyer told me last night, they're probably related. It may even be a serial killer. For obvious reasons, they don't want officially to go public with it yet."

"I'm aware there was another murder," Wilson said, a chill in his voice. "This Porter woman's sister doesn't work for my agency. As a probation officer, you have access to confidential court records. All I'm interested in is your brother. How do you think it's going to fall?"

"I have no idea," she said, curling her fingers around her mouth. "I know Neil didn't kill her. He was in love with her. They dated when they were in high school. When he went to Europe to study art, she married an officer in the navy."

"Ah," Wilson said, taking a drink of his coffee. "So the woman who died was an old flame. I've had a few of those surface myself. Nothing but trouble. If your brother was in love with"—he reached forward and took the paper back from her, opening it to the second part of the article—"this Laurel Goodwin, why was he in LA with the Asher woman? Did she buy one of his paintings or something?"

Carolyn didn't answer. She started to pick up her coffee cup from the end table, then decided she was jittery enough as it was. "Who do you think is the best defense attorney in the county? Vincent Bernini?"

"You're talking big bucks. Sure you need such a heavy hitter?" He moved his coffee cup to the edge of the desk. "The police haven't charged your brother yet. Word gets out you've hired Vincent Bernini and everyone will assume he's guilty."

"I know," Carolyn said, her brows furrowing as she thought. "But Neil's got the money to hire a decent attorney, at least for the short haul. A trial, well, I'm hoping it doesn't go that far. I'm beginning to suspect someone is trying to frame him."

"How so?"

Carolyn's eyes widened. "More ways than you could imagine."

Wilson came from behind his desk and picked up his putter, tapping a ball into the circular target. "I can imagine just about anything," he told her. "I generally restrict my fantasies to making a hole in one or winning the lottery. I got a call this morning from the board of supervisors. Talk to me, Carolyn."

He was making her nervous. Carolyn thought about leaving. What happened to her brother could have easily happened to Robert Wilson or Brad Preston. The chief was a known womanizer. Brad moved in different circles, yet it was still what people would consider the fast lane. She thought of Paul, certain he would never find himself in such a position. The physics professor was brilliant, stable, and her children adored him. Theirs was a comfortable, enjoyable relationship. Brad had been an emotional roller coaster. As desirable as he was, she was relieved that their affair was over.

"Why would the board of supervisors care?" she asked, a tinge of aggravation in her voice. "I'm not directly involved. As long as I can do my job, you shouldn't have a problem."

"Forget it, I'll run interference for you," Wilson said, propping his putter against the wall. "Brad told me he assigned you that mayhem case. You know how long it's been since we've had a mayhem? When it first came in, I didn't recognize the code section."

"It's aggravated mayhem," Carolyn told him. The crime was intentional mutilation or disfigurement, or depriving a person of a limb, organ, or member of his body. The sentence was life with the possibility of parole. In this instance, the victim had been attacked with a machete, severing his right arm at the elbow. "Tupua Mea'ole, the defendant, is Samoan. He doesn't speak English. I'm waiting for an interpreter."

"What's the status on the victim?"

"He's alive," Carolyn told him, pushing her hair back behind her left ear. "They're fitting him with a prosthesis. The victim's name is Harold Jackson. He has an extensive record. He served five years at Folsom for armed robbery. He was also a suspect in the LAPD shooting three months ago. They didn't have enough evidence to convict him. Since he lost an arm, the DA decided not to file battery charges."

Wilson smiled. "Sounds like we should give your Samoan a medal. Wasn't Jackson about to rape his wife?"

"That was a misunderstanding," Carolyn said, sighing. "The woman wasn't his wife. She's a prostitute. She claims Jackson was beating her. The defendant lived next door, heard the ruckus, and came to the rescue with his machete. The public defender tried to plead self-defense. The DA didn't buy it. Just because the victim is a criminal doesn't change the facts. You can't chop off a person's arm if they don't have a weapon."

Wilson returned to his desk. "Can you handle the unit for a few weeks?"

"A few weeks?" she said, tilting her head. "I was told Brad would be laid up for at least six."

He smiled, causing the skin around his eyes to crinkle. "Idiot doctors," he said, turning so he could see his monitor. "That's Tiger Woods, you know." When Carolyn ignored him, he swiveled his chair back around. "The doctor you talked to was probably an intern. I stopped by the hospital on my way to work this morning. The X ray showed only one broken vertebra. Brad isn't a pantywaist. He won't let a little thing like that throw him out of the box."

Carolyn looked down as she thought. If she became acting supervisor, her pending cases would have to be reassigned. The mayhem case was a nightmare. Due to language and immigration problems, the investigation would take twice as much time. Stepping into Brad's shoes would increase her responsibilities. On the other hand, it might be easier than her present position. She wouldn't have to deal with deadlines, victims, or defendants. Overall, it would give her more time to help Neil.

"So," Wilson said, "can you handle it? You know, with the situation with your brother."

"Yes," she said with confidence, deciding to make light of the situation. "What can I do? You know, outside of trying to keep his spirits up?"

"Sounds good."

Carolyn headed for the door, then stopped. "Tell me something," she said. "Why did you promote Brad instead of me? You obviously think I'm qualified or you wouldn't ask me to fill in for him."

Wilson pointed his finger at her. "You caught me with my pants down," he said, chuckling. "Damn, you're good. Brad warned me about you."

"You didn't answer my question," Carolyn said, wondering what else Brad had told him.

"Men don't have babies and all that PMS stuff," he said,

scrunching his nose up. "My wife drives me crazy. I'd prefer not to deal with female problems at the office."

Carolyn was speechless.

"Hey," he said, seeing the look of shock on her face, "ninety days and I'm out of there. Do a good job while Brad is gone and I'll bump you up before I retire. I hate to admit it, but a woman like yourself may end up running this agency one day." He smiled as he intentionally shivered. "Scary thought for a guy like me. Glad I won't be around to see it."

Carolyn could see why Brad felt comfortable acting the way he did. The head of the agency was prejudiced against women. The man was a dinosaur, she thought, glaring at him in disgust. If she had the time, she'd report both of them.

"Oh, by the way," Wilson said, his eyes twinkling with mischief, "everything I said was just a joke. Thought you could use a laugh. Brad said you were a good sport. Have a happy Christmas."

"How?" Carolyn said, disappearing through the doorway.

Lawrence Van Buren was sipping coffee in the lobby restaurant of the Biltmore Hotel in Santa Barbara, enjoying the view of the ocean. The day was so clear, all five of the Channel Islands could be seen. When weather permitted, they could also be seen from Ventura. Channel Islands National Park consisted of more than two hundred thousand acres, half of which were underwater. Over two thousand species of plants and animals could be found, and 145 of these species were unique to the islands and could be found nowhere else in the world. Archaeological and cultural resources spanned a period of over ten thousand years.

A historic Santa Barbara structure, inside its stucco exterior, the Biltmore Hotel had mission-style doors, curved archways, dark tiled floors, and outstanding service. Everyone flocked to its restaurants, and its Sunday brunch was one of the hottest tickets in town.

The hotel's holiday decorations were lavish. A towering tree stood in the entryway, its lights twinkling. A sleigh full of brightly wrapped packages was a few feet away, complete with life-size reindeer and an animated Santa Claus. Christmas music softly played in the background, and a crackling fire burned in the fireplace. Unlike Los Angeles, Santa Barbara had seasons. The air outside was brisk enough to wear winter clothing. Van Buren came here because it got him into the holiday spirit.

His eight-year-old son, Zachary, ran up to him. "Mom needs money," he said excitedly. "We're going shopping. She said we could pick out two toys. I want a Spider-Man suit and those sticky gloves he uses so I can climb walls. Felicity wants more stupid Barbie dolls. She already has hundreds of them. As soon as she gets them, she rips their heads off."

"What are you running around by yourself for?" Van Buren said, his brows raising. "It's dangerous for a kid your age. This is a public place. Where's your mother and sister?"

"In the gift shop."

"Tell her I said it's okay to use her credit card."

"But . . . she needs money for taxicabs and things."

He reluctantly reached into his pocket, pulling out three one-hundred-dollar bills and placing them in his son's outstretched hands. His wife was a spender. He preferred cash because it left no paper trail. The only problem was that he didn't know if she was handing out his money to some no-good beach bum or tennis pro. Their sex life was terrific, but a man should keep track of his wife, particularly one as young and beautiful as Eliza. Ruffling his son's hair, he said, "Run along now, champ. Daddy has a business meeting. Tell your mother to be back by lunch so we can beat the traffic. You don't want to miss Santa Claus, do you?"

"I'm not a baby, Dad," the boy said, trying to look tough.

"I know Mom is Santa Claus. Don't worry, I won't tell Felicity."

After his son ran off, Van Buren saw a tall, striking blonde striding rapidly toward him. Her movements were stiff, almost robotic. She leaned forward slightly when she walked, and her head swiveled from side to side as she constantly checked her surroundings. He wished his men were this alert. If they'd kept their eyes open, he wouldn't be in the present predicament. He stood and pulled out a chair. "How did you like the new helicopter?"

"Fine," she said, sitting down and crossing her shapely legs. "It would have been nice if you'd met me in the city, Larry. To make me fly to this godforsaken town on Christmas Eve is bullshit, let alone inconvenient. I have a family, you know, and the last few days haven't been pleasant."

In all the years he had known her, Van Buren had never seen her smile. She was the coldest woman he'd ever known. When he looked into her eyes, it was as if he were staring at a slab of concrete. No emotion, fear, humor, compassion, basically no human characteristics whatsoever. How could she possibly have a family? Just the thought of it was ludicrous. Her work was excellent, though, and her services were in great demand. She had worked in Russia, Iran, China, Africa, and all over Europe. No matter how difficult the job, she always performed flawlessly. Through no fault of her own, this time she had failed. What had kept him awake the night before was whether or not he should allow her to continue. What he'd asked her to do was so simple, it was almost laughable for her degree of talent. That's what made the situation unbearable. Dismissing her was a sticky situation. His nerves forced him into small talk. "Are you still living in Vegas?"

"No," she said bluntly. "I never lived in Vegas."

"What have you got against Santa Barbara? We come here every year around Christmas. Most people think it's paradise. Hardly any crime, pristine beaches, even a polo field. Look at this place," Van Buren said, gesturing. "The ambience is magnificent. You can't find this in LA."

She flagged a waiter over and asked him to bring her a glass of orange juice. The look on her face said Van Buren had dropped down another notch for not asking her if she wanted anything. "I don't live in LA."

"Oh," he said, "when you mentioned meeting there, I assumed—"

She cut him off. "Never assume. And where I live is confidential. It's not a game, Larry. You know the rules."

"Absolutely," Van Buren said, fearing she might get angry and throw him across the room. She was as strong as most men, but she dressed as if she'd stepped out of a fashion magazine. On a rare occasion when he'd caught her intoxicated years back, she'd explained that women didn't bulk up like men, regardless of how much weight they lifted. The only time a woman's muscles showed was when she flexed. The majority of female bodybuilders took steroids. Even then, most of them resembled an ordinary woman in street clothes.

She drank the orange juice in one swallow, slamming the glass down on the table. "I don't have time to shoot the breeze. Tell me what you want me to do."

"Nothing," he said, shrugging. "We struck out, so that's the end of it. I'll keep pursuing it, of course, but your end of it is finished. I'm in no way unsatisfied, although it would have been better if things had gone as planned." He dropped his hand to his side, sliding a slim leather briefcase to her side of the table. "I needed to find this material fast," he added. "I would have never gone to such extremes if I wasn't pushed against the wall. Like I said, I know it's not your fault."

The waiter came by and placed the bill on the table. Van Buren looked down and scribbled his name and room number. When he looked up, the briefcase and the woman were gone.

Chapter 12

Hank Sawyer entered the detective bay at the Ventura Police Department and checked to see if Mary Stevens was at her desk. When she wasn't in the field, the detective wore short skirts and tight-fitting sweaters, causing the men in the unit to develop suspicious bulges in the lower half of their bodies. She should get along great with Carolyn, Hank thought. He was certain the probation officer was going to get hurt one of these days.

Before talking to Mary, he stopped at the coffeepot and pulled out a Styrofoam cup, filling it first with half a cup of milk and three packages of sugar. The coffee had probably been there since seven o'clock that morning, and Hank needed the milk to coat his stomach.

He had been appalled when he'd heard how Carolyn had taunted Raphael Moreno, talking on the phone and demeaning him until he'd snapped and crushed her cell phone. He had to give her credit, though. She'd managed to get Moreno to talk, even though he hadn't told her much of anything worthwhile and Preston had screwed it up. He adored Carolyn, but she took too many risks when it came to her job. She manipulated and baited dangerous criminals on a regular basis. Many times she went to the jail with her boobs popping out and a skirt that barely covered her ass. One of the deputies swore she'd showed up one time without underwear and spread her legs in front of a rapist. Hank doubted if a Catholic girl would have gone that far. With Carolyn, though, anything was possible. Defense attorneys knew the moment a case fell into the probation officer's hands that their clients were going to serve twice as much time in prison. The attorneys instructed their clients to keep their mouths shut, but Carolyn could get a Doberman to drop a steak at her feet. Not only was she able to aggravate violent offenders' prison terms by her unconventional interview techniques, she'd provided vital information in dozens of unsolved crimes. If Carolyn was willing to risk her life and let disgusting criminals gawk at her body to nail them, Hank found it hard to fault her.

Mary dressed the way she did to prove a point. In the past, many rapists went free due to the fact that their female victims had been dressed provocatively at the time of the crime. Mary felt women should be able to walk the streets naked without fear of being sexually assaulted. Hank was old-fashioned. When a woman dressed scantily and paraded down the street, she was asking for trouble.

Having graduated UCLA with a degree in biology, Mary had hired on with a medical research company, then quit to enter the police academy after her father was killed in the line of duty. Police work was in her veins. In addition to her father, two of her uncles were detectives in Los Angeles.

The woman worshipped her father. No wonder, Hank thought. Jim Stevens had been a decorated officer. He'd been working a gang slaying when he was killed. Mary conducted her own investigation and managed to uncover the killer, the primary reason she'd decided to quit her job and enter law enforcement.

"What have you got for me?" Hank said, poking his head in the opening to her cubicle.

"A mother of a hangover," she said, massaging her temples. "I stopped by the party after I cleared the Goodwin homicide. Bad decision."

"You don't have time to nurse a hangover," Hank snapped at her. "Finish what you're doing and come to my office."

"At least we didn't have another murder," she called out. "I was afraid we'd have three by now."

"It's early."

Hank's office was a partitioned space like Mary's, but it was considerably larger. In addition, he had a window. These were the perks you got after twenty-three years as a cop, he thought sourly. When Mary appeared, he picked up a folder and threw it at her. "While you were partying, I stayed up all night organizing the particulars of these crimes. I thought you wanted to be a lead investigator. If I'd been given a chance like that, I'd still be snooping around the crime scenes."

Mary leaned over and picked up the papers off the floor. Vernon Edgewell walked by and whistled. "Where's the preliminary lab report on Porter, Vernon?" Hank barked. "Go to the lab and sit there until they give it to you, understand? And if we page you again and you don't answer, I guarantee you'll be out of a job by the end of the week. Then you can kiss your big career with the FBI good-bye." He turned his attention back to Mary. "Stop wearing short skirts. The chief caught sight of you the other day and asked me to have a word with you."

Mary's shoulders rolled forward. "Guess we're gonna cancel Christmas."

"Damn right," Hank said, dropping down in his chair and yanking his tie off.

She quietly sat down. "Are you through spewing lava or should I get Bender so you can jump on him, too? He's the only guy left in the office."

The other detectives were chasing down leads, interviewing witnesses, and picking over the crime scenes. The department wasn't that large, and with the holidays, the two homicides were a nightmare. "What do you have on Porter?"

Mary closed the file, balancing it on her lap. "Not as much as we have on Goodwin."

"Shoot," he said, gulping down his cup of lukewarm coffee, then tossing the empty cup in the trash can.

"The lab confirmed that it was Neil Sullivan's fingerprints on the syringe. Just so you'll know, I picked up the report at five o'clock this morning."

"Incredible," Hank said, shaking his head in disbelief. "His whole story was shit."

"There's more," she said, clearing her throat. "The substance in the syringe was a mixture of heroin, cocaine, and strychnine. Looks like we've got ourselves one hell of a crime."

Things like this didn't happen in Ventura, he thought. "Was Porter injected with the same stuff?"

"Don't know yet," Mary said. "The killer didn't leave us a specimen, so we have to wait for the autopsy."

"Did you have any luck with the Asher woman?"

"No," she said. "I've left three messages on her machine. My guess is she's avoiding us. Just because Sullivan's fingerprints are on the syringe doesn't make an airtight case, Sarge. He could have come home late, gone into the bathroom to brush his teeth without turning the lights on, then touched the syringe without knowing it. Haven't you ever gone to the bathroom without turning the lights on?"

His mind spun back to the days when he'd been drinking. He'd staggered to the bathroom plenty of times in the dark, sometimes so tanked, he missed the toilet. "I'm not going to hang a case on it," he told her, rubbing the side of his face. "It might substantiate an arrest, though. I don't buy all these accidents and coincidences. Those are for defense attorneys. When you start thinking like a defense attorney, you'll be back in uniform."

Mary handed him several sheets of paper. "Here's what we have at present," she said. "A Siemens wireless router was found inside Neil Sullivan's property. Evidently, it was connected to his security system. It provided an unknown person with the ability to watch Sullivan in any room that had a camera, including the backyard, where the killing more than likely took place. Because of his artwork, there were cameras everywhere. As you know, there was nothing on the surveillance tape. Sullivan must have turned it off. The last date it recorded was in November."

Hank leaned back in his chair. When a homicide was fresh, he fueled himself on outrage and adrenaline. Before he could solve it, however, he had to understand it. That meant a clear, focused mind.

"I'm not sure how the setup worked," Mary went on. "Our technical people think someone might have been spying on Sullivan, possibly the killer."

"I don't understand," Hank said. "Isn't this router, or whatever it's called, part of the security system?"

"No, I called the security company this morning. It's not their hardware."

"Interesting," he said, his arms folded on top of the desk as he listened intently. In cases this serious, time was limited. It was better to memorize things than to have to scrounge them up at a later date. The new breed of detectives used their Palm Pilots and laptops; then when they lost them or their computers crashed, they ended up with nothing. The only thing he had to worry about losing was his mind.

"Unfortunately," Mary said, "the router had been wiped clean, like everything else in the house. We do have unidentified prints, of course, but unbelievably few. We have Carolyn's prints on file, but we only found one set in the house." She ran her finger around the neckline of her sweater as she read through the rest of the report.

"Stop doing that," Hank said, his eyes drawn to her cleavage.

Mary looked up. "What?"

"Forget it."

"Don't you think it's strange that the guy's sister left only one set of prints in his house? You'd think her prints would be all over the place."

"He cleaned it."

Mary smiled. "If I ever need a housekeeper, I'll know who to hire. Some prints were the victim's. The other prints probably belonged to the housekeeper and Melody Asher. Then there's another set, which may or may not be the killer's. If it is our killer, his prints aren't on file. Hard to believe we're dealing with a first-time offender."

"There is no such thing as a first-time offender," Hank told her. "It's first-time caught."

"Amen on that one," she said, twirling a strand of hair around her finger. "I'd really like to hear what Melody Asher has to say about Sullivan, particularly as to his alibi."

"Tell me about it," Hank said, tossing his feet on his paper-strewn desk.

"I left before the father got there last night. Did he tell you anything worthwhile?"

"Stanley Caplin?" he asked, tugging on his left ear. He'd never handled a serial killer before, so he was overly anxious. For now, though, they had to treat the two murders as separate crimes. A good night's sleep would put things in perspective. "What was I saying? Ah, Daddy claims Sullivan is a drug dealer. Maybe our playboy artist stiffed his suppliers so he could buy himself that fancy Ferrari. The guy's sleeping with a gorgeous broad who has more money than God and he wants to marry a schoolteacher. Doesn't add up. Tell me more about this router."

"Since we haven't been able to question Neil Sullivan," Mary said, "we have to consider that the lab might be mistaken and he set up the router himself. He spends most of his time in that pool house he converted to a studio. Maybe he wanted to keep his eye on the house. The problem is we didn't find a computer or monitor anywhere on the property that was linked to the router."

Hank couldn't rule out the possibility that Laurel Goodwin's death was a result of Neil's indirect actions. Thugs could have killed her as a warning. He'd handled a single drug deal that had gone bad. When he'd arrived on the scene, the floor had been covered with blood and bodies. The next time, it might be Neil. "There's another possibility," he said. "Laurel Goodwin's divorce wasn't final. Her father claimed the husband called her a few days ago to make certain she signed off on the property settlement. She wasn't there, so the father talked to him. The husband may have found out about Sullivan and killed her."

"Why kill her?" Mary reasoned, tapping her pen against her teeth. "If the guy was jealous, he would have gone after Sullivan."

"She may have had dozens of lovers. Her husband filed for divorce, not her. In most cases, the woman files. According to her father, Jordan Goodwin is on a ship somewhere in the Atlantic."

"Have you confirmed that?" Mary asked, jotting down notes on the file folder he'd given her.

"Not yet," Hank said. "We've put in a call to the navy, but they haven't got back to us yet. What we need to do is to map out what the crimes have in common. There was no router on the Porter property. Also, no syringe left behind. Someone picked the lock in the door leading to the garage, but there was no forced entry with Goodwin. It really doesn't matter about the swimming pool, because the Porters didn't have one. The killer dragged the body outside, even though it appears that the murder occurred inside the house."

Mary snapped to attention. "It's the same, don't you see? He thinks water destroys the evidence. He threw one victim in the pool, and the other he left out in the rain."

"Manny in narcotics says there's some potent smack on the street. Was the heroin in the syringe high-grade?"

She excitedly flipped through the pages. "Yes," she said. "So was the coke."

"Okay," he said, rubbing his hands together. "Now we're getting somewhere. Both ladies are closet users. They may have started out snorting coke to stay thin, and before they knew it, they were hooked. The drug dealer is the guy on the motorcycle. Upscale women like these two don't know how to shoot dope. He makes a home visit, then finds out the drug kills them."

"That doesn't make sense," Mary argued. "If he injected one and she died, why would he inject the other?"

"Let's say he shot up the first victim. We're not sure who died first, only when the crime was reported. He leaves her and continues on his rounds to the next. She croaks. After he does everything possible to cover his tracks, he goes back to find the first lady dead as well." Hank smiled smugly. "How does that grab you?"

"Feasible," Mary said. "We still have Sullivan's prints on the syringe."

"Let's use your scenario and say he touched the syringe without knowing it. We'll make Goodwin the first to die." He stared up at the water spots on the ceiling. "He injects her in the bathroom. She dies. He panics and leaves the syringe in the sink. After dumping her in the pool to make it look like a drowning, he jumps on his bike and returns to Porter's house. He picks the lock and enters through the garage. She's dead in her bathroom. He dumps her out on the lawn, then does a bang-up job of cleaning the place, now that he knows he can't fool us into thinking the two deaths are accidents."

"That makes sense," Mary said. "He would have only had to break into one house because the victims knew him."

"Somewhere in this mess is the key to what really happened. Right now, we go with what we have. I'll call Kevin Thomas at the DA's office . . . see if he thinks we have enough to arrest Sullivan. He lied about the wet clothes, so that will go against him, and the syringe will most likely turn out to be the murder weapon."

"I forgot to tell you," Mary said sheepishly. "If he went in the pool twice that night, he didn't do it in the clothes we found in the laundry room. Only trace elements of chlorine, the type you find in tap water, not a swimming pool."

What did he expect? Hank thought, bracing his head with his hand. To put the case together on the first day? "Doubtful we'll get an arrest warrant, then. The big honcho over there is Sean Exley. According to Thomas, if even a remote chance exists that the state might fail to get a conviction, Exley won't allow them to file."

"Exley's a dick," Mary said, scowling. "He's afraid he won't be reelected. He isn't getting my vote. I'd rather see a donkey in that job than a self-serving asshole like Sean Exley."

"When you come back to work, I want you to question the principal of Ventura High where Goodwin taught. Find out who her friends were and see what they say about her. Also, see how many sick days she took last year." He stopped and took a breath, trying to remember what else he needed her to do. "Find out what happened to her car and clothes. She didn't walk to Sullivan's house in her bra and panties."

"Aren't we putting all our energy into the Goodwin homicide and neglecting Porter?"

"No," Hank told her. "I've got four men on Porter. Right now, we've got nothing to go on. Solve Goodwin and you'll solve Porter. If it's not a serial killer, the way things are stacking up, both these women were killed by the same person. Neil Sullivan was playing around with two women. Why not three? Find out if he knew Porter."

"I understand," she said. "We'll make a full-court press after the holiday. Who's going to talk to Melody Asher?"

"I'll handle her," Hank said, moving some papers around on his desk.

Mary got up to leave. "I'm sure you will," she said, flashing a smile. "If you don't get around to it, I know about five other guys who would be glad to do it for you."

Chapter 13

Neil was drinking a cup of coffee in Carolyn's kitchen when he heard a knock at the door. He hesitated, trying to decide whether to answer it or not. Looking through the peephole, he saw Melody. His pulse quickened. Carolyn's words of caution resonated in his head.

Although she was the last person he wanted to see, he couldn't leave her standing there. As soon as he unlocked the dead bolt, Melody rushed in and embraced him.

"I heard what happened, on television," she said, a sharp intensity in her voice. She was wearing jeans, a pink cashmere sweater, and a full-length matching coat. Her feet were clad in pink K-Swiss tennis shoes. She'd fashioned her blond hair in a French braid, and her face was void of makeup. "I've been trying to call you all night. Where were you? Why didn't you answer your cell phone?"

"I was with the police." They went into the living room and Neil dropped down on the sofa, clasping his hands tightly in his lap. Melody walked over and looked at the family pictures on the fireplace mantel. How could he explain what had happened with Laurel? He was disgusted with himself.

"Look , it's your sister, the famous probation officer." She held up a silver frame. "How's her boyfriend?"

"Fine," Neil said, trying to figure out how he could get her to leave.

"The paper said this Laurel woman was your girlfriend. Is that true?"

Hearing Melody say her name was surreal. He felt a wave of emotion. Laurel had been the love of his life. The woman standing in front of him was repulsive. "I think you should go."

"I'll go after you answer my questions," Melody said, a devilish look on her face. "Who was this woman? Was she or was she not your girlfriend?"

"I . . . she was a friend of mine since high school. We saw each other every now and then." Neil couldn't force himself to tell her the truth. He'd never seen her really angry before. Her nostrils were flared, her lips compressed, and her movements jerky. She was a different person, not at all attractive. Maybe this was how she really looked, he thought. Everything was an illusion. Her eyes frightened him.

"Was she stalking you or something?"

"It wasn't like that," Neil said, fumbling for the right words.

"Then what was it?" Melody snapped. "Were you sleeping with her?"

"Well . . . um . . ."

"You were fucking her," she said, giving him an icy look. "And to think you had the nerve to call me a slut last night. Of course it's socially acceptable for a man to sleep around. But if a woman does, she's a whore. You never answered my question. Were you sleeping with her?"

"Yes."

"Damn it. I knew it."

"We were lovers."

"That's great. Now the police are calling me," Melody said, pacing in front of him with her arms crossed over her chest. "They must think that I killed her in a jealous rage. I didn't kill her. You killed her."

"You're talking crazy," Neil said. "Settle down. Let me explain our situation."

"No, let me explain *your* situation!" Melody yelled. "This

is your problem, not mine. You're the one who was sleeping around behind my back. You're the one who found your so-called lover dead in your pool." She stopped and pointed at her chest. "You think I'm going to be your alibi? Think again."

"But I was with you last night."

"Who says?"

"What do you mean?" Neil said, shocked. "You even made a video of us."

"I don't know what you're talking about," Melody said, her voice low and controlled now. "I was with Richard last night. You must be having another breakdown, Neil. Did you tell the police you spent time in a mental institution? They should know that their prime suspect has a history of violence against women. They're going to find out eventually, you know."

Neil felt like ripping her throat out. "I didn't kill Laurel. I loved her."

"Love, huh?" Melody spat at him. "Nice of you to tell me, Neil. What were you going to do, invite me to the wedding?"

"You were with me last night, not this Richard guy."

"Oh, really?" she said, arching an eyebrow. "You've met Richard Fairchild. Blond hair, about your height and build. Of course he's younger and better looking than you. His picture was on the cover of *Esquire* last year. Richard's not a loser like you. You can't even sell your stupid paintings." She stopped and paced, then yelled at him, "I refuse to have my name smeared. I don't want to get involved."

Neil's jaw dropped. "You're not going to tell the police the truth?"

"Nope, at least not right now." Melody smirked, pleased with his reaction.

Everything suddenly made sense. Melody insisted on taping them, even called out the name Richard. "You found out I was seeing her. Then you threw her in my pool so the police would think I did it."

"That's the difference between you and me," Melody said,

only inches from his face. "You're so whacked-out, you don't even know what you did last night. You have no control of your life. I'm always in control. I can do anything I want. You can't even walk across the street without getting lost."

"You murdered her, didn't you?"

"No, you murdered her!" she shouted. "You killed her before you came to my house. They're going to arrest you, and when they do, they'll find out about your little drug problem."

He grabbed her by the shoulders and shook her. "I won't let you ruin my life."

"Temper, temper," Melody said in a playful tone. When he released his grip, she pushed him hard. He lost his balance and slammed back onto the sofa. "You're outmatched, Neil, both mentally and physically. Want to play rough? You have no idea who you're dealing with."

Hank received a phone call from the desk officer, advising him there was a problem at Carolyn's house. When he got the probation officer on the phone, she confirmed that Neil was at her house. Now he knew why the media was camped out on her lawn. He decided to drive by and attempt to run them off. He didn't want his suspect to panic and leave town. Then his attorney could file for a change of venue, claiming his client couldn't get a fair trial in Ventura County.

Neil Sullivan belonged behind bars if he was guilty. Facts didn't lie. The truth would make the decision for him, regardless of his feelings for Carolyn.

When he pulled up at Carolyn's house, Hank saw at least ten reporters standing on the sidewalk, itching for any scrap of information they could obtain. The story became hot when a leak from within the police department exposed Neil's romantic relationship with Melody Asher. The media put two and two together and realized they had a sensational story. It spread like wildfire. The headlines in the morning paper read SCHOOLTEACHER DIES IN LOVE TRIANGLE. A different paper declared: HEIRESS MELODY ASHER TANGLED IN HOMICIDE. If the press were judge and jury, based on the articles they'd written, Neil would get the death penalty.

Ironically, whoever killed Laurel Goodwin and Suzanne Porter might meet a similar fate—death by lethal injection. Personally, Hank preferred the smoking, convulsing, crap-in-their-pants electric chair. Shooting a vicious murderer full of drugs and watching him die peacefully wasn't that satisfying. Martha, his ex-wife, had called him sadistic until he'd made her look at pictures of an adorable little girl who'd been raped by five gang members and carved up like a watermelon.

As Hank approached the front lawn, the door opened and a woman emerged. Her blond hair glistened in the morning sunlight. When the door slammed shut behind her, he caught a glimpse of Carolyn's brother. Reporters swarmed the woman. She held up her hands with an annoyed expression, saying something he couldn't make out.

The flashing of cameras and clamoring reporters were no match for the detective. Hank forced his way through, almost knocking a female reporter down. He reached out and grabbed Melody Asher.

"Who the hell are you?" she yelled, yanking her arm free.

"Listen, lady," Hank said, "want to get out of here? Or should I leave you to be picked apart by these vultures? I'm not one of them."

"Fine," Melody said, following him.

"Are you Neil Sullivan's other girlfriend?" a reporter with thick glasses asked.

"Melody Asher, were you with—" another reporter blurted out.

"Miss Asher won't be answering any questions today," Hank said, escorting her toward his unmarked police unit. When he opened the door, she slid into the seat, flashing her blue eyes at him. He thought he saw a tinge of gratitude, then realized it was nothing but the glance of a beautiful woman.

"I've heard a lot about you," Hank said, steering the Crown

Victoria toward the main road. "Big bucks, looks, and a boy-friend who's in one hell of a lot of trouble."

"Oh, yeah, what's it to you?"

"I'm Hank Sawyer, with Ventura PD homicide," he told her. "Why were you at Carolyn Sullivan's house?"

"I was giving Neil a blow job," Melody said, smiling as she waited for a reaction. "You know, you're not a bad-looking man. When was the last time your wife took care of you? Marriage is bad for your sex life. That's why I'm single."

"Very funny," he said, a fake grin plastered on his face. "You're a real comedian."

"I don't think my comment was funny at all," Melody told him with a stoic expression. "Just the truth."

"Okay, you were in a relationship with Neil Sullivan?"

"Not really. I was having sex with him. If you call that a relationship, then . . . I guess the answer is yes."

The car fell silent as Hank tried to size up the woman sitting next to him. How could someone who looked like Miss America have such a filthy mind? If she were his daughter, regardless of age, he'd lock her in her room in a state of perpetual grounding.

Melody's testimony would be crucial. Extracting information from her wouldn't be easy. He hadn't given it much thought, but a possibility existed that she'd killed Laurel Goodwin in a jealous rage. Afterward, she could have driven around the block looking for another victim, someone who resembled Goodwin in order to trick the police into believing they were dealing with a serial killer. Now that he thought about it, his scenario wasn't that outlandish. Suzanne Porter had been out jogging. Her running clothes had still been damp when they'd arrived on the scene. Neither of the women incurred any substantial injuries. Men usually spent time punishing their victims before they killed them, especially in sex crimes. Nothing precluded the killer from being a woman. A needle was a fairly sanitized way to take someone's life. He could see how it would appeal to a female killer. She wouldn't have to risk getting hurt, and no blood would even be splattered on her clothing. He looked over at Melody in her fancy pink outfit, asking himself if he could be sitting next to a murderer. There were more female killers than anyone realized. They didn't get caught because no one was looking for them.

Motive—well, motive wasn't a problem. From what Neil had said, he'd been in love with Laurel Goodwin. If the woman sitting next to him had found out . . . His eyes wandered to her pink sweater. The material was clinging to her small breasts. He could tell she wasn't wearing a bra because he could see her nipples. She reminded him of the Hilton sisters—rich, young, skinny, and spoiled rotten. "Where were you last night? Were you with Neil?"

"I don't think that's any of your business." Melody placed her hand on his thigh.

Something sparkled and the detective looked down. She was wearing what had to be a five-carat emerald on her left hand, letting prospective suitors know she was single in a big way. Her manicured pink fingernails even matched her sweater. Delectable decadence, he thought, forcing himself to keep his eyes on the road. At that moment, he didn't care if she was a killer. What he wanted to do was lick her like an ice-cream cone. He inhaled her perfume, knowing it was permeating the fabric in his jacket. It had an orange scent to it. No, he thought, taking another sniff. Maybe it was chocolate or vanilla. Mary used to wear the same thing. She said it was called Angel. Mary was a knockout, but this girl could get a rise out of a corpse.

"We can do this nicely," Hank said firmly, "or I can drag your pretty little ass down to the station."

"Look at you," she cooed, "this police work has you ready to explode. Some extracurricular activity never hurt anyone. Wanna have some fun?"

"Cool it!" Hank shouted, more for his sake than hers. He had to keep a professional demeanor. He coughed. "How long have you been seeing . . . ah . . . sleeping with Neil Sullivan?"

"About a year," Melody said, placing her hand back in her lap. "Those artist types are great lovers. Neil was too good for a quickie."

"Did you know Laurel Goodwin?"

"Is that really the question you want to ask me?" she said, spreading her left leg in the car seat as she turned to face him. "You want to know if I killed her, don't you?"

Hank saw the seductive smile on her face. Her straight white teeth were gleaming. She was stalling, he thought. She wanted him to beg for the answer. "Well, did you?"

"Of course not," Melody said emphatically. "I only kill people when I'm on-camera. I'm an actress, in case you don't know." She placed her hands behind her neck and sighed. "Now that we've got that out of the way, take me back to my car. If not, I'm going to call my attorney."

Hank made a U-turn and returned to Carolyn's house. Melody didn't seem to be the jealous type. At least not to the extent that she'd kill off the competition. With her looks and money, she could have anyone she wanted. She wasn't their murderer. The woman was so bored, she looked as if she were about to fall asleep. The question was whether or not she could provide him with incriminating information about Carolyn's brother. "Do you think Neil is okay mentally? You know, could he have gone off his rocker and murdered his girlfriend?"

Melody's face shifted into hard lines. In no time, her self-control surfaced and she flashed another seductive smile. "Neil's always been unstable. That's the way I like them. It's exciting in a way. You ever had a crazy girl, Detective? You know, someone who'll do you like you've never been done before. Something about being on the edge of sanity lets the sexual predator free. Neil never held back."

"Has anyone ever told you that you have a one-track mind?" Hank said, sick of her sexual innuendos. "Try giving me a straight answer. Could he have killed Laurel Goodwin?"

Melody looked him straight in the eye. "Sure."

Chapter 14

The Moreno sentencing was uneventful. Because of the incident with Brad, Raphael Moreno was not present in the courtroom. He watched the proceedings on closed-circuit TV.

After advising the county operator to forward her calls, Carolyn went to Brad's office. Sitting down at his desk, she picked up a stack of files from his in basket. Only seven cases, she thought. Covering for him would be easy. Pulling out a roster of probation officers, she read through a chart listing the cases that had already been assigned. She looked up when someone entered the room.

"What happened to Preston?" a female clerk with short red hair asked, removing a large stack of file folders. "Someone said an inmate at the jail broke his back. Is that true?"

"Not exactly," Carolyn said, watching as the woman placed the files in her basket. She quickly counted them. She'd just received seventeen new cases to assign. "Is this abnormal?" she asked. "You know, are there always this many cases?"

"Nah," she said. "This is nothing. Twenty is average. Sometimes it's as high as thirty."

Carolyn's mouth fell open. "Every day?"

"You got it," the clerk said. "It's probably light today because of the holiday."

Carolyn placed her head in her hands. She should have found out what was involved before she agreed to take over

Brad's position. What if Wilson was wrong and Brad didn't return to work for six weeks? She'd have to analyze each officer's workload, as well as their abilities. In addition, she had to read every report and approve the officers' recommendations before they submitted them. Brad made decisions in an instant. She was far more meticulous. Dealing with people's lives was serious business.

Seeing Brad wasn't that important, Carolyn thought, feeling overwhelmed. He had his racing-car buddies and his girlfriends. It was Christmas Eve. She needed to spend time with Paul and her children. She'd give Brad another day, hoping he could pick up some of the work while he was recovering. She wanted to do a good job. If she screwed things up, she'd jeopardize her chances of being promoted.

Carolyn called Vincent Bernini's office and spoke with his secretary. The woman informed her not to expect a response until after the holiday. Stuffing as many files as she could into her briefcase, she decided to go home and make an attempt to salvage Christmas.

At a few minutes past eight that evening, Carolyn, John, Rebecca, and Paul's thirteen-year-old daughter, Lucy, were gathered around the Christmas tree. After his confrontation with Melody and the media that morning, Neil had taken off to spend the night at their mother's place in Camarillo. The police had impounded the Ferrari and he wasn't allowed back on his property to pick up the van. Paul lent him his extra car, an older blue BMW.

The kids didn't want to wait until Christmas morning to open their presents. The floor was littered with wrapping paper and boxes.

Rebecca held up a red sweater trimmed with fake fur. "This is adorable, Mom," she said, putting it on to see if it fit. "Most of the things you buy me are hideous." Inside another box were matching red ankle boots.

Carolyn had given John a used laptop computer. "I really needed this," he said, walking over and kissing her on the cheek. "Are we going to get DSL now?"

"No," his mother said, sinking into the sofa. No matter what she gave her kids, they always wanted more. Lucy never asked for anything. When Carolyn had pointed this out to Rebecca, her daughter hissed at her, like a cat confronting a dog, "Why would she? She has everything. She even has her own American Express card."

Carolyn turned her attention back to her son. "You're lucky I found a computer I could afford. DSL would cost five hundred dollars a year. That's more than our budget allows. Maybe when you get a job."

Their meal had been wonderful. Isobel, Paul's live-in housekeeper, had made turkey with all the trimmings, along with two homemade pies, one chocolate and the other pecan. Around nine, Lucy asked Rebecca to spend the night. John had already made plans to stay with his friend Turner Highland.

Once the girls were in bed and the trash collected, Paul walked over and embraced her. "Why don't we go to your place?" he said, brushing a strand of hair off her forehead. "Your kids aren't there. We'll have the house to ourselves."

Carolyn frowned. "You know how I feel about that, Paul. We can't make love at my house. John or Rebecca might come home for some reason and walk in on us. We have to be even more careful now that John drives."

"Calm down," he said. "I won't mention it again. We'll go to my place in Pasadena. If we leave right away, we should be there in an hour. We can spend the night and come back early tomorrow morning. The girls have already opened their gifts. Lucy told me they were going to sleep in."

Carolyn was more than ready for an evening of pleasure. Unnoticed even by herself, she was stroking the bottom of her bra with her thumb. It had been too long. "What are we going to tell Isobel?"

"Come on, honey," Paul said, scowling. "You act like we're teenagers." He took her hand and. led her into the kitchen. "We're going for a drive, Isobel. If you need to reach us, call me on my cell phone."

"What?" she said, placing her hands on her ample hips. "I just had the phone turned back on at the Pasadena house."

Carolyn's face flushed in embarrassment. She ducked behind Paul. Isobel had been with the professor for nineteen years. She was the boss of the house and didn't mind voicing her opinion. Having recently turned sixty, she was a tall, wiry black woman with a mind almost as sharp as her employer's. Just like Paul and his daughter, Carolyn had come to think of her as a second mother. How did she know they were going to Pasadena?

"What you hiding for, woman?" Isobel asked her. "You think I don't know what you two are up to? Wish I wasn't so old or I'd get me some loving. Now get on out of here before I make you clean up the dishes."

Pacing the floor in her bra and panties, Melody breathed shallowly. She tipped the bottle of scotch. Finding it empty, she let it fall onto the floor. Her life was out of control and there was no one to help her. Nobody to hold her and make the pain go away.

Going to the penthouse level, which she called her viewing room, she removed a large box. Inside were two smaller boxes. One contained Lego pieces, and the other held a silver charm bracelet. Her real name was inscribed on the heart-shaped charm—Jessica Graham.

Jeremy was dead.

The charm bracelet was Jeremy's last gift on that terrible night before Christmas. She had worshipped her brother. He was the only one who had truly loved her. Melody and Jeremy were more than just siblings, they were best friends. He was her stability in an unstable and emotionally deprived childhood. Eighteen long years had passed since his death. Her eyes welled up with tears. Alone, she thought to herself. Alone on Christmas Eve once again.

Every year, she pulled out the bracelet and held it in her hands. Rubbing the shiny silver heart with her index finger and thumb made her feel as if Jeremy were still alive. He'd promised to buy her more charms. Each time she looked at the heart, though, she was also reminded that there wouldn't be any more. Her father had taken him away from her. The police told her that he'd cut out Jeremy's heart in an attempt to save him. When her father shot her mother in a blind rage, Jeremy was caught in the cross fire. Her brother died trying to protect their mother.

She dumped the Lego pieces out, sobbing as she began building a castle. Unlike their last night together, she had all the pieces. As soon as she finished, she stood and kicked out, scattering the pieces across the room. Her life was broken. Like the castle, every time she rebuilt it, it was repeatedly knocked down. Staggering across the room, she tripped on the wastebasket and almost fell.

Her attachment to Neil had grown strong. Because he was such a wonderful brother to Carolyn, she had begun to see him as an older version of Jeremy. Her brother had always looked out for her, protected her when her mother went on a binge, listened to her fears and dreams. She had thought Neil could step in where Jeremy had left off and find a way to heal her shattered heart.

Like everyone else, Neil had abandoned her. The only ones who stayed with her were the men who were after her money. She could spot them before they opened their mouths. When she was younger, she'd let them take advantage of her. Now she insisted that they treat her as they would any other woman. If they invited her to dinner, they paid the bill. When they traveled together, they split everything down the middle. If they complained, she told them to get lost. Why should she foot the bill just because she was wealthy? She wasn't anyone's damn meal ticket.

Melody hated the closeness between Carolyn and Neil. Jealousy of their relationship raged deep in her soul. In many ways, Carolyn was what she could have become if not for the tragedy that had taken her brother and destroyed her family.

Neil spoke of the hours he and Carolyn spent together. His sister was always there for him, and he for her. Why did he need to be with his sister and her children so much? His priorities were all screwed up. He needed to spend more time with her.

The Sullivans were a perfect family, something Melody would never have. Even their mother was smart. Marie Sullivan held a master's degree in chemistry. The father had died, but they still had warm memories of him.

Melody's childhood had been lonely and tainted by violence. She squatted down on the plush carpeting again. Tears fell from her eyes as she picked up the Lego pieces and placed them back in the box. Her mother had staggered through each day in an alcohol-induced haze. Her father had been a good man, a doctor. That all changed the night he'd shot her mother and brother. He was then sentenced to prison for thirty years. She didn't communicate with him. How could she? He had tried to blame everything on her. As far as she was concerned, she didn't have a father. He'd gone to prison and eventually he would be released. She would never be released. She'd been sentenced to a life of misery, sleeping next to the demons that continually taunted her.

She reached for the empty bottle, then collapsed, the room spinning around her. Her eyelids flickered as she felt herself drifting through time. Eighteen years disappeared and she found herself in the cold, frightening house of her childhood. When she saw Jeremy's face, she was filled with joy.

"Where are the rest of the pieces?" her brother asked,

looking at the partially completed castle he was building for his sister. A stream of profanity erupted from their parents' bedroom. At fifteen, Jeremy could escape by spending the night with one of his friends. Jessica was only nine. Although she could go to her friends' houses during the day, she was not allowed to have sleepovers. She hated it when her brother left, especially when her mother and father were fighting.

She was dressed in her pink flannel pajamas with the embroidered silk collar. They had become too small for her, but she refused to wear her new ones because they weren't as soft. Stretched out on her stomach on the floor, she pedaled her feet in the air. She had inherited her mother's strawberry blond hair, and her nose and cheeks were dotted with freckles. There were vague memories of a time when her mother had been pretty. She certainly wasn't pretty now. Her eyes were always puffy and red, her mascara smeared, her breath reeking of alcohol. Jessica loved her mother, but lately she'd grown to despise her.

She rolled a Lego piece between her index finger and her thumb. "Mama might have thrown some of the castle pieces away," she told him, resting her head on her fist. "She got mad at me yesterday because I didn't put them all back in the box."

"Why did she do that?" Jeremy said, annoyed. "Mom trained you to drop your toys on the floor. We're too rich to pick up after ourselves, that's Mrs. Mott's job. Even Dad says the same thing. All he wants us to do is study. Money can't buy intelligence."

"I don't care about the castle, anyway," Jessica said. "We live in a stupid castle."

"Be grateful that you have a roof over your head and food to eat. Think of all the kids who're cold and starving."

She fell silent for a few moments, chewing on the ragged skin around her cuticles. "Melody's parents won't let her come over anymore."

"I thought you didn't like that girl."

"Mel brags too much," she told him. "I still play with her, though. All the other kids live too far away." She stopped and put her hand inside the waistband of her tight pajamas. "People know Mama isn't right, Jeremy. Dad doesn't think they do, but they do."

The town kids called them stuck-up and spoiled. Jessica would have preferred a shack, something small and cozy, with a mother who cooked their meals, washed their clothes, and loved her children more than she loved a bottle. Jessica had tried to take it away from her one time and her mother had knocked her to the ground.

Six months earlier, her father had ordered the servants to leave the premises by six. The Grahams were society people. He couldn't allow the help to see his wife drunk. Even Mrs. Mott had been forbidden to play with her. Jessica didn't care. She was certain the nanny was a witch who'd put a spell on her mother to make her sick.

"Go to bed," Jeremy said, pushing himself to his feet. "It's past nine o'clock."

Two pale blue eyes peered up at him. "School's out for Christmas vacation, remember? Mama said I could stay up as late as I want."

"You do what I say," Jeremy snapped at her, pointing at his chest. "Mom isn't right, okay? She might tell you to jump off a cliff or stick your head in the oven. Listen to me or Dad."

No matter how often their parents fought, the children never got used to it. It was Christmas Eve and they were going at it again. The room fell silent. Jessica had tears in her eyes. Her brother walked over and placed a comforting hand on her shoulder. "I'm sorry I got mad. Want to watch a movie? You like *It's a Wonderful Life*, that old movie they play every Christmas. We have the video. We could go upstairs and watch it in the theater."

"You know I'm scared of the third floor," she said. "Something terrible happened up there. Daddy said if I ever go up there again, he'll send me away forever." She went to her dresser and pulled out a stack of Swiss chocolate bars, tied up with a gold ribbon.

"Why do you tell so many lies, Jess?" her brother said, the sounds from their parents' room growing louder. "That's the reason you don't have any friends."

Jessica refused to answer. They'd talked about this a dozen times. Since her mother lied, she assumed it was okay.

"I guess we'll watch the movie here, then."

The house was as large as a hotel, but they all lived in the left wing on the second floor. Jessica's room had been her mother's bedroom as a child. It was located next to their parents' room. Outside of the few years she'd attended college, Phillipa Grace Waldheim Graham had never lived anywhere but this house.

"We don't even have a Christmas tree," she said. "Do you think they bought us any presents?"

"Of course," Jeremy told her, although his expression said he wasn't certain.

Their father, a cardiologist, worked long hours in Manhattan. She knew he had probably forgotten to buy them any gifts. They had everything, anyway.

"I got you a special present," her brother said. "Do you want me to give it to you now?"

"Yes," Jessica said, smiling as she clapped her hands. "But I didn't get you anything. I asked Mama to take me to the store. She said it was too cold and she didn't want me to get sick."

"Wait here," Jeremy told her, leaving to go to his room.

When he returned, he handed her a small box. He watched as she eagerly ripped off the wrapping paper. Inside was a silver charm bracelet. With only one heart-shaped charm dangling from it, it looked naked.

"It's beautiful," she said, her face glowing. "Hearts mean love."

"Look at the back."

The girl turned the charm over and found her name engraved in the silver. "You're the most wonderful brother in the world," she said, walking over and hugging him. "I love you *so-o-o* much."

"I love you, too, Jess. Every year, I'll buy you another charm."

A few minutes passed and the smell of the chocolate got her attention. Jessica began methodically unwrapping the chocolate bars, her slender fingers as agile as her father's. Dr. Graham's emphasis on learning had paid off. She read at a high-school level, and she was far above average in subjects such as math and science. Her father had mentioned several times that she might one day become a surgeon like himself.

She laid out the candy wrappers side by side, then used each bar to shape bricks into various sizes. "See," she said, licking her chocolate-covered fingers. "If you hadn't torn down the castle, we could have finished it with these."

Something heavy crashed against the wall. Her mother must have thrown a lamp or a vase. Jeremy inserted the movie in the VCR, depressed the play button, then turned up the volume to block the noise.

As far as she knew, her father had never hit her mother. Unless she got drunk and went on a rampage, Dr. Graham was a soft-spoken and loving father, a man who would do anything for his family.

When she heard another thud against the wall, Jeremy hit the mute button on the remote control. It sounded like her mother was moaning. He asked Jessica to stay there, but she refused. They left the room to find out what had happened. When they reached their parents' room, they found it locked. Jeremy pounded on the wood with his fists. When there was no response, her brother insisted they go back to her room. Before they walked away, it became quiet. Jeremy told Jessica the argument had either ended or her mother had passed out.

Thirty minutes later, they tiptoed down the hall again to

see if they could talk to their father and make certain everything was okay. This time, they saw the door to their parents' room standing ajar. In the middle of the floor were a broken bottle and a stain where its contents had spilled out onto the carpet. Jessica's mother was on the bed, on her back, with her eyes closed, her arms sprawling out at her sides. She was wearing a black lace nightgown, and her left foot dangled off the side of the mattress. Their father was slumped in one of the blue velvet chairs, staring into space.

Jeremy told Jessica to go to bed, then went in to speak to their father. Instead of doing what he said, Jessica slid down the wall outside the door and listened.

"Are you all right, Dad?" her brother asked.

Dr. Graham was twelve years older than his wife. Standing six-five, he was an imposing figure. Phillipa Graham was a petite woman. Jeremy and Jessica inherited their height from their father. Her brother was already five-ten, and Jessica was the tallest fourth grader at her school. "Your mother's sick, son," Dr. Graham said. "If she doesn't stop drinking, she's going to die. Her liver is already shot."

"What are we going to do?"

"I've made arrangements for her to go into a residential substance abuse program, one of the best of its kind in the country." Dr. Graham paused and rubbed his temples. "That's what we were fighting about. She's chasing the booze with tranquilizers now. Either she bought them on the street, or one of her friends from the country club gave them to her. I've instructed every physician in town not to prescribe medications to her without my consent."

"But you have to work late or go to the hospital in the middle of the night," Jeremy protested. "The closest house is a mile away. How can I spend time with my friends? I'll have to leave Jess here alone. I deserve a life, don't I? What if something happens? I know Mom's drunk most of the time, but it's nice to have an adult around."

"Don't worry," his father told him. "I'll have Mrs. Mott

move in as soon as your mother's committed. Before you know it, she'll be home and everything will be fine."

Jessica ran sobbing to her room. Now she hated her father as much as her mother. She couldn't stay in the big house alone. It was full of ghosts and Mrs. Mott was a witch. She wished her mother and father were dead. Then they would give her new parents, who would love and protect her.

Chapter 15

When they arrived at Paul's house in Pasadena, Carolyn went to the bathroom to take a quick shower. She tried to put Laurel's murder out of her mind as the hot water relaxed her aching muscles. Leaning her forehead against the tile, she prayed that her brother wasn't responsible for Laurel's death. She then asked forgiveness for even thinking that he could do such a terrible thing.

Stepping out, she dried off with a large white towel. When she was in Pasadena, she was in Paul's world. The house had never been remodeled, just meticulously maintained. Never had she seen a home that was this reflective of the owner's taste and personality. Beautiful cherry-paneled walls, bold California colors, exquisite coffered ceilings, elaborate crystal chandeliers—and not a throw pillow out of place. About as far away as a person could get from the chaotic, teenage world she lived in. There was a delightful odor that she couldn't quite put her finger on. Was it cedar? It must be something permanent or Paul would never allow it.

Opening his medicine cabinet, she stared at the perfectly aligned bottles and tubes. The toothpaste not only had a top, it was rolled up tightly without a smudge on it. She closed the glass door too hard, causing a bottle of mouthwash to fall into the sink. Paul called out from the other room, "Is everything all right?"

She broke out laughing, then cupped her hand over her mouth so he wouldn't hear. The first time she'd spent the night here, she'd showered and sprayed herself with perfume. Paul had run into the bathroom, looking at her as though she'd ripped out the toilet. "What did you do?" he'd said, scolding her like a child. He proceeded to tell her it would take weeks to get the smell out of the house. That's when she discovered that Paul had an aversion to odors.

Now she had two neat freaks in her life—Neil and Paul. What a ridiculous thing, for Hank to be suspicious of her brother because he wasn't a pig. Tons of people needed order. It certainly didn't mean they were murderers. Maybe Paul was obsessive-compulsive like Neil. No, she thought, he was just a physicist.

She opened the lower cabinet and saw five bottles of Lubriderm fragrance-free lotion, which Paul had stocked up on after the perfume disaster. After she moisturized her skin, she slipped one of his white dress shirts over her naked body.

When she reached the living room, the sight and smell of the crackling fire awoke her senses. Paul was waiting for her. He'd tossed a thick white blanket on the floor in front of the fireplace. Holding two wineglasses in one hand and a bottle of vintage Merlot in the other, he set the bottle on the mantel and poured the dark red liquid into the glasses. "How could you make me wait like that?" he said, gesturing for her to join him. "You're cruel, Carolyn."

She giggled, watching as he sat Indian-style on the blanket. He was wearing the black silk boxer shorts with the hearts on them that she'd given him for Valentine's Day. Although he was not physically impressive, his mind made him irresistibly appealing. He was also the sexiest man she'd ever known. Not many women would agree, though, unless they'd slept with him.

Carolyn dropped down on the floor, taking her wineglass out of his hands. "Living dangerously, huh?" she teased. "Red wine on a white blanket."

"Well," he said, smiling, "it *is* Christmas."

She felt as if they were teenagers about to have sex for the first time. The energy was electric.

"Merry Christmas, baby," Paul said, tapping his glass against hers. After they both took a sip, he pulled her down into his lap. "I love you, you know."

"You're just making sure I don't fall asleep on you," she said, tugging on the elastic waistband of his shorts.

"I am not," he protested. "I really love you, Carolyn. The past year has been the happiest time in my life. Not only do I love you, Lucy loves you. She told me the other night that she wished you were her mother."

"I adore Lucy," she said, gazing into his pale eyes. She rolled over and kissed his stomach, then stuck her tongue inside his belly button.

"We're having a serious conversation here, young lady. Is that all you want me for, sex?"

"Sometimes," Carolyn told him, then fell serious. "I love you, too, Paul."

He bent down and kissed her, brushing a strand of hair off her forehead. "You don't know how long I've waited to hear you say that."

Paul clasped her hands and pulled her upright. He slowly unbuttoned her shirt, then pushed it off her shoulders, exposing her breasts. She lifted her hips and placed the shirt on the floor next to the blanket. Running her hands over the fabric, she found it incredibly soft, almost like velvet.

"Why don't you rub your hands over me instead of the blanket," he said, playfully pinching one of her nipples. "It's cashmere, by the way. One of my students gave it to me. I liked it so much, I gave her an A."

"Liar." Carolyn stretched out on her side, then patted a spot beside her. "Did that student do anything else for you on this blanket?"

"Of course not," Paul told her. "Stay here, I have to freshen up. I'll only be a minute."

She knew he would never accept a gift from a student. His ethics were impeccable. But as their relationship became more serious, she had to ask herself if she could live with him. He drove her crazy sometimes over inane things. When they went to the movies, they had to get to the theater at least an hour early. To make certain they got the best seats, he'd ask her to buy the tickets while he drove around trying to find the perfect parking space. If another car was behind them, he made her jump out. Rather than inconvenience the person behind him, one time he'd almost driven off with her hanging onto the doorknob. His quirkiness was one of the things she loved about him. He was maddening, but somehow wonderful.

She rolled around on the blanket, smiling as she played back scenes from their relationship. Carolyn had a bad habit of holding on to the rubber seal where the car window closed. The previous week, Paul had hit the button for the electric windows and almost cut her fingers off, then lectured her for thirty minutes. She gritted her teeth rather than tell him that he should have checked before he rolled up the window.

Everything had to be spotlessly clean. He was constantly searching for particles of food or dirt in her kitchen, and he was fanatical when it came to his clothing. He wore his pants too high on his waist, which made him look like a nerd. When she suggested he might wear a casual shirt loosely outside, instead of tucked in, he looked at her as if she'd lost her mind. No matter how much he weighed, he bought the same size. Every item in his drawers was folded precisely. She was certain he measured each piece to make certain the dimensions were accurate, and he absolutely never wore anything twice. He had stacks of gray socks, folded once, white Jockey underwear, also folded once, and a specific style of jeans and slacks. They spent hours at the department store and usually left with nothing. He could take months and go to ten different stores before he finally decided on a fifty-dollar purchase. She wondered if all physicists were as persnickety.

Personally, she doubted if he would ever finish his book. Her ex-husband, Frank, had been a writer. Paul didn't have the type of mind to write books, even about physics. His head was crammed full of numbers. Most of what she'd learned in the area of math, she'd long forgotten, burying it under mountains of legalities. She suspected his mind churned out equations even when he slept.

He came back into the room and lay down beside her. She held up her arm, staring at the Cartier watch he'd given her for Christmas. "The watch is great, Paul, but it must have cost a fortune. I can't show up at the jail in a watch like this. People will think I'm dealing drugs or having one of my probationers rob banks for me."

"For what I paid for the watch," he said, "I could have bought you an engagement ring. Seriously, when are you going to marry me?"

At first, she thought he was joking, then she saw he was serious. "Are you proposing to me?"

"I hadn't planned on asking you tonight," he told her. "I bought you the watch instead of a ring. It feels so right when we're together, like we're already married. Would you marry me under the right circumstances?"

"I don't know," she said, tossing her arms around his neck and kissing him. "You're not the easiest guy to get along with, you know. I might do something terrible . . . like put the pineapple rinds in the disposal or spray the house with air freshener."

"That's it," he said, holding her in a bear hug. "You're mine. We'll set the date later."

She whispered in his ear, "Are we going to look at The Book tonight?"

"We don't need The Book. I think I can improvise."

When they'd first started sleeping together, Carolyn had

been amazed at how proficient Paul was in bed. Several months later, she'd found a book on sex in his bedroom, tucked in between *A Tour of the Calculus* and Stephen Hawking's *Black Holes and Baby Universes*. Paul told her he hadn't been with a woman in years and decided to study sex to make certain he could please her. Instead of flipping through the pages like most men, he'd studied the book like a physics text. "Wow" was the only word for it. Carolyn thought every man should do the same.

Each time they made love, they tried a different technique and position. Their secret code for sex became "The Book." The other day at dinner, John had asked them what book it was they were always talking about and they'd both cracked up.

"Hurry," Carolyn told him. "If you don't, it's going to be morning and we'll have to go home. I need more than a few hours. I've been under a lot of stress lately, so I guess I'll have to pay for the full treatment."

"I thought you were broke."

"I wasn't going to pay you with money, dummy. How about a trade?"

Paul threw his head back and laughed. "You're a case. That's probably why I love you so much."

He refilled their glasses and they brought them to their mouths at the same time, drinking deeply. Afterward, he dipped his fingers in the wine and began to stroke her between her legs, touching just the right spots. She started breathing heavy when she felt his fingers slide inside her. "God, that feels so good." Within minutes, she had her first orgasm.

Still panting, she scooted down his body, licking his stomach all the way down to his genitals, then taking him into her mouth. He moaned with pleasure. When he was about to explode, he pulled her up and rolled her onto her back. "It's my turn," he said, his lids heavy with lust. He kissed her, then stared at her body in the firelight. "God, you're beautiful," he said, fanning her hair out on the pillow. "You look like an angel."

"I thought you didn't believe in God or angels."

"Now that I have you," he said, "I may have to reassess my position. You're the most exciting woman in the world. If I'd known angels were this sexy, I would have never become an agnostic. Now shut up and let me make love to you."

Not only did Paul know what to do in bed, he knew what to say. Her ex-husband had never understood female anatomy, let alone female psychology. There was no such thing as foreplay. He'd never complimented her or told her he loved her. All that came out of his mouth were a few grunts. He demanded oral sex, but he never reciprocated.

Her muscles contracted. She cried out, "Oh, God . . . Oh, God . . ." The sound of the fire crackling combined with his mouth caused her to have another orgasm, this one more powerful than before. She felt as if she were swimming in warm liquid. She pushed him onto his back and climbed on top, closing her eyes and imagining she was riding him into a brilliant white light. Slipping off him, she reached under his arms and pulled him on top of her.

"Take me . . . now. . . . Please, Paul . . . I can't wait." A few minutes later, she felt another wave of pleasure. The problems with Neil, her work, her kids—everything disappeared except the intensity of that moment. Not even Brad had made her feel this way.

Paul quickly entered her. Their bodies were slick with perspiration. She heard a smacking noise as they slid back and forth. Their rhythm matched his thrust.

When he cried out, she embraced him tightly, pressing his head down on her shoulder. Once he relaxed, she panted out, "How much do you love me?"

"More than the universe."

"How can I top that?" she said, smiling in delight. How could a man be more romantic than a woman? When he said he was busy writing, he must be sneaking away to some kind of class, probably poetry or songwriting. She racked her brain trying to think of some kind of response. "I love you more than I love myself," she announced proudly.

Carolyn was watching the shadows from the fireplace dance on the ceiling. She heard a sound and felt certain Paul had mumbled something else just as magnificent. When she turned her head, her jaw dropped. Mr. Wonderful was snoring, and he wasn't snoring softly. He was flat on his back, his mouth open, sawing away loud enough to wake the neighbors. She tried to sleep, but the sound was too irritating. Taking the edges of her pillow, she pulled them up over her ears. A few hours later, she saw the sun streaking through the window.

Chapter 16

Christmas Eve—Eighteen years ago

When Jeremy didn't return from her parents' bedroom, Jessica decided to search the house on the chance that her parents had bought them Christmas presents, after all. She checked most of the closets on the two lower floors. The first level had a modern kitchen, an enormous dining room, a formal living room, and a large circular area at the foot of the stairs. When her mom and dad had parties, the area near the stairs was used as a dance floor.

In addition to the theater room, seven of the fifteen bedrooms were located on the third floor. At one time during the house's history, the rooms on the third floor were filled with servants. Jessica had nightmares about the third floor. The year before, her mother had made her go to a shrink, a crusty old man who did nothing but sit and stare at her. Then she started having nightmares about the psychiatrist. Now she tried her best to be brave.

Jessica headed to the garage. After looking around, she saw a box perched on top of one of the storage cabinets. Her father liked everything neat. Most of the garage's contents were organized inside the white cabinets. Her eyes kept returning to the box. Not far away was an aluminum ladder. It was too heavy for her to lift, so she got behind it and pushed. It made a scraping noise as it moved across the cement floor. She positioned it beneath the area where the cardboard box was located. At the top of the ladder, she still couldn't see inside. Standing on her tiptoes, she felt a long, narrow box, similar to the kind dolls were packaged in. Unable to lift it, she reached in and wrapped her fingers around the cold object inside.

"Cool," Jessica exclaimed, staring at the long brown rifle in her hands as she tried to maintain her footing on the ladder. Jeremy had wanted a gun for a long time. Some of his friends went duck hunting with their fathers every year. Excited, she couldn't wait to show him what she'd found.

Holding the rifle in her right hand, she scampered down the ladder. Finding their Christmas presents had been a game they'd played every year. Once they discovered where their gifts were stashed, she and Jeremy would secretly play with them, then return them on Christmas Eve. The servants always spent Christmas Eve wrapping presents and preparing the holiday meal. They didn't care if something had been opened. This year, the servants were gone. Her daddy said they were going to have Christmas dinner at the country club.

Rushing down the hall on the second floor, Jessica saw her brother bending down over her mother. Her gaze shifted slightly to the left and she saw her father standing in the doorway of the bathroom. A stern look leaped into his eyes. "Give me that this minute!"

The only time Daddy had ever yelled at her was the time she found him on the third floor. He reached for the rifle as Jessica turned to run away. She recalled seeing her father's twisted face and terrified eyes at the same time she heard the explosion.

Blood gushed out of her brother's back. The smell of gunpowder filled the air. She saw her father lift Jeremy off her mother and place him on the floor. Blood was coming out of a hole in her mother's forehead. Jessica crawled across the floor and huddled in a corner. When she saw her father cut her brother's chest open, she screamed until she couldn't breathe, then everything went black.

* * *

Melody bolted upright, her eyes roaming around the room as she tried to figure out where she was. She was drenched in sweat. Tossing the empty scotch bottle against the wall, she swore she would never drink again. They always said a child mimicked its parents. If she turned into her mother, she would kill herself.

The nightmares always ended abruptly. She had dreamed about the shooting again. When she awoke, all she remembered were disconnected fragments. She had even tried hypnotism. The psychiatrist told her the events of that night were buried so deep in her subconscious, they might never resurface.

After her father was sent to prison, the court had placed her with his brother's family. When she accused her uncle of abusing her sexually, she was placed in a foster home in Manhattan. She ran away at fourteen. By fifteen, she was one of the top fashion models in the country. A twenty-nine-year-old man named Rees Jones had later become her surrogate father. He designed a line of high-end evening gowns. His fresh style and unique designs had made him a major player in the fashion industry. On her seventeenth birthday, she used a phony I.D. and they were married. Two years later, Rees was found dead in his bathroom. The death was ruled a suicide. His fortune fell into the hands of his beautiful young wife.

It wasn't right that Neil and his sister had everything and she had nothing but money. Neil was supposed to be her fix. For the first time since her brother died, Melody had allowed herself to love another human being. She hadn't loved Rees. She knew Rees had exploited her, using her face and body to promote his business. Because she was only seventeen, she wasn't allowed to spend a penny without first getting approval from his accountant. She'd once asked for money to buy tampons. Rees told her to wait until Monday when the accountant returned to his office. The entire weekend, she'd had to stuff rags into her panties.

She was restricted from seeing her mother's will until after her eighteenth birthday. When she found out how wealthy she was, she was furious she'd married Rees. The wedding was for show, anyway.

The wedding dress he had made for her carried a price tag of twenty thousand dollars. When he was diagnosed with AIDS, he'd killed himself. People like Rees thought they could cheat death. He'd never changed his will, so Melody happily added his fortune to her own.

If Neil would only stop wasting so much time with his painting and family, he would realize how much she needed him. He had to fill the void that her brother had left. She wasn't going to let anything get between them, not even his sister.

Neil had been hysterical today. Playing the game too much longer would be dangerous. She'd have to provide him with an alibi. If not, she would lose him. Exposing herself in the process, though, was not an option. Carolyn was smart. If Melody wasn't careful, she could end up in prison.

"I need more scotch!" she yelled, upset that she didn't have live-in help anymore. The last woman had been too nosy. It was ironic. Her father had made all the servants leave every night at six, not wanting to expose them to her mother's drunken rages. Now she did almost the same thing.

Melody sat back, her buttocks shifting on the leather chair. Her mind drifted to her former lover, the physics professor at Caltech. She wondered what he was doing on Christmas Eve. He hadn't been at the Pasadena house for several months. Once she set up her system, it wasn't worth the risk to take it down. Unless someone moved or stumbled across her transponder tucked away in the attic, her lovers would provide her with entertainment for the rest of their lives.

She normally saw darkness when she opened the view into his home. Her pulse quickened. There was an outline of two bodies in front of the fireplace. She knew he was dating Carolyn, but seeing it was different. She turned away, trying to prevent another emotional outburst. Her eyes were drawn back to the screen. It was similar to spectators slowing down on the freeway whenever an accident occurred. Even though they knew it would be disturbing if they saw dead or seriously injured people, they couldn't stop themselves from looking.

She watched as Paul's and Carolyn's bodies moved together. It was almost as if she were watching them in slow motion. His touch was so gentle. Melody's experience with him had been vastly different—satisfying, but rough and quick. What she was witnessing was real love. Her level of agitation escalated. Neil had made love to Laurel in the same manner. Melody's sex partners didn't treat her that way because they didn't love her. No one had ever loved her, no one except Jeremy.

Paul Leighton had been her professor when she'd attended Caltech. He wasn't handsome like Neil, but she hadn't been attracted to him for his looks. To her disappointment, the affair had lasted only three weeks. Just long enough for Melody to set up her equipment and get some good video footage.

When she had shown up at Thanksgiving dinner at Carolyn's house and seen Paul sitting at the table, she'd felt like strangling him. Taking him aside, she asked him why he'd stopped returning her calls. He had just shrugged and returned to the table. She endured the entire afternoon without revealing their relationship. Asshole.

Her hands clenched into fists, the veins in her forearm raising from the furious pumping of her blood. She slammed them down on the desk, causing the plasma screen to shake. Tonight of all nights, Paul was with Carolyn.

She turned away from the monitor. Moving to another

view, she opened the window into Neil's home. Getting no signal, she knew the police had found her router. All of this equipment would have to go immediately after Christmas. She was sure to have visitors from the police department in the near future.

Melody glanced back at the screen, displaying Paul's Pasadena house. "Stop!" she screamed, seeing them still thrashing around.

It was time to take the bliss out of Carolyn's little romance.

She opened a cabinet containing rows of CDs. Each one was labeled with a date and name. Finding the one that said Paul, she placed it into the CD drive. She then selected Carolyn's e-mail from the list and attached the movie file. Messing with people's heads helped chase away her demons. Why should they be happy when she was alone and miserable? She threw her head back and laughed, imagining Carolyn's reaction. "The truth hurts, sweetie pie," Melody said, pressing the send button.

Chapter 17

Paul dropped Carolyn off at her house around nine on Christmas morning. They'd called Isobel from the road and she'd told them Rebecca and Lucy were still asleep. Since John probably wouldn't come home until lunchtime, Carolyn booted up her computer and checked her e-mail. Seeing a message from Melody Asher, she opened it.

> *Hello, Carolyn,*
> *   Paul isn't what you think he is. He likes having sex with his students. Why do you think he bought a house in Ventura? Maybe it got too hot for him in Pasadena.*
> *   Merry Christmas,*
> *   Melody*

Carolyn's fingers were shaking so badly, she had trouble opening the attachment. When the video started, she knew instantly that it was Paul. He had a birthmark on his left shoulder. Watching the man she was in love with having sex with her brother's girlfriend was sickening. She ran into the bathroom and threw up. After she rinsed her mouth out, she stared at her image in the mirror. "Fool," she shouted, shattering the glass with her electric toothbrush. "How many women are there? How could I have been so stupid?"

The least Paul could have done was tell her he'd had an

affair with Melody. They'd sat across from each other at Thanksgiving. The video must have been made a few years ago, as Paul was thinner and his hair shorter. While he was on sabbatical from Caltech, supposedly to focus on the physics book he was writing, he'd let his hair grow several inches below his ears.

Carolyn placed a hand on her forehead, feeling her pulse pounding through her veins. She'd never liked Melody, but she hadn't perceived her as evil. How could she have done something this cruel, particularly on Christmas?

What was she thinking? What was her motive? It certainly wouldn't cause Paul to come running back, if that's what she wanted. When he found out, he'd be furious. This had nothing to do with Paul, Carolyn decided. Melody had sent the video as a direct attack on her. "Why?" she cried out. "What have I ever done to make you hate me? Are you a murderer? Did you kill Laurel?"

Everything came clear. Melody Asher was out to destroy Neil's life by killing those that he loved. Was Carolyn next on her list?

She went to her bedroom and called Paul. "I have to see you."

"I just got out of the shower," he said. "What's wrong? You sound upset. Did something happen with Neil?"

"No," Carolyn said flatly. "Come over right now."

Paul had no idea what was wrong with Carolyn. The night before had been wonderful, one of the best Christmases he'd ever had. Lucy adored her, and he had become extremely fond of Rebecca and John. Lucy had always wanted a big brother, someone to look after her.

After his divorce, he'd looked for a woman like Carolyn—intelligent, courageous, attractive, as well as someone he respected enough to care for his daughter. He'd already charted their future. As soon as his book was finished, they'd get married and move into the Pasadena house. His father had left him some money. His investments had tripled during the past five years, so there was no need for Carolyn to continue working. He paid Isobel only a few dollars less than what Carolyn earned as a probation officer. Besides, the job was dangerous. A vicious criminal had tried to kill her the year before. If Brad hadn't gone to the jail to interview Raphael Moreno, Carolyn might have been in the hospital instead of him.

He threw on a pair of jeans and a green sweater, then peeked in on Rebecca and Lucy. Lucy had changed so much, he had to remind himself that she was his daughter. She was tall and lanky like her mother. Her straight blond hair reached the center of her back. His little girl had disappeared, replaced with the blossoming body of a young woman. Boys had already started calling. At present, Lucy had no interest in the opposite sex. He knew that would change. The image of his precious daughter walking out the door with a guy who wanted to jump her bones was terrifying. Maybe he could send her to an all-girl boarding school.

Isobel was curled up on the sofa reading. "I'll be at Carolyn's. Call me when the kids wake up."

"Don't expect another big meal," the housekeeper told him. "I'm taking the day off, remember? There's plenty of leftovers in the refrigerator. If you want something else, you'll have to go to a restaurant."

"You're tough, Isobel," Paul said, walking over and kissing her on the cheek. "By the way, Merry Christmas. Did you like the robe I got you?"

"I'm wearing it, aren't I?" she said, glancing down at her feet. "I needed a new pair of slippers. You did pretty good this year, though. Last year you bought me a set of pots and pans. Why do I need more pots and pans? I have enough stuff to scrub." Isobel looked at the expression on his face and laughed. "Come over here and give me a kiss. You might be the genius, but I can always pull one over on you."

Paul walked over and kissed her cheek. "I love you, Isobel. You know that, don't you? All you have to do is ask, and I'll buy you anything you want."

Isobel grabbed his head and pulled it down, planting a wet kiss on his forehead. "You already have," she joked. "This little house is a perfect retirement home. Just be sure to put the deed in my name when you move back to Pasadena."

"You—you can't retire now, Isobel," Paul stammered. "How could we get by without you? You promised you'd stay with us until Lucy goes to college."

"I'm not going anywhere now," Isobel told him with a laugh. "You're not getting rid of me that fast." She pushed her glasses back on her nose. "Run along so I can finish this book. You should be thinking about the same thing. When are you going to finish that book you're supposed to be writing? I haven't seen a lot of work going on lately, just a lot of loving."

Paul walked the short distance to Carolyn's house. Isobel was right. He had become so engrossed in Carolyn's life, he had forgotten about his own. He patted down his hair, then rang the doorbell.

"Get in here," Carolyn snapped, yanking him by the arm.

"What the hell—"

She shoved him in the center of the back, not stopping until he reached her desk in the kitchen. "Sit," she said, pushing down on his shoulders. "This is what I had to see on Christmas, a gift from your former girlfriend Melody Asher."

"Oh," Paul said, frowning. "She told you, I presume. I was going to tell you. It was several years ago, Carolyn. I thought about it and decided to keep quiet. I mean, she was dating your brother."

"She didn't tell me anything," Carolyn said, pacing. Leaning over him, she double-clicked her mouse and the video began playing.

The blood drained from Paul's face. "Jesus, the woman's insane. I didn't give her permission to film me. We only had sex a few times. She came on to me. She even made up a story, offering to make me dinner if I helped her with a problem. Physics is difficult, you know."

"Difficult, huh?" Carolyn said, her blood boiling. "It doesn't look like she's having any difficulty here, Paul. How many other students did you sleep with? What are you doing, hiding out here in Ventura? What do you think I am, just someone to screw while the dust settles at Caltech?"

"Stop, Carolyn," he said, raising a palm. "We were both adults. Sure, it doesn't look good for a professor to date a student. I didn't think of Melody as a student. She was auditing my class without credit. I gave her a grade because I thought she had potential."

"I bet she did," she said, pouring a glass of water from the faucet and gulping it down. "Looks like she has lots of potential, Paul. As a porn star."

"I don't have to listen to this," he said, standing to leave. "I love you, Carolyn, but I don't deserve to be raked over the coals for something I did years before I even met you."

Carolyn realized she was being irrational, but she couldn't stop herself. Seeing the man she loved in bed with another woman was devastating, and Melody was years younger and far more attractive. The video had stopped playing, but the last image was still on the screen. It was the same blanket! "Damn you, what you said last night about a student giving you the blanket was true. Did you give Melody an A, like you said? What other lies have you told me?"

"I forgot Melody gave me the blanket, okay?"

"No! Absolutely not okay," Carolyn said, turning around in a circle. "Get out of my house. And here," she said, removing the Cartier watch and throwing it at him, "take your fancy Christmas present. Melody likes expensive things. Give it to her."

Wanting to catch Isobel before Paul got home, Carolyn punched in his number. "Is he there?"

"No," Isobel said. "I thought he was with you."

"Listen," Carolyn told her, talking fast. "Something came up at work. Tell Rebecca I'll be home by lunchtime. She can always reach me on my cell phone." She started to hang up, then continued, "Don't tell Paul I called you."

"What's going on?"

"Trust me, Isobel, you don't want to know."

She called John at his friend's house, told him that she was going to the hospital to see Brad, then rushed out to her car. She thought about calling Veronica. Carolyn knew what she would say—cut off his left testicle and feed it to her dog. She needed to talk to someone, and under the circumstances, she thought it would be better if she spoke to a man.

Carolyn arrived at the hospital before ten, carrying her laptop in her backpack. When she entered Brad's room, she found him sleeping. "Merry Christmas," she told him, managing a weak smile. "How are you feeling?"

"Like I got run over by a train. Tomorrow they're going to put me in a brace and send me home. They say I might be able to go back to work in three weeks." He stared at her and sighed. "I should have listened to you about Moreno. Did you come here to gloat? Why aren't you with the family?"

"We celebrated Christmas last night," she said, moving a chair close to his bed. "I pushed Moreno to the breaking point, Brad. He crushed my cell phone with his bare hands. I told Bobby to keep him in the room all day without water, food, or bathroom privileges. I'm sorry. I guess I didn't tell you because I thought you were trying to upstage me. I was certain Moreno would crack and tell me everything."

"Don't sell yourself short," Brad said, grimacing in pain. "The guy would have escaped. He murdered seven people, for Christ's sake. There's no doubt he'll kill again. My bet is he was going to make his move on the bus to Chino. It's not that easy to bust out of jail."

"Wilson put me in charge of the unit," Carolyn told him, rubbing her hands on her jeans. "I thought it would be a snap; then I realized how many cases come in each day. If I'd known in advance, I would have turned him down."

"You'll do fine," Brad said. "Anyway, Wilson intends to give you my job when he retires."

"Where will you go?"

"Deputy chief."

"Nice," she said, brushing her finger underneath her nose. "Did you talk to Hank this morning?"

"No," she said, curious. "Do they have something new?"

"We didn't talk about Neil," Brad explained. "Seems our boy Raphael had a contract out on him. Hank thinks it was the Mexican Mafia. They offered an undercover FBI agent half-a-mil to hand him over. I think you may be right about him hiding out in the Hartfields' house. Shit, I saw a guy once who'd been skinned alive by those people." He reached behind him, attempting to adjust his pillow. Carolyn walked over and did it for him. "Anyway," he said, "what's going on in your neck of the woods? Did you have a nice holiday? How is 'physics boy' doing? Are you guys still an item?"

"Something happened." Carolyn nervously cleared her throat. "Paul and I had a fight and I threw him out."

"What did he do? I thought he was Mr. Perfect."

"It might be better if I showed you," she said, removing her laptop and positioning it on his tray. "Can I raise your bed?"

"No," Brad said, wincing. "I can see. Go ahead and show me."

She hit the play button. His eyes were glued on the monitor. "Man," he exclaimed, "this chick is hot. She's got a great ass. Is this my Christmas present?"

"Don't you recognize her? That's Melody Asher, the woman Neil's been dating."

"The million-dollar broad?"

"Try fifty million."

"Shit, I'd do her for free," Brad said, smiling. "All that

money and a body that won't quit. Who's that with her? It doesn't look like Neil."

She took a deep breath, then said, "It's Paul Leighton."

"No kidding."

"Yes," Carolyn said, lowering her eyes.

"Lucky guy," Brad said. "You dumped me for a man who makes porno movies? Low blow, Carolyn. And he's humping your brother's girlfriend behind your back. A real class act."

"You don't understand," she said. "This was made several years ago. Melody Asher sent it to my e-mail address. Paul claims he was only with her a few times. He swears he never gave her permission to film him. I went ballistic when I saw it. Am I overreacting?"

Brad fell silent, thinking. "As much as I'd like to see you dump the guy, I'm not sure you should do it over something like this. When you and I started dating, you knew I'd been with other women. Give him a break. He's a man. It's not like he's been cheating on you. From what I've read about this Asher broad, she's a first-class bitch. She probably seduced him just for the fun of it." He turned back to the monitor and smiled. "He certainly isn't anything to look at. I can't believe you went for this guy. He reminds me of Mr. Rogers."

Carolyn closed her laptop and placed it in her backpack, then set it on a chair. She grabbed onto the railing and shook it. "I'm so angry. I mean it, I feel like beating the crap out of him. What a Christmas, huh? My brother's a suspect in two homicides and I had to watch my boyfriend screwing a woman who has shoes more expensive than my entire wardrobe. I hate him."

"Give it time," Brad said, touching her hand. "Don't take him back until I'm better."

The room fell silent. Carolyn started to leave, but his eyes pulled her back. "We had some good times together, you and I," she said softly. "Maybe it was because we worked together. You know, we had something to talk about at the end of the day. I don't understand Paul's work, and he doesn't have much of an interest in mine. Most of the time, we talk about the kids, politics, things like that."

"Forget the video," he said. "Do you love him?"

"I don't know," she answered, wiping a tear off her cheek. "I thought I loved him last night." Memories flashed through her mind—Paul's proposal, their torrid lovemaking. Now it all seemed disgusting, like waking up the morning after having sex with a stranger. The blanket was the worst. All she could think of was Melody's naked butt rolling around on the same white blanket. Men were hideous.

Right now, the emptiness of a fractured relationship made Brad seem more attractive. He was far worse than Paul could ever be. God only knew what *he'd* done in the past. Regardless, she wanted him. Another man was the only cure. It was a basic truth that every woman knew.

"Take down the rails."

Carolyn hesitated. "They're supposed to keep you from falling out of the bed."

"Just do it," he said, yanking on her hand.

"Fine," she said, releasing the lock on the bed rails.

"Bend down, I want to tell you something."

When Carolyn leaned over, Brad cupped his hands around her face and lifted his head a few inches off the bed so he could kiss her. She started to pull away, but she needed it. Already she could feel the empty hole inside of her filling. His soft lips pressed against her own. His skin smelled fresh and healthy. Even in his condition, his body seemed to be surging with energy. When the kiss was over, she felt lightheaded. She stood up, feasting on his muscular body, his amazing eyes, his thick blond hair.

"I curse myself every day for letting you go," Brad told her, watching as she pulled the rails back up. "Since my encounter with Moreno, I've had time to think. If you want to keep seeing this professor, there's nothing I can do to stop you. I don't think he's going to make you happy, though. You're not like him. You take on his personality so you can get along with him. If he sees who you really are, he'll run for the hills."

"Bullshit," she shot out. "I'm not pretending to be someone I'm not."

"Yes, you are," Brad said. "You're not some passive housewife who does whatever her husband tells her or spends hours organizing her drawers. This guy's nothing more than a curiosity. Underneath, you're laughing at him. How can you not? You're out there every day risking your life, dealing with murderers and rapists, looking at pictures of dead people. And he's lining up his pencils. An equation never saved anyone's life. But you have, Carolyn. Trust me, you'll eat this guy alive."

Carolyn's jaw dropped as she tried to digest what he was saying.

"Not only that," he continued, "this joker who thinks he's so smart doesn't even believe in God. You know for a fact there's a God. We may think we can thumb our noses at Him on occasion, but we don't doubt His existence. When I'm out there on the racetrack, I know who's looking out for me. God allows me to do that, okay? It's my reward for sending scum like Moreno to hell."

Carolyn's stomach was bubbling with acid. "Where was God when Mrs. Moreno's son decapitated her?"

"You know I can't answer that," Brad said. "All I know is living without God is like driving a car with no wheels. If you want to follow your friend down that bumpy road, be my guest."

She stared at him, then turned to walk away. "I have to go to my mother's. I'll call you in a few days."

Chapter 18

"How can it be over so quick?" Eliza asked her husband in a thick Southern drawl.

"I don't know what you're talking about," Lawrence Van Buren said, slouched on the sofa in front of the Christmas tree.

She watched as their two live-in housekeepers picked up the blizzard of wrapping paper and boxes left by their children. "I shopped since Thanksgiving and it took them less than fifteen minutes to rip open their gifts, collect their loot, and run off to their rooms. All this time and effort for a lousy fifteen minutes."

"I have to go out," he said, pushing himself to his feet.

Eliza pouted. "It's Christmas, Larry. Please don't leave. My family is coming for dinner."

"That's not until three," he told her. "I should be back by then. You know I don't have a choice, honey. Crime doesn't stop because it's Christmas."

Heading upstairs to the master bedroom, he stripped off his pajamas and entered the walk-in closet, selecting an off-white shirt, an Armani jacket, and a pair of gray Calvin Klein slacks. Sitting down on the bed, he slipped on a pair of Gucci loafers.

As he started down the stairs, he stopped to gaze at the woman he called his wife. She'd changed into a white knit dress that clung to her body. He saw the reflection of her face in the mirror across from the sofa where she was standing. Eliza was a platinum blonde. She bleached her hair, but Larry didn't mind. Her eyes sparkled like two 5-carat sapphires. She turned to the side, exposing the outline of her exquisite breasts and the deep curve near her hip bones. Her breasts and hips were the same exact size, emphasized by her tiny waist.

Ever since he was a teenager, Van Buren had fantasized about marrying an American girl with blond hair. Eliza was perfect. No heterosexual male could look at her body without becoming sexually aroused. A former Miss Alabama, she stood a statuesque five-ten. In heels she was taller than Larry. This, too, he didn't mind.

Every man who saw them together was envious. He would ravish her tonight, but today he had to take care of business.

Van Buren continued down the stairs. Eliza met him and kissed him on the lips. "I'll call you if I run late."

"I wish I hadn't married a CIA agent."

"I've told you not to say anything around the kids," he barked at her. "I have enemies, Eliza. Everyone in the agency has enemies. You want the kind of animals we go after to find out where I live and butcher our children?" His son came bounding down the stairs in his new Spider-Man costume, almost knocking his mother to the floor.

"Watch where you're going, champ," he called out as the boy sped around the corner into the family room.

Eliza walked her husband to the rear door leading to the garage. "You must be working on something big, honey," she said, running her hands over his chest. "You're a nervous wreck. I can feel your heart racing. How much longer will this last? We haven't had sex in weeks." She puckered her lips. "I want my hubby back."

"We ran into some problems," he said, reaching for the doorknob. "If everything goes right, we should wrap this up by the end of the week. You better catch up on your beauty sleep. Once I get this case off my back, I'm going to make love to you for twenty-four hours straight."

"Promises, promises," Eliza said, giggling. "I'm going to take Felicity and Zachary to the zoo tomorrow. You're not the only one who has to work, you know. Try corralling an eight-year-old and a three-year-old all day. Chasing criminals will seem like a piece of cake."

He pecked her on the cheek and entered the garage, climbing into his white Mercedes. Eliza had questioned their affluent lifestyle for years. He explained that it was necessary in order to blend in with the high-level criminals the agency was attempting to apprehend. It was amazing how many lies a man could tell a woman and get away with it, Van Buren thought, checking the rearview mirror before he backed out of the garage. Eliza had been repeatedly warned that telling relatives, friends, and acquaintances what he did for a living could put all of their lives in jeopardy. His cover was exporting exotic cars to wealthy overseas clients.

Pushing a button, he talked into the speaker. "Dial Leo." A minute later, a man with a gruff voice answered. "Where is Dante?" Van Buren barked, gripping the steering wheel so tight his knuckles turned white.

"Standing right beside me," Leo Danforth answered. He was a tall, powerfully built man with long dirty-blond hair tied back in a ponytail. "He wants to talk to you."

"It's cold as a bitch, Larry," Dante complained. "We couldn't even wait in our fucking cars. Why in the hell did we have to meet in a graveyard on Christmas morning? We had to scale a six-foot stone wall."

"It's safe, asshole," Van Buren said. "You want the cops to show up? We're in enough trouble as it is. A new lead turned up yesterday. We'll discuss it as soon as I get there. I'm maybe twenty minutes away."

Van Buren pressed his foot down on the accelerator. No one had been buried in Shady Oaks Cemetery since 1983. Money for a groundskeeper had run out years ago, and the closest house was a mile away. As additional security, the stone wall prevented visitors from bringing their cars inside. It was a perfect location for what he was about to do.

"They must be having a funeral today," Dante said, making small talk until Van Buren arrived. He tilted his head toward an open grave a few feet away. "Who'd want to be buried in this dump? They don't even pull the weeds."

"I hear you," Leo said, seeing Van Buren's headlights on the hill above them. He stepped quickly in front of Dante to block his view. Now forty-seven, Dante Gilbiati had previously been a member of the Gambino crime family. When the Feds went after them, he'd fled to LA, where he'd somehow managed to avoid apprehension. He had bulging muscles and a pockmarked face. He looked as if he hadn't shaved in days, and his thick black hair was disheveled. Dressed in a light blue jogging suit, he took another drag on his cigarette, then dropped it on the ground and snubbed it out with his sneaker.

Slamming on the brakes, Van Buren popped the trunk and got out, walked to the rear of the car and removed a ladder. Placing it against the wall, he climbed it to the top and jumped down, glad he'd made time to go to the gym even in the midst of the present crisis. Seeing the two men, he walked briskly toward them. As soon as he reached them, he coughed, his prearranged signal for Leo to take action. Leo quickly positioned himself behind Van Buren and opened his jacket, removing his gun from his shoulder holster.

Dante was clasping a thermos of coffee in one hand and plucking out another cigarette with his teeth. The steam from the open thermos rose in the frigid morning air. Before Dante figured out what was happening, Van Buren whipped out a nine-millimeter Ruger and trained it on him. Leo stepped forward and did the same.

"Keep your hands where I can see them," Leo shouted, peering at him through the sight on his weapon.

"What the hell—" Dante exclaimed, spitting the cigarette out of his mouth as he raised his hands over his head. He narrowed his eyes at Leo. "You set me up, you no-good piece of shit. I should have known when you brought me to this godforsaken cemetery." Craning his neck, he stared at the open grave behind him. He jerked his head back around, the muscles in his face twisted in fear.

"You like to kill children, do you?" Van Buren shouted, a blast of cold air striking his face. Despite the temperature, he was already perspiring. He hated sweat almost as much as he hated the man standing in front of him. He generally delegated disposing of out-of-control animals like Dante to men like Leo Danforth. In this instance, he wanted to make sure Dante suffered. He didn't want to kill him instantly or beat him until he became unconscious. Men like Dante Gilbiati didn't deserve mercy. "Have I ever given you permission to murder babies?"

"That peanut-size cockroach didn't come out of the house," he said. "What was I supposed to do, drive off? I thought we'd found it. If it wasn't there, why didn't he come out? How was I supposed to know there were people inside?" He threw the thermos with all his might, striking Leo in the face. Then he crouched down, charging toward Van Buren like a linebacker.

Van Buren fired, shooting him in the left forearm. The gunshot was muffled by a silencer, but the scent of gunpowder drifted past his nostrils. Leo's right cheek was scalded from the hot coffee. He raised his gun to fire when another bullet sailed past him.

"You're going to pay for this," Dante yelled, his weapon flying out of his bloody left hand. He pressed his right hand against the wound when another bullet bore its way into his arm. More blood pumped out, soaking his blue jacket. He fell to the ground, groaning in pain.

"Don't kill me," Dante pleaded. "God . . . please, Larry, I'll do anything you tell me to do. Say the word and I'll take out the president."

"You're a swell guy, Dante," Van Buren said, incredulous. "Why don't you kill the pope while you're at it? Too bad Mother Teresa is dead or you could take her out, too. Tell you the truth, you're too stupid to live." He pulled out his knife and threw it, knowing he'd hit his target when blood squirted out of Dante's groin. Dante's face drained of all color and his eyes closed. Van Buren walked over and kicked him to see if he was conscious. There was so much blood, he appeared to be floating in it. Seeing Dante blink, Van Buren turned to Leo, who was holding a handkerchief over the burn on his cheek. "How long do you think he'll last?"

"Maybe thirty minutes, an hour max," Leo said. "If the bullet wounds don't kill him, he'll bleed to death. We'd better get out of here, boss."

Van Buren pulled out a Snickers bar and unwrapped it. "Sorry," he said, smiling at Dante, "I only brought one. I know how much you like chocolate. Bet those kids had some candy. Ah, but you probably ate it while they lay there dying."

Dante moaned again. When he tried to push himself up, Van Buren turned to Leo. "Bury him."

He turned and started walking in the direction of the fence. Leo chased after him. "But he's not dead yet, Larry. We can't take a chance that he might survive. Don't you want me to finish him off?"

"I didn't say anything about finishing him off," his boss said. "Two of those kids were still alive when Dante left the house. One of our contacts at the police department said they died next to the dead bodies of their parents. You've got kids, Leo. What would you do if Dante killed them?"

Leo's eyes glazed over. He spoke without a trace of emotion, "I agree. I'll bury him."

"Oh," Van Buren added, "kick him so he'll stay conscious. I want him to feel the dirt on his face. Besides, suffocation takes more time. Need a shovel?"

"No," Leo said, marching back toward the open grave.

Chapter 19

Carolyn pulled into the driveway of her mother's house in Camarillo, a small town located off the 101 Freeway just north of Ventura. After she'd visited Brad the day before, she had decided to take a nap before heading out to Camarillo. When she woke up, it was six o'clock at night. She'd assumed Neil would still be at her mother's. When she had called, though, her mother told her he'd taken off after she went to bed Christmas Eve.

People affiliated with the art world hung out in Brentwood, Melrose, or Santa Barbara. Neil had tons of friends in the LA area, most of them she'd never met. He carried a cell phone, but only turned it on when he made a call. She hoped he wasn't holed up with Melody Asher, if for no other reason than out of respect for Laurel. If he was, there was nothing she could do about it. She'd babied and covered for him his entire life. This time, the situation was so serious she might not be able to fix it.

After she'd learned that her mother was alone, she'd asked John to go visit her, then promised her she would spend the next day with her. Now it was time to fulfill her promise. Rebecca was at the mall with Lucy. As usual, John was out somewhere with his friends. As long as he came home by ten and maintained a four-point average, Carolyn felt he deserved his independence. Before he'd got his car, he had spent most of his free time taking care of his younger sister. She doubted if he was thrilled the night before when she'd asked him to take her mother out, but he hadn't complained.

Dressed in a red sweater with rhinestone Christmas trees on it, Marie Sullivan had naturally curly silver hair, fair skin, and was petite like her daughter. "I'm sorry about yesterday, Mother," she said, embracing her in the entryway. "I meant to come, but this thing with Neil . . . I guess I was exhausted. Did you have a good time with John?"

"Oh, yes," she exclaimed. "He's a wonderful boy. He only stayed a few minutes, though. He said he was going to a big party."

Carolyn had given John money to take her mother out to dinner and a movie. He'd never mentioned anything about a party. When she got home, she'd have to talk to him.

Marie Sullivan lived in a gated retirement community called Leisure Village. The town people jokingly called it "Seizure Village," since hardly a day passed without someone either dying or being rushed away in an ambulance. Leisure Village had been designed for active seniors. Most of the residents were in their late fifties or early sixties. On the property, they had a swimming pool, several tennis courts, and a nine-hole golf course. The only things the community didn't provide were meals and transportation. Her mother was about to turn seventy and her hearing was failing. She had hearing aids but refused to wear them.

"I can't talk to you unless you put in your hearing aids, Mother!" she shouted. "I'm going out to the car to get your Christmas presents. One of them is a box of See's Candies. If you don't have your hearing aids on by the time I come back, I'll let the kids eat it."

Mrs. Sullivan frowned. "I don't like noise. It makes it difficult for me to think. And the awful things hurt my ears."

"Then I'll have to leave," Carolyn said loudly. "I'll lose my voice, Mother. I love you, but I can't scream all day."

Carolyn returned with a large box wrapped in foil paper. Inside was a peach-colored lightweight coat. Her mother's passion for chocolate was greater than her dislike for her hearing aids. She placed the box of See's on the coffee table.

"This is lovely," she said, putting on the coat and going to the other room to look in the mirror. When she returned, she smiled at her daughter. "It fits perfectly, honey. I bought you a present, too, but I forgot where I put it. Would you check the hall closet for me? It may have fallen behind the box where I keep my Christmas decorations."

Carolyn saw her mother's hand already moving toward her left ear. Now that she had the candy, she was going to trick her and take the hearing aids out. Carolyn stood her ground. "We'll find it another day."

"I think I know where it is," Mrs. Sullivan said, knowing her daughter was onto her. "Wait here and I'll go and get it." She returned a few minutes later carrying a Nordstrom shopping bag. "I hope you don't mind. I didn't get around to wrapping it."

Carolyn pulled out a red silk scarf with tiny roses embroidered on it. Chanel N° 5, her mother's signature fragrance, drifted past her nostrils. Every year, Marie gave John and Rebecca a thousand dollars to put into their college fund. Her daughter always received a scarf. She was lucky to get anything. Neil was the contemporary Michelangelo, according to her mother, but she hadn't given him a Christmas present since childhood, probably because she didn't have any male clothes or accessories in her closet. Carolyn actually didn't mind. When she wore one of her mother's scarfs, she didn't have to add any perfume.

They went to lunch at Coco's restaurant, then returned. Her mother seemed tired. "I should probably go home," Carolyn told her, running her hands through her hair. "I haven't been spending enough time with Rebecca and John."

"Don't leave," Mrs. Sullivan pleaded, her voice trembling. She perched on the edge of the blue velour sofa. "I have something to tell you."

Carolyn sat next to her and took her hand. "What is it, Mom?"

Marie cleared her throat. "I should have told you years ago. I thought . . . well, you know . . . it was painful for me to talk about it. Neil decided to clean out the chest of drawers in the guest room last night. He was going to stay with me until this mess with the police was cleared up. He found something I'd forgotten was in there. Since he knows, I think you should know, too. I tried to explain things to him, but he wouldn't listen. He became upset and ran out of the house. I'm scared he might hurt himself. He's too much like your father."

She got up and disappeared into the spare bedroom. When she returned, she was carrying a plastic storage container, the kind she stored her sweaters in during the summer. She took a deep breath and sat back down on the couch, composing herself. "Your father didn't die of a heart attack," she said. "He killed himself."

Carolyn's face froze in astonishment. How could her mother have failed to tell her something this serious? "Are you making this up?"

"No," she said, clasping the box against her chest. "After he retired from his teaching position, your father worked day and night on his math. The man next door had a Doberman that barked all the time. It drove your father crazy. Normally, things like that didn't bother him. He was suffering from sleep deprivation, though, and he hadn't been eating properly."

She walked over and handed her the box. "I'm going in the other room to rest. When you're ready to talk, come and get me."

Carolyn took the lid off, seeing several documents. One was a death certificate, listing her father's death as a self-inflicted gunshot wound to the head. The other was the Camarillo PD report. She began weeping. After an altercation with his neighbor, he had turned the gun on himself and blown his brains out.

She checked the date. It was six years ago to the day. Her mother had told her that her father had died of a heart attack. The funeral had been closed casket, so they couldn't see the wound. At the time of their father's death, Neil had been away in Europe, and Carolyn was in the midst of her divorce from Frank. Everything had been a blur. Her emotional state was wrecked by the divorce and then crushed by her father's sudden death. Her mother had never told them he had a heart condition until after he died. Now she knew why.

Carolyn's hand involuntarily opened and the police report floated to the floor. In most instances, suicides were not publicized unless they involved a crime. The only one who'd known the truth was her mother. Why hadn't she told them? Carolyn pushed the plastic box off her lap onto the table, leaning over at the waist. She feared she was going to vomit. What had driven her father to kill himself? He'd been the most gentle, loving man she'd ever known. He wasn't a talkative man, but when he did speak, he generally said something worthwhile.

After his retirement, he had drifted into a world of his own. Her mother was still teaching chemistry at Ventura Junior College. She quit after her husband's death.

Carolyn brought forth the last memory of her father. She'd moved back in with her parents for a brief period after filing for divorce from Frank. Once she got a court order giving her possession of the house, she and the kids had returned to their home in Ventura. This was several months before her father's death.

Awakening at four in the morning, she'd gone to the kitchen for a glass of milk. Her father was working at the table, stacks of papers in front of him, all covered with complex equations. He used to concentrate so intently that when she and Neil were kids, they made a game out of trying to distract him. They would blast the radio, even stand in front of him and scream that someone was breaking into the house. He would continue working as if no one was in the room with him.

On this particular morning, Carolyn had been surprised when her father had dropped his pencil, removed his glasses, and asked her to sit down so they could talk. "You don't sleep much, do you?" When she admitted that she suffered from bouts of insomnia, he asked her, "Does it bother you?"

"Well, yes," she told him, surprised he was speaking on such a personal subject.

"Why?"

"I don't know," Carolyn had said, smiling. "I don't want to be tired the next day, I guess. Besides, everyone else is asleep."

"Are you tired the next day?"

"Not really," she replied, never having thought about it.

"Neither am I," her father said. "People sleep their lives away. I sleep three, maybe four hours. You'd be surprised what you can accomplish at night. No interruptions. No noise. It's nice, you know. Stop trying to make yourself into a common mortal. You have a fine mind and an energetic body. My mother was like that. She used to do crossword puzzles all night, then work a ten-hour day."

Carolyn put the papers back, then went to her mother's bedroom. She found her sitting in a maple rocking chair, with cranberry-colored cushions, her hands folded neatly in her lap.

A picture of Neil was sitting on the bureau. No wonder he'd left in the middle of the night. His breakdown carried more significance now. If the police found out, and they probably would, it could lend credence to their suspicions that he was a murderer. They would also find out he had served time in a mental institution to avoid prosecution for assault.

Carolyn rested her back against the doorway. "I'm sorry, Mother," she said. "This must have been a terrible burden for you to carry. But why would Dad kill himself over a barking dog? When he concentrated, he shut everything else out."

"After he stopped teaching," Mrs. Sullivan explained, "Peter became convinced that he was on the verge of solving the Riemann hypothesis, a famous mathematical puzzle. He'd been awake for days. On numerous occasions, he'd asked Mr. DiMaio to do something about his dog. DiMaio was a large man with a nasty temper. When Peter went over there to speak to him that night, Mr. DiMaio knocked him to the ground and threatened to kill him. Your father came back to the house and got his shotgun. I grabbed his papers and tore them into pieces, screaming at him to stop wasting his life over a problem he'd never be able to solve. He slapped me, then he ran out the door with the gun." She placed her hands over her face, her shoulders shaking as she sobbed. "I couldn't let him shoot someone. I had to do something. Maybe if I hadn't torn up his papers he wouldn't have done it. I always thought we'd be reunited in heaven when I died."

She must have lost her Catholic ideology along the way, Carolyn thought. According to the church, her father would have gone to hell. Eventually he would go to purgatory. After eons had passed, he might be admitted to heaven. Suicide was a cardinal sin. "Dad may have been thinking about killing himself for some time. When they retire, especially men from Dad's generation, they sometimes feel useless, decide their life is over. Most people don't just shoot themselves, even in heated situations. You couldn't have prevented what happened, Mother."

"That's not true," Mrs. Sullivan said, reaching for a tissue to blow her nose. "I called the police. I'm certain he wouldn't have shot himself if I hadn't made that call."

"In a situation like this, nothing is certain. Things may have ended up the same no matter what you did."

Mrs. Sullivan stared across the room as the events of that night played out in her mind. "I was only a few steps away when he did it. When he saw the police officers, he looked straight at me. I could tell from his eyes that he thought I'd betrayed him. Then he put the barrel of the gun in his mouth and pulled the trigger." She stopped and took a breath. "He was the only man I ever loved. I was drenched in his blood. His brain was . . . Oh, God, it was so awful."

Carolyn walked over and dropped down on her knees, tenderly stroking her mother's arm. "It's all right, Mother. You don't have to talk about it anymore."

"Yes, I do," she said, reaching under the chair and pulling out an envelope. "Even in death, I cheated him."

"I don't understand."

"He solved it!" Marie Sullivan said. "I taped the papers back together that I took from him. He only had one more step, which I completed from his notes. Your father solved the Riemann hypothesis, the most important unsolved problem in mathematics. If I hadn't done what I did, he would have won the Fields Medal."

"You must be mistaken, Mother," she said. "Have you shown Dad's work to anyone? People all over the world are trying to solve that problem. Some people say it's unsolvable."

Mrs. Sullivan leaned forward, her mouth set in defiance. "He solved it, Carolyn. It's right here. Don't pass me off as an old fool because I'm not. Your math skills aren't good enough to comprehend it, but it's undeniable. How can I go public with your father's accomplishment? I would have to tell the world that I stole this from my husband, then pushed him to commit suicide. Here," she said, handing her a key. "His papers are in the safe at the bank. After I die, you can show them to everyone. I'm sure your physicist friend can confirm what I've told you. Unless someone else solves it in the next few years, you and your brother can split the money."

Carolyn handed the safe-deposit key back to her, kissed her on the cheek, then stood to leave. Her thoughts were scattered—first Neil, then Paul, then Brad, now this. She knew what happened when a man put a shotgun to his head. She saw her father's kind face, but then another grotesque image appeared. This was a new death. She felt the same as she did the day her mother called her at work and told her he'd suffered a fatal heart attack, as if she needed to start shopping for a coffin, call all the relatives. She would have to grieve again. "I'm not interested in money or mathematics, Mother. Right now, I'm trying to make certain you don't have more articles to add to your box of secrets. If you hear from Neil, tell him I need to see him. The police may issue a warrant for his arrest if he skips town. In addition, he'll appear guilty. He's got enough going against him as it is."

"Merry Christmas," her mother said despondently. "I didn't mean to ruin it for you."

Carolyn forced a smile. "Christmas was yesterday," she said. "Anyway, someone else made a mess of it long before you. Will you be okay here by yourself? Do you want to stay with us for a few days? We have the extra room, you know."

"No, no," she said. "Take care of Neil, darling. He's terribly fragile. Great artists have delicate temperaments. The only person he'll listen to is you. Be strong for him."

"Haven't I always?" Carolyn tossed her sweater over her shoulder as she headed out the front door. One of the reasons Neil was so screwed up was her mother. She'd tried to push him into science and math when all he had ever been interested in was art. When he began reaping money and acclaim from his paintings, she'd started telling her friends he was the contemporary Michelangelo. Before, her mother had treated him like a failure.

Her poor father. If what her mother had told her was true, he'd worked all his life for nothing. How could Marie have torn up his papers? Faced with the same situation, though, she might have done the same thing. Even if she could have chosen a different set of parents, Carolyn knew she would want things to be just as they had been, with the exception of her father's tragic end. She thought of John and Rebecca, reminding herself to look under the surface, make certain there weren't problems she was missing. In today's world, though, young people faced a myriad of dangers and parents were often inattentive. How could she be everything to everyone? She could sleep less, but look at what had happened to her father. Was lack of sleep a factor? From what her mother said, it had been. Everything she knew about her father had changed in a few hours. Now she would spend endless hours replaying their moments together, analyzing and wondering. Underneath his quiet demeanor, her father had been a complex and tormented man.

Opening the car door and sliding behind the wheel of the Infiniti, Carolyn stared out the window. Her windshield was filthy. Why hadn't she noticed it before? She got out and rubbed the spots away with her sweater.

How could her father be dispatched to hell when he'd never done an immoral or cruel thing in his life? The teachings of the church suddenly seemed barbaric, she thought, tossing her sweater in the backseat and driving off. It was idiotic to believe that hell even existed. As far as she was concerned, they were already living in it.

Carolyn vowed to remember her father for his brilliance—in time she'd manage to set aside his suicide—but she had learned a bitter lesson. After almost forty years of marriage, her mother had not known her father. If she had, she would have never torn up his papers. Carolyn could not allow herself to make the same mistake with her brother.

What didn't she know about Neil?

Chapter 20

Hank didn't have anything to do at home, so he dialed Charley Young's home number. Mrs. Young answered and said her husband had gone to work. During the holidays, the coroner's office was always jammed. Seldom did a Christmas pass without at least one suicide. The number of homicides generally went up as well. They were deluged this year, the body count reaching into the double digits. While the rest of the world enjoyed the long weekend, police officers, firemen, coroners, and the people who kept the county running were at work.

Rather than call Charley, the detective decided to go in person. Phone calls were frequently ignored, even ones from police officers. It was harder to say no to a person standing in front of you. Besides, he and Charley were pals.

Since no one was present at the reception desk, Hank went to the phone mounted on the wall by the door and punched in Charley's extension. When no one answered, he sat down in a chair in the lobby, hoping he hadn't made the drive for nothing. A few minutes later, Charley appeared.

"Come with me," the small Korean man said, peering up at the detective through thick glasses. "Good timing. I've been working on the Goodwin case this morning. I just went out to pick up some lunch."

They walked side by side down a long corridor. Hank

looked through the glass at the autopsy rooms. "Looks like's you've got a full house today."

"It's been a nightmare," Charley said, unlocking the door to his room. "We had to cache some bodies at a local funeral home. We haven't run out of space since the millenium."

Hank stared at Laurel Goodwin's naked body on the stainless-steel table. She looked as if she'd been gutted. "What's that?" he said, gesturing to some organs on the scales.

"Lungs," the pathologist said, putting on a cap with a clear plastic shield that covered his eyes and mouth. "I found evidence of pulmonary edema. In the classic wet drowning, white or hemorrhagic edema fluid is present in the nostrils, mouth, and airways. Compression of the chest causes it to flow out. Pulmonary edema is nonspecific, though. An individual dying of a drug overdose can also have pulmonary edema."

"And that's what happened here?"

"Let me explain something," Charley said, lifting up his face shield. "Drowning is a diagnosis of exclusion. The first thing we have to do is rule out all other causes of death. Even then, we can't be certain. Look at her hands. That's called washerwoman appearance."

"Then she drowned, right?"

"All it means is that the body was in water for longer than one to two hours. By the look of the hands, I'd estimate three to six."

"Back up a minute," the detective said, his deep voice bouncing off the walls. "You know we have two homicides. Time of death is going to be crucial. On the stand, vague statements like that can result in an acquittal."

The pathologist placed his hands on his hips. "Have you ever handled a drowning before?"

"One," Hank said. "Some old guy took too many pills and drowned in his bathtub. We had no choice but to work it as a homicide. Waste of time."

"Let me explain more clearly," Charley said. "In most instances, all we can honestly say is we *assume* the person drowned. And the only way we do that is by means of exclusion, ruling out any other possible causes. If this lady drowned, we know it wasn't an accident. CSI sent the toxicology over. It's on the table behind you."

Hank picked up the papers and then set them back down. "I've already read the preliminary. I was hoping they'd be able to match the unidentified prints. One of them must be the housekeeper's. The others belong to someone who's not in the system." He chuckled. "We should hire his housekeeper. She does a better job than most of our crime scene investigators."

Charley moved the magnifying glass over the body. "See these bruises under her arms. She was either unable to walk unassisted or she was unconscious and someone carried her. My guess was she was killed somewhere else and dumped in the pool."

The detective pulled his reading glasses out of his pocket. "What about the drugs? Is that what killed her?"

"Probably," Charley said. "We've never seen heroin this pure before. It's fifty percent stronger than China white. The cutting agent is cocaine."

"The classic speedball?"

"Nothing is classic about this concoction. We also found a sizable amount of strychnine. Not many drug dealers cut coke with strychnine these days. Believe it or not, we have seen it before. Rarely, though, and mostly in LSD. I guarantee they don't cut with this strychnine, though. They'd have too much of a problem getting their hands on it."

"Strychnine is used as a pesticide, right?" Hank said. "You can buy it at Home Depot."

"Not this," Charley said, arching an eyebrow. "This is a much higher grade than commercial strychnine and none of the other additives used in pesticides were found. It came from what's called the Saint-Ignatins'-bean. The name developed because of the attention it attracted from the Jesuits, but it was discovered by two French chemists in the 1800s. It's highly esteemed in China as a medicine." He bent down and removed Laurel Goodwin's brain, setting it down near the slicer so he could section it later. "Now, here's another interesting ingredient, Novantrone. It took the lab a while to identify it, so it wasn't on the preliminary report."

"What in the hell is Novantrone?"

"It's an injectable medication used to treat multiple sclerosis. Another strange thing is if you drastically reduced the dosage and removed some of the controlled substances, this mixture might be considered medicinal."

"You're shitting me?" Hank said, thinking the pathologist was out of his mind.

"Stay with me, all right? Let's say the killer suffers from multiple sclerosis. Traditional treatments aren't working. A doctor prescribes Novantrone to prevent the progression of the disease, so the person taking it is becoming more disabled each day. Heroin helps kill the pain. Morphine is almost the same as heroin, but you can't get it unless you're hospitalized. Cocaine gives them energy and also serves as a pain reliever. Somehow they believe the strychnine can help them as well."

"So you think the killer might have MS?"

"Maybe," Charley said. "But if he used it for medicinal reasons, he'd need a chemist or a pharmacologist to prepare it for him. As evidenced in Ms. Goodwin here, the wrong combination is lethal." His cell phone vibrated. "I'll be there," Charley told his wife, stepping to the back of the room. "I told you I'd pick up Kelly by three. All you have to do is make sure she has money for the ice-skating rink. I forgot to go to the ATM again."

Hank shut out the pathologist's conversation. Something was bouncing around in the back of his mind, triggered by what he had said. Was the person who'd loaded the syringe the murderer? This would be the rational assumption, but nothing about these murders was rational.

In four years, the detective would turn fifty. Outside of his liver and the extra twenty pounds he carried, he'd passed his physical with flying colors. He hadn't had sex since his wife had divorced him. Every now and then, he rented a porno movie and jerked off to make sure the darn thing still worked. He'd been dating a nice lady who worked as a waitress at Denny's. Although they hadn't slept together yet, the possibility was good. They went dancing every Saturday night, unless something came up at work. Betty was mad at him now because he'd stood her up three times in a row. The woman didn't understand the life of a homicide detective, the same problem he'd encountered during his marriage. Next week he'd planned on buying her a cell phone so he could call her when he got tied up. She nagged him about his belly, certain if they did have sex, he'd have a heart attack.

The biggest problem was his memory. What he was experiencing right now was the worst. Most detectives carried around Palm Pilots. They even had computers in their cars. The county had issued him a Palm Pilot, but he'd never had the time to figure out how it worked. Next to his computer was a twenty-year-old Smith Corona typewriter. When everyone's computer crashed or became infected with a virus, Hank would gloat while his fellow officers cursed and ran around like nuts trying to snag an available tech.

"Old Hank," as they called him, didn't have to worry about that kind of thing. Inside his filing cabinets were typed reports, original documents, copies of arrest records, as well as a complete history of every case he'd handled during his career as a police officer. Even though he wasn't supposed to take certain documents out of the building, once a year he boxed up the overflow and stored it in his garage.

The pathologist had returned to his position at the table. He moved some equipment around so the detective could get closer to the body. "Okay, let's continue. Like I told you at the scene, I'm almost certain your victim was dead when she entered the water. The killer dragged her facedown to the pool. That's when the abrasion on her forehead must have occurred. I've searched every place imaginable and I only came up with this one injection site." He moved the magnifying glass over the vein in her left arm. "She doesn't show signs of being an addict. Look at her. This was a healthy woman. Her muscles are toned. The size of her calves compared to her arms and upper torso indicate that she may have been either a bicyclist or a jogger. The Porter woman was also in excellent condition. The killer must be attracted to athletic women." He paused and took a drink of his Coke, perched on top of a stainless-steel table next to his scalpels, saws, and other instruments. An unwrapped and partially eaten roast beef sandwich was sitting beside it.

"Was Suzanne Porter injected with the same stuff?"

"Yeah," Charley said. "We did a preliminary toxicology on her, but we haven't had time to start the autopsy. We got so far on Goodwin because we had the sample in the syringe."

"Then both women were killed by the same person."

"Looks that way," he answered nonchalantly. "Of course we still can't rule out a drug overdose. It's like the Halloween-candy-laced-with-poison phenomenon that surfaced when we were kids. Remember? Your parents let you go trick-or-treating, but you couldn't eat the candy. Now, everything has to be sealed or kids can't even put it in their baskets. Just when things eased up, parents started finding razor blades."

Hank shoved a toothpick in his mouth. "Why are we talking about Halloween?"

"You're rude, you know," Charley said, his feelings hurt. "I'm in here working on your case on Christmas and you don't even have the courtesy to listen. All you guys are the same way."

Hank jokingly held his hands in a praying position. "Please

forgive me, O God of dead people. I'll never interrupt you again."

"Where was I?" Charley mumbled, depressing a pedal on the floor that rewound the audio recording he made during every autopsy.

"Halloween candy?"

"Okay," he said, depressing the stop button before the recording began playing. "Some nut decides to kill people and doctors up what today's generation perceives as candy—dope. The dealer may not have known what was in this batch."

Hank was confused. "But you said neither of them looked like they were drug users."

"Not the kind we usually see," he explained. "Someone could be selling a concoction to lose weight. Both ladies want to stay in shape, which is evidenced by their physical condition. Say the weight starts to creep up on them and a friend introduces them to someone they pay to come to their house and give them an injection. This individual could be a doctor or nurse, or just someone posing as a professional. The health department has all kinds of problems with these diet clinics. As soon as they close one, a new one springs up. The people running them aren't always accredited, so some of them have gone underground." He glanced back at the body and sighed. "I guess we should try to focus on the autopsy. I'm sure you have somewhere to go."

"No," Hank said, tugging on Charley's lab coat. "What you're saying sounds feasible, Charley. Tell me more."

He ripped his gloves off and flopped down in a chair, then gestured for Hank to do the same. Once they were settled, Charley leaned forward, obviously excited. "My wife wants me to write a murder mystery. What do you think? Pretty good imagination, huh?"

Hank frowned. "Just pick up where you left off."

"The person tells them the treatment is in the experimental stages, but it will soon pass FDA approval. Upper-class ladies suddenly feel great. Their appetites are suppressed because they're using methamphetamine without realizing it. If this was an occasional thing, the injection sites would disappear. As you know, you don't get tracks unless you use on a regular basis. Then along comes a maniac who decides to kill all the pretty ladies by poisoning the stash." Charley grabbed his sandwich off the tray and took a bite. "Sorry," he said. "Want me to order you some lunch?"

The detective groaned, chastising himself for encouraging Charley's theorizing. It was hard to watch someone eat a roast beef sandwich when Laurel Goodwin's lungs were sitting on a scale only a few feet away. "Who poisons the stash?"

"Maybe the diet doctor's wife got jealous."

"Great, Charley," Hank said, standing and pulling up his pants. "We'll give you a medal if you're right. What I need is something to help me find the son of a bitch. If you've got anything else to tell me about Goodwin, tell me now. I'm about ready to bolt. Either that or puke. Give me that," he said, snatching the sandwich out of the coroner's hands and placing it back on the plastic paper. "Finish your lunch later."

Charley laughed, then turned back to the body. "I couldn't find anything in her stomach. This is another factor that lends itself to a drug overdose. The first time people shoot up with heroin, they usually vomit. The Novantrone would compound that as one of the side effects is nausea. The crime scene guys didn't find any vomit inside the house. I located some regurgitated food lodged between her teeth and lower jaw. One of the ingredients was oats and the other was sugar. Probably whatever was left of her breakfast. She was either dead by lunchtime or she didn't eat for some reason."

"What's your best estimate as to time of death?"

"I told you I can't give you an exact time," Charley said, his voice elevating. "You guys are always pushing for things we can't do. I'm listing it as two to six hours. I assume Sullivan is a suspect."

"One of them," Hank told him.

"Did you bag his hands?"

"No."

"That was a mistake."

"I know," Hank said, grabbing the report and scrunching it up in his fist. "He's Carolyn Sullivan's brother."

"Carolyn's a nice lady," the pathologist said, looking up. "I thought it was kind of strange that you let her wander around the crime scene like that. But, hey, what do I know? All I do is slice and dice them. She's pretty. You're alone, aren't you? Why don't you take her out to dinner? You're not employed by the same agency."

Hank was attracted to Carolyn, even though he would never admit it. Why would she want an old buzzard like him? He would ruin their friendship if he made a pass at her. "What about semen?"

"Nothing," Charley told him. "Anyway, I doubt if it would have proved anything. Since the victim and suspect were dating, they were more than likely having sex. Are you going to drain the pool?"

"Yes," the detective said, turning and punching open the door, then glancing back at what was left of Laurel Goodwin. He'd let his feelings for the probation officer cloud his judgment. The woman on the table with her insides removed deserved justice. From this point onward, he'd have to exercise more constraint when he talked to Carolyn.

Hank was halfway down the corridor when he turned around and entered the room again. "Oh, do you know if the lab worked up the cars we removed from Sullivan's and Porter's garages?"

"Doubtful," he answered. "But you'll have to call them. Like us, they ran out of room. I had lunch with Harold Sagan the other day. He was furious. Seems there's talk their budget is going to be cut again this year. He claims it's because the board of supervisors can't get it through their thick skulls that victims and criminals have cars that have to be processed for evidence. I'll call and give Sagan a nudge for you. They'll probably get to the vehicles later this week. Because of its value, Sagan locked up the Ferrari in one of our warehouses. Have you seen it?"

"I've seen it," the detective grumbled. "One of the guys at the lab is probably driving it. That's why they're dragging their heels on the report."

"Don't get so worked up over everything," Charley told him. "Appreciate what you have. People aren't dragging their heels, Hank. Both of these homicides are only a few days old. How would you like to have six unidentified corpses on ice?"

Hank heard only a few words the pathologist had spoken. His mind was still trying to lock onto something related to a chemist. He thanked Charley and left. Suddenly he remembered. Carolyn's mother had taught chemistry at the junior college.

He reached his black Crown Victoria in the parking lot. Ducking inside, he recalled snippets from his childhood. He saw himself on a sunny afternoon, watching through the picture window in the living room while the kids on the block played. He sat at the piano, his chunky fingers desperately trying to make music. His mother had been an accomplished pianist. Parents thought their child could do anything they wanted with the right amount of effort. He wondered if Neil Sullivan's mother had felt the same way about teaching her son chemistry.

Chapter 21

Dr. Michael Graham had been a free man for two years. He was standing on the front porch of his brother's house in Brooklyn, having celebrated the holiday with him and his family. Elton had suggested they talk outside before his wife, Sally, made him clean up the dishes. The ground was covered in snow, the air frigid. "Women," Elton grumbled, placing his collar up and rubbing his hands together to warm them. "Sally orders me around like I'm one of the damn kids. Shit, I've been in the doghouse so long, I've started to piss in the backyard."

A tall, lanky man, Dr. Graham had the stooped and ashen appearance that came from sixteen years of hard labor behind prison walls. His brother was shorter, and had gained thirty pounds since the last time he had seen him. His stomach now spilled over his waistband. "I should take off, Elton," he announced. "I have to work a graveyard shift tonight at the hospital."

Elton looked up at the night sky. The day had been overcast and the stars weren't visible. He lived in a row house, with a zero lot line. Seeing his neighbor backing out of his driveway, he yelled to him, "Yo, Jimmy, I got some great snow tires for you. Stop by the store on your lunch hour next week. I'll sell them to you at cost."

"Things are hectic at work, Elton," the neighbor said. "I'll catch you later."

When he drove off, Elton turned back to his brother. "Guy's an asshole," he said. "Thinks he's a major executive 'cause he got promoted to assistant manager at the bank. They got kids fresh out of school working the same job. It's better than mine, though. I hate selling stupid tires."

Dr. Graham asked, "Isn't there any way you can get another teaching job?"

"I'm a convicted sex offender, Mike. My teaching career is history. After all these years, I still can't get over what happened to our family. You were my hero. I remember the day you graduated from medical school. Mom was so proud. I'm glad she didn't live to see you go to prison. It would have broken her heart. Of course she would have disowned me. You were always her favorite. Teaching didn't pay much, but at least I got a little respect from my students. And it was all because of that lying little bitch. I bet you wish she'd never been born."

"She's my daughter, Elton," Michael told him, his voice laced with intensity. "Besides, I'm the one who was negligent. I kept a loaded rifle where my children could find it. Jessica was only nine. The state didn't punish an innocent person. I'm guilty, don't you understand? I told her I was to blame. That's why she told the police I shot Phillipa and Jeremy."

"That's not my situation," Elton insisted. "I didn't do anything wrong. I've never forced a woman to have sex with me, let alone a kid. Anyway, it's an icebox out here. We can talk in the basement. It's the only place I have any privacy outside of the bathroom. I've got something I think you should see."

"We need bread and milk," Sally called out when the two men entered the kitchen. "You'll have to go to the market. And don't think you can shirk your chores, Elton. I work, too, you know. Tomorrow night, you're cooking dinner."

"Yeah, yeah, yeah," her husband said. "I'll stop at the store later." He removed his key ring from his belt, unlocking the door leading to the basement. Reaching in, he flipped on the light switch, then began descending the steep steps.

The damp, musky odor of the basement reminded Dr. Graham of the Arthur Kill Correctional Facility in Staten Island, where he'd been incarcerated. Two tattered brown vinyl recliners were positioned around a paint-splattered oak desk.

"Sit," Elton said, turning on a portable space heater. He collected some papers from a drawer in the desk.

"What's this?" he joked, picking up a homemade wooden paddle from the bookcase with three holes in it. "Some of your teaching tools."

"Not anymore," his brother said. "I gather you haven't been following the news lately."

"I don't have a television and I seldom read the paper," Dr. Graham told him, taking a seat in the other recliner and placing the paddle on top of a box his brother was using as an end table. "I guess I lost interest in what was going on outside while I was in prison. I've also been working a lot of overtime. Manhattan rents are exorbitant. I have to pull down extra shifts, or I'll have to move out of the city."

"Why? You've got money tucked aside."

Dr. Graham said, "I need that money for my future." He stared down at his hands. Having once been a skilled surgeon, he was now a sad middle-aged man who had to empty bedpans just so he could work inside a hospital. Prison changed a person forever, sometimes even took away the will to live. He had longed for the day he would be released, but for the past two years, he had been lost, finding it hard to cope with the pressures of the outside world. His left thumb had been mangled in the pressing machine while he was working in the prison laundry. Elton didn't know, as he had stopped coming to visit him, even though Staten Island was not that far away. He had learned to keep his deformity hidden, probably more for himself than others. His fingers had once been long and dexterous, the perfect tools for a surgeon. His brother wouldn't notice. Elton was a self-possessed man who hardly ever looked at him.

"If I ever get my medical license back, it will cost a fortune to open up my own practice," Dr. Graham continued. "Another doctor won't take me in, not with my background. And I may have to go back to med school. It's been eighteen years since I practiced medicine, Elton. I tried to stay up on things by reading medical journals while I was in prison. Medicine has leaped forward in almost every area. I'll never be able to operate again. That doesn't matter, though. I'd be happy if I could set up a general practice."

After his conviction for the murders of his wife and son, Dr. Graham's license to practice medicine in the state of New York had been revoked. As soon as he was released on parole, he had filed a petition to be reinstated. The seriousness of the crimes made his chances of practicing medicine practically nonexistent. Since he had some money of his own stockpiled before the death of his wife and son, he had wanted to study full-time after his release, maybe try to get back into medical school. His parole officer put a halt to his plans. Regardless of his financial situation, the terms of his parole made it mandatory that he maintain full-time employment.

Even a skilled physician had trouble getting a job after spending time in prison. It was the crime itself, however, that caused the doors to slam shut in his face. Not many businesses were willing to hire a murderer, even at minimum wage.

He had finally called in one of his markers. Thelma Carrillo was now head of the personnel department at St. Anthony's Hospital in Manhattan. Her ten-year-old son had needed a heart transplant shortly after she'd been hired as an admitting clerk. Dr. Graham had waived his fee. From then on, she wrote to him two or three times a year, thanking him for saving her son's life and keeping him up to date on the boy's progress. She had been saddened to learn the doctor was in prison, but she continued to correspond with him.

"This job is beneath you, Dr. Graham," Thelma had said. "Are you sure you can handle it? You'll be sweeping floors and emptying bedpans."

"I swept floors when I was in prison," he'd answered. "Believe me, being in prison is about as humiliating as it gets." He surfaced from his thoughts when he heard his brother speaking.

"Your kid is up to her ears in shit again," Elton said, handing him several newspaper clippings. "Sally made me promise not to tell you. I decided you should know. Maybe this time, they'll throw Jessica's ass in prison. Fitting payback, don't you think?"

Dr. Graham stared at the photograph in the newspaper, then quickly scanned the text. "This isn't Jessica. I know this girl. Melody Asher grew up in Tuxedo Park. Phillipa and I were friends with her parents. Melody used to come over to the house to play with Jessica."

"Oh, that's Jessica all right," Elton said, stretching out in the other recliner. "I've been following her for years. Don't tell me you don't recognize your own daughter?"

Graham read through the other articles. One had two pictures of the murdered women, Laurel Goodwin and Suzanne Porter, then a close-up shot of the woman they identified as Melody Asher. He pulled the paper to his face, wondering if his eyes were deceiving him. His daughter had been a redhead, and the Asher woman was blond, but now that he could see the image more clearly, he was certain it was Jessica. She had her mother's chin and high cheekbones, along with her small nose. But it was her eyes that were unmistakable. He dropped the newspaper articles in his lap, appalled that his daughter was involved in these terrible crimes. "You're right," he said, "it's Jessica. She must be living in Los Angeles.

That's why I haven't been able to find her. The papers don't say anything about her being a suspect. She was dating the man who owned the house where the second woman was killed, that's all. You have to let go of this anger you feel toward Jessica. I learned that in prison. It does nothing to the people you hate. All it does is make you miserable."

"Let me tell you something," Elton said, a biting tone to his voice. "I've been tracking her since she concocted that story about me having sex with her. She married some fruity-looking dress designer around ten years ago. She was already a model. Her pictures were plastered all over the place. I was afraid if I told you I was keeping tabs on her, you might think it was for some kind of sick reason. I mean, I wasn't entirely certain where you stood during my trial. You said you believed me when I told you Jessica was lying, but she was your kid."

No wonder Elton had stopped coming to see him. "I tried to stand behind you," Dr. Graham told him. "I was in prison. There was nothing I could do. Jessica never answered any of my letters. And you never brought her to see me."

"Hey," his brother said, defensive. "The little shit didn't want to go. What was I supposed to do? I tried to give her a decent home. I have no idea why she told her teacher those lies about me. My shrink said she probably did it to get attention. You know, because everyone made such a fuss over her at your trial. She was also jealous of Dusty and Luke. The boys tried to win her over, but they could never replace Jeremy."

Graham's eyes moistened. Jessica and Jeremy had been inseparable.

"Not long after she married this Rees Jones," Elton said, "I read an article that said the guy croaked. They called it a suicide. Maybe she killed him and got away with it. The police say the two women in LA were injected with some type of poison concoction. When Jessica moved in with us after you got shipped to prison, she made us buy her a toy doctor kit. She complained because the needles weren't sharp. She said you taught her how to give shots using an orange."

Dr. Graham remembered how eager Jessica had been to learn. She wanted to be a doctor like him, and pestered him to teach her. He had been certain she would become a surgeon. "I have to find her," he said. "If I can get Jessica to recant her testimony in front of the medical board, I may be able to get my license reinstated. Do you know where she's living? Los Angeles is a big city. I'm sure she isn't in the phone book."

"Call the cops," Elton told him. "I lost track of her years back. I guarantee the police know how to find her." He stood and picked up the newspaper articles, walking over to the desk and slipping on his reading glasses. "Here it is, Mike. Call the Ventura police and ask for Detective Hank Sawyer. Tell him you have important information about these murders. Oh, and what happened to the real Melody Asher, huh? Your girl is not only a liar, she may be a murderer. She's your flesh and blood. Are you going to let her keep killing people, or are you going to stop her?"

An hour later, Dr. Graham was on the subway headed back to Manhattan, still reeling from the conversation with his brother. He found it ironic that Jessica would use the name of her childhood playmate, Melody Asher. She'd always been intensely jealous of Melody. Her brother, Jeremy, had told him that she named one of her dolls after Melody, then threw it around in her room and stomped on it. Back then, a nine-year-old girl with a voodoo doll was good for a few laughs at the dinner table. But Jessica had always been a problem. She'd been a manipulative, demanding child. The only person she had ever gotten along with was her brother.

Memories from the past flooded his mind. He blocked out the people around him, the sound of the track, the people talking, returning to the awful night eighteen years ago.

People who knew the truth would call it an accident, but

they were wrong. The circumstances were always similar, yet no one ever learned. The worst part was that it wasn't a problem without a solution. Most people read articles in the newspaper and promptly forgot them. They only understood when it happened to them. And it would happen. Almost every hour of the day, irresponsible people caused the deaths of their children and loved ones.

He could never forget. Jeremy would not allow him to forget. As in Charles Dickens's Christmas novel, the ghost of his dead son paid him a visit every holiday season. He stared out the window into the darkness, seeing his nine-year-old daughter standing in the doorway with his rifle in her hands. Jeremy was leaning over his wife, Phillipa. He tried to take the gun away from Jessica, but it was too late.

"Oh, my God!" Dr. Graham cried, rolling Jeremy's body off his wife. The boy had been kissing her good night. The bullet had passed through his body and lodged in her forehead. "Push the red emergency button on the phone. Hurry, Jessica! Do it now!"

Dr. Graham knew he couldn't administer CPR to two people at the same time. Due to the amount of alcohol and tranquilizers Phillipa had ingested, she'd been semicomatose when the bullet had burrowed its way into her brain. Now she was in cardiac arrest. The chances that she could survive such a massive head wound in her condition were minuscule.

Placing his son on the floor, Dr. Graham began CPR. "Come on, Jeremy!" he yelled. "Don't give up on me, son. Fight. Fight for your life."

Where in God's name were the police and ambulance? Perspiration poured off Graham's face. He had to do something fast or his son would die.

Out of the corner of his eye, Dr. Graham saw Jessica huddling against the wall. A muscle in her face was jerking and her eyes were open. She was obviously in shock. The rifle was resting on the floor a few feet away.

No wonder no one had come. His daughter had never made the phone call. He couldn't think of it now. He grabbed a battered brown leather case that had once belonged to his father. So the children didn't stumble across it, he kept it in a hidden storage area inside his closet. If only he'd kept the rifle in the same place. He removed a scalpel and sliced through the cartilage, his fingers grasping the interior part of the rib cage as he separated his son's chest. He yelled at Jessica several times, praying the girl would snap out of it and get help. He couldn't notify the authorities. He was holding his son's heart in his hands.

The light seemed to suddenly grow dim. Dr. Graham's efforts to save his son had failed. He stared at the rifle, seeing it for what it really was—a hideous killing machine.

He had once been a registered member of the NRA. One of his uncles had built the five-pound rifle. His father had presented it to him on his tenth birthday. When he realized that the world would be better off without firearms, he'd sold his extensive gun collection. All but the lightweight rifle, one of his few links to his now-deceased father. Jeremy must have used the rifle without his permission, irresponsibly leaving the ammunition in the chamber.

A moment ago time had been racing. Now an eerie silence had settled over the room. Death had won. Dr. Graham felt as if he had somehow stepped outside the world. He kissed his wife for the last time and pulled the sheet over her head. Removing the bloodstained bedspread, he stroked the hair back from Jeremy's forehead, then covered his son as well.

Hoisting Jessica into his arms, he carried the child down the stairs to the living room and gently placed her on the sofa. "Jessica," he said, his voice shaking, "can you hear me? It's Daddy. No one's going to hurt you, baby. It was my fault, understand? Daddy should have never left the gun where you could find it."

Dr. Graham said her name again, then moved his hand back and forth in front of her face. When she didn't blink, he unbuttoned her pajamas and examined her body to make certain she hadn't been injured. He couldn't remember the precise sequence of events. His brain was mush. His heart was shattered. His shoulders shook as he sobbed.

He headed to the kitchen to call the police, then turned and walked back up the center staircase to the master bedroom. His daughter had witnessed something so devastating that her mind had shut down. She might never come out of it. Her healthy body could continue to grow within the confines of a hospital, her mind locked in a catatonic state. During his internship, he had seen children frozen like statues.

He dropped to his knees. "Take me, God," he cried, staring at the ceiling. "Strike me dead. Please, please, please, anything but my precious daughter."

What reason did he have to live? His medical practice would be ruined, his wife and son would rot in their graves, and his daughter might never recover. Even if she did, the horror of this night would haunt her forever. The person she loved the most in the world was her brother.

Without thinking, Dr. Graham picked up the rifle and carried it to the garage, placing the barrel into his mouth. Holding back his desire to kill himself, he set the rifle down on the concrete floor. Removing the shells, he placed them in his pocket, then found a sledgehammer in one of the cabinets. He struck the gun with all his might, emitting a tortured cry with each blow.

An overweight police officer with a pie-shaped face grabbed him from behind and wrestled him to the ground. He saw a smaller officer with dark hair standing next to Jessica. He watched as the officer bent down and clasped the girl's hand. When Dr. Graham tried to speak, the larger officer placed his foot on his neck.

"What happened here, sweetheart?" the smaller officer asked in a gentle voice. "Can you tell us who hurt the people upstairs?"

With her pink pajamas soaked in blood and a streak of chocolate across one cheek, Jessica raised her arm and pointed an accusing finger at her father. "He did."

"Who is this man?"

"My daddy."

"Are you certain, honey?" the officer continued, exchanging glances with his partner. "Did you see him fire the gun? How can you be sure your father did these bad things?"

The girl stared up at him with a flat, unemotional gaze. When she spoke, her voice had an eerie sound to it, almost as if another person or a machine were speaking for her. "I know he did it," Jessica said. "I know he did it because he told me he did. Is he going to kill me, too? Don't leave me here alone with him!"

After Hank left the coroner's office, he grabbed a cheeseburger and fries from Carl's Jr. and wolfed them down in his car. A short time later, he rang the doorbell at the residence of Stanley and Jane Caplin. The day was overcast and the air was brisk. Their home was located in the marina and had a boat dock. The property appeared modest from the outside, but the land alone was probably worth close to a million dollars.

Mrs. Caplin kept the chain in place as she cracked the door and peered out. "I'm Detective Sawyer," he said. "May I come in?"

"Yes," she said, her voice just above a whisper. "Stanley has been expecting you."

Jane Caplin was small, maybe five-two. Her body was reed thin, and her limp brown hair made him think of cancer victims. Her pain was so deep, the detective had to look away. The mothers seemed to suffer the most. There were two ways to deal with a tragedy of this magnitude—either find release through anger or throw yourself into a bottomless pit of despair. As time went on, the strong ones reached a level of acceptance. Judging from her anguished eyes, he doubted if Mrs. Caplin would ever recover from her daughter's death.

They must have purchased the property twenty years ago, Hank thought. The furnishings looked dated and the floor was covered with shag carpeting. A day after Christmas and he didn't see a tree or any decorations. He spotted some pine needles scattered across the tile entryway. They must have had a tree and then taken it down after Laurel was killed. There was nothing to celebrate in this house. Under the circumstances, a Christmas tree was almost obscene.

As the detective followed Mrs. Caplin down a hallway leading to the study, Laurel Goodwin's life was displayed in pictures. He glanced at the smiling girl frolicking in a swimming pool, the teenager dressed for her first prom, the proud college graduate, the glowing bride, and finally the lovely teacher surrounded by her adoring students. Now she was no longer the dissected body in the morgue. She was Laurel.

The pictures suddenly stopped, just as Laurel's life had ended so abruptly. There was a large empty space near the door leading into the study. Mrs. Caplin must have saved it for her future grandchildren. When one person was killed, the detective had heard, an entire world was annihilated. All the generations that would follow her would never be.

Hank felt an odd sensation in his stomach. Perspiration popped out on his forehead. The walls were dark wood and the hall was narrow and confining. Mrs. Caplin's picture wall, he decided, had become a wall of sadness.

Stanley Caplin stood around five-seven and weighed over two hundred pounds. He was wearing a brown golf shirt and a dark pair of pants. A cigar was smoldering in an ashtray beside his brown upholstered recliner. No wonder he'd felt sick, Hank thought, shaking the man's hand. He'd been so distracted by Mrs. Caplin and the photographs, he'd failed to realize how badly the house reeked of cigar smoke. "Can we talk outside?" he asked, pulling out a handkerchief and placing it over his mouth and nose.

"Oh," Mr. Caplin said. "Don't worry. I'll put it out. It was too chilly to go outside. Besides, some of those newshounds might come around."

Hank reluctantly took a seat on the sofa, folding his handkerchief and placing it back in his pocket. The man thought he could solve the problem by putting out his cigar. To get rid of the stench, the house would have to be knocked down and rebuilt.

He assumed Mrs. Caplin had followed him into the study. He looked back at the door and discovered she'd disappeared. "Doesn't your wife want to be present?"

"Janie's not well," the man said, scratching the day-old stubble on his chin. "She's been in bed most of the time since we heard Laurel had been murdered. She's a wonderful woman. Laurel was our only child. Janie had something wrong with her fallopian tubes. It took us ten years and two operations before she got pregnant."

Hank pulled out a tape recorder and placed it on the coffee table. "My memory isn't so good these days," he told him. "Hope you don't mind."

"No," Mr. Caplin said, his dark eyes narrowing. "Did you arrest that Sullivan guy yet? Murdering son of a bitch. He killed Suzanne Porter, too, I hear. Her husband called me again last night. Young fellow. Taking it real hard. We both hope Sullivan gets the death penalty."

The problem with the Porter case, Hank thought, was there was absolutely nothing to go on. The husband was at his office with ten other people, the house had been impeccably cleaned, and the couple's friends and relatives said they were like newlyweds. Other than a six-digit stock portfolio and a lot of sexy underwear, the wife had nothing to hide. No former lovers, no enemies, no drug or alcohol abuse. Eric Rittermier, the neighbor's boy, had looked promising as a suspect in the beginning. Even owned a motorcycle, but his girlfriend swore he was banging her in his bedroom at the time Suzanne Porter was killed.

He turned back to Stanley Caplin. "Tell me about your daughter's relationship with Neil Sullivan."

"The first or the second time?" Caplin asked, leaning forward in his chair.

"Start from the beginning."

"Laurel was a good student," he said. "Then she started dating Neil in her junior year in high school. We weren't really happy about the situation. You know, her dating. The boy came from a respectable family, so we thought it was okay. Besides, he was kind of a prissy boy. Janie thought he might be gay."

"What happened?" Hank asked, pulling out a toothpick and sticking it into his mouth. "Why did they break up?"

"I caught the little shit smoking dope in my backyard," Caplin shot out. "He was giving drugs to my daughter. Laurel's grades had started dropping. We didn't know what was wrong until I saw it with my own eyes." He sighed, his mind drifting back in time. "I put a stop to it. I forbade Laurel to see Neil again or I threatened to turn him in to the police. She buckled down and graduated at the top of her class."

"When did she start seeing Sullivan again?"

"Sometime last year, I guess," Caplin answered, shrugging. "My wife and I didn't know."

"You accused Sullivan of dealing narcotics. Do you have any proof?"

"Proof," the man said, his voice loud and abrasive. "You're asking me for proof? Didn't you find a syringe in his bathroom? The last time I talked to you, you told me the coroner found a puncture wound on Laurel's body and that might be what killed her. The piece of shit shot her up with something. The man lives in a million-dollar house and drives a Ferrari. You think he earned all that selling paintings? That art stuff is his cover. He's a drug dealer. What more proof do you need?"

"We're investigating all of Neil Sullivan's activities," Hank said. "If he was dealing narcotics, we'll find out eventually. Sullivan said she was living here. Is that true?"

Caplin took some deep breaths before speaking. "She moved back in with us after her husband threw her out. Can't say I blame him. I would have done the same thing if I was him."

"Can you elaborate?" Hank said. "I'm not sure I understand."

Caplin answered in a hushed voice, "Laurel was cheating. I never told my wife."

Rats, the detective thought, seeing his case spin off in another direction. Adultery was historically one of the prime motives for murder. "Do you know this man's name?"

Caplin was staring at the floor, lost in his thoughts. Hank waited a few minutes, then spoke, "Sir, I asked—"

"I heard you," Stanley Caplin said, picking up his cigar and clamping his mouth on it. "I don't know his name, okay? You'll have to ask Jordan. All I know was he was young, too young. Maybe eighteen or nineteen."

"How long had Laurel been teaching school? She taught eleventh grade, right?"

"Yeah," Caplin said, garbling the words through clenched teeth. "I know what you're thinking, that the guy was a former student or something. I heard as much as I wanted to hear. When it comes to sex, a man doesn't want to know what his daughter is doing. Jordan will have to fill you in on the rest."

"The night of the murder," Hank said, "you told me Laurel's ex-husband had called you recently. Do you recall what transpired during that conversation?"

"First of all," Goodwin said, "Jordan is still her husband. They split up two years ago, but their divorce isn't final. Laurel refused to sign the settlement papers. She thought they could patch things up. I told her it wasn't going to happen. She wouldn't listen to me."

Hank stood, feeling as if he were going to suffocate if he didn't get out of their house. He'd have to go home and change his clothes. "I need to get in touch with her husband," he said. "I also need the exact time and date he called you."

Stanley Caplin walked him to the door. "It was about three days before she . . ." He stopped and wiped his eyes. "This is hard. Never thought I'd have to bury my daughter. When are you people going to release the body?"

It might be hard, Hank thought, but the man standing in front of him possessed the strength to go on with his life. The detective listened to every word that came out of a person's mouth. In the span of a few minutes, Caplin had gone from referring to his daughter as Laurel to what she had now become—nothing more than a lifeless body.

"Things are backed up now due to the holidays," the detective told him. "I was at the coroner's office this morning. My guess is no later than Wednesday. I'll call you as soon as I know for sure. About that phone call—"

Caplin cut him off. "Jordan wasn't angry or anything. All he wanted to know was whether or not Laurel had signed the papers."

"Did he give you a number where she could reach him?" Hank asked. "We've contacted the navy several times. They aren't being very cooperative."

"An officer like Jordan could be anywhere. With all this trouble with North Korea and Iraq, his location is probably classified."

"Let's just say he wasn't overseas," Hank said, moving the toothpick to the other side of his mouth. "Do you think there's any chance he might have killed her?"

"No," Stanley Caplin said, shaking his head. "Doesn't make sense. Jordan didn't so much as slap Laurel when he found out she was sleeping with this idiot kid. Why would he want to hurt her now?"

"Maybe he wants to get married again and she was holding him up."

Caplin looked the detective straight in the eye. "Your murderer is Neil Sullivan. If he's not in jail by the end of this week, I'm going to kill him myself."

"I don't think you want to do that," Hank told him. "Then you wouldn't be much different than the person who killed your daughter."

Caplin glared at him, then closed the door in his face. Hank stood there a few minutes, kicking a snail off the porch. It wasn't uncommon for relatives of homicide victims to make remarks like Caplin had made. In most instances, nothing came of them. But there were also instances where people followed through on their threats. He hoped Stanley Caplin wasn't one of the latter.

Chapter 22

Monday, December 27—2:00 P.M.

Neil had disappeared.

Carolyn had been at work since eight o'clock that morning. It was hard to concentrate when she hadn't spoken to her brother since Christmas Eve. She'd driven by his house on her way to work. Several police cars and a truck from Leslie's Pool Service were parked in the front. When she had tried to enter the house, an officer had told her to leave. She'd gone through the alley to the backyard, hoping Neil was hiding in the pool house. A different officer had sent her away, telling her they were still collecting evidence. She left when she saw a crime scene tech inside Neil's studio.

She had set up an appointment for six o'clock that evening with Vincent Bernini, the defense attorney. She kept leaving messages on Neil's voice mail until it was full.

Carolyn hadn't left Brad's office other than to go to the bathroom. Files and papers were strewn everywhere. When the records clerk delivered twenty new cases, she was ready to scream. Gulping down a cold cup of coffee, she began assigning cases as fast as she could. She didn't have time to think about every assignment. If the officers had problems, they would tell her. So what if she gave one person more work than another? She'd handled twice as much as everyone else for years.

Carolyn was trying to stay focused on her work, but

thoughts of her father kept surfacing. She remembered how her breasts had seemed to develop overnight when she was twelve. And they weren't the swollen nubs most of her friends had. They were large and round, emphasized by her small stature. Her mother was completing her master's degree in chemistry at the time, and too busy to pay her much attention. She was far too shy to ask her mother for advice. The boys had started to tease her, though, as her nipples protruded from her shirts.

Her mother's bras didn't fit, and she was afraid she would miss one if she took it. She'd been so desperate that she had stolen a garter belt from her mother's drawer and fashioned herself a bra. Her mother didn't wear the garter belts anymore, only panty hose. It was fairly easy, as all she did was cut off the snaps for nylons and stitched the elastic together for straps. The clasp at the back was almost the same as a real bra. The only problem was the fabric was too thin.

Her father taught math at the high school and got home every day around four. One afternoon, he took her to Robinson's and pressed a twenty-dollar bill into her hand, telling her she could buy whatever she wanted. Then he told her he would meet her in the men's department, claiming he needed a new tie. Money was tight then, and her father seldom wore ties to school. She knew he was lying. When she returned with her purchase, two white cotton bras wrapped in tissue inside the sack, she was terrified her father would ask her what she had bought. He never said a word, not even to ask for the change back. As they drove home, she glanced over at him, still waiting for him to say something. All he did was touch her hand and ask her if she wanted an ice cream. She would never love another person as much as she had loved her father that day.

Hank Sawyer appeared in the door to Brad's office, startling Carolyn out of her thoughts.

"I can't talk now," she told him, turning back to her computer and trying to figure out where she'd left off.

"There's been some new developments in the Goodwin case," he said. "Thought you'd want to know about them."

"Sit down," she said. "And close the door. The records clerk forgot to close it." She spread her arms out. "Look at this mess. First day on the job and I'm already behind. I can't work like this, Hank. It makes me a nervous wreck."

The detective had a smug look on his face. "I spoke to a man about an hour ago who swears Melody Asher is an impostor. But you're too busy so I'll . . ." He turned to leave.

At the mention of Melody's name, Carolyn was enraged. When Hank reached the doorway, she shouted, "Get your butt back in here!"

"Okay," he said, returning and taking a seat. "A man named Michael Graham called me from New York. He swears the woman we know as Melody Asher is his daughter, Jessica Waldheim Graham."

"Wait a minute," Carolyn said, trying to absorb what she'd heard. "You've got a crank caller on your hands, Hank. Don't you screen for those kinds of people?"

"Don't take this lightly," he cautioned. "All Graham wanted was his daughter's address and phone number. He was sentenced to thirty years in the joint because of his kid. He thinks she can help him get his medical license back. That's why he was trying to find her. He was a doctor, a cardiologist, before he went to prison. We confirmed this with the medical board in New York."

"There're plenty of doctors in prison," she said, annoyed he was wasting her time with such nonsense. "I have work up to my eyeballs, Hank. Tell your stories to someone else."

"Will you just listen, for Christ's sake?" the detective said. "He's not just any con."

"Are you saying you consider Melody a suspect now on the grounds of what this person has told you?"

"That's what I've been trying to tell you," he said, speaking faster. "I'm flying Graham out here tomorrow. Even her father admitted she may have the capabilities to kill again. I'm going to pick him up at the airport, then take him to Asher's house to make a positive ID."

Carolyn swiveled her chair so she could look out the window. The fog hadn't lifted and she saw several menacing clouds. Any minute, she thought, it would start raining again. She hoped John would pick up Rebecca from school. She hadn't told Hank about the video Melody had sent her. It was embarrassing and she didn't think it had any bearing on the case. "I don't believe it," she said, spinning back around. "Melody Asher is famous. Wouldn't the real Melody know if someone was using her identity? What about the press? Dozens of articles have been written about this woman."

The detective told her, "Graham says the girl found a loaded rifle in the garage and accidentally killed both her mother and brother. Then she lied and told the authorities he was the shooter. She was only nine at the time. Sounds like something Melody Asher would do, don't you think? She also accused Graham's brother of sexually abusing her, which Graham claims was unfounded."

"Tell me more," Carolyn said, intrigued at what she was now hearing.

"Okay, Jessica Graham grew up in an exclusive area in upstate New York. I had one of my people do some research before I came over here. Tuxedo Park is a hideaway for the rich and famous. It was developed over a hundred years ago by a French tobacco baron. Because it's an incorporated city, they have their own police department. No one else has jurisdiction. Graham claims there could be bodies buried everywhere. The houses are acres apart and most of the residents are major icons."

"What does this have to do with the Goodwin homicide?"

"Wait until you hear everything." Hank's eyes flashed with excitement. "Melody Asher grew up in Tuxedo Park. According to Dr. Graham, the two girls were friends. Jessica was always jealous of Melody. This is the scary part. The real

Melody Asher disappeared not long after she turned eighteen. As you know, she's the sole heir to APC Pharmaceuticals. What I'm saying is this woman may have developed a taste for killing. Jessica Graham might have murdered three people before she turned nineteen." He counted them off on his fingers. "Her mother, her brother, and the real Melody Asher."

"Jealousy," Carolyn said, starting to think they'd stumbled onto something that could clear her brother. "Maybe the real Melody Asher stole her boyfriend or something. That would tie in with the situation with Neil and Laurel. How could she have got her hands on Asher's money, though? A fortune that large would have been protected by dozens of lawyers."

Hank stood and removed his jacket, tossing it on the chair as he walked around the room. "That's the beauty of this. Jessica was also an heiress, not as wealthy as Melody, but a millionaire several times over."

Carolyn sucked in a deep breath, then slowly exhaled. Her head was throbbing, her stomach growling, and she was shaky from the caffeine. "So you think Melody killed Laurel?"

"Jessica," Hank said, correcting her. "She's not only a jealous person, according to her father, she may be a pathological liar. Instead of telling the authorities the truth, she let her father go to prison. For all we know, the Asher woman is buried somewhere in Tuxedo Park. The father said the girls were both tall and resembled each other. Jessica must have bleached her hair to look more like Asher. Her father said she used to be a redhead." The detective then went on to explain what he'd learned from Stanley Caplin.

Carolyn was shocked. "But Laurel seemed so sweet."

"And sweet people don't sleep around?" Hank said, giving her a chastising look. "My father was a captain in the army. He beat the shit out of me and my sister. Jordan Goodwin is a lieutenant commander. Guys like that don't walk away when they find their wife in bed with another man. I'm not saying the husband killed her, but I'm not saying he didn't. The first thing we have to do is find the sucker."

She locked eyes with him, placing her hand on her chest. "So you consider Jordan Goodwin a suspect as well?"

"He has a motive," Hank said, smiling. "The good news is Kevin Thomas thinks we should back off Neil for now. If you've been praying, it must be working."

Carolyn was pacing the reception area of Vincent Bernini's law firm. She'd left messages at Neil's home as well as his cell phone. Their appointment was at six, and it was now six-thirty. The new leads in the case were promising, but she still had to protect her brother. Things could turn around.

Taking a seat, she flipped through a magazine, then nervously tossed it back on the table. She replayed the day before when she had visited her mother. How could she have kept such a huge secret for so long? Her father had been a humble man. She recalled how scuffed his shoes had been, how he never spent money on himself. He'd surprised her by showing up at her office not long before his death. She'd been so caught up in her divorce that she hadn't appreciated his desire to be with her. The worst was that she had been embarrassed at his shabby appearance. A pang of guilt seized her. Could this have been around the time he'd solved his lifelong goal—the Riemann hypothesis? He'd come to share his special moment. Tears stung her eyes. She could not help but think how excited he must have been. He hadn't said anything. What made him a great man was his humility. She doubted if he gave thought to winning the Fields Medal.

A realization struck her—he may have killed himself as soon as he felt he'd accomplished everything he set out to do in his life. Maybe that lunch, which had meant so little to her, had been her father's way of saying good-bye.

Carolyn heard the young blond receptionist speaking and pulled out a tissue to blow her nose. A plate on a metal stand read WENDY FITZGERALD. "Mr. Bernini had to leave. Would you like to schedule another appointment?"

"Yes," she said, reaching down to pick up her briefcase. When her jacket opened, the receptionist's eyes zoomed in on her gun.

"Are you a police officer?"

"No," Carolyn said. "I'm a probation officer."

"Have you ever killed anyone?"

"No," she answered. "Why don't we focus on setting up another appointment?"

"The first opening we have is February fourth at ten in the morning," the woman said, a plastic smile on her face. "Is that okay?"

"No, it's not okay," Carolyn said, her voice sharper than she intended. "I'm sorry. It's been a long day. Don't you have anything sooner?"

"Mr. Bernini will be in trial most of January," Wendy explained. "The only reason he agreed to see you this evening was because he knew you. Maybe you should call and speak to him another day."

Bernini's office was located in Sherman Oaks, a city on the outskirts of Los Angeles. Carolyn left and pushed the button for the elevator, then stepped inside and hit the speed dial for her mother's number. "Did Neil show up?"

"No," Marie answered. "You mean you haven't found him? Oh, my, now I'm upset. My heart is beating too fast. I may have to call the paramedics."

"Calm down," Carolyn told her. "You're fine, Mother. You have a pacemaker, remember? You called the paramedics three times last month and there was nothing wrong with you."

"But Neil . . . he's . . . he's my baby boy."

"Neil just came in the door," Carolyn lied. "We're at the attorney's office. I'll call you later tonight. Will you be all right, or do you want me to call Mrs. Bentley from next door? She could come over and sit with you for a few hours."

"That old biddy," she snapped. "Why would I want her snooping around my house? She's a thief, you know. She stole my purse one time when I left my door unlocked."

"She didn't steal your purse, Mother," Carolyn told her, sighing. "We found your purse under the bed. Maybe you should reconsider going into that nice retirement home near my house. They cook your meals, wash your clothes, and there's a van to drive you around. The kids and I could spend more time with you if you moved to Ventura."

"Heavens no! I'm fine. That place is for old people."

Carolyn smiled when she heard the dial tone. Dealing with a parent in this stage of life was never easy. Her mother had become more demanding recently. In a way, it was fun, almost like a new game they were playing. When Marie Sullivan wanted attention, she'd pretend she was having a heart attack or make up some kind of story. Any mention of assisted living and she miraculously recovered.

She dialed the number for Neil's cell phone. Once again, she got the message that his voice mail was full. She rode the elevator to the parking level, got out, and jogged to her car. Paul had let Neil borrow his BMW, so he could be anywhere. Melody was the best bet. Now that Laurel was gone, he needed someone to lean on. She had to find Melody's address. Opening her glove box, she pulled out a stack of envelopes, the majority of them Christmas cards. To save time, she generally read her mail on her lunch break. "Great," she said, finding a card from Melody.

Thirty minutes later, she rang the bell at Melody's Brentwood home.

Melody came to the door in a tight-fitting animal print workout suit. She smiled as if nothing had transpired between them.

"Where's my brother?"

"What do I look like? A babysitter? I gather you got the video I sent you. Paul's a dirtbag, huh?" Melody flashed another smile. "Now that we've got that out of the way, come in. I'll fix us a drink."

How could anyone be so insensitive? Carolyn thought, following her inside. Life was just a big game to Melody.

This time, though, she was playing with a pro. If Carolyn could go head to head with a vicious killer like Raphael Moreno, she decided, she could make mincemeat of this skinny, pampered blonde.

She gazed in disgust at Melody's lavish home. Her entire house could fit into her cavernous living room. The bronze sculptures seemed to be a collection of body parts. Two nude girls were huddled together in one piece, their legs extending several feet from the wall.

Carolyn walked over and stared at a large blue sculpture made out of blown glass. The top section consisted of a man's nude torso, complete with an erect penis. When she saw the head underneath the body, she chuckled. At least she agreed with Melody as to where men's minds were most of the time. Another piece consisted of nothing but a bronzed butt. How much money had Melody paid for that one?

On one wall was a huge painting, more or less the centerpiece of the room. The only thing on the canvas was white paint and the number five. She should bring Rebecca over and let her paint Melody some pictures, scoop up a few buckets of that money she didn't appear to know what to do with. God knows, they'd be better than this crap. And Neil, the classic artist, was spending his time with someone who'd thought this kind of stuff was art. No wonder he'd fallen in love with Laurel.

Melody led her into another room, which resembled a Miami nightclub, with mirrored ceilings and polished black granite floors. Situated in various places were garishly colored velvet chairs and sofas, and the room was illuminated with strangely shaped light figures. Melody ducked behind the bar and returned with two glasses. "Gin and tonic, right? Or would you rather have what I'm drinking, scotch?"

"I'm driving," Carolyn said, scowling. "I don't drink when I drive."

"Oh," Melody answered, acting surprised. "Neil and Paul do, so I assumed you did, too. I can drink most men under the table. My doctor says it's my fast metabolism. That's what probably keeps me so thin. Would you like something else then, a soda, juice, or coffee?"

Melody couldn't really believe she came over to socialize. "I got the video." Carolyn took a seat on a purple sofa, leaning forward for emphasis. "Why did you send it? What Paul did before we met doesn't interest me. You wasted your time."

"That's not what Paul said when he called this afternoon," Melody told her, flopping down in an orange high-backed chair. "He said you broke up with him. Good for you. Paul uses his teaching position to solicit sex from female students. You're probably the oldest woman he's dated since his divorce. I knew sending you the movie clip would upset you, but I was trying to help you. I thought you'd want to start the new year on a clean slate, find someone decent. You're a nice lady, Carolyn. I know you don't like me. Women have never liked me. I guess it's a combination of my looks and money. Anyway, I couldn't stand by and let Paul hurt you the way he hurt me."

The oldest woman Paul had ever dated, Carolyn thought, infuriated. She was only thirty-eight. Who had he been sleeping with? Eighteen-year-olds? Simmer down, she told herself. Her relationship with Paul was over. She had come to find her brother, but the challenge to find out the truth about Melody Asher had also become important. Why couldn't she crack her like she did criminals? With this new development, Melody might hold the key to Neil's freedom in more ways than simply providing him with an alibi.

Who was this woman sitting across from her? Was she an impostor? Was she a murderer? Even if she'd killed Laurel, why would she kill Suzanne Porter? "Stay away from my brother, understand?"

"Where'd that come from?" Melody answered. "Don't you think Neil is old enough to handle his own affairs?"

"No," Carolyn said. "Not with someone as dangerous as you. You killed Laurel Goodwin, didn't you? You found out

Neil was seeing another woman and decided to get rid of her. Then you set it up to look like Neil did it."

"Don't be ridiculous," Melody said, laughing. "Neil means nothing to me. He was like a snack, something to hold me over until dinner. I'm dating Richard Fairchild. Neil knows. If you don't believe me, ask him. Your brother's mentally ill. Some time in jail might be good for him. I learned about people like Neil at the FBI Academy." She saw the shock register on Carolyn's face and quickly added, "No, I'm not an agent. I made it through the training program, but I dropped out to be a model. I hate to even mention this, but your little brother is the one you should be accusing of murdering those women."

Melody attended the FBI Academy! Could it be true, or was it another of her elaborate fabrications? The woman was so complex, Carolyn thought, she wondered if they would ever be able to unravel her. "Neil didn't kill anyone. You're the one with the motive . . . jealous rage. Besides, you're not even who you say you are. The police already know the truth, Jessica."

Melody stood, her teeth clenched, a muscle in her cheek twitching. "What did you call me?"

Now the game was on. She wouldn't have reacted this way unless what Hank had learned was true. "It's your name, isn't it?"

"No, it's not," she argued. "You're confused, Carolyn. I think it's time for you to leave."

"Your father's out of jail," she told her. "He's talking to the police. You can't pretend to be Melody Asher any longer, Jessica. Jessica Graham, right? Your father is Michael Graham. He was a cardiologist before he was convicted of killing your mother and brother eighteen years ago."

Melody dropped down on the edge of the sofa. Her demeanor changed. The tension was gone, and her mouth hung slightly open. "You talked to my father? He's already out of prison?"

"Yes, he is."

Melody looked down at the floor. "Why did he call you?" she asked, raising her head. "Why didn't he call me if he knew where I was?"

"He called the police," Carolyn told her, ignoring her question. "Where's the real Melody Asher? Did you kill her?"

"Of course not," Melody said. "She's an archaeologist. Mel married a Jewish anthropologist and moved to Israel years ago. I didn't do anything wrong. All I did was use her name. That's not a crime."

"You're wrong," Carolyn said. "If she decides to press charges, you could go to jail. That is, if what you say is true. Her people told the police she was still missing."

Melody flicked her hand. "That's just for the media," she said, her confidence returning. "Mel made up that story years ago to get the paparazzi to leave her alone. She won't press charges. We're friends. We grew up together." She pushed a strand of hair behind her ear. "It started as a joke. Melody was planning her wedding. She didn't want the press to show up and ruin it. They'd pestered her all her life. After her parents died, things got even worse. As you know, her family owned APC Pharmaceuticals. A reporter took a picture of me at a play one night after I'd become a blonde. I was with a guy Melody used to date, so the paper mistakenly identified me as Melody. When I called Mel up to tell her, she loved it. She called me back a few days later and asked me if I would use her name so she could live a normal life. It worked for me because of the situation with my father. I was about to marry a well-known fashion designer and was afraid someone might bring up my past."

Carolyn was incredulous. Yet Melody appeared to be telling the truth. Her tone of voice was steady; she looked Carolyn straight in the eye without blinking. But she was also a world-class liar. "Wait a minute," she said. "How old were you when this took place?"

"Eighteen," she said. "The same age as Melody. Girls in

Tuxedo Park mature fast. There's a private school inside the park that teaches above grade level. Mel had her undergraduate degree by then. I didn't do as well. You know, because of what happened. I hired a tutor, though, and managed to catch up pretty fast. At nineteen I was accepted at NYU. I majored in math and minored in psychology."

"Weren't Melody Asher's attorneys concerned about her money and holdings?"

"No," Melody said, taking another drink of her scotch. "Why would I need her money? I inherited a fortune from my mother. My brother was dead and my father couldn't lay claim on the money because he killed her."

"Then you got everything?"

"Yes," she said. "But I don't have anywhere near the amount of money Melody has. To be safe, her attorneys had me sign a document outlining what we'd done to make certain I didn't make any claims on her estate. Then we went to court and legally changed my name. Her watchdogs weren't crazy about the idea, but they didn't have a choice. Melody could do anything she wanted." She stood and walked to the bar, refilling her glass. "Anyone can change their name, you know. All you have to do is file a petition. Would you like to see the paperwork?"

"Yes," Carolyn said, watching as Melody left the room. In a weird way, it made sense. She could see how the public might be fascinated by an eighteen-year-old girl worth over fifty million. On the other end of the spectrum, if she'd been Jessica, she wouldn't want anyone to know that her father had gone to prison for murdering her family. Rich people, particularly society types like the Grahams and Ashers, lived in another dimension.

Melody returned with a large manila envelope, handed it to the probation officer, then quietly returned to her seat on the sofa.

Carolyn looked over the papers, most of them legal documents. There was a formal request for a name change filed in

the state of New York, then an agreement signed by both parties, with the conditions that Melody had mentioned. Her
suspicions were weakening. Because of the video, she realized how eager she'd been to expose Melody as a fraud and a
killer. Perhaps her intentions had been sincere as to Paul as
well, and she'd been smart enough to know that pictures
were more powerful than words. Being Melody Asher or
even Jessica Graham might not be so easy, after all. "It looks
like your name is officially Melody Asher," she said, handing
back the papers. "How long has it been since you talked to
your friend?"

Melody reached back and twisted her long blond hair into
a knot. "A year, I think."

"What name does she go under?"

"Well," she said, her voice trailing off in exhaustion, "her
husband's name is Sam Goldstein. I think she still uses her
first name, but I could be mistaken. A mutual friend told me
she had a kid. I sent her a gift, but I never got a thank-you
card. Maybe it didn't get there. As far as I know, she still
lives in Israel."

Melody continued talking and Carolyn continued listening. Melody told her about the sexual abuse at the hands of
her uncle and how she'd run away from the foster home.
After a year on the street, she had been discovered by the
Ford Modeling Agency.

Carolyn asked herself if Melody had exaggerated parts of
the story to garner sympathy. "You say you were fourteen
when you ran away. How could a girl that age possibly survive in Manhattan?"

"I had sex with rich men," Melody said, rubbing her
hands on her thighs. "By then, I was used to it."

From the look on her face, Carolyn sensed she was telling
the truth. A young girl forced to sell her body for food and
shelter was in one of the most tragic conditions in the world.
Melody had done everything possible to detach herself from
her past. The bleached blond hair, the tough demeanor—

they were nothing more than fragments of her armor. It was impossible to leave that much of yourself behind and continue living. She understood why Melody had wanted to take on someone else's identity. "But couldn't you have just called someone and had them send you money?"

"Nope," she said, a flicker of sadness in her eyes. "The only relative I had outside of my uncle was my father. My father was in prison. At that age, I didn't know anything about money or attorneys. Anyway, I was afraid they'd send me to another foster home. Everywhere I went, men tried to have sex with me. Maybe it was something I said or did. The bastards always told me it was my fault. Most of the time I believed them."

Carolyn's cell phone rang and she excused herself, stepping into the hallway to talk privately. "Where's your brother?" Hank asked. "I need to talk to him. You've had adequate time to hire an attorney."

"Not really, Hank," she told him. "Finding someone to represent him over the holidays isn't easy. A lot of attorneys are out of town. We had an appointment with Vincent Bernini today, but he got tied up and couldn't see us."

"Humph," the detective said. "Where's Neil staying?"

Carolyn felt like she had a wad of cotton in her throat. She ran her hands through her hair, then blurted out, "With my mother."

"That's not true, Carolyn. I called your house and talked to Rebecca. She said she hasn't seen Neil since Christmas Eve. She gave me your mother's phone number and your mom told me the same thing. You're covering for him, aren't you?"

"I can't talk right now," she said, hitting the off button.

When she returned to the living room, she confronted Melody. "Was my brother with you the night of the murder?"

"I saw him for a few hours," she said. "From what the papers say, the two women were killed earlier in the day. Besides, my testimony won't be that valuable. We were lovers. Lovers lie to protect each other." She paused and chuckled. "As you've discovered, I'm pretty good at embellishing the truth. I'm not sure you want me standing up for your brother in a courtroom."

"I need to get going," Carolyn said, her concern for her brother intensifying. "If Neil contacts you, tell him I need to speak to him immediately."

"Oh," Melody said. "I thought we'd catch a bite to eat together. There's this great Chinese restaurant—"

"Another time," Carolyn answered, turning to leave.

"I apologize for sending you the video," Melody told her. "I just wanted you to know the type of man you were sleeping with. I fell for Paul pretty hard. He's smooth, you know. He tells you what you want to hear; then when he gets bored with you, he discards you as if you were garbage. He refused to take my calls. He wouldn't even talk to me in the classroom. Did he tell you he was going to buy you an engagement ring?"

Carolyn's hand flew to her chest. "Yes," she said, her eyes zeroing in on Melody's wrist. She was wearing a Cartier watch that looked almost identical to the one Paul had given her for Christmas, the same night he'd proposed to her. The only difference was the color of the band. Hers had been brown and Melody's was black. "Where did you get that watch, if you don't mind me asking?"

Melody held her arm up so Carolyn could get a better look. "Paul, of course. Did he give you the same watch? I told you. It's not all that expensive. I just wear it when I work out at the gym. It's Cartier's sport line. They call it a Tank."

"I can't believe it," Carolyn said, placing her hand on top of her head. "I feel like a complete fool. What did he do, buy them by the dozens?"

"Don't feel bad," Melody reassured her, touching her arm. "I was a far bigger fool than you, Carolyn. Paul's from Pasadena. That's a big-money town. I had him checked out. His parents left him a sizable estate. He lives fairly simply, but he's pretty well-heeled for a college professor. He can either seduce a woman or buy her. If you want to know the truth, I don't think it matters to him. You live next door, right?"

Carolyn knew what she was going to say. "I was convenient."

"Sounds that way," she said. "Anyway, now that everything's out in the open, I lied when I said I didn't care about Neil. It hurt me when I learned about Laurel, but when he's ready, I'd like to try to work things out between us." She reached over and stroked a silky strand of Carolyn's dark hair. "What they say must not be the truth."

"A lot of things aren't true," she answered, stepping back. "What exactly are you referring to?"

"That men prefer blondes."

Carolyn turned to leave, then remembered something. She wasn't about to be had. Even if Paul was the bastard Melody had depicted, she had learned from him: never accept anything without definitive proof. And not just a stack of official-looking papers. With the kind of equipment available today, people could print themselves a new life. "The police are going to want copies of those documents. They'll want to verify them."

"Not a problem," Melody said, leaning in the doorway until Carolyn got in her car and sped off.

Whoever Melody was, Carolyn thought as she navigated the 405 Freeway north toward Ventura, she didn't seem menacing anymore. She was just a hardened woman who'd had to struggle through life on her own. Some people would foolishly claim they would give up their family for the right amount of money. She doubted if the woman who had taken the name Melody Asher would make such a statement.

Chapter 23

Michael Graham's plane was scheduled to arrive at LAX at seven-fifteen that evening. Hank assigned a patrol unit to pick Graham up and stick him in a motel for the night. Since Carolyn had already cleared up the identity problem, he had no reason to see Dr. Graham outside of curiosity. The man was a convicted murderer. Hank couldn't give him his daughter's address without her permission. If they were on good terms, Dr. Graham would already have it.

Thinking Melody had murdered the two women was a stretch, but she did have the money to hire someone. The killer had to be a male. The lingerie was a giveaway. Suzanne Porter hadn't been wearing a plain white bra and cotton panties like Laurel Goodwin, one of the few discrepancies between the two cases. What she'd had on was what they called a Wonderbra, the kind they sold in stores like Victoria's Secret. Her panties were lacy T-backs. Their killer got turned on by killing women. Not just any women. Young, sexy women with pretty faces and good bodies. Women who lived in Ocean View Estates.

Did the killer live in the area? Or was Ocean View Estates merely his farm, the place where he harvested his victims?

Dropping down at his desk, Hank loosened his tie. Most of the other detectives had either gone home or were still in the field. He called narcotics and spoke with Sergeant Manny Gonzales.

"None of our snitches know of a dealer who rides around on a Yamaha injecting his customers in the privacy of their homes," Manny told him. "The majority of our dealers work out of Oxnard. I'm telling you, the kind of mixture your man put together definitely doesn't sound like a local."

"Dig around with some of the dealers. Offer them a get-out-of-jail pass if they give us some names."

"You're softening in your old age," Manny said. "Whenever I worked with you, everything had to be by the book."

"I'm not softening," Hank said gruffly. "I'm trying to catch what may turn out to be a serial killer."

"It's true, then?" Manny said. "I thought all that 'serial killer' stuff was put out there by the media. I'll get right on it. If you come up with more information, let me know right away. My best sources can only be tapped once."

Something had been bothering Hank since the night of the murder. His old brain wasn't functioning like it did when he was younger. The funny thing about aging was it hit you all at once. You got up one morning and found a crease on your face, thinking it would go away by the time you ate your breakfast. When it was still there a week later, you knew it was going to be there forever. Same thing with the memory. He'd been doing fine until the Moreno homicide. Of course nine murders in less than two months would drive anyone crazy.

Glancing down at his notes, he realized what had been nagging him and rushed over to the wall, where a map of the city was mounted. Neil Sullivan lived at 1003 Sea View Terrace. Hank reached up and stuck a green thumbtack in the map. Suzanne Porter's address was 1003 Seaport Drive, three blocks away. After marking it with a blue thumbtack, he returned to his computer and reviewed the particulars on the Hartfield murders. The residence was closer to the beach, but the address was 1003 Seaport Avenue. Returning to the map, he pushed in a red thumbtack. The area formed a triangle. Was it only a coincidence? Raphael Moreno was already in custody when the recent homicides occurred. In addition, the manner of death didn't match. Moreno had shot all five members of the Hartfield family, lining up their bodies military-style in the living room. None of the victims had been killed by lethal injection. There was no swimming pool, and Mrs. Hartfield had been fully clothed. In a town near the beach, however, every other street had the word "sea" in it.

Mary Stevens appeared in his cubicle, pulling up a chair and kicking her shoes off. "Ready for a bombshell?" she asked. "Suzanne Porter knew Neil Sullivan. Before he became famous, he taught oil painting at Ventura College and she was one of his students. I guess her husband didn't know about him or forgot. One of her girlfriends, Brooke Lamphear, claims Suzanne and Neil were friends. She used to stop by his house and have coffee now and then."

"Were they having an affair?"

"Her friend doesn't think so," Mary continued. "Story is the same we've heard from everyone else we've interviewed." She stopped and glanced down at her notes. "Great couple, loved each other to pieces, blah-blah-blah. Almost sounds too good to believe. A former bond trader turned suburban housewife might not have found life exciting enough for her. But, hey, don't forget all that sexy underwear. Looks like Sullivan's back in the hot seat."

"Did you get in touch with anyone at the school Goodwin taught at?"

"Finally," she said, stretching. "Everyone's gone for vacation, you know, but I managed to track down the principal, Lawrence Hughes. He said there were rumors that Goodwin had been fooling around with a former student named Ashton Sabatino. Since they couldn't substantiate anything and the boy was over eighteen, they didn't take action against her.

Sabatino was a piss-poor student, it seems, but the girls were all crazy about him. You know the type—movie star looks and the brains of a rock." She cleared her throat, then continued, "I spun by his last-known address, an apartment on the west side. The landlord said he moved out nine months ago. No forwarding address. I'm going to check with the parents next. I'll let you know what I find out."

Once Mary walked out of the room, Hank called district attorney Kevin Thomas at home and went over the new information. Thomas didn't put much stock in the address similarities or the lead on Laurel's teenage lover, yet his boss, Sean Exley, had demanded that they take some type of action. Because the press was classifying the two murders as the work of a possible serial killer, the pressure in the DA's office was escalating. The fact that Neil Sullivan hadn't appeared for questioning gave them a valid reason to suspect that he might be the killer. Thomas said if Hank wanted to write a request for an arrest warrant charging Neil Sullivan with two counts of first-degree murder, he'd get Judge O'Brien to sign it. "If the case doesn't come together, we can always cut him loose. Guy's still on the street, and if another homicide goes down, we'll all get fired."

"I'll think about it," Hank said, slowly placing the phone back in the cradle. He was on his way to an AA meeting. Today was the four-year anniversary of his younger brother's death.

The meeting was held at the Christ the King Presbyterian Church. Hank sat in a circle with fifteen other people from all walks of life—carpenters, doctors, firemen, housewives. Alcoholism didn't discriminate. That a room filled with strangers could meet and spill out some of the darkest moments of their lives was one of the elements that made the program so successful. That and the Serenity Prayer, which Hank said every time temptation reared its ugly head. He didn't know about God, though. He wanted to believe, but it was hard. Once you'd picked up the pieces of a butchered child from a garbage dump, you had to ask yourself if anyone was listening.

Having a sponsor to call on whenever you needed help was another element. Hank's sponsor was a fifty-year-old advertising director. He wasn't there tonight. He must be out of town.

The topic for this particular meeting was how family members played a part in the alcoholic's behavior. Many times Hank didn't share. By merely listening, he allowed newer attendees or those in crisis time to interact with the group. This evening, he was the person in crisis. As soon as the holiday season began, he was flooded with painful memories. Keeping his feelings inside was similar to carrying a concrete ball inside his stomach. "I became an alcoholic after my brother was killed in a traffic accident," Hank said, his eyes roaming around the room. "He was killed this day, four years ago. After a night of partying, Andy drove his Corvette into the ocean on the outskirts of Ventura. The search was called off the next day. My brother was assumed dead. Once I recovered from the shock, I drove to the beach area near the sewage treatment plant in Oxnard, where a number of surfers and boaters had washed up on the shore. This was where the currents generally carried them, depending on where they went into the water. I knew this the night Andy died, but I failed to tell the search and rescue team. I guess my mind shut down. Maybe because the people who had been found near the treatment plant were all dead, it was just too painful to think about." He leaned forward over his knees, emotion welling up inside him. Here a man could cry. He couldn't allow himself to break down, though, even today. He had to catch a killer.

"When I got to Andy, he was dead," Hank continued. "The autopsy reports indicated he was alive when he washed up on the shore the night before. He was a strong swimmer.

Even though the undercurrents had swept him two and a half miles down the coast, his death wasn't caused by drowning. He died from the injuries he received when the Corvette slammed into the water. If I had checked the area near the treatment plant sooner, my brother would still be alive."

Hank listened patiently to all the other members' stories. This was the price you paid to cleanse your soul. It was similar to confession. The penance came from admitting publicly that you had made mistakes—battered your wife, squandered your finances, lashed out at your children. Some of their stories he knew as well as his own. Others he had never heard before, and many were far worse than his. Another benefit came from the realization that you were only human, that human frailty was inherent in everyone.

As soon as they broke out the coffee and doughnuts, Hank said a few words to some of the regulars, then slipped out of the room to drive back to the police station.

It was almost eleven before Hank finished the paperwork. The detective realized Carolyn was probably in bed, but the situation warranted waking her. He called her from the car, telling her he needed to see her, then showed up a short time later on her doorstep.

Carolyn came to the door in a white terrycloth bathrobe, her eyes swollen from sleep. "Are you drinking again? Good God, Hank, it's almost midnight. Don't tell me there's been another murder."

"I'm not drinking," the detective said, following her into the house. "And no, there hasn't been another murder. At least, not yet. I came to talk about your brother."

"Has he been hurt?" Carolyn asked, dozens of terrible images passing through her mind. Cops came to your house late at night to tell you someone had died. She grabbed onto the detective's jacket. "Please, Hank, Neil didn't kill himself, did he?"

"Settle down," Hank told her. "It's time Neil comes in, Carolyn. Can't you give us a clue as to where he is?"

"Well," she said, smoothing down his jacket, then taking a seat on the rose-colored sofa in her living room. "I'm sure Neil is staying in LA with some of his friends, Hank. I don't think he believes he's actually a suspect. He's grieving for Laurel. He has a right to do that, doesn't he?"

"I'm going to be honest," the detective said, too anxious to sit. He paced around the room, picking up knickknacks and then setting them back down. "The DA has decided to file. Your brother's prints are on the syringe. Charley Young has identified it as the murder weapon. We have probable cause to arrest him, Carolyn. Mary found out today that he also knew Suzanne Porter, which ties him to the other murder as well. She was one of his students in the art class he taught at Ventura College."

When Carolyn reached up to turn on the lamp, her hands were shaking. "Neil grew up in Ventura. He knows half the people in this town. Not only that, Suzanne Porter was practically his neighbor. You may not realize it, but my brother is something of a celebrity, especially in the artistic community."

Hank remained somber. "I had the dispatcher broadcast it a few minutes ago. When he contacts you, get him to turn himself in. Until I'm convinced otherwise, we're classifying him as armed and dangerous."

Carolyn fell silent, giving herself time to absorb the implications. The fact that Neil knew Suzanne Porter was no revelation. They couldn't hang a case on something that flimsy. Hank was trying to tell her what she feared the most, that her brother could be shot and killed by a police officer. All it took was one wrong move. "Why armed and dangerous? Neil has never fired a gun in his life. Anyway, no weapon was used in either murder."

Hank knew he had to talk straight to her. She was far more involved than she knew. "A weapon was used in the Hartfield homicides."

"What in God's name does that have to do with Neil?"

He explained the similarities in the house numbers and locations. "Raphael Moreno is the key. You're the only one who's managed to break through to him. We certainly can't send Preston in there again. Before you get spooked, hear me out. We'll arrange it so you interview him in a room with half a dozen of our top marksmen. The bastard so much as hiccups and he's a dead man."

"The address similarities are just coincidences," Carolyn said, trying to keep the detective from seeing how upset she was. She couldn't allow them to put her brother in jail. It was too similar to a mental hospital, where his past experience had been devastating. "It's absurd to think Neil was involved with Moreno. You think this has something to do with drugs, don't you? Neil may have smoked a little pot when he was in high school, but so did I. It's hard to find anyone from our generation that didn't, even some of our presidents."

"We're not talking about marijuana, Carolyn."

"You're giving the killer the upper hand," she said. "He planned this so you'd see a pattern. He's a damn serial killer. He doesn't want to be portrayed as a garden-variety murderer. He's trying to establish himself as another Dahmer, Gacy, or Bundy."

Hank unwrapped a stick of gum and popped it into his mouth. "I hope you're wrong." He paused to chew, then resumed. "Once I get approval from the chief, I'll start arranging things for tomorrow."

"You're wasting your time."

Hank's back stiffened. "What's that supposed to mean?"

"Why should I put my life on the line?" Carolyn asked him. "Preston was seriously injured. Moreno's got razor-sharp reflexes. He might strangle me this time."

"Christ, woman, we're trying to save lives here," the detective argued. "You usually beg for the chance to pry information out of violent offenders. You'll be covered by the SWAT team and Moreno will be shackled."

"You mean like he was when he attacked Brad?" she

countered, recalling her tense confrontation with Moreno. If she'd known he could get out of the restraints, she would have never stepped foot in that room. The department had issued her a new cell phone. She kept the one he had crushed with his bare hands as a reminder to be more careful. "He's a contortionist, remember? He can get out of anything."

Hank swallowed hard. "We'll have him in a chair so we can see his hands and legs."

"He's five feet six inches tall and fast as lightning. Even handcuffed, this guy scares me."

"So we'll put him behind glass."

"Have you tried sending someone else over there?" Carolyn asked. "He could have responded to me because I was a woman. Get Mary to talk to him. You guys are the cops. I'm just a probation officer."

"Sure," he said. "A probation officer with a remarkable ability to get people to talk. I bet the FBI or the CIA would hire you in a minute. Think of how valuable you could be interrogating terrorists. As for other people trying to crack Moreno, when we first arrested him, we sent five detectives, two of them female. Mary went over and spent a whole afternoon with him. Guy didn't even blink. She said it was like trying to get a corpse to talk."

"They talked to him through the glass, right? No one else had the guts to go in there alone."

"It's you or nothing, Carolyn."

As terrifying as Moreno was, Carolyn felt herself stirring with excitement. She still didn't know what had caused him to commit the crimes, or if he might have had an accomplice. This would give her another chance. It was like staying up all night reading a book, then finding out it had no ending. "Surround him with cops, Hank, and the same thing will happen. He'll never talk that way. I'll have to do it exactly like I did before—one-on-one. Even then there are no guarantees."

Hank compressed in his seat. "What do you want from me?"

"Retract what you broadcast about my brother," she told him, fully awake and energized. "Say that he's only wanted for questioning and that the dispatcher made a mistake by classifying him as armed and dangerous. Give me twenty-four hours to bring him in. You don't have a signed warrant yet. What proof do you have that Neil's carrying a firearm?"

"I can't let you do this," Hank said. "One of our officers could get killed."

"Fine!" Carolyn shouted. "Find someone else to do your dirty work. I don't have to do this based on your speculations. I'm a single mother with two children. It's unconscionable that you'd even ask me to do such a thing."

Rebecca appeared in the doorway, dressed in a cropped top and a pair of tights, a ragged pink baby blanket crushed to her chest. "What's wrong, Mom?" she asked. "Why are you yelling? It's about Uncle Neil, isn't it? John said he might be in trouble because of that lady who was murdered." She looked over at the detective. "Hi, Hank," she said. "Why are you and Mom fighting? I thought you were buddies."

"You're growing up," he said, managing a smile. "Don't let those boys get their hands on you. You're going to have to keep an eye on her, Carolyn."

Rebecca put her arms around her chest to cover her breasts. "You guys woke me up," she said, not at all happy. "How am I gonna go back to sleep? Mom, can't you give me a pill or something?"

"Absolutely not," Carolyn told her. "We'll have a chat as soon as Hank leaves, if you're still awake." She had told John about the situation with Neil, but she had as yet to break the news to his sister. Rebecca worshipped her uncle. She seemed to have inherited his artistic abilities. Her art teacher had raved about her drawings. She would explain everything tonight. There wasn't really that much to say, just that the police were doing their jobs, and that meant eliminating Neil as a suspect. When she saw Rebecca still standing there, glaring at her, Carolyn added, "You don't have to

246 *Nancy Taylor Rosenberg*

get up and go to school in the morning. You can sleep until noon if you want."

"Whatever," Rebecca said, waving good-bye to the detective.

Hank let out a long sigh. "You've got a deal," he said, once he heard a door close. "I'll call you tomorrow and tell you what time this is going down."

"No SWAT team," Carolyn said, standing to walk him out. "The only thing I'll consider is a room with two-way mirrors."

"We'd have to transport him to the station," Hank said at the door. "The jail doesn't have those facilities. He's an escape risk. The chief won't approve it under those terms. We can throw up a room inside the jail, make it look like the room where you first interviewed him. But the SWAT team has to be present. No deal unless you do it my way. Are we clear?"

"Perfectly," Carolyn said, hating to concede but knowing that she had run out of bargaining power. If she didn't let Hank handle the Moreno interview the way he wanted, every cop in five counties would be searching for Neil, a man Hank had depicted to be armed and dangerous. She would rather risk her own life than risk the life of her brother. In what was left of her original family, Carolyn was the designated driver.

Chapter 24

Melody opened the door, surprised that the Chinese food had arrived so quickly. The aroma of the Ma Po Tofu permeated the lower level of her home. Tonight would be like many other nights—she would be alone. She hadn't seen Neil since two days before Christmas. She missed his touch and his company.

She set the food down on the table, glancing into the living room. She should have turned the lights on earlier. December brought darkness at five o'clock. She'd become afraid of the shadowy corners of her large house. When she went to the viewing room, it evoked memories of the third floor of her childhood home in Tuxedo Park.

She didn't want to eat alone. Feeling despondent, she stretched out on the sofa. Her mind spun back in time. She was nine years old. She could see her tall, skinny body and her mass of curly red hair. Tears fell as she mourned for the child she'd once been, wishing she could change the events that had created who she was today. Her eyelids became heavy; then she connected with a frightening childhood memory.

"Mommy," she called out, having returned from her girlfriend's house. She hated Melody, but she liked Melody's mother. Even though they had tons of money, Mrs. Asher wasn't drunk all the time. Instead of smelling like alcohol, she smelled like flowers. Her mother tried to cover the smell of booze with perfume, but it only made her stink more.

"Your mother went to the city," Mrs. Mott told her, busy at the kitchen sink. "Go upstairs and do your homework."

"It's Friday," she said, grabbing a handful of cookies off a plate on the table. "I don't have any homework."

"Then catch up on your reading."

Since Mrs. Mott was occupied, she decided to rummage around the house. There was a locked bedroom on the third floor and she wanted to see what was inside. It was scary and dark up there, especially for a nine-year-old. Her fear was not as strong as her curiosity. She'd searched for months for the key and hadn't been able to find it.

As she walked through the foyer, the marble floor echoed her footsteps. Then she saw the solution right in front of her. Why hadn't she thought about it before? The key was on her father's key ring on the table at the foot of the stairs. He was probably in the library working at his desk, like he did every night before supper.

She set the cookies down as her fingers grasped the keys. Then she rushed up the two flights of stairs. She halted, looking down the dark hallway with its nine doors and patterned red carpeting. She flipped on the light. It flickered and went off, plunging her again into darkness. Even the servants hardly ever came upstairs. Glancing at the keys in her hand, she heard a noise coming from one of the rooms at the end of the hall. It sounded like the voice of a woman. She tiptoed toward the door, her stomach fluttering. Jeremy made fun of her. She'd show him she wasn't a chicken. She could now see the moving illumination of a candle through the cracked door. She peeped through the opening.

She drew a quick breath. What she saw was terrifying. There was a dark-skinned woman with a large head of frizzy hair. Her hair looked as if it were on fire as it bounced with the gyrations of her naked body. She was in pain, moaning as she tossed her head back and forth. Someone was hurting her. The lamp and nightstand obscured Jessica's view. She saw a man holding onto the woman's hands. She was trying to escape, but he wouldn't let her go.

Jessica's fear for the woman grew. She had to be crying because her face was contorted in agony. In order to get a better vantage point, Jessica moved to her left. When she realized the person who was hurting the woman was her father, her fingers involuntarily opened and the keys fell out of her hand. Her father tossed the woman off, causing her to tumble onto the floor. He retrieved his burgundy silk robe, then charged toward his daughter.

"What are you doing up here?" he said, yanking open the door and grabbing her arm.

"I-I was . . ."

"Shut up," her father yelled, picking her up and pressing her against the wall. "If you ever say anything about this to Jeremy or your mother, I'll send you away." He shook her. "Do you understand? You'll never see this house again."

Tears ran down Jessica's face. "Yes . . . Daddy . . . please, you're hurting me."

He set her down on the floor, then patted her on the top of her head as if nothing had happened. "Now give me those keys and get downstairs where you belong."

She'd never seen her father that mad before. Why was he hurting that poor woman?

Jessica never went onto the third floor again. Even today, darkness left her with a feeling of helplessness.

Pushing the past aside, Melody turned all the lights on and went to eat her food. She took a few bites of the spicy sauce, then tilted the half-empty bottle of red wine to her mouth. She didn't know why she'd ordered so much food. She didn't have an appetite lately. Her thoughts moved to Neil and the night of Laurel's death. As she walked up the stairs to her viewing room, she decided to watch the video again.

Dropping her clothes at the doorway, she slipped on her robe and burped. The Chinese food tasted different the second time. Opening the small refrigerator she kept upstairs, she took out a cold bottle of water and washed down the bitter taste. A few minutes later, she was positioned at one of her monitors, waiting until the video player loaded the file. She clicked through it to find where she wanted to start watching.

The night of the murder, Melody had stayed up until five o'clock watching the footage she had recorded that day, frame by frame.

The leather-clad figure with a motorcycle helmet stood at the side of the house. The figure moved to the backyard. That's when she saw Laurel coming out of the French doors. She had a portable phone in her right hand, then placed it to her ear. She must have been trying to call the police.

Helpless bitch, Melody thought. She should have learned to protect herself. A struggle ensued, and Laurel and the assailant moved into the house. Pausing the video, Melody moved to another monitor, which showed a different feed, and clicked play. They were in the bedroom.

Laurel was so weak, she didn't stand a chance. She was forced to strip down to her cheap cotton underwear. Melody was surprised the red circular Target logo wasn't imprinted on her ass. She watched the helmeted figure inject Laurel; then they both disappeared into the bathroom.

Melody panned to the other monitor and clicked forward to the point where Laurel was being dragged facedown across the pavement. That couldn't have felt very good, she said to herself, even with whatever the guy shot her up with.

Laurel was propped up at the side of the pool, her head bleeding. Then Melody's eyes locked on the screen. She saw the splash. Bubbles rose from beneath the water as the last bit of oxygen left in Laurel Goodwin's lungs floated to the surface, never to be recaptured again.

Melody was sad for Laurel, but it had been wrong of her to try to take Neil away. The woman had to know Neil was dating her. Everyone knew. The local paper had even run a picture of them together. Melody was the innocent party again. When would it end?

She had a philosophy. Each person was allowed a certain number of mistakes. It was similar to tokens. Whenever you did something bad, you'd lose a token. Once they were all used up, an agonizing death was imminent. She'd seen it happen to Rees.

At the end, Melody had discovered the truth. Her husband was a homosexual by choice and heterosexual whenever it benefited him. He'd risen to the top in the fashion world by sleeping with high-profile women, then married a seventeen-year-old girl to mask his sexual preference. Rees had never made love to Melody, which showed he possessed a modicum of decency. She had found out he had AIDS. Rees had used up his tokens. She had threatened to expose him. So what if he killed himself? Even though she didn't need it, Melody took his money as payback for all the poor women he'd deceived. He might not have known he had AIDS at the time he slept with them, but his lifestyle made him a high risk. His current male lover received nothing in his will.

Like Rees, Laurel had not been a good person. She deceived people with her tacky clothes and schoolteacher image. Her uncle had also been a teacher, and Elton had forced Melody to have sex with him. She remembered the nights he thrashed on top of her small body in the damp, scary basement while his wife and sons slept only a floor above. Even when the nurse at school saw her bruises and reported them to the police, her uncle's stupid wife, Sally, insisted Melody had lied, disturbed over the tragic deaths of her family. Sally was probably still cooking his meals and washing his clothes while he molested other children, giving them cuddly teddy bears and expensive toys, then telling them if they told, their parents would punish them for lying.

Pedophiles were similar to people suffering from a terminal illness, Melody had later learned. There was no such thing as a cure. Until they died, pedophiles would be attracted to children. Years ago, the state hospital for the criminally insane had attached electrodes to their penises and shocked them every time they got an erection while looking at pictures of underage children. Nevertheless, when they were released, they did it again.

Laurel must have given drugs to Neil, intending to trap him into marriage and destroy his relationship with her. Where else would Neil get the drugs? She'd filmed him snorting the damn stuff.

She didn't let him know how much she admired his work, for fear he would become overly confident and leave her. It was a shame to destroy such talent. Neil thought his recent paintings weren't selling because of the slump in the economy. They didn't sell because they were shit. Dope made you think everything you did was wonderful. She would never pollute her body or mind the way Neil had.

Her dilemma was staring her in the face. She wanted to release the video of the murder to the police, but she couldn't let people know about her hobby, fearing she would end up in prison. It was a crime to spy on people without their consent, and now she'd withheld vital information in a homicide. She could send the video anonymously, however, and they wouldn't be able to trace it back to her. The police didn't have any evidence linking her to Laurel's murder, but she couldn't take any unnecessary chances. She had to find a way to help Neil. The tape she'd made of them having sex the night of the murder and the tape she was looking at now would more than likely clear him.

Melody opened a drawer in her desk and removed a bottle of scotch. A little alcohol was okay as long as she didn't abuse it. She only got drunk during the holidays, when the past became too difficult to suppress. How many tokens did she have left? Not many, she figured. She'd better use them wisely.

Chapter 25

Monday, December 27—7:25 P.M.

Neil stood alone on a large sand dune in Oxnard Shores, a beach community fifteen minutes from Ventura. Farther inland, Oxnard was not a desirable place to live. When his mother had brought him and Carolyn here when they were children, the area was just starting to develop. Now houses were crammed together along the sand and cars backed up in the narrow streets. At night, though, it was peaceful, and Neil came here often. The salty ocean breeze swept over him. The temperature had dropped into the mid-fifties, but even without a jacket, his skin felt hot and clammy.

He remembered playing on these same dunes. Some were three feet high and others as big as five. Grassy plants grew on top of them. He and his friends liked war games. Diving into the sand, they'd fire their fake machine guns at each other, making staccato sounds with their mouths. Life was simple then.

Things had changed—the gun in his hands was real.

Staring at the sea, the moon reflecting on the water, he wondered if he would see Laurel on the other side. He took a long drink out of the wine bottle he was holding, wiping his mouth with the back of his hand. He didn't believe in all that Catholic bullshit. If there was a God, how could He punish someone for taking his life when it became unbearable? His poor father didn't deserve to go to hell.

Maybe Neil could have understood himself if his mother hadn't kept the truth hidden. Some people were merely too fragile. He was sure he hadn't killed Laurel, but he now remembered hitting her. The night she'd died, he had taken so much Depakote to come down off the amphetamines, he was surprised he remembered anything. He recalled stumbling into the bathroom in the dark, leaning down to get a drink from the tap, and almost cracking his head open. The police had found the syringe in the sink. He may have touched it without knowing. If they found his fingerprints on it, they would lock him up forever. He'd rather die than go to jail.

When Laurel told him she was still legally married to Jordan and might eventually reconcile with him, he'd gone crazy. After snorting several lines of meth in the garage, he returned to the house and they'd argued some more. He slapped her. Then everything had become murky.

For the past three days, he'd been holed up in a cheap motel, trying to kick his drug habit. He was certain the police were going to arrest him. Once they tested him, the truth would come out. His hip bones were protruding. He must have lost ten pounds. He felt as if he were being squeezed to death by a boa constrictor. He'd sweated buckets and experienced violent muscle spasms. After saturating himself with booze, he decided he was either going to start using drugs again or kill himself.

The wine bottle was almost empty. The effects of the alcohol were kicking in, intensified by the three vodka martinis he'd tossed down a few hours earlier.

Laurel's image appeared inside the mist, hovering over the ocean in a ghostly form. The memory of her soft voice rang in his ears. He had been desperate to bring back the happy times they'd spent together in high school. Their love had been pure, untainted by sex, drugs, alcohol, the kind of things many of their friends had already dived into. After constant heckling, Neil and Laurel had shared a marijuana cigarette late one night in her backyard. Stretched out on a blanket, they were laughing and munching on M&M's when Neil looked up and saw Laurel's father standing over them. Her parents had come home early from a wedding. Furious, Stanley Caplin accused Neil of being a drug dealer and forbade Laurel to ever see him again outside of school. They could have resumed their relationship after graduation. Everything was ruined, though, so they went their separate ways. Laurel remained in California and obtained her teaching certificate, while Neil perfected his art skills in Europe. He cursed the day he'd run into her at Barnes & Noble. Maybe she would be alive today if they hadn't started seeing each other again.

He knew he had to leave Carolyn's house before she found out the truth—that her brother was a drug addict. Only when you stopped using did you realize that the drug you were so eager to consume was poison. If you continued to use, it would kill you. Because of his anxiety over his paintings not selling, he'd started using twice as much. He'd been flying so high, he lost track of what he was doing. People would come up to him in a restaurant or club, rambling on about things a stranger couldn't possibly know. Neil would quickly excuse himself, unable to remember the person's name or where he had met him.

Proposing to Laurel had been an impulsive act, clearly induced by narcotics. He'd been drifting untethered until he seduced himself into believing that Laurel would become his anchor.

When he shut his eyes, he hallucinated that he was struggling in the dark, cold water. Gasping for air, he hoisted Laurel onto the edge of the pool. After two compressions of her chest, her eyes opened and her beautiful mouth spread in a smile. "I love you, Neil."

Why did everyone think she was dead? She'd just gone for a swim and slipped under for a few minutes. Not a problem. Her future husband was there to rescue her. Reality struck him in the face and he was staring into Laurel's dead eyes, her body stiff and frigid.

"It's you and me forever," Neil said to Laurel's fading image. He closed his eyes. He cried for the children they would never have, the anniversaries they would never celebrate, all that they could have been.

"I'm still right here, Laurel," he yelled into the wind. "Why did you leave me?"

He reached to his side and picked up the loaded pistol. They would be together again as soon as he pulled the trigger. He wondered how much blood would gush out. Would the remains of his brain be found by children out for an afternoon at the beach? That would mess them up good. So what, he thought, he'd spent most of his life screwing things up. Why change things now?

He put the gun away, lured back into his thoughts. If he had a canvas, he would paint it cold and gray like his soul, waiting patiently for the cruel world to disappear. Before he used the gun, he would take out a knife and slash the canvas once, symbolizing his father, then add another for Laurel.

Neil had found the police report describing his father's suicide when he'd spent Christmas Eve with his mother. Why hadn't she told him the truth years ago? He'd tried to understand, but it smashed his sanity. He tried to forget the pain, but the pain was the only thing that seemed real. He was broken and nothing could repair him. The truth about his father and the white powder had left a gaping hole that was about to swallow him, scratching and skidding down to the core.

He removed his wallet and stared at a small snapshot of himself and Laurel. He'd kept it since they were in high school. She was perfect and they fit perfectly. He could smell the sun on her skin that day when he'd kissed her neck; then his senses were crushed by the aroma of salty water. No matter how far he ran, Laurel was inside, calling him to join her.

He ripped the picture in half and let the pieces fall to the ground. His life had been a failure. A strong gust of wind brushed past him. When he looked down, the picture was gone. He was insignificant. Just like the picture, he would soon be gone and forgotten.

Was he being fair? Taking his life would destroy Carolyn. "Shit, what am I doing?" he said, pulling out the gun and tossing it into the sand. Carolyn had been more than a sister. She'd been like a mother to him. She risked her life protecting society while he sold paintings to rich people. He thought of the silly woman who'd traded the Ferrari for some of his worst paintings.

Neil's hands closed into fists. He lashed out into nothingness. "Why did you do this to me?" Suddenly he fell, as if God had opened up the sky and pushed him to the ground. He removed a pen and a small spiral binder from his windbreaker, sobbing as he wrote.

> *Dear Carolyn,*
> *I didn't mean to have it end this way. There was no way out. No place I can go. I'm nothing but a nuisance, constantly interrupting your life. I'm sorry, but you won't have to worry about me anymore. I made the choice to end it. It's not your fault. Carry on, I'll be fine in the eternal fire where I belong.*
>
>

Love,
Neil

He placed the paper and pen down, then stretched out on his back, staring up at the early evening stars. Reaching out, he retrieved the pistol. The sound of the waves would muffle the explosion. Beginning to accept death, he reminded himself that as soon as a person was born, he began to die. Maybe when you died, you finally began to live. Tonight would be his first step toward his new existence. His time was up. He raised the gun up to his temple and closed his eyes.

Bang.

Chapter 26

Dr. Michael Graham stepped out of the shower in his room at the Holiday Inn Express. He had tried all day to get in front of Hank Sawyer. A female detective kept telling him Sawyer was tied up and couldn't speak to him. No one would tell him Jessica's address. Another door had slammed in his face, reminding him that he was a convicted murderer, too dangerous to know where his daughter lived.

His clothes were folded neatly on the bed, a plain white shirt and a pair of jeans. He went over to the window with a partial ocean view. He'd been to California once when he was a child, but he'd forgotten how scenic it was, and what great weather it had. Pressing his hands against the glass, he couldn't understand why the detective had flown him out. Sawyer said on the phone that Jessica was a possible suspect in these awful crimes.

When his brother had shown him the newspaper articles, he'd refused to believe it. All he could think of was seeing his daughter again and possibly having his license to practice medicine reinstated. On the airplane, his excitement grew. He remembered Jessica's soft red hair, the fresh smell of her skin, the sound of her playful laughter, and his love for her as a father. Did she still love macaroni and cheese, Lego blocks, chocolate, and watching *I Love Lucy*? His anticipation was overshadowed by the alarming conversation he'd had with the homicide detective. Now he had a far more serious reason to see her.

He couldn't understand how Jessica had gotten away with passing herself off as Melody Asher. He knew the Asher family. They'd lived close to them in upstate New York. Phillipa, his deceased wife, had inherited the house in Tuxedo Park, as well as several million in stocks and bonds. Unless she'd squandered it, Jessica should be an extremely wealthy young woman. But she would never have the kind of money the Ashers had.

The Ashers were one of the richest families in the country. Morton Asher had founded Asher Pharmaceutical Corporation in 1903. Unlike most major corporations, it was privately held. When Morton and Elizabeth Asher died, their fortune had fallen into the hands of their two sons, Raymond and Kendall. Kendall Asher was killed in Vietnam. Raymond married and gave birth to Melody. In a highly publicized traffic accident, Raymond, along with four other individuals, had been killed. Five years later, his wife, Blythe, had died of lung cancer. Melody had inherited somewhere close to fifty million dollars, and that was just the amount released to the public. On her eighteenth birthday, the heiress had disappeared.

Graham had to admit that the two girls resembled each other, at least when he'd last seen them. Phillipa thought their height was one of the reasons they had struck up a friendship. Jessica had been the tallest girl in her class, Melody only an inch shorter. Everyone made a fuss over Melody, though, and Jessica became jealous.

People in Tuxedo Park were ranked by their fortunes, not their personalities. The children mimicked their parents. It was uncouth to speak of money, but anyone with half a brain knew what it meant when a person announced that they'd never worked a day in their life—old money. Old money didn't mix with new money.

The night of the shooting, Dr. Graham had feared Jessica would never speak again. The only thing she claimed to remember was her father telling her that he was at fault. During the trial, she testified that she'd never seen the gun before it went off in her father's hands. Even the district attorney suspected that the killings may have been an accident. Because Graham had destroyed the murder weapon, and had also failed to notify the police as soon as the deaths had occurred, Jessica's story appeared credible.

When he was first arrested, he'd thought the only way he could redeem himself was to accept whatever happened. He had to protect his daughter, all that was left of his family. Jessica had either buried the truth deep in her subconscious, or she had lied, terrified of what the police would do to her.

Jessica's attitude toward her father changed almost before the gun stopped smoking. He saw it in her face as she looked at him in the courtroom. The police and prosecutors had coached her. Already she exhibited the steely resolve of a survivor.

In prison, Dr. Graham realized he'd made another serious mistake. He'd shown his daughter that it was okay to lie as long as she didn't get caught. Jessica might never take responsibility for her actions. She lived in denial, while all around her things were going wrong. Many of the events that later occurred must have been directly related to that fateful night. The accusations against his brother had shocked him. Jessica had been blinded by her own mind. She not only told lies, she believed them.

Dr. Graham remembered the attention his daughter had received from the police investigators and the prosecution team during his trial. He pictured her in the witness-box, smiling at the female prosecutor.

His days living with men who committed horrendous acts of violence had taught him a great deal. He found that many of their problems had stemmed from their childhoods. What happened to his daughter was like a seed planted in fertilized soil. Add a little water and the plant might grow into a full-blown criminal.

The phone rang. He hoped it was the detective. Instead, it was a local reporter from the *Ventura Star*. He began firing off questions, "Is it true that you've been in jail for the past sixteen years?"

"Do you know where my daughter lives?" Graham said. "No one will tell me."

This wasn't the first call he'd received. He didn't understand how the press knew where to find him.

"Yeah," the reporter said. "Hello, are you there, Dr. Graham?"

Could he be foolish enough to believe a scrambling reporter's claim? What other option did he have? His pulse rate escalated. "Yes, I'm here. Where is she?"

"Not so quick, pal. Information doesn't come for free. Fortunately, you have something that I need."

Dr. Graham started to hang up, then listened as the man continued speaking.

"Give me an exclusive on the story of you and your daughter's reunion and I'll personally drive you to her home. How does that grab you?"

"Deal."

Less than twenty minutes later, the reporter knocked on the door at Graham's hotel room. Jack Overton was small in stature, with brown hair and a well-groomed mustache. They got into a tan Buick. Without hesitation, the reporter interrogated him on every aspect of his life—his daughter, his prison sentence, and the events that led up to his conviction. He refused to answer all of Overton's questions. The man persisted as the miles ticked off on the odometer.

"We're here," Overton announced.

Jessica's home was secured with a fence that had white metal bars placed on top of a U-shaped brick wall. The structure was large and the grounds manicured. They walked through the unlocked gate to the front door. Graham's hands were cold and clammy. He rang the doorbell. Movement could be heard from inside the house. Would she open the door?

It swung open, exposing a disheveled woman who vaguely resembled what had once been his little girl. She was dressed in an animal print workout suit. The smell of booze permeated the air. When Graham tried to speak, his words were stuck inside.

"I'm Jack Overton," the reporter said, extending his hand. "Are you Melody Asher?"

"No, I'm the maid," she said, declining to shake his hand. "What the hell do you want? You're a damn reporter, aren't you? Get off the property."

A tall figure stepped forward. "Jessica, it's Dad."

Melody's father reached out to touch her. She pulled away from him and almost fell backward onto the hard marble floor. "What are you doing here?" she spat. "You're a murderer. Get out of here before I call the police."

Dr. Graham extended his arm forward, forcing his way into the house. Melody was caught off guard. He turned, glared at the reporter, then slammed the door in his face. The subsequent pounding was ignored.

They were finally alone.

"I'm sorry for barging in," he said. "You need to know the truth. We have to talk."

"I know the truth," Melody said, remembering him leaning over Jeremy's body. "We don't need to talk. Please leave now."

He moved toward her. "Honey, you need to know what really happened the night Phillipa and Jeremy died. I'm not a murderer. You have to believe me."

"You're lying," she said, rushing into the other room. She'd been tormented by the past for eighteen years. Now it had shown up on her doorstep. Her father looked terrible. He had been so handsome. How could this man be her father? He'd been a prominent heart surgeon. He looked like an ex-con, with his cheap shirt and his worn jeans. She picked up the portable phone in the kitchen. He stood quietly in the shadows, staring at her, making her furious. "If you're not a murderer, why did they convict you? Go back to wherever you came from. You have no business being here. I'm not your daughter anymore."

"They convicted me based on your testimony. What are you doing?" He walked forward and took the phone from her.

She swung at him, her balled-up fist striking his face. The impact dropped him to the floor. "You killed Mother and Jeremy," she yelled, standing over him. "I wasn't going to lie to protect you, even if you were my father."

Rubbing his bleeding nose, he said, "I didn't fire the shot that killed them. *You did*, Jessica. It was an accident."

"No, you're just trying to trick me," she said, pointing to the front door. "Get out of my house. I'm going to set off the alarm." She walked a few feet away and held her finger above the panic button on the security panel. If the useless rent-a-cops didn't get there in time, she'd have to solve the problem herself, just as she had always done. She dropped her hands to her side, forgetting to press the button. The volcano inside her erupted. "You know the hell I've been through? Your fucking brother raped me, not once, but every single day. He took me in the basement and locked the door; then he stripped me naked. If I refused to have sex, he beat me with a paddle."

"Oh, my God, the paddle!" her father exclaimed, pushing himself to his feet. "I swear, Jessica, I didn't know. Elton swore it wasn't true. I'm sorry. I'm so sorry."

"Now you know why I don't need him, you, or anyone. I can take care of myself."

"Before I leave," he said in a voice full of shame, "I want you to know your mother and Jeremy's death wasn't your fault. You were looking for the Christmas presents when you stumbled across my rifle. You brought it into our bedroom. That's when it happened, Jessica."

Melody's mind began spinning. She walked into the living room and sat down on the edge of the sofa, a distant look in her eyes. She remembered him carrying her down the stairs that night. Her pink flannel pajamas had been splattered with blood.

Dr. Graham sat in the chair across from her. "Jessica, you're a grown woman. You're living in denial. Think about this logically. Why would I shoot Jeremy in the back while he was leaning over your mother? You know I would never intentionally hurt you, Jeremy, or your mother. I dedicated my life to healing people. I tried to save Jeremy. I held his heart in my hands. There was nothing I could do, nothing anyone could do.

"Your mind shut out what really happened. It's a survival mechanism, particularly with children. It's lingered in your subconscious for years. When I saw you, I ran toward you to get the rifle. Your finger got caught in the trigger mechanism and the gun went off. The bullet first hit your brother in the back, then entered your mother's head."

She leaned into the sofa, her eyes darting back and forth in thought. "You can say anything you want. It won't change things. I know I took the rifle from the box in the garage. But you yanked it away from me and shot them. You're the one who's living in denial. You didn't believe Elton raped me, either." She stood and walked over to him, a frenzied look in her eyes. "After I ran away, I lived on the street. Want to know how I survived? Having sex with men. You and your piece-of-shit brother turned a child into a prostitute. Are you happy now, *Daddy*?"

"I couldn't help you, once they locked me up," he said. "I paid the price for what happened that night, regardless of who pulled the trigger. I thought you might have come to see me, but you never did. I served sixteen years, Jessica. I've been searching for you ever since I was paroled two years ago. Every day I thought of you."

"You paid the price?" Jessica shouted, shaking her fist at him. "I slept in cardboard boxes in the winter in New York. I ate out of trash cans while you lolled around in a warm prison with three meals a day. I let hairy, disgusting, and perverted old men fuck me for money."

She went to the bar and poured herself a glass of scotch, drinking it like water, then refilling the glass. She heard footsteps and thought he had left.

Dr. Graham stood, waiting for her outside the door to the bar. When she returned, he reached out and seized her, pulling her into a tight embrace. Melody panicked, struggling against him and cursing. Then her muscles went limp. All the feelings of being loved by a father came rushing back. The glass bounced on the carpet, the liquid spilling out. He pulled her head onto his shoulder, stroking her hair.

"I love you, Jessica," her father whispered. "What happened to you shouldn't have happened to anyone. If only I could have been there for you."

She pulled away and returned to the sofa. "Just so you'll know, my name isn't Jessica anymore. Call me Melody. That is, if you want me to answer you. Jessica is dead."

"Any name you want me to call you is fine. You're still my daughter. I did see in the paper that you were using the name Melody Asher. Isn't that the girl you used to play with in Tuxedo Park?"

"Yes," Melody said, explaining their legal arrangement. "With all this bad publicity, I may be changing my name back."

"At least tell me one thing before I leave," Dr. Graham said. "Do you know anything about these murders? The police flew me from New York. They said you may be a suspect. What am I going to tell them?"

"Tell them anything you want. I'm not a killer." The booze was catching up to her. She could hardly keep her eyes open. "Look, you may be my father and I know that you must have loved me, but right now you're a stranger. I need to get some sleep. Tell me where you're staying and I'll call you."

They went to the kitchen. Dr. Graham wrote down the

number to the hotel. When he handed her the piece of paper, she saw his mangled thumb. "What happened to your beautiful hands? How can you operate?"

He dropped his left hand to his side, where she couldn't see it. "I'm not a doctor anymore."

Even in her intoxicated state, Melody realized how much they had both lost. A single shot from a handmade rifle had destroyed all four of their lives. She walked him to the door in silence. Once outside, he turned and looked back with familiar eyes. Had her hatred been unfounded? Her father might never operate again, but he was an intelligent man and would one day reclaim his dignity. She had told too many lies, hurt too many people, broken too many rules. She turned the dead bolt and slid to the floor, her mouth open wide as she wailed in despair. All she could see was darkness.

Chapter 27

After Hank left, Carolyn made two cups of hot chocolate and carried them to Rebecca's room. "I'm sorry we woke you up, honey," she said, handing her a cup. "I want to explain what's going on with Neil. I didn't tell you earlier because I thought everything would be cleared up by now."

Rebecca tossed aside the *Glamour* magazine she was reading, then took a sip of her hot chocolate. "It's okay, Mom," she said, setting the cup on her end table. "John already told me everything. I know Uncle Neil would never do anything that bad."

Carolyn sat down on the edge of the bed, clasping her cup with both hands. "The police have to protect the community. When they're under this kind of pressure, they sometimes arrest the wrong people. Two women were killed. Neil's only one of the suspects the police are considering."

The girl's eyes widened. "Are they going to put him in jail?"

"If they do arrest Neil, he'll be released on bail," Carolyn told her, asking her to scoot over so she could lay in the bed beside her. Realizing the cocoa had caffeine in it, she placed her cup next to Rebecca's. "The problem is, we don't know where he is right now. Remember what I've always told you about running away from your problems? Neil disappearing like this gives the police a reason to be suspicious. I can understand how upset he is about Laurel's death, but he should have called and checked in, let us know where we could reach him. If he calls when I'm not here, make certain you tell him he has to get in touch with Hank right away."

"Lucy was crying today," Rebecca said, placing her head on her mother's shoulder. "She said you and her dad had a big fight."

How could she possibly tell her daughter what had happened? When Carolyn had lashed out at Paul, she'd failed to think of how it would affect her children. She'd been even more enraged after her visit to Melody. The woman might have a drawer full of Cartier watches with bands in every color. She probably bought them herself. Melody was shrewd. She could have assumed Paul had mentioned buying her a ring as they had been seeing each other for over a year now. Then when she asked Melody about the watch, she had jumped on it.

Carolyn had listened to everyone but Paul, the only person who really mattered. Even if Melody wasn't an impostor or killer, her past could have made her a very disturbed woman. Did Paul deserve to be treated so poorly? Should she throw away a loving relationship and break her kids' hearts? She had to suppress the urge to pick up the phone and call him. She already missed him. There was no one to hold her, no one to console her when things started flying apart as they had tonight.

Carolyn heard Rebecca sniffling, then tipped her head up and saw she was crying. "Please don't cry, baby. Everything's going to work out."

"No, it's not," her daughter said, dabbing at her eyes with a tissue. "I thought you and Paul were going to get married, that Lucy and me would be sisters. Lucy says her dad is talking about moving back to their house in Pasadena. She's my best friend, Mom. How am I going to see her?"

"I've got a lot on my mind right now," her mother said, remembering the gory details of her father's death from the police report. She was also worried about her mother. The woman had a heart condition and had been under tremendous stress. "After things get back to normal," she added, "Paul and I may be able to work things out."

The girl's face brightened. "Promise?"

"I can't make any promises," Carolyn said, getting up and turning out the light. "Do you think you can sleep now?"

Rebecca yawned. "I guess," she said, rolling over on her side and adjusting her pillow.

Carolyn closed her door and headed down the hall to her bedroom. Was she leading her daughter on, creating false hope? No, she decided. She would do her best to forget what she had seen on the video. Still, Paul might not want to patch things up after the way she had acted.

She collapsed in the bed, but her pills had worn off, and she doubted if she could sleep. Her mind began sifting through the events of the day and the dangerous agreement she had made with Hank to stall her brother's arrest.

A few years after they were married, her ex-husband, Frank, had challenged her to go paragliding. When she had pushed off the edge of the cliff, her eyes focused on the landmass moving slowly toward her, she'd felt a rush of adrenaline. It was similar to how she felt now, knowing tomorrow she would be sitting across from Raphael Moreno again. Even with the SWAT team peering in from the specially constructed room, her fate would be in God's hands.

She was startled at the sound of her cell phone ringing. On the other end of the phone line was a weak, desperate voice. "Carolyn, I almost did it," Neil said. "I put the gun to my temple. . . . I was about to pull the trigger when I panicked. I—I pulled the gun away at the last second. It went off, but the bullet missed my head."

"Oh, my God!" Carolyn exclaimed, knocking the clock to the floor. "Where are you?"

"I don't want to live anymore," Neil said, sobbing. "They're going to send me to prison."

"That's not true," she said, forcing herself to remain calm. "Take a deep breath. Concentrate on my words, Neil."

"It's no use."

"Do what I say and everything will be all right," Carolyn instructed, relieved when she heard him stop crying. "You didn't kill Laurel. It's not your fault that Laurel died."

"You think that helps me?" he said, his voice shaking. "She was the love of my life. Maybe things weren't right for us now, but eventually we could have married and had a wonderful life. Now she's in a morgue, her body cut up in pieces. If I hadn't gotten so angry, she'd be alive today. Why should I live when I'm the one who's responsible for her death?"

Carolyn was so distraught, she couldn't think straight. She heard him crying again. "Neil, where are you? I'm going to come to you."

Her brother's voice trailed off with each word. "You've got to let me go."

Carolyn was afraid he was going to end the call. She had to use another tactic. "What about me?" she shouted. "Is this how you pay me back for all the years I've looked after you? I love you. John and Rebecca love you. When Mother dies, we'll have no one. Is that what you want? Tell me where you are, damn it!"

"Oxnard Shores in the sand dunes."

"Are you alone?" she asked, knowing that he was in an area near the housing development where they used to live.

"Who would possibly be with me? I have no friends. Even Melody doesn't want to see me anymore."

Carolyn kept talking as she rushed to John's bedroom. She jotted down a note and handed it to him. When he woke up and asked her what was wrong, she placed her hand over his mouth. John's face paled when he read what she had written. She kissed him on the forehead and raced to the garage for her car. "You're wrong about Melody," she told Neil. "I spent time with her today. She cares about you."

Neil fell silent. Carolyn could hear the sound of waves crashing in the background, so she felt fairly certain he hadn't moved to another location. "You're a survivor, Neil. This is just a bump in the road. As long as we stick together, we'll make it."

"I scared myself today," he said. "You don't know how close I was, Carolyn. I pulled the trigger. I was gonna do it."

His sister got inside and slammed the door to her Infiniti. "We'll get you back on track, trust me. Where's the gun?"

Neil sucked in a deep breath. "Beside me in the sand."

"Get rid of it!" she yelled, cranking the engine and backing out. "Get up and walk toward the ocean. When you reach the water, throw the gun as far as you can. Do it now, Neil."

"Okay."

His breathing became heavier as he walked through the deep sand. "Is the gun gone?"

"No."

"Get rid of the gun!" Carolyn shouted again, almost rear-ending the car in front of her. "Do you hear me, Neil? How can you kill yourself? Do you want to damn yourself to hell?"

"I don't believe in that stuff," Neil told her. "My father killed himself. If I go to hell, we'll be together."

"It doesn't matter what Dad did," she said, speeding onto the ramp to the 101 Freeway. "Please, I'm begging you. Suicide is an offense against God. It's also an offense against seriously ill people all over the world who're battling insurmountable odds so they can live one more month, a week, a day, an hour. Think of all the children, Neil. Children who will be dead by sunrise. How can you throw away something so valuable? You're a healthy young man. If you do this, I could kill myself, too. What about John and Rebecca? We can't keep repeating this awful cycle for generations. Stop it now!"

"The gun's gone."

"Thank God," Carolyn exclaimed as silence overtook the

phone line. She began speaking again, this time slower and softer. "Now watch the waves as they break and turn into white water. Do you remember the days we spent playing in the sand and bodysurfing on those waves?"

"That was a long time ago," he said, the sound of his voice becoming more coherent. "I miss being a kid."

"You remember the sand crabs?"

"Yeah," Neil responded, emitting a small chuckle. "That was great what we did to little Joe."

"What was that?" she questioned, pretending not to know.

"We put sand crabs in his pants. He jumped around the beach whimpering like a girl."

A few miles and she'd be there. Neil was coming back to reality. Her negotiations today with Hank would only buy him twenty-four hours. She thought of insisting that he turn himself in, but she was afraid he would become hysterical again. She would have to hide him, shelter him from the police until his mind settled. He couldn't stay at her house. She was sure Hank had unmarked cars in the area, ready to arrest him as soon as the twenty-four-hour time period expired.

Carolyn knew she couldn't leave her brother alone. There was only one person she could leave him with—Melody. The police didn't appear to consider her a viable suspect anymore. Could this woman she'd formerly despised be trusted? Did Melody really care about him? Carolyn didn't have a choice. She certainly couldn't take Neil back to her mother's house.

When she arrived at the beach, she could barely see where she was going in the darkness as she trudged through the sand, finding Neil slumped over at the top of the dune. Her stomach rose in her throat, thinking he was dead. "Neil," she shouted, squatting down beside him. When he didn't respond, she grabbed a handful of his hair and jerked his head up. He didn't appear to be injured, but the gun was in his hand. She pried it out of his fingers and shoved it in the waistband of her jeans. "I thought you threw the gun in the ocean."

Neil stared at her, his face twisted in misery. His sister embraced him, then helped him to his feet.

"It's okay now," she said, placing her arm around his waist as they headed back to the parking lot. "Where did you get the gun?"

"At a pawnshop."

"When?"

"Today."

Now that Carolyn knew their father had killed himself, and after tonight, there was no doubt that Neil needed psychiatric treatment. But she couldn't commit him against his will. If she did, when he got out, he might try to kill himself again. Eventually he would be successful. Maybe in the next few days she could talk to him, convince him that a short stint in a decent hospital would be better than the county jail. Then if the state followed through and prosecuted him, he could plead not guilty by reason of insanity.

Leaving the door open, Carolyn got in her car and called Melody, asking if Neil could stay with her for a few days. Until the warrant was issued, she couldn't be charged with aiding and abetting a criminal. Carolyn had promised Hank she would bring Neil in, but her brother's life was more important.

"I'm not in the greatest shape for company," Melody said. "He can crash here, though. What's going on? Is something wrong?"

Carolyn said they would explain everything when they got to her place. When she saw Neil getting into Paul's BMW, she rushed over and angrily pounded on the glass. "Get out of the car."

"I'm not going to leave Paul's car here," he protested, hitting the button for the automatic window. "Someone might steal it."

"Follow me," she said, too drained to argue. As long as he didn't have the gun, she felt she could let him drive. Carolyn decided Melody owed her a few favors. Even if it had been important for her to see the sex video, which she wasn't certain was true, sending it to her on Christmas Day had been cruel. "I'll meet you at Melody's place in Brentwood," she told Neil. "If I don't see your headlights in my rearview mirror, I'll call the police, understand? What's it going to be, Neil? Melody's house or jail?"

Neil rolled up the window, waiting until his sister backed the Infiniti out of the parking lot, then pulled up behind her.

Chapter 28

Mary Stevens sat at her desk in the middle of the investigation unit. Taped to the board next to her was a picture of her father in full uniform at his graduation from the police academy. There was one of her bulldog, Hitchcock. She could smell the fresh coffee brewing in her personal coffeemaker. The chatting in the break room was too time consuming.

Lieutenant Commander Jordan Goodwin was in town for his wife's funeral and could be reached on his cell phone. The navy had already confirmed he was at sea at the time of the crime, so he was officially no longer a suspect.

"I need to ask you some questions," Mary said. "If this isn't a good time, I understand."

"I'll do anything I can to help you find out who did this," he said, his voice deep and authoritative. "I loved my wife very much. I was hoping we could patch things up when I came home on leave this time."

Mary's goal was to confirm Stanley Caplin's statements about Laurel's young lover. "You say you wanted to work things out with your wife," she said. "What started the problems between you two? Why was it so hard to mend the relationship?"

"She was cheating on me with one of her former students," he explained, his deep voice laced with tension. "I guess she got restless because I was traveling so much. Laurel was like the sea, constantly in motion. She wasn't good with downtime."

"Who would have wanted to kill her?"

"There's no question in my mind . . . Ashton Sabatino."

"What do you know about this person?"

"He's the kid she was sleeping with," he snapped. "This guy was a drug dealer. He stole both my wife's mind and body from me."

His statement corresponded with what she had learned earlier. As soon as she'd arrived at the office that morning, Mary did a search through the criminal database for Ashton Sabatino, discovering several arrests for possession, one of them for cocaine. Manny Gonzales said his intelligence sources described the boy as a low-level dealer, and he provided her with Sabatino's most recent address. She turned her attention back to the young officer. "Did you see a change in your wife?"

"Yes," he said. "In the old days when I would return from a long stint at sea, Laurel would be waiting for me with open arms. I knew something was wrong when I came home and she was gone. Our house looked like a category-five hurricane had swept through it." He paused and then resumed speaking. "I couldn't stand seeing our life fall apart like that without an explanation. I hired one of those fancy private investigators to follow her. When I saw the snapshots of Laurel with Sabatino, it was one of the worst days of my life. I loved her. I really loved her. Please catch this murdering bastard and put him behind bars."

"My condolences for your loss," Mary said, "but why do you think Ashton Sabatino killed her?" Vernon Edgewell came up behind her, trying to swipe a cup of coffee. She swatted him away.

"Sabatino must have been insanely jealous," Goodwin said. "Once Laurel started seeing that artist, the guy went nuts. He even came to my house and spray-painted the exterior with obscenities. One said, 'Die Bitch.' Laurel had already moved back in with her parents. I didn't say anything because I thought the guy was just an immature prick. I mean, people who write graffiti on walls are a nuisance, but it's hard to see them as dangerous. Now if he'd riddled the house with bullets, that would be something to worry about. He was a kid, you know. That's how I saw him . . . just a snot-nosed kid."

"Are you aware another woman was killed only a few blocks away from the house where Laurel died? We have reason to believe the two murders may be connected."

"Hey," he said, "I don't know what to tell you about that. Sabatino has the hots for older women. Maybe he was dealing drugs to this woman and screwing her like he did my wife. He could be the serial killer they've been writing about in the papers. Kids his age think life's like it is on TV and in the movies. Those Hollywood people think it's not enough to have one murderer these days, it's always a serial killer. Are those kind of maniacs really that common?"

"No," Mary said, having noticed the same phenomena in the entertainment industry. Violence had become like a drug, and the public had developed a tolerance for it. The only way to keep their attention was to ratchet it up several more levels. They could watch murders play out on television. Hollywood had turned serial killers into stars. As long as they sold tickets, nothing would change. "In reality, Commander Goodwin," she said, "serial killers are extremely rare. That doesn't mean they don't exist. Can we contact you at this number if we need to ask you more questions? How long will you be home on leave?"

"Two months," he said, choking up. "This afternoon I'm burying my wife, Detective. After that, feel free to call me anytime you wish."

Mary dialed Hank's number and got his voice mail. After the beep, she said, "I've got an address on Ashton Sabatino. I'm heading over there now. Guess where he's living? Ocean

View Estates. This might be our man, Hank. Call me and I'll give you the details."

The unmarked car sped toward the address Manny Gonzales had given her. She'd checked the county recorder's office and discovered that the house was owned by Arthur and Constance Sabatino, presumably the boy's parents. When she arrived, she saw a guest house in the rear of the property and wondered if that's where he stayed.

She approached the front door cautiously and knocked. Hearing a sound of scraping feet on the pavement, she turned to her right and saw a figure running toward the street. Adrenaline flushed through her body as her muscles responded with a burst of speed.

Looking over his shoulder at the person giving chase caused the fleeing man to miss a step. At that moment, Mary dived. She grabbed his legs, sending him tumbling to the ground. She rolled aside, pulling out her service weapon and training it on the suspect. Looking down into the eyes of a young man, she saw that his pupils were dilated and she suspected he was planning to run again.

"Don't get any ideas, Ashton," she said. "Turn around and lay flat on the ground." As soon as he was facedown on the pavement, she shouted, "Put your hands behind your head." She planted her shoe in the middle of his back. Multiple clicks of the handcuffs were heard as she adjusted them to fit his wrists.

"You're hurting me," Sabatino whined.

"Don't be a baby," she responded, pulling her cell phone out and calling for backup.

"I didn't do anything!" the boy yelled.

"We'll have to see about that," Mary said. "I've been doing this long enough to know when someone runs, they're running for a reason. What are you running from, Ashton?"

"Nothing," he said, looking away. "I just don't like people sneaking around my parents' house."

"Are you sure you don't have something to hide?"

"No, damn it," he snarled. "Get off me."

The police car screeched to a halt at the curb, angled sideways in the middle of the residential street. The officers emerged with guns drawn. "You okay, Stevens?"

"I'm good. Thanks, Perna. Is that Briggs with you?" She reached down and grabbed the handcuffs, then jerked the boy to his feet. The officers patted him down, searching for weapons. When they reached in his front pocket, they found a plastic bag filled with white powder.

"Yo, Mary," Briggs announced, holding up the suspicious substance. "Looks like your boy liked to party."

"Nothing to hide, huh," the detective said with sarcasm, waving the bag inches from his nose.

"Shit . . . this is bullshit."

"Anything else we should know about, Ashton?"

"No," he said in a firm tone. "One of your goons planted that stuff on me."

"Keys," the officer said. "Other than the Baggie, that's all we found on his person."

"Let me see them," Mary asked. Briggs handed them over. The first thing she noticed was the leather key fob, which displayed the Yamaha emblem. Attached to it was what appeared to be a motorcycle key.

Mary sat in her cubicle, anxiously waiting for Hank. He was going to join her as soon as he could break free from a phone call. She could see how Laurel Goodwin could have been seduced by Sabatino. He was a striking young man. His hair was a spiky-dusty brown with lighter highlights on top. He stood about six feet tall and had strong facial features.

As Jordan Goodwin had told her, Sabatino was trouble. After his most recent arrest, he'd been placed on probation Being in possession of a controlled substance violated the terms of his probation. This meant they could keep him locked up until the present offense was adjudicated, which would give the DA time to build a case against him for the murders of Suzanne Porter and Laurel Goodwin.

"What you got, Mary?" Hank asked, strolling into the detective bay.

"Possibly our murderer," Mary said, exhilarated. "Drugs in his possession, Yamaha in the garage, and a former lover of Laurel Goodwin. Also, he lives in Ocean View Estates, where Porter and Goodwin were murdered. Looks like we might put these two homicides to bed before New Year's Eve, Sarge. Then we'd really have something to celebrate."

"Nothing's that easy," he told her, picking up Sabatino's file from her desk.

"I know, but this is the closest we've been," she said. "Can't I enjoy the possibility before you shoot me down? I even got in a foot pursuit with the little shit."

"Interesting," Hank said, ignoring her comment as he reviewed the file. "He has a record . . . a drug-related record. Did you tell the lab to compare the substance found in Sabatino's possession against the drugs in the syringe used to kill the Goodwin woman?"

"All over it," Mary said, kicking off her heels and staring at a blister on her right toe. "I'm going to wear tennis shoes from now on. I thought when I graduated to homicide, I wouldn't have to chase these guys anymore. Anyway, trace elements of strychnine would cut Sabatino's career as a killer short, don't you think?"

"We'll know more when we have the lab reports," Hank told her, placing the file back on her desk. "With these new developments, I'm not sure we can justify filing against Neil Sullivan."

"That should make Carolyn's day."

"I'm going to call her," he said. "I need her to put forth her best effort this afternoon. She's going to interview Moreno again at four-thirty in the jail. We're erecting a prefabricated room and bringing in the SWAT team."

Mary's jaw dropped. "Jesus, Hank, why are you messing

with that guy again? I mean, especially when it looks like we've got our man. Moreno was in jail when Porter and Goodwin were killed. How could he possibly have been involved?"

The detective rubbed his fingers over his chin. "This address thing is driving me crazy, Mary. I don't care what Kevin Thomas says, it's too big a coincidence that every person who's been murdered in this city in the past two months has had the numbers '1003' and the word 'Sea' in their address."

"You're the boss," Mary said, turning to her computer to start writing her arrest report on Sabatino.

"Oh," Hank said before leaving, "I have to go to the mayor's monthly luncheon. Call me on my cell, but only if it's an emergency. Otherwise, I'll see you at the jail at four-thirty for the interview with Moreno."

Chapter 29

Melody had awakened with Neil beside her. It would have been great if she'd been sober and he hadn't been teetering on the edge of sanity. After a cold shower and a pot of coffee, she'd played psychologist, lover, and co-conspirator, nothing she hadn't done before.

He looked so innocent while he was sleeping on her pink Italian bed linens made by Claudio Rayes in Beverly Hills, surrounded by satin hand-embroidered floral pillowcases. That bed had a lot of mileage. She loved it. It was satisfying to see powerful men being forced to sleep under her white silk drapes in what was clearly a feminine setting.

"Neil, get up," she said, poking his bare back. "Don't expect to sleep all day like you do at your place. We've got things to do today."

"All right, already," Neil grumbled. "Cut me some slack."

"Not while you're in my house, understand?"

"Yes, master," he said, his attitude turning playful. He reached up and pulled her back into the bed. "Why don't you give me something to wake me up?"

"Down, boy, we'll have time for that later," Melody told him, picking his clothes off the chair and throwing them at him. "Get dressed, sleepyhead."

The phone rang and Melody answered it. When she heard Carolyn's voice, she handed the phone to Neil.

"Good news," Carolyn told him. "The police arrested Ashton Sabatino. It looks like you're off the hook."

Neil sat up on the edge of the bed. "You've got to be kidding. That's great."

Melody dropped down beside him, whispering in his ear, "I'm going to put her on the speaker phone so I can hear."

"Sure," Neil told her, advising his sister that Melody would be listening. "Can you hear me, Carolyn?"

"Loud and clear."

"But you told me the two murders were identical," Neil said. "Why did Sabatino kill the other woman? It doesn't make sense."

"To trick the police into believing it was a serial killer," his sister explained. "No one would suspect that a nineteen-year-old kid would murder two women. Looks like the underlying motive was narcotics. Did you know Laurel used drugs?"

"No," Neil lied, having snorted lines with her. The fact that Laurel would occasionally get high with him was one of the things that had made her so desirable. Melody had a fit if he even brought drugs into her house. The night before, she'd made him choke down three glasses of a disgusting green concoction she'd made in the blender, swearing it would make him detox by morning. He'd gone to the bathroom six times, but he had to admit, he felt a hell of a lot better. "How did they put it together?"

"A neighbor at the Porter homicide witnessed a guy on a motorcycle around the time of the crime. The police went to talk to Sabatino and he fled on foot. When they caught him, they found a key to a Yamaha motorcycle in his pocket along with a Baggie filled with high-grade cocaine. As you know, Laurel was killed with a mixture of cocaine, heroin, strychnine, and some type of prescription medication. The police got a warrant this morning and searched Sabatino's garage. They found a red-and-black Yamaha motorcycle that matched the witness's description."

Melody stood and paced. All she had to do was send the

video of the Goodwin homicide to Detective Sawyer and the Sabatino kid would be toast. Then she and Neil could be together.

Neil asked, "Where did he get the strychnine?"

"At any hardware or garden store," Melody interjected.

Carolyn continued, "And anyone in possession of cocaine can probably get their hands on heroin."

"So what's going to happen next?" Neil asked.

"Things have to run their course," his sister told him. "You won't be completely in the clear until Sabatino either confesses or the state convicts him. The police released the Ferrari this morning. I'd say that's a good sign, wouldn't you?"

"I guess," Neil said, his face falling as he thought of the day that stretched before him. "Melody and I will pick up the car when we go to Ventura. She read in the paper that Laurel's funeral is today. Tell Paul I'll try to drop off his BMW tonight."

"You shouldn't go to the funeral, Neil," Carolyn told him, agitated. "Just because Sabatino has been arrested doesn't mean you won't upset Laurel's family if you show up. Her husband will be there as well. And after last night—"

Her brother cut her off. "I have a right to be there. I've known Laurel since high school. I want to pay my respects, okay. The service is being held at a church. I'm sure they'll have a big turnout since Laurel was a local teacher. The family won't even know I'm there."

Melody walked over and draped her arm around Neil's shoulder. He pulled her hand to his mouth and kissed it.

"Don't worry, Carolyn," Melody said. "I'll wait for him in the car. He needs this for closure. Your brother is going to be back on his feet in no time. I'm taking him to the Chart House for lunch so he can get some decent food. Do you want to join us?"

"I'm sorry, I've got too much to do."

After concluding the call, Melody brushed her hair and put on her makeup while Neil went down the hall to take a shower. After she dressed, she went to the kitchen to grab some breakfast. From the granite counter she picked up the piece of paper with the phone number to her father's hotel. She hadn't decided yet if she was going to call him. The paper felt strange in her hands, almost as if a part of him had been imprinted on it. Then she realized it was his handwriting. Unlike most doctors, it had always been so perfect. They no longer taught children to write that way. She remembered how she had tried to copy her father's handwriting as a child. Seeing his disfigured hand had disturbed her, but it was his left, and he was right-handed.

Before the incident on the third floor of her home in Tuxedo Park, Melody had adored him. She'd been daddy's darling, and he had lavished her with attention and gifts. Afterward, their relationship had been tempered by fear. If what he had told her was true, his rough treatment of her that day when he was having sex with the woman may have caused her to tell the police he was the one who'd pulled the trigger. Parents had no idea how their actions affected their children. Memories from the night Jeremy and her mother died were stalking her. Details she must have suppressed were resurfacing. Neil showing up as he did, regardless of the circumstances, had provided her with a much-needed distraction.

Neil was hers now. The best part was that Carolyn had handed him to her. This had given her the upper hand with both of them. Carolyn and Neil needed her in multiple ways, the most important they would never know about, the footage of the murder. Need was a powerful tool in the hands of a user. Melody had also discovered a new weakness in Neil—his suicidal tendencies. She could use this to her advantage.

So much had happened during the last twenty-four hours. Today would be another bitch of a day, but she would muscle through it. She poured two bowls of cereal, setting them on the table, then filled two glasses with orange juice.

"You're getting your Ferrari back," she said when Neil came and sat down beside her. "Aren't you excited?"

"No," Neil said flatly. "Once everything is over, I'm going to sell it."

It was obvious by the look on his face that mentioning the car triggered negative memories. Today was Laurel's funeral. He'd driven her to his house in the Ferrari the day she'd been murdered. By the time they got to Ventura, picked up the car, and had lunch, it would be time to go to the church. Soon Laurel Goodwin would be nothing more than a memory.

The ninety-minute drive to Ventura was filled with light conversation and long moments of silence. Melody knew that Neil needed time to sort through his feelings about Laurel.

The Ferrari wasn't parked at the regular police impound lot. Because of its value, it had been placed inside a secured building owned by the city. She dropped Neil off, reminding him to meet her at the Chart House restaurant as soon as he was done.

Melody parked down the street from the Ventura Police Department and exited her Porsche. She was dressed in a gray business suit, a black blouse with the top three buttons undone, and low-heeled black leather shoes, with a matching inexpensive shoulder purse. She could have e-mailed the video from a library or some other publicly used computer, but what she was about to do was far more challenging. Showing the police she could step into their world and do anything she wanted made her feel powerful.

She opened the trunk and removed a manila file folder and a black wig. The file was empty, yet it served its purpose as a prop. Reentering the car, Melody slipped on the wig, then secured it with a clasp at the base of her neck. She removed a badge that said FBI, which she'd purchased the day before at a costume store, clipping it onto her belt. Looking in the mirror, she purred, "Perfect."

Once inside the building, she stopped at the reception desk. "I'm Agent Rodriguez with the FBI. I have a conference scheduled with Detective Sawyer at eleven-thirty. I'm a few minutes early. Is he in?"

"No," Desk Officer Carl Duval said. "He's with the mayor right now. Is this an emergency?"

"No," Melody said, smiling as she pressed her chest against the counter. "Can you direct me to his office? I have some paperwork to catch up on while I'm waiting."

The officer handed Melody a clipboard to sign. She quickly wrote the name Samantha Rodriguez, then was buzzed through the security doors. The officer seemed to be more interested in her breasts than her credentials. Typical.

Filling her lungs with a deep breath and pushing her shoulders back, she entered a door marked HOMICIDE. The detectives must be out on cases as no one was around. Ten workstations were separated with half-height walls and had chipped blue Formica tops. Prominently displayed over each desk were gold nameplates. To the left, she saw an enclosed office with a window looking out into the open space. Hank Sawyer's name was on the door. What a slob, she thought, entering. No wonder he had trouble doing his job. A disorganized desk was reflective of a disorganized mind.

Digging into her purse, she pulled on a pair of latex gloves and sat down behind Hank's desk, inserting a DVD into his computer.

"Oh, hello," a voice said, breaking the silence.

Melody placed her hands in her lap, quickly removing the gloves and depositing them in the trash can.

"I didn't mean to scare you."

Standing there was a fresh-faced young man, wearing a white shirt, a tie, and slacks. He ran his hands through his tousled brown hair. Not a problem, Melody thought. This wimp was no threat. She wasn't even sure he was a man. He looked about sixteen. "No, that's fine," she said, turning back to the computer. A window opened on the computer screen asking if she wanted to play the video or save it to a file. Noticing the man's eyes track to the screen, she stood and walked toward him, extending her hand.

Fortunately, she distracted him from the monitor. "I'm

Samantha Rodriguez," she told him, closing her jacket so he didn't see the phony FBI badge. "I'm from tech support. Detective Sawyer notified us he was having problems with his computer."

"I'm Chris Alabanie," he said, blushing. "I'm a police cadet. Most of the time, I end up making phone calls or filing. These guys are always chasing after one murderer or the other. I guess one day, they'll get around to training me to do something else. You know, this computer I'm using is running out of memory. It would be great if you—"

Melody cut him off, "I'm sorry, but I have to get this taken care of before Detective Sawyer comes back. Call tech support and see if they can send someone else."

Once he wandered off, she retrieved the gloves and clicked on the Lotus Notes icon. Hank's e-mail program filled the screen. She typed out "Hank S" and his full e-mail address filled out the box. Then she attached the video file from the DVD and pressed send. A window appeared signaling that a new e-mail had arrived. Mission accomplished. Wearing a disguise had been warranted, she told herself, grabbing the DVD and shoving it into her purse.

Melody rushed to get out before the wannabe cop returned. Sawyer may have busted Sabatino, but as Carolyn had pointed out, these idiots needed proof. The video should seal Sabatino's fate. Neil was innocent. That didn't mean innocent people weren't sent to prison due to incompetent law enforcement officials. Her father had been wrongly convicted, or so he claimed. The cops and their investigative units were pressured by the victims to get results. It was just like a slogan her stockbroker always used, "Churn and burn." The police had to make cases quickly and move on to the next. She knew what the word "make" meant. Take any evidence collected and either add to or modify it to make a conviction. Right or wrong, the police felt they'd done their job.

Nobody was taking Neil away from her.

Chapter 30

Hank burst into the detective bay, rubbing his eyebrows. What a waste of time, he thought. An hour and a half listening to the mayor speak on how to reduce crime in the city. Hank was convinced that the best way to reduce crime was to stop having stupid luncheons with the mayor.

His IN tray was filled with new yellow and blue files. Yellow meant faxes and blue signified an internal communication. The color-coding system was supposed to help him get organized. His desk now looked like a circus tent.

He decided to dig into the pile before his phone started ringing. Picking up one of the blue files, he found the forensic report on the Ferrari. CSI had certainly taken their time, he thought. He looked at the signature. Who was Alex Pauldine? He remembered a message from someone named Alex with a last name he couldn't make out, advising him that they were releasing Neil Sullivan's Ferrari. What did he care if they released the car? They'd done a complete workup and Sullivan didn't appear to be their primary suspect at the moment.

The report was dated yesterday, December 27. His eyes locked on the name Raphael Moreno on the second page. Blood! Raphael Moreno's blood inside Neil Sullivan's Ferrari! What in the hell is this all about? He picked up the phone and called Alex Pauldine at the lab.

"Have you already released the Ferrari?"

"Neil Sullivan picked it up less than twenty minutes ago," Pauldine said. "Is there a problem?"

"Yeah, there's a problem," Hank shouted. "According to your report, Raphael Moreno's blood was found inside that car. Why wasn't I notified?"

"Don't yell at me," Pauldine said defensively. "I sent you the report yesterday. I also called you to let you know we were finished working up the car. Since you didn't call us back, we assumed you didn't object if we released it. As I understand it, Sullivan is no longer a suspect. What's the big deal?"

"Do you know who Raphael Moreno is?"

"I think the morgue has a Moreno on ice," Pauldine answered. "I'm not sure if his first name is Raphael. Traffic accident. We've got the wrecked car. It's a common name in the Hispanic community. What's going on?"

"Raphael Moreno slaughtered an entire family. One of the victims was a six-month-old baby. How could you not know about something like that? Mr. Hartfield's Cadillac was sent to you guys."

"I didn't handle that case. Bernie Wolcott did, I believe. Since the defendant pleaded guilty, the DA's office pressured us to work the Caddy up in five days."

"You obviously remember it, then," Hank argued.

"Now that you mentioned it, I do. When the case involves kids, I try my best to forget. What's that got to do with the Ferrari? We held the car long enough. We got everything we needed. You don't need the car anymore."

"That Ferrari may be tied into the deaths of nine people."

"Where do you come up with nine? Weren't there only five members of the Hartfield family?"

"Here they are," the detective said. "The five you mentioned, along with Moreno's mother and sister. Those occurred in Oxnard, so they were out of our jurisdiction, but they were all tried as the same case. That makes seven. Then there's the Goodwin and Porter homicides. Got it?"

"You're telling me they're all connected?"

"It's looking that way. We thought we had the killer, but I'm not certain now. This is big, Pauldine. As soon as you realized Moreno's blood was in the Ferrari, you shouldn't have released it. What if you missed something? It's not like it's never happened before."

"Remember, we process evidence. We don't solve murders, Sawyer. That's why we sent *you* the report. We also sent it to you twenty-four hours before we released the car. We were well within protocol. After you read the report, if you still have questions, call me. Otherwise, do your job, partner, and let me do mine."

"Fine," Hank said, slamming the receiver down. Damn crime scene techs. Most of them weren't even cops. Because the work they did was so essential to solving crimes, they could bring an investigator to his knees.

He picked up the report and continued reading, something he should have done before he'd jumped on Pauldine. When they'd removed the driver's seat in Neil Sullivan's Ferrari, they'd found a small quantity of blood. DNA testing determined that the blood belonged to Raphael Moreno.

Hank had to resist the urge to call Carolyn. She was the only one who'd ever spoken to Moreno. He couldn't call the probation officer, however, as her brother owned the car in which they'd found Moreno's blood. It was no longer a speculation that the murders were connected, it was fact.

How did Neil Sullivan fit into the picture? A drug deal had been one of the first things that had crossed Hank's mind. This was somewhat supported by the fact that the lab had found trace elements of methamphetamine in the trash can of Sullivan's next-door neighbor. They hadn't pursued it because they didn't have a search warrant.

Stupid rookies, he thought. They were always tossing things without a warrant. The instructors at the academy drilled them on what was known as the "Fruits of the Poisonous Tree," or the exclusionary rule, but the lesson never seemed to stick.

Basically, any evidence that was obtained without the benefit of a search warrant was inadmissible in a court of law.
When they ended up with stacks of evidence and no warrant,
district attorneys would go to extraordinary lengths. They'd
have the cops perjure themselves and swear the person wasn't
a suspect when they searched their property. Sometimes they
had already booked the suspect and then had to set him free
long enough for a jury to buy their story. No one wanted to
be responsible for putting a guilty person back on the street,
so the majority of judges would simply pass the buck.

Hank knew how the system worked. A suspect was arrested and arraigned, then a date was set for the preliminary
hearing. The preliminary hearing was held in the municipal
court. Many judges weren't concerned if their case was overturned on appeal as long as they appeased the public while
the case was hot. After the defendant was held to answer in
the superior court or supreme court, the name depending on
the jurisdiction, the case then went to trial. If it was still hot
in the court of public opinion, even a superior court judge
might allow the evidence to be admitted, with full knowledge that the ruling would be overturned once it reached
the appellate court.

Evidence that was illegally obtained was eventually brought
to light, no matter how desperately the prosecution attempted
to hide it. The sad part, at least as Hank saw it, was that the
person or persons who screwed the case from the get-go were
cops. Some were rookies, like the officer who went through
the neighbor's trash in the Goodwin homicide. It was worse
when the officer had been on the force for years and simply
decided to make his own rules, thinking he could lie his way
out of it.

Hank no longer wasted his time with illegally obtained
evidence. He didn't mind knowing about it—he just knew he
couldn't build a case around it. Why take it to a DA and
watch him salivate over it, or start scheming for a way to get
it admitted as evidence? Some of the DAs were fresh out of

law school, and not Ivy League schools, but cram schools like the one Carolyn was attending. Give an overeager DA a sloppy case and they'd screw it up so the suspect could never be convicted. Try them once and the jury finds them not guilty and they could never be tried again.

Hank called Captain Gary Holmes. "Things blew up on us, Captain."

"Which case?"

"All of them," Hank told him, his voice sparking with excitement. "The lab found Raphael Moreno's blood inside Neil Sullivan's Ferrari. The Hartfield killings occurred at 1003 Seaport Avenue. Laurel Goodwin was found dead in Sullivan's pool located at 1003 Sea View Terrace. Three blocks away, Suzanne Porter was murdered in the same fashion. Her address was 1003 Seaport Drive."

"The killers are looking for something."

"Exactly my thoughts," Hank answered. "Even then, how does it explain Moreno's blood inside Sullivan's Ferrari?"

"Have you asked Sullivan about it?"

"No, he disappeared," the detective said. "The lab released the Ferrari before I found out about Moreno's blood. Since we arrested Sabatino, they assumed Sullivan was no longer a suspect."

The captain's voice elevated. "Why didn't you read the report? You're not back on the sauce, are you?"

Hank angrily yanked his tie off, tossing it on his desk. His affair with the bottle had lasted six months. The way it seemed, it would follow him forever. "I'm not drinking, okay? We've had two homicides in less than a week. You're the captain. Tell me what to do."

"We need to have a conference," Captain Holmes told him. "I'll have Louise take care of the notifications from my end. All you have to do is call in whatever people you have on the street. It's one-fifteen now. Let's call it for two thirty. Make sure you fire off an e-mail to everyone in your department. Just because you're computer handicapped doesn't mean your people are. The city paid a fortune to create an integrated network connecting the entire department, including unmarked as well as regular patrol units. Try using it every now and then, Sawyer."

Hank disconnected and stared at his computer screen. First, the captain implied he was drinking, then he made him sound like a dinosaur because he didn't worship this stupid box on his desk. He checked his e-mail at least once a week, and he occasionally used the Internet for research. He didn't like deleting messages, though, fearing he might need to review them again. He squinted and saw a small envelope at the bottom of his screen indicating he had e-mail. He'd never tried to send e-mail to several people at one time.

He clicked the icon for Lotus Notes and discovered he had forty new e-mails. Most of them were junk, either advertisements or cops forwarding jokes to everyone in the department.

"That's strange," he said aloud. The most recent message was from Hank Sawyer. Must be a mistake. He highlighted it and double-clicked. When it opened, he could see that a file was attached. The technicians had told him to always be careful about opening attachments because many of them contained viruses. The file was named *GoodwinMurder.wmv*. Out of the corner of his eye, he saw Mary Stevens. "Come here, I need you."

Hank was slouching over the keyboard, his face inches from the screen. "You're not trying to use that thing, are you?" Mary asked.

"Yeah," he grumbled. "The captain just told me it's mandatory that I learn how to send e-mails. Oh, I almost forgot to tell you, we're having a meeting in the conference room at two-thirty. There's been some major developments in our homicides. Can you send e-mails to all our people? If you don't get a response, do it the reliable way and call them."

"I'll take care of it, Hank," Mary said. "We wouldn't want you to break a fingernail."

"Thanks," he said, still staring at the screen. "How do you know if you've got a virus? I think I have one here."

"Don't touch anything," Mary said, moving around in back of him. "Get up, Hank. This isn't a virus, it's a video file. The letters WMV stand for Windows Media Video."

"Should we open it?"

"Already have, it'll play in a minute," she told him. "Since when did you start sending video files to yourself?"

"I didn't. I don't mess with this stuff unless I have to. You know how I feel. Cases aren't solved inside a box, they're solved on the street."

The first image they saw was a leather-clad figure wearing a motorcycle helmet moving along the side of the garage.

"Jesus," Mary exclaimed, "it's Neil Sullivan's house. That's got to be Sabatino."

"Hold your horses," he answered, wanting the video to play out. The next scene showed the person in the backyard. Laurel Goodwin could be seen standing at the open French doors, her face stricken with fear as she placed a portable phone to her ear. "Looks like we're going to watch a murder," Hank said, remembering the death mask Goodwin wore after they'd pulled her from the pool.

They watched as the man grabbed her, placing a gun to her head and marching her into the house. The screen went blue. "Is that it?" Mary said, sliding the mouse to see the video progress bar. It was only 25 percent complete. "There's more, Hank."

The video shifted to a different camera angle, and they could see Goodwin and the assailant in the master bedroom. She stripped down to her bra and panties. "There's the syringe," Hank said excitedly, placing his finger on the screen.

"Don't do that," Mary said, knocking his hand away. The video continued as the helmeted figure injected Laurel Goodwin. The gun appeared again as the killer forced her into the bathroom. "She's going to vomit like Suzanne Porter did," she said, placing her hand over her mouth. "God, this is so awful. I feel like I'm about to throw up."

The next image they saw was Laurel being dragged by her ankles facedown across the backyard pavement. "Look," Hank said, "her body's gone limp from the narcotics."

"This is it," she said, taking a sharp intake of oxygen.

Laurel was propped up at the side of the pool, her head bleeding. The killer faced the camera, still wearing the helmet and darkened face mask. With one push, he shoved Laurel Goodwin into the water.

"Where did this come from?" Hank asked, still shocked at what they had witnessed.

"From you," Mary said, her eyes widening.

"How did it come from me? If I had a video of the murder, we would have all seen it."

"All I know is it was sent from your workstation."

"Could somebody have done this remotely?" Hank asked

"No," Mary told him. "Unless they somehow hacked into the system. I don't think that's possible. As far as I know, our network has never been infiltrated."

"So let me get this right," Hank said, perplexed. "You're saying someone managed to get through the security checkpoint, sat at my desk, and used my computer to send me a video of the Goodwin murder?"

"Looks that way," she answered, as distraught as Hank. She stepped back from his desk and raised her hands in the air. "Damn, this is a crime scene. We probably obliterated the fingerprints. The killer himself could have sent you the video. How could I have been so stupid?"

"Carl Duval is the desk officer today, right? I'll talk to him. Get forensics over here. Then copy the video and bring it to the meeting. Don't forget to notify everybody about the meeting."

"I'll pull the video down off the file server and burn it onto a DVD," Mary told him. "That way, it can be entered as evidence as soon as everyone sees it."

"Great," Hank said, trying to catch his breath.

He walked rapidly out of the detective bay to the front desk. "Carl, what happened here? Someone was in my office. Did they check in?"

"Oh, you mean that pretty FBI agent, Samantha Rodriguez? She said she had an appointment with you. I told her you were at the mayor's luncheon. She asked if she could wait in your office so she could catch up on some of her work. I assumed it was okay."

"How long ago?"

He picked up the sign-in sheet. "About thirty-five minutes."

"She could still be in the building!" Hank said. "Secure the exterior, and send officers to check the parking lot." He waited until the desk sergeant relayed his instructions, then asked, "What did she look like?"

"Tall and slender," Duval said. "Maybe a hair under six feet. Long black hair, blue eyes. A real looker, Sarge."

Hank's thoughts flashed back to the video he and Mary had just watched. The description could easily fit the murderer. Because of the motorcycle outfit, there was no way to tell if Laurel's assailant was male or female. "Pull down the surveillance tape and broadcast her image," he told the desk officer. "She's wanted for questioning in two homicides and may be armed and dangerous. Also, have someone call the FBI and see if they have an agent named Samantha Rodriguez."

Chapter 31

Sixteen law enforcement officials were assembled at the conference table: Hank Sawyer, Mary Stevens, Ventura chief Brady Riggs, Captain Gary Holmes, District Attorney Kevin Thomas, eight detectives from Ventura homicide, Oxnard PD homicide detective Dick Rutherford, along with FBI agents Boris Tushinsky and Gordon Gray.

Hank gave Mary a telling look. There were enough conflicting egos and agencies in the room to blow the roof off the building. With a case this sensational, everyone wanted a piece of the action.

The first order of business was to show the video of the Goodwin homicide. Hank had previously asked Mary to handle all the visual presentations. As the clip ended, even the most experienced officers sat in stunned silence.

The powerful voice of Chief Brady Riggs echoed throughout the room. At sixty-three, Riggs was a silver-haired, red-faced Irishman, whose quick temper had not mellowed with age. "What you have just seen is the brutal murder of Laurel Goodwin, a local high-school teacher. At present, we have an eighteen-year-old individual in custody named Ashton Sabatino. He was the former lover and student of the victim. We believe he may have also killed Suzanne Porter, a housewife who lived a few blocks away, to make us believe the crimes were committed by a serial killer." He paused and took a sip of his water. "I'm now going to turn this meeting over to the lead investigator in our chain of recent homicides, Detective Hank Sawyer."

Hank stood and adjusted his jacket, taking the spot at the front of the table vacated by the chief. "We just received the video this afternoon. The person who sent it entered the building in disguise and e-mailed me the video file from my own computer. A woman presenting herself as an FBI agent gained access to the building around twelve forty-three. Each of you has her photo and description in the bulletin in front of you. The FBI has confirmed that there's no agent named Samantha Rodriguez."

Hank raised several pieces of paper. "To make matters more complex, our lab found Raphael Moreno's blood inside a red Ferrari owned by Neil Sullivan. Sullivan was Goodwin's current boyfriend and it was his residence you saw in the video. The reason why we're here today is to use our collective resources to determine the link between the homicide you just witnessed and eight other seemingly related murders."

Hank sat down and watched as Mary Stevens clicked through the slides of the various crime scenes as well as the evidence, forensic findings, and pathologist reports. Once they were finished, Dick Rutherford, of the Oxnard PD, cleared his throat to get attention. Rutherford had a seedy look, more in line with a criminal than a homicide detective. He wore his thinning brown hair tied back in a ponytail, and he had the type of mustache that hadn't been in style for twenty years. The man must be a chain-smoker, Hank thought, having caught the scent of tobacco the moment Rutherford had stepped into the room. His face was scarred from acne and his left eye drooped. He made Sawyer think of a junkyard dog. To give him credit, his appearance might serve him well on the streets of Oxnard.

"We know about Raphael Moreno 'cause he killed his mother and sister in our city," Rutherford said, struggling with a piece of Nicorette gum. "Excuse me, but they make this stuff almost impossible to open." He extended the package, like he would a pack of cigarettes, smiling when three of the detectives took him up on his offer. "Our investigation was limited," he continued, "since Moreno also killed the Hartfield family and Ventura snatched the case away from us." He stopped and smirked, his next sentence directed toward Hank. "That was a mistake," he said. "We had a peculiar carjacking that went sour on November eleventh, about a week before the Hartfield murders. Three days ago, we busted an informant for DWI and traded a week in the slammer for some interesting information." He coughed, then continued. "Our man claims a local car thief with the first name of Raphael is the culprit in the carjacking. He also insisted that the Raphael he knew had never committed a crime of violence."

"What did the crime scene tell you?" Hank asked, turning sideways in his seat.

"That's the strange part," Rutherford told him. "The way forensics puts it together, there were two men in the car. Thieves who jack seldom hit a car with two occupants as there's a greater chance of something going wrong. We believe the driver was killed due to the amount of blood and brain tissue scraped off the pavement, but we can't be certain because the body was gone when we arrived on the scene. The passenger must have got out and circled around to the back of the vehicle, then exchanged gunfire with the guy trying to take the car. That's where we found a sizable quantity of blood." He stopped, folding his hands on the table, then letting his eyes roam from one person to the other. "We found an even larger amount of blood near where we believe the driver's side of the vehicle was located. The passenger's blood, however, was the only one we could identify in the system. His name is Dante Gilbiati and Agents Tushinsky and Gray say he has ties to organized crime. Why don't you tell them what you've got, Boris?"

"Dante Gilbiati is a professional assassin," Agent Boris

Tushinsky answered with a heavy accent. "Years ago, he was employed by the Gambino crime family and has been linked to approximately thirty homicides. He prefers knives over guns because they're quiet. In a number of the murders back East, a scalpel was determined to be the murder weapon. When we heard that a scalpel was used to behead Moreno's mother, we stepped up our efforts to locate Gilbiati. Unfortunately, our trail has gone cold. He may have left the country or died from the gunshot wound."

Agent Gray spoke up. "We believe Gilbiati is presently working with a suspected arms dealer named Lawrence Van Buren. Interpol notified us the other day that there's a chance Van Buren may now be trading in nuclear material. Both the CIA and the military are involved. As usual, they're not willing to share much information."

Hank turned to Rutherford. "Didn't you find any witnesses who could identify the car?"

"Nada," Rutherford answered. "One guy said he thought it was a 'Vette. Another swore it was an NSX. Most of our witnesses were Hispanic housekeepers and clerks. One lady was seventy-nine years old. They only got a glimpse of the car after they heard the gunfire. All we know for certain is the car was red."

Hank bolted to his feet. "That's Sullivan's Ferrari!"

"You know," Rutherford said snidely, "there's more than one red car on the street, Sawyer, just like there's more than one criminal named Raphael, particularly in our neck of the woods."

"Don't you see?" Hank blurted out. "This is what the killers have been looking for . . . the red Ferrari. They went to these houses to get the car back. When the occupants interfered, they killed them."

"Are you trying to tell me nine people have died because of a car?" Rutherford asked, tapping his knuckles on the table.

"That's exactly what I'm telling you," Hank said, pointing

a finger at him. "It's not the car, though, it's what's inside it. Our lab did a thorough workup, so they say, but they didn't find anything outside of Moreno's blood. If this Dante guy has connections to a man who may be trafficking in nuclear material, who knows what's inside that car? Obviously, it's well hidden. Another thing that could have caused us to miss something is the car itself. Ferrari only made one of these models and its value is estimated at half a mil. Our technicians were probably reluctant to rip it apart for fear they wouldn't be able to put it back together again. Six months ago, narcotics had them tear up a Lamborghini and the county ended up paying for it."

"That makes sense," Chief Riggs said, eager to justify the lab's mistake. "Our people aren't Ferrari mechanics. Besides, this was a suburban murder, not a narcotics case."

"The video we watched earlier may have been staged," Agent Tushinsky interjected. "If the killer is employed by the same person as Dante Gilbiati, he's more than likely a professional." He paused to make sure he had everyone's full attention. "There's a top female assassin named Claire Mellinger. She kills by means of a lethal injection. I understand in the murders of the two women, one of the additives was a medication known to treat multiple sclerosis."

"People use what they know or what they have available," Agent Gray added. "There's been reports that Mellinger is ill. She resides in Europe, therefore, Interpol has been notified. They're presently contacting all physicians who have prescribed this medication. Because Novantrone is only administered by injection, the patient must come to the doctor's office once per month. This narrows down our search criteria. As soon as we hear something, we'll let you know."

"She could be closer than you think," Hank said. "Is this Mellinger woman the one in the picture in front of you?"

"Don't know," Agent Tushinsky explained. "Mellinger has never been photographed. We don't even have a physical description. She leaves nothing behind, gentlemen. The crime scene is usually cleaner than when she arrived."

Everything was slamming together. Hank was so excited, he looked as if he were about to have a heart attack. This was the type of payoff that kept him chained to a high-risk job with a lousy salary. The rush when a sensational case began to mesh was phenomenal. Hitching up his pants, he walked to the front of the room and picked up the clicker. It was upside down. He looked to Mary for help. She signaled for him to turn it over. He pulled up a photo of the Hartfield residence.

"The address of the first murders was 1003 Seaport Avenue." Flipping to the next image, Hank showed the address of Neil Sullivan's home at 1003 Sea View Terrace. "The red Ferrari had been in Sullivan's garage until a few hours prior to the Goodwin murder."

He clicked ahead to the Porter homicide, his voice elevating. "You'll notice that this is once again the same numerical address of 1003, except this time the street is Seaport Drive, three blocks away from the first murder. The killers must have had a partial address, say '1003' and the word 'Sea.' Like I said, they were searching and the only thing we know of that has a documented connection to the murders is Sullivan's Ferrari. Hartfield is tied into the Goodwin murder because Raphael Moreno's blood was found inside Sullivan's car. Goodwin was killed by the same person who killed Suzanne Porter because both were killed by a highly unusual combination of drugs and poisons. The murder of Moreno's mother and sister is now tied to all nine homicides."

"You released the car?" Agent Gordon Gray exclaimed, a look on his face that said he thought Hank Sawyer and the Ventura police were idiots.

Ignoring him, Hank turned back to Rutherford. The FBI might think they were fools, but they were so busy kissing up to their superiors, it took them years to solve a case.

Besides, it took time to go to fancy hairstylists and shop for expensive Brooks Brothers suits.

"Rutherford," Hank said, tilting his chin up, "run a DNA test on your blood samples. I'll bet you a hundred bucks the man who jacked a red sports car and killed the driver was Raphael Moreno. You didn't catch it as we didn't have his DNA on file until he was arrested for murdering the Hartfield family."

The other officers in the room suddenly felt the rush. The only one who looked unhappy, Hank noticed, was Mary Stevens. The suspect she'd chased down that morning, Ashton Sabatino, had just slid out of the noose.

"I'll get right on it," Rutherford said, getting up and stepping to the back of the room to make the appropriate phone calls.

"If we get Moreno to talk again," Hank continued, "he might be able to tell us everything we want to know. We need to find the Ferrari as well as the killers. If I'm right, they're going to keep killing until they find that car." He grabbed a glass of water off the table and drank it down, then turned to the FBI agents. "No one could get a nuclear bomb inside a car, could they? I mean, it'd be too big, right?"

Agent Tushinsky paused before answering. "Not really," he said somberly. "We've never seen a briefcase-size nuke before, but I understand it's possible. We're not talking complete annihilation, of course. The damage would still be considerable."

Hank's excitement turned to fear. "We shouldn't have a problem finding the car," he said, trying to appear confident. "What should we broadcast to our officers?"

"Nothing," Agent Gray said, his hands gripping the arms of his chair. "Let us notify the appropriate agencies. Until we advise you differently, I'd suggest you don't broadcast it to your field officers. We don't know what's inside that car, gentlemen. We can't take a chance that one of your men will end up in a pursuit, a pursuit that might conclude in a collision." He fixed Hank with a steely gaze. "You said it was re-leased back to the owner. Don't you know where he is so we can pick it up?"

"No," Hank said, "but I can find his sister."

The agents were standing and Agent Tushinsky was already busy making phone calls. "I suggest you do that right away, Detective," Gray said. "That vehicle shouldn't be on the street."

"We're going to talk to Raphael Moreno at four-thirty. Is the room ready, Mary?"

"All set," she said, scurrying to pick up the information she had brought and then rushing out of the conference room. She collided with Sawyer in the corridor, the files and DVDs spilling out onto the floor. "I called all our contact numbers for Neil Sullivan and wasn't able to reach him. I also called Carolyn and she didn't answer. What should I do?"

Hank glanced at his watch; it was three-thirty. "The funeral should be over by now. Both of them probably turned their cell phones off. If you hurry, you should be able to catch them at the cemetery. If we get lucky and the Ferrari is there, stand guard over it until we can get some people over there."

Hank headed down the corridor at a fast clip. He remembered something and turned around. "When you find Carolyn, don't take no for an answer. This is too serious. If she gives you any trouble, just pick her up and deposit her in the back of your car."

Chapter 32

While Mary stayed outside to make a few calls, Carolyn looked through the glass into the lobby of the men's jail and saw Hank waiting. She marched straight up to him and whacked him across the chest. "Don't trust me, huh?"

"God, woman!" the detective exclaimed. "Are you psychotic or something?"

"Mary brought me down here in her police unit. She wouldn't let me drive my own car. If it wasn't for me, you wouldn't have a chance to break Moreno. I suggest you use more tact the next time."

Hank smiled. "I could have you arrested for assault on a police officer. Mind your manners or I'll book you."

"You wouldn't dare arrest me," Carolyn said, still fuming. "Remember that blond shoplifter with the big tits that you took to a hotel room instead of the jail? You're bucking for lieutenant, aren't you? How would that sit with the review board?"

Hank scowled. "Low blow, Carolyn. Since you never fail to rub my face in it, you should know that I was on the sauce back then. It's the only time in my career I stepped out of line. All the girl lifted was a damn lipstick, for God's sake. My shift was over, so I had her pay for what she'd taken, then asked her to have a drink with me at the Holiday Inn. One drink turned into six. I think I passed out as soon as we got to the room."

Mary returned and took a seat in the interconnected row of plastic seats used by visitors. Hank was relieved that she hadn't overheard what Carolyn had said. "Anyway, you're here," he said, sighing. "Where's Neil and the Ferrari?"

"I don't know," she told him. "He probably hasn't picked it up yet because of the funeral. They must have driven Melody's Porsche."

"We sent some of our people to the services," he told her. "That's why we couldn't find him. They were looking for the Ferrari. Neil picked it up earlier today, Carolyn. Do you have Melody Asher's cell phone number?"

"Only her home," Carolyn said, massaging her temples. "Neil doesn't turn his cell phone on. He just carries it to make outgoing calls. What's going on, Hank?"

He filled her in on some of what had transpired since she'd last talked to him. He knew he was restricted from telling her what they feared might be hidden inside the Ferrari. "I'll try to find Neil while you're in with Moreno."

"Neil said something about getting a drink after the funeral," Carolyn said. "I don't know if they planned on stopping at a place in Ventura or heading back to Brentwood."

Hank called out for Mary, then tapped on the glass window for the jailer. After Bobby Kirsh buzzed them through the security doors, he told him, "Don't transport Moreno to the interview room until I give the go-ahead." He needed more time to explain things to Carolyn and he didn't want Moreno waiting, for fear he would figure out it was a setup.

Neil was sitting at the bar at the Chart House restaurant waiting for Melody to return from the restroom. The funeral had sent him into a tailspin of self-analysis. Yesterday he'd almost committed the ultimate act of self-pity. Today he had said good-bye to his high-school sweetheart.

He had lived thirty-two years of selfishness. The material things of his life had only caused complications. He'd accomplished nothing worthwhile other than painting a few good pictures.

Laurel had deceived him.

With her soft voice and innocent smile, she had slipped into his life, pretending to be an angel, giving him hope in the midst of despair. A woman who cheated on her husband with a teenager and former student, then lied to the man who wanted to marry her, was most assuredly not an angel.

The burial of Laurel brought his own mortality to the surface. What would be his eulogy?

He could imagine Carolyn, Melody, and his family sitting in the Catholic church at his funeral. It was midnight. The cavernous building's walls danced with the shadows of the flickering candlelight. The priest stood to speak, but no words came out. The last time Neil had stepped a foot inside a church was at his father's funeral. His suicide had been concealed by another lie. This time, the demon came to Neil in the guise of his own mother.

Marie Sullivan had pushed him relentlessly as a child, constantly berating him over his poor grades and lack of interest in subjects that were central to her and her husband's lives. At the same time, she'd ignored his talent as an artist and tossed his drawings in the trash. Becoming an artist was worthless, his mother had told him. It was a hobby, not a career. He would end up selling used cars for a living, struggling to support his family. Eventually his wife would get tired of her lazy and unrealistic husband and leave him. He brought forth an image of his mother shaking her finger at him, her face twisted in anger. "Go ahead, paint to your heart's content, but don't come running to me when you're out of money and you can't feed your kids."

No matter how poorly she'd treated him, Neil had no choice but to respect the woman who had given him life. Like everyone else who had hurt him during his lifetime, his mother would survive him and sit silently with the others at his funeral.

He imagined his ceremony concluding without a single word being spoken. What could they say? There was nothing to say.

When Neil saw Melody walking toward him, his spirits lifted. He had not allowed himself to take Melody seriously because of her wealth. When a woman was that rich, a normal guy found it hard to see himself fitting into her life of luxury and privilege. Until five years ago, the highest price Neil had ever received for a canvas had been two thousand dollars. His price had skyrocketed when a rock star's girlfriend convinced the singer to outbid another client. The star ended up dishing out fifty grand without figuring out the client he was bidding against was Neil's agent.

Melody could spend ten grand during a few hours of shopping on Rodeo Drive. So what? he told himself. She probably squandered money for the same reason he'd allowed himself to become dependent on crystal meth. Her success and his weren't on the same level, but they shared many things. Surrounded by people, they had both felt terribly alone.

Maybe his life was about to turn around. The police would catch the killer and he would be free to build a new life. No more mistakes, he told himself. No drugs, alcohol, nothing that could upset the delicate chemical balance inside his brain. He would eat right, get a decent night's sleep, start exercising. If all that didn't work, he would go on lithium.

Melody's perfume teased his nostrils as she leaned over and kissed his cheek. "Let's get a table," she whispered. "I don't feel like driving back to the city by myself right now."

When they'd eaten lunch there earlier, Melody had insisted that Neil leave the Ferrari with the valet, telling him it was too ostentatious for a funeral.

They slid into a booth and sat side by side. Neil stood back up.

"What's wrong?" Melody asked.

"I just need some space right now," he said, taking a seat

across from her. The floor-to-ceiling windows gave them a view of the ocean. The day was bright, with a sprinkling of clouds in front of the blue backdrop.

"Are you sure you're okay?" she asked.

"I'm okay," he lied. It felt strange to be mourning Laurel while he was with Melody. She was almost too nice. Neil's senses told him that in his weakened state she could manipulate him without her normally aggressive nature. The waitress arrived at the table.

"I'll take an apple martini," Melody told her. "Honey, what do you want?"

"Pellegrino with a lime, please."

"What are you talking about?" she asked. "I'm not drinking alone. Bring him a slightly dirty martini with Grey Goose vodka."

The waitress looked at Neil for approval.

"A drink will do you good," Melody pressed. "It'll take the edge off."

"Okay, but things are going to change," Neil said in a firm voice once the woman had left. If they were going to be together, he thought, he'd have to take more control in the relationship. It was embarrassing how she handled him. He was the man and it was time he acted like one. "I'm going to clean up my act. I don't want to give up drugs and then become an alcoholic. That's what they say happens. People trade one addiction for another. Maybe I need to go to those Narcotics Anonymous meetings for a while."

"You'll be fine," Melody said, extending her hand to embrace his on the coarse surface of the white tablecloth. When the waitress came back with the drinks, they both took a sip. "I have to tell you something about myself."

"What?"

She leaned forward and whispered, "I like to watch videos I recorded of us having sex."

"What's so earth-shattering about that?" Neil said, disinterested. "I know you taped us. You even called out that guy's name to make me jealous."

"It was more than that night, Neil. I . . . I set up video cameras in your house."

"You what?" he said, raising his voice enough to get a look from the table next to them.

Melody began speaking fast. "They were in your bedroom, living room, in front of the house, overlooking the pool. It was for my own protection. You weren't the only one. I filmed almost all of my lovers."

"Your protection?" he said. "How could you invade my privacy like that?" His mouth twisted. "You know how sick that is, Melody?"

Her expression remained stoic. "That's not why I'm bringing this up."

Neil slouched low in his seat, refusing to look at her. Did the bottom have to constantly fall out of everything? He felt like buying another gun and returning to the sand dunes. "Okay, then why are you telling me this?"

"I have a tape of Laurel."

He craned his neck around. "You mean you videotaped everything? Even when I was with Laurel?"

"Yes, I'm sorry," she said, her voice trailing off.

"God, you're the one who killed Laurel!" Neil said, almost knocking his drink over.

"I didn't kill Laurel and I know you didn't, either." Melody sucked in a deep breath, then slowly let it out. "I recorded more than just sex, Neil. I recorded Laurel's murder."

Chapter 33

Wednesday, December 29—4:03 P.M.

"Thanks for coming down," Hank told Carolyn, talking in the locker area inside the jail. "I know this isn't the best day to be interviewing a violent criminal."

"You've got that right," she said, locking up her gun.

"We have new information connecting Moreno to the Goodwin and Porter homicides," he said, stopping to get her full attention. "We found trace elements of Moreno's blood under the driver's seat in Neil's Ferrari."

"That's impossible!" Carolyn said, clutching at her chest. "Moreno's blood couldn't have been found inside Neil's car. It has to be a mistake, Hank."

"DNA is foolproof. Weren't you listening before? Things are finally coming together. You have to get Moreno to spill his guts. He's the missing piece of the puzzle."

Just when she needed to be strong, Hank had delivered another blow. After the night before, she had to do everything possible to keep Neil from learning this shocking turn of events. "Wait," she said, grabbing the detective's sleeve, "Neil didn't own the car at the time of the Hartfield murders. He got it around Thanksgiving. Then it got tied up in a lawsuit. The court filed an injunction and locked it up until they made a ruling." She explained how her brother had traded the car for his paintings. "He got it back the day of Laurel's murder. Moreno was in jail. That's the same day I interviewed him the first time, remember? We talked on the phone and you invited me to a party."

Hank grimaced, moving his feet around on the linoleum. "Who did Neil get the Ferrari from?"

"I don't remember the woman's name," Carolyn told him. "I think they were a couple in their late forties or something. The man was cheating on the wife, so she traded the Ferrari to get back at him."

"It's urgent that we find out who these people are, Carolyn," the detective said, his brow dampening with perspiration. "Are you saying Neil is the only person who knows?"

"I can't help you there," she said, not wanting to tell him what she had gone through the night before with her brother. In reality, she should have driven Neil straight to the police station. "You'll have to ask Neil, Hank. It's not like I haven't been busy. Brad is out and I have cases stacked to the ceiling. Wilson almost had a stroke when he heard I was taking off today to interview Moreno again. Things are so bad, the asshole hasn't been able to play golf. He's furious that he might actually have to do some work."

Hank erupted. "I don't give a rat's ass about Wilson or anyone else over there, understand? The interview with Moreno takes precedence over everything. If your boss doesn't like it, I'll get the chief to call him."

"Does this mean Sabatino's off the hook?"

"Not exactly," Hank said, leaning against the row of lockers. "We're not going to file against him until we're absolutely certain. I spoke with Abby Walters, his probation officer, and she's already slapped a hold on him until the new offense is adjudicated. I talked to him thirty minutes ago. He doesn't come across as a murderer, especially when you consider the body count. Abby also informed me that he has an alibi for the night of the Goodwin murder. We're running down the witnesses. He was supposedly at a Ventura High basketball game. Probably selling dope to the players.

"According to the FBI, one of the men involved is a former assassin for the Gambino crime family. Pros like that would never let a drugged-out kid do their dirty work. That is, unless they planned on taking him out as soon as the job was done."

Mary Stevens walked up as Bobby Kirsh was about to escort them down a long corridor. The inmates were raising such a ruckus, they had trouble hearing one another. "Am I seeing things, Bobby?" Carolyn asked, squinting as she stared into one of the cells. "Are there three men in there? I thought the max was two."

"Well," Kirsh said, shooting Hank an annoyed look, "we had to put them somewhere. Detective Sawyer made us evacuate the third floor just so you could have another tea party with your buddy Raphael. Hope you don't end up in a hospital bed next to Preston. It's nuts to mess with this guy again."

"I won't disagree with you on that one, Bobby," Carolyn said, cutting her eyes to Hank.

"My men should have him restrained by now," the jailer continued. "Call me when you're ready for us to bring him up. Good luck, Carolyn. You're going to need it."

Hank stepped into the elevator, pressing the button for the third floor. "Okay," he said, "we built a dummy room that looks exactly like the one where you first interviewed him. This way, the SWAT team can monitor you without Moreno's knowledge. You need to do everything possible to keep him focused on you. Guy spots the guns and the show will be over."

"If he makes a move to hurt me," Carolyn said, her voice shaking, "you're going to kill him, aren't you?"

"Precisely," Hank said, holding the door open as Carolyn and Mary stepped out. "We'd prefer to keep him alive, though. Without his cooperation, we may never find out who committed these murders."

"I'm going to have to play rough with him," Carolyn said, her face stern. "I don't want him shot until I give a signal.

I'll shout your name, got it? That's the way it's going to go down or I'm not going in."

"It's your neck," Hank told her. "Just say my name and the SWAT team will take dead aim."

Carolyn turned to Mary. "Do you have some paper and a pen?"

"Sure," she said, reaching into a compartment in her computer case and handing them over.

"Hank," Carolyn continued, "I need you to write something for me."

"I'd be happy to help," Mary offered. "Hank's handwriting is almost illegible."

"Thanks, but no," Carolyn told her. "A woman's handwriting is different than a man's. Listen, Hank, I'm going to tell you what to write."

Hank did what she asked, then disappeared. A member of the SWAT team stashed Carolyn in a chair as they went about checking their communications devices, ammunition, and anything else they might need if the situation blew apart. She wadded the note up Hank had written, then straightened it out. Finally she folded it and tucked it inside the waistband of her skirt.

Hank returned and led her to the prefabricated room. Unlike the rows of rowdy inmates she'd seen earlier, the floor was eerily silent. She looked up and saw at least six officers stretched out on their stomachs on a metal platform that had been installed directly above. Their assault rifles protruded through the openings in the metal; then the ends of the barrels disappeared inside the plasterboard ceiling.

Hank pointed out how the ceiling had been designed so it looked as if the holes were part of the material. They needed additional openings so the officers could maintain visual contact.

Other men stood in strategic places around the perimeter. Carolyn wondered how easy the guns were to spot from inside the room. "How can I keep Moreno from seeing the holes in the ceiling?"

"People don't look up that often," Hank told her. "You only spotted our guys because you knew they were going to be here. My suggestion for you is to keep the conversation flowing. Don't talk too loud and he'll have to concentrate to hear what you're saying. Even people who aren't deaf resort to reading lips. They may not know it, but they do. It's instinctive. If your daughter is talking to you and you can't hear her, do you look at the ceiling or do you look at her face?"

"Her face."

"Do what I say and you won't have a problem."

Mary gestured for him and the detectives walked away. Carolyn's stomach began gurgling with acid. She knew exactly what she had to do. No matter how the events of the past week had short-circuited her nervous system, she needed to be on top of her game. This was the big leagues and she was playing for more than her own life. At stake were the innocent lives of possible new victims.

Her mother's revelation about her father's death, Neil's suicide attempt, and the disgusting video of Paul seemed like nothing next to sitting in a box with Moreno. Distracting herself from the tension, her thoughts drifted to Melody. By suppressing the truth about her mother's and brother's deaths, she'd learned to reshape reality to suit her needs. Ironically, the sexual abuse inflicted on her by her uncle may have caused her more harm than the loss of her family.

Children who were sexually abused on an ongoing basis learned to barter with their bodies. Given a choice between a beating and being molested, it wasn't hard to figure out which decision a child would make. People found it hard to believe, but some of the children even found it pleasurable, even though they were being exploited. Pedophiles with regular access to their victims might not reach the level of penetration for months, even years. They courted the child slowly with hugs, kisses, teasing, and fondling. Being held and stroked wasn't so awful, especially when the child was rewarded with special privileges or gifts. Over time, the victim learned to control the abuser by holding back sexual favors or threatening to expose him. In return, the rewards got larger. Carolyn knew of a case of incest, where the victim had a wallet full of credit cards and a new Thunderbird convertible, her youthful body already perfected by a plastic surgeon. From the age of ten, her father had made her bend over the toilet every morning before school so he could sodomize her. The abuse had stopped at the age of thirteen when the girl had threatened to report him to the police. After that, she was in control, extorting anything she wanted from him. The situation came to light after the father began embezzling from his company to pay his daughter's credit card bills.

Female victims became provocative and manipulative women, using their bodies to get what they wanted. Some turned into pathological liars, prostitutes, criminals, even killers. Death row had its share of sexual abuse victims, both male and female. When a sixteen-year-old girl who'd been sexually abused since the age of six walked into a courtroom, the jury expected to see a shy, modest, and severely traumatized teenager, her head hung low in shame.

What they saw was a Melody Asher, a precocious manipulator who had learned to use sex as a bargaining chip.

Now that she thought about it, Carolyn doubted if Melody had made the video so she could distribute it to Paul's future lovers. She probably had set up the monitoring equipment to blackmail Paul if he decided to stop seeing her. Carolyn was surprised Paul was still allowed to teach at Caltech. Of course, for all she knew, Melody might have followed through on her threats, and this could be the real reason why he had left Pasadena and relocated to Ventura.

Good God, she thought, the tape!

Hank was speaking to Mary Stevens. Carolyn rushed over

and seized him by the arm. "Melody e-mailed me a video. As soon as I talk to Moreno, I'll go home and get it. The lab can tell if the same digital camera was used in the video you received today of the Goodwin murder."

"Melody sent you a video!" he yelled. "Shit, woman, why didn't you tell me? What video? When did this happen?"

"Christmas Day," Carolyn told him. "I didn't tell you because I didn't think it had any bearing on the murders." They could have two trains running on the same track. Sabatino might be the killer, but Melody could have hired him. Knowing the next question was inevitable, she looked around to make certain no one was listening, then told Hank and Mary what was on the tape.

"This is wild," Mary said, wrapping her arms around her chest. "If the videos were made with the same camera, then Melody had to be the one who set up the Siemens router inside Neil's house. That means she watched the murder and then sat on the evidence, even when she knew Neil might be charged with Laurel's murder."

"How tall was the man in the motorcycle outfit?" Carolyn asked. "Also, was he slender, medium, heavy?"

"Around six feet," Mary answered. "Hard to tell his weight because of the leather suit. He looked about the size of your brother. You know, tall and thin."

"Sabatino isn't six feet tall."

"The helmet added height," Hank told her. "The lab hasn't had time to analyze the video. We just got it today. Where are you going with this, Carolyn? You're all over the place when you should be concentrating on Moreno."

"Melody is almost six feet and she's thinner than Sabatino or Neil." Carolyn stopped and cleared her throat. "She has a motive, remember? If she installed the surveillance equipment, she saw Neil with Laurel. She must have known they were seeing each other all along."

"See if you can find me some Tums or something," Hank said to a young deputy, his hand pressed over his chest.

"Christ, if we don't put this case together soon, I'm going to have a heart attack."

"We can't do anything until we find out whether or not the tapes match," Mary said. "Give me the key to your house, Carolyn. You could be tied up here for hours."

"My kids should be home," Carolyn said, scratching her arm and seeing a patch of reddish blisters. Melody was with Neil. Should she tell Hank and Mary or wait to see what the lab found out? As Hank had told her, she needed to remain focused on Moreno. "I don't want my children anywhere near the video of Paul and Melody, understand? I was going to delete it, but I never got around to it." She told Mary where her laptop was located and gave her the code to access her files. "There's a blank DVD in the top drawer. The file is too large to fit on a disk. You'll have to burn it on a DVD. I'll call the kids and let them know you're coming."

In addition to hives, when Carolyn got nervous, she had a tendency to lose her voice. She'd been swallowing down water from a plastic Evian bottle, praying it didn't happen. They were expecting too much from her. The way things had gone down last time, there was a good chance Moreno might refuse to talk to her. The others weren't risking their lives. The cops dressed in riot gear, with their high-powered assault weapons, had nothing to fear. It was hard to be a sitting duck and a miracle worker at the same time.

"Ten minutes and it's a go," Bobby Kirsh said. "Check in with Sergeant Griffin over there. We want you to wear a wire."

All she needed was something taped to her chest, Carolyn thought, scratching her shoulder. She stepped up to a desk on the left side of the interview room. A stone-faced sergeant confiscated her briefcase. "I need something in there," she told him, pulling out a manila envelope. Once the sergeant had looked inside, he handed it back to her.

"No pencils, pens, tape recorders, or any kind of sharp objects?"

"Nothing," she said, thinking if the officer smiled, his

face would crack. He handed her a roll of tape and the kit containing the electronic monitoring device, reminding her to remove the underwires in her bra while she was in the ladies' room to prevent the suspect from using them as a weapon.

After Carolyn used the bathroom, she changed her clothes and made some adjustments to her appearance. Deciding not to go for the seductive look this time, she had tied her hair back in a ponytail and had washed off her makeup. She was wearing a white cotton shirt, the fabric thick enough to conceal the bulletproof vest, and a knee-length blue skirt, her version of a Catholic schoolgirl's uniform. Her goal today was to remind Moreno of his sister, Maria.

"What makes you think Moreno won't know this is a setup?" she asked Hank when she came out. "A freestanding structure with men in SWAT gear positioned on the roof is a dead giveaway, don't you think?"

Hank stared at her, then broke out laughing. "Why are you dressed like that? You look like a kid. What are you trying to do? Get Moreno to ask you to the prom?"

Carolyn sneered. "While you guys have been chasing your tail, I've been doing my homework. Anyway, you didn't answer my question."

"We blindfolded him," the detective told her, unwrapping a toothpick and shoving it into his mouth. "Bobby told Moreno it was for security reasons. Since he's an escape risk, taking his eyesight away makes anything along those lines more difficult. The main reason is so we can trick him into believing it's just the two of you again. He'll be more inclined to talk that way. Of course, once you're in the room, we'll remove the blindfold."

Hank became somber again. She saw his hands trembling as he placed the small container of toothpicks back in his pocket. What they were about to do was riding his nerves for a number of reasons. The most maddening part was that there was nothing he could do but wait. "You ready, hotshot?" he asked. "If there was ever a time to strut your stuff, this is it."

Carolyn thrust her shoulders back. Mary hugged her, whispering in her ear, "Don't take any chances."

The temperature couldn't be over sixty degrees, she thought, rubbing her hands together to warm them. The air-conditioning was probably set to work with the combined body heat of the prisoners. Either that, or they wanted to make certain everyone stayed alert. She reached out and turned the door handle, stepping inside the room.

Moreno was sitting in a plastic chair. There was no table, as it would prevent the SWAT team from seeing his hands and feet. The jail had added a metal neck restraint and attached it to a thick belt around his waist. The chains on the other restraints were linked to the one on his neck and also secured through a metal fastener on his belt. If the prisoner tried to kick out with his legs, his neck would be snapped backward. If he attempted to raise his arms, the same thing would happen. Carolyn relaxed, fairly confident that he couldn't hurt her. If he made a move, she would signal the SWAT team to start shooting.

Bobby had told them he wasn't eating. It wasn't unusual for inmates to go on hunger strikes. Some would do it to protest jail or prison conditions. Others would starve themselves to gain attention for a cause, such as abolishing capital punishment. But some deliberately lost weight to facilitate an escape. Ted Bundy stopped eating, lost weight, and shimmied out of the jail in Aspen through its ventilation system.

Carolyn saw hatred shooting from Moreno's eyes. He knew she'd set him up after the first interview, locking him in the room for hours in scorching heat, without water, food, or the use of a toilet.

She doubted if Moreno weighed more than 115 pounds. The bulging biceps she'd seen before were even more sinewy. She started to look up at the ceiling for reassurance, then stopped herself. The clock was ticking.

Steeling herself, Carolyn began speaking. "I'm here today because one of the jailers came across this letter." She reached into the waistband of her skirt and removed the note she'd dictated to Hank. After she handed it to Moreno, she watched as he read. "As you can see, the people you're involved with have planted men inside the jail with explicit instructions to kill you."

"Old news," Moreno said. "I took care of those guys, remember? They carried them outta here on stretchers, bleeding and crying like a bunch of pussies."

"These aren't the same men," Carolyn insisted. "They're waiting for you to be released into the general population or they'll make their move inside the tunnel. Your prelim on the assault charges begins next week. That means you'll be in the tunnel twice a day."

"Lying bitch," Moreno snarled, pulling against the restraints and causing them to rattle. "If they didn't have me chained like a damn pit bull, I'd break your skinny neck. Why would I buy this shit? You played me before. It ain't gonna work this time."

Carolyn stood, slapping her hands against her thighs. "I'm not conning you," she told him. "But if you don't want to talk, there's nothing I can do. You think the jailers care if the inmates kill you? Most of them think you deserve to die. All these men have to do is slip a few guards some hundred-dollar bills and you're a goner. No one will even know who killed you." She walked toward the door, then turned back around as if she'd forgotten something. "Oh, do you have any friends or relatives who might be willing to bury you? The allotment for indigent deaths barely covers a cremation. It's better if we take care of this type of thing in advance."

Moreno's mouth fell open in shock. Carolyn reached for the buzzer to be released. "Wait—come back," he called out.

His eyes glistened with tears. Lack of food wreaked havoc on a person's emotions. If Carolyn played her cards right, she just might get what she came for.

"Why do you care what happens to me?" he said. "The cops said I killed my mother and my sweet sister."

Carolyn had to contain her excitement. One word said it all. She doubted if he would describe his sister as sweet if he'd killed her. Things were working better than she had expected. She bent sideways and retrieved the envelope off the floor, holding it in her lap as she pulled out two eight-by-ten photos. Picking up her chair, she repositioned it beside him, placing the first photo in front of his face. "Is this what you did to your mother?"

Mrs. Moreno was lying on her back on the floor, only a few feet from her wheelchair. Her neck had been slit with what the lab had identified as a scalpel, the cut so deep it had severed her head from her body. Her eyes were open and her face was sprayed with blood.

Moreno tried to knock the photo aside. The chains pulled against the metal restraint on his neck. "Get that fucking thing away from me. I ain't talking about my mother."

Carolyn pulled the photo back, replacing it with a second one. A twelve-year-old girl wearing a Catholic-school uniform, similar to the clothing Carolyn was wearing, was gagged and bound in a high-backed wooden chair. Blood streamed down her face and soaked her clothes. Forensics had identified the murder weapon as a household hammer.

Moreno became enraged. "Ain't you got ears?" he shouted. "I don't want to see no pictures. Maybe I should kill you, then the state would give me the death penalty. Tell them to put me in the main jail section now. Go ahead. Let them assholes try to kill me. They'll find them like they did those other idiots. The only difference is this time they won't be breathin'."

Carolyn moved her chair back to where it had been previously. For a while, she sat quietly with her hands folded in her lap. When she began speaking again, her voice was soft and nonthreatening. "I saw in the file that Maria went to Saint Agnes's. I'm a Catholic like you." She reached inside her white cotton blouse and showed him her mother's silver cross. Because it was large, she had stopped wearing it outside her clothing. Some of the guys at work had teased her, telling her she looked like a nun. Catholics had a bond, though, even strangers. "I checked with the school and they told me you paid Maria's tuition every month in cash. Since your mother was confined to a wheelchair and couldn't work, how did you come up with the money? It doesn't make sense for you to kill someone you loved that much. I bet you loved your mother as well."

Moreno transformed. The look in his eyes was no longer threatening. What she saw was a quiet, emotional young man. He was more than likely an introvert. How else could he have gone so long without speaking? She could see why the DA had decided not to risk putting him in front of a jury. He could pretend to be anything he wanted. All she had to do was figure out what was real.

"You didn't kill them, did you?" she stated. "You never told anyone you were innocent because you were afraid the men who killed your family would kill you, too. Am I right, Raphael?"

His shoulders began shaking. He tried to suppress the tears, but the floodgates had opened. For at least ten minutes, he sobbed uncontrollably.

When he raised his head, Carolyn stopped breathing. She watched him rub his eyes with his right hand.

He had slipped it out of the handcuffs.

She jerked her head toward the door, terrified the SWAT team was going to start shooting. She wasn't a fool. The room was the size of a closet. If they started shooting, Moreno might not be the only one to die. She whipped back around, seeing both of his hands in the cuffs. Her fear and lack of sleep could have caused her to have imagined that one hand had been free. Terminating the interview now would be a disaster. He was about to tell her everything. She took in a breath, then slowly exhaled. His voice broke through her panic.

"I know who the real killer is."

Chapter 34

Raphael had been standing in front of El Toro Market on Cooper Road in Oxnard, killing time until his sister's school let out at three. The sky was clear, not a cloud to be seen, and the sun felt warm against his skin. It was hard staying inside all day with his mother. Sometimes he wondered if he'd made the right decision bringing her and Maria to the States.

Three years ago, his parents were involved in a car accident in Mexico. His father was killed instantly and his mother's legs were crushed. At the time, Maria was only nine. How could he leave them there with no money and no man to protect them?

For a seventeen-year-old, he'd done fairly well. Dropping out of school had been the hardest. He had gone to work for a chop shop located in the hills above Malibu. For the first year, he'd dismantled cars and sanded off VIN numbers. One day, he'd got lucky. The boss, Angel Romano, heard about the burden he was carrying with his family and decided to try him out boosting cars. His slender build and fresh-faced appearance made him an excellent candidate, enabling him to move in the same circles as the wealthy without drawing suspicion.

He'd been smuggled into the United States at the age of

ten, crammed in the back of a sweltering truck with forty other immigrants. The last thing he'd aspired to be was a criminal.

The first year, he'd worked in the strawberry fields, then a family had taken him in. As soon as he'd become fluent in English, they'd enrolled him in school. They'd been amazed to find out how smart he was. They told him he could be a lawyer, a doctor, or anything he wanted. He'd loved reading in his room, writing on the crisp white paper, learning and expanding his mind.

His downfall was his inherent thirst for fighting. Because of his small size, he'd strengthened his body. He'd spent hours in a makeshift gym he'd set up in the garage. Filling two plastic milk containers with a mixture of water and sand, he had used them as barbells. He did wide-arm pull-ups on the beam above his surrogate father's workbench, developing a powerful punch and great hand strength. Holding old tires to his chest, he squatted to strengthen his legs. He'd become muscular, yet fast and agile.

When he was threatened by other students, he'd beat them to prove his masculinity. It wasn't long before he had earned the name "Mighty Mouse" at school. People began to fear him, everyone except Javier Gonzales. Raphael didn't know when to stop. When he did, Javier was a bloody mess of broken bones. Fifteen hours in surgery, and the boy barely survived.

The Gonzales family pressed charges, then dropped them with a nominal payment by Raphael's foster parents. If not, he would have never been able to become a U.S. citizen. That was the happiest day of his life. Soon after, his world was shattered. His foster father had lost his job, making it impossible for them to care for him. Social Services placed him with another family, but they were awful. They fed him spoiled milk and food that looked as if it had come out of a trash can.

Raphael swore he would never be arrested again. He practiced getting in and out of restraints. When he was picked up by the police after robbing a convenience store, he slipped out of the cuffs and ran. The officer gave chase, but he was too fast.

When he learned about his parents' accident, he'd decided the only thing he could do was sneak his mother and sister into the States. Things weren't going well with his mother. Her left leg was infected and the doctor was afraid he might have to amputate. Raphael hadn't had the heart to tell her, but tomorrow morning, he would have to drive her to the hospital. If she did lose her leg, he would have to hire a nurse. He'd managed to save about twenty grand, but he knew it wouldn't last forever. He needed a score.

Out of the corner of his eye, Raphael saw a flash of red. What was going on? Someone was unloading a red Ferrari off the back of a truck. Angel had a customer who wanted a fancy Ferrari. Could this be it? He'd never expected to see a car that valuable on the streets of Oxnard. He found most of the cars in Beverly Hills or Brentwood. When he delivered this one, he'd pocket five grand. Angel knew he had to pay his people well or they'd find buyers for the cars themselves.

His eyes scanned the area. Two drunks were sleeping in a doorway at the end of the street. An old lady, her back stooped and her face withered, was carrying a grocery sack across the street. Old ladies never talked to the police. Gangsters could mow down five guys, and an old lady would step over them and keep on walking.

Raphael carried a backpack so he'd look like a student. The only thing inside was his gun—a Tech 9. He yanked the gun out and dropped the empty backpack on the sidewalk, then sprinted toward the driver's side of the red Ferrari. The windows were tinted, so he couldn't tell who was inside. He was almost certain there was only one man. Smashing the glass with his gun, he shouted, "Get out of the car or I'll kill you!"

Everything happened in a heartbeat. He saw the barrel of a gun and instinctively pressed the trigger, shooting the man in the face. Yanking the bleeding man out onto the street, he was about to duck inside when he saw the passenger door was open. Spinning around, he saw another man at the rear of the car pointing a gun at him. They fired simultaneously. Raphael reeled backward as the bullet ripped into his right shoulder. Regaining his balance, he didn't wait to see if he'd hit the man. He leaped into the driver's seat, gunned the ignition, and sped away in a cloud of dust.

The Ferrari almost jumped out from under him. Checking his rearview mirror, Raphael saw the passenger scooping his friend off the pavement and placing his body in the back of the truck. Wasn't he going to call the cops? The guy was limping, so Raphael assumed he must have shot him in the leg.

Blood was oozing out of his shoulder. Steering the car with one hand, he removed his shirt and pressed it over the gunshot wound. He couldn't bleed all over the Ferrari, not after he'd killed a man to get it.

The house he rented was only four blocks away. Angel had insisted on a house over an apartment because of the garage. He couldn't park expensive cars on the street, so his instructions were to garage them until it was safe to drive them to the chop shop. If there was still heat after a few days, Angel would send a truck to pick them up.

Raphael kept his garage door opener clipped to his belt next to his pager. Hitting the button, he drove the Ferrari inside, then rushed into the house to call Angel.

"What kind of Ferrari did you get? Get the operating manual out and tell me what it says."

"It's nice looking, man," Raphael told him. "Never seen one like this before. You still got money for me?" He knew he couldn't tell him he'd killed a man. If there were injuries, Angel wouldn't touch it.

He raced to the garage, seized the manufacturer's booklet and flipped through the pages. "It says it's a 2001 five-fifty Barchetta Pininfarina Speciale. The car's in perfect condition. I swear, man. There's not a scratch on it."

"You're shitting me," Angel said. "Ferrari only made one of those babies. Bring it in around ten tonight. We have a buyer creaming his pants for a car like that."

Disconnecting, Raphael went to the bathroom to check the gunshot wound. It was not deep. Since the bullet wasn't embedded, he didn't have to worry about infection. He found some hydrogen peroxide and bandages in the medicine cabinet. After he'd dressed the wound, he put on a clean shirt. He peeked in his mother's room and saw she was sleeping. Maria handled her medication at night when he was working.

His eyes went to the crucifix mounted over her bed. Dropping to his knees, he made the sign of the cross and begged God to forgive him. If he hadn't shot the man, he would be dead. Then who would care for his family? He knew protecting them would not buy him redemption. When he died, he would burn in hell. His eyes came to rest on his mother. At thirty-six, she looked more like fifty. Her lovely dark hair had turned gray, and her once-shapely body was emaciated. Suffering and hardship were etched on her face. She'd given birth to two boys before him, but both of them had lived only a few months. The village his parents lived in had no work. His mother told him they were so poor, without God's help, they would have all died. Despite all she'd gone through, she had never complained. Until the accident, she had gone to mass every day, praying for the souls of the lost and damned. How did the son of a saint become a murderer? He knew that now that he had killed, he would do it again. He had disgraced his God, his church, and his family. He was the one who had smashed the window out with a gun and threatened to shoot the driver. The man had acted in self-defense. What if he was arrested and sent to prison? How would his mother and sister get by without him? Since they were illegal immigrants, they would be deported to Mexico.

Closing his mother's door, Raphael rushed out to his ten-year-old black Mustang, then headed to St. Agnes's to pick up Maria. His mother and sister were used to seeing fancy cars in the garage. He covered his occupation as a criminal by telling them that he detailed expensive cars for rich people.

After dinner, he **went to** the garage and scrubbed down the Ferrari. Once he told his mother that she would have to go to the hospital in the morning, he tucked Maria into bed and headed out to Malibu. He had driven a Ferrari before, but the Barchetta was fantastic. His problems were momentarily forgotten as he whipped around the curves, the city lights nothing more than a blur.

Angel was officially the caretaker of a twelve-acre parcel of wooded real estate. The property had been in probate for seven years, and the courts had erected high fences to keep people out. He'd started out small, receiving stolen cars and selling off the parts, working out of a double-wide trailer and a few metal sheds. Three years ago, he'd moved up to luxury cars, hiring guys to steal them and then delivering them to brokers throughout the country. His people never stole anything until Angel told them he had a buyer. The only work he had to do was to remove the VIN numbers and replace them with new ones so the car could be legally registered. On cars like the Barchetta, this was far more difficult. The new VIN number had to come back to a Barchetta. Angel had contacts with salvage companies throughout the world. When a luxury car was totaled, Angel would purchase the VIN plates. He had five file cabinets crammed full of clean

VIN plates that could be placed on a vehicle whenever it came in.

Angel was still laughing when Raphael drove off in the spare car he kept at the shop, a Volkswagen bug, with five grand tucked in his pocket. Cops didn't stop you when you drove a Volkswagen, particularly in Oxnard. Gangsters, even run-of-the-mill hoodlums, wouldn't be caught dead in a Beetle.

Chapter 35

Lawrence Van Buren inserted his gold key into the brass lock, securing the double glass doors, and disengaged the alarm. Navcon International was located on the twelfth floor of a high-rise office building in Los Angeles. He stepped several feet back and gazed at the gold lettering on the door, knowing it would soon be gone if he didn't deliver the Ferrari.

Entering and turning on the master switch for the lights, his eyes swept over the opulent furnishings in the lobby. His life was a sham. He had been born John Hidayah, the only son of a wealthy Egyptian family. He had changed his name so his father in Egypt wouldn't be able to find him. He'd selected the name Van Buren after the American president. Although his hair and eyes were dark, his skin was fair. He told people he was born in New York. Everyone trusted Lawrence Van Buren. His honest face and impeccable manners served him well.

Taking a seat behind his leather-topped Louis XVI desk, he unlocked a drawer and removed a small phone book. His cover of brokering exotic cars to overseas buyers had once been legitimate. Some of his best clients resided in Saudi Arabia. The only thing that was an outright lie was telling his wife he was a CIA agent. Women weren't that concerned with the truth, particularly if you gave them everything they wanted.

Van Buren used his established history of shipping exotic cars overseas to avoid suspicion. His organization used tankers sailing out of Port Hueneme, a small city with a naval base and shipping yards a short distance from Ventura. They altered the car so no one outside of the Ferrari plant in Italy would be able to tell that it was carrying illegal cargo. In addition to those cars, they shipped at least four cars a month that were clean. Another reason they passed undetected was geography. No major players in the arms market operated in this particular area. Criminal activity in Oxnard, a sister city to Port Hueneme, centered around gang activity, murders, and local drug-trafficking. These types of criminals might be vicious, but they didn't possess the funding or sophistication needed to broker weapons to foreign entities.

After the terrorist attacks on September 11, Van Buren had lain low for two years before resuming trade in the arms market. He had, however, continued to export exotic cars. Americans were big talkers with short memories. Politicians yapped all the time about airport safety, yet security guards continued to be individuals with no education and a minimum level of training. To prove his point, he'd had one of his most trusted men smuggle a suitcase full of automatic weapons on board a Delta flight to New York.

His best recruits were former police officers and disgruntled FBI and CIA agents. Of course they weren't aware of what was inside the vehicles. Only a few international criminals knew the truth.

Each day, he searched the newspapers for cops who had been fired for using excessive force, dealing drugs, or receiving payoffs. Such men were willing to sell their souls for the right amount of money. The bonus of working with pros was that they knew not to ask questions.

Van Buren pushed the button for the speaker phone, then stood behind his desk. He could never talk with his North Korean contact sitting down, particularly when he was seven weeks late on a delivery of plutonium. His three earlier shipments had gone perfectly. The cars were shipped to Saudi Arabia, then to Shanghai. For security reasons, he wasn't informed as to how they reached their final destination. As it was, he knew more than he wanted.

He sucked in a deep breath, then punched in the number. His contact had been waiting in Shanghai for delivery. There was a sixteen-hour time difference, and he refused to accept calls during business hours. Although it was a few minutes past four-thirty in the afternoon, it was eight at night in Shanghai. To avoid wiretaps, his call was transferred electronically to an unknown number. A recognizable voice finally came on the line. The code name the Korean had chosen was Bill Clinton. He doubted if the former president would be held accountable if the situation ever came to light.

"How are you doing, Bill?" he said, sweating inside his Valentino sport jacket. When the Korean answered, his accent was so thick, Van Buren had to strain to figure out what the man was saying.

"How do you think we doing?" he shouted. "Your company fail to deliver goods. I wait six weeks in crappy hotel in Shanghai. Boss say you no good. If not get it by next week, he send someone to kill you and your family."

"There's no reason to panic," Van Buren told him, pacing in a small circle. "We got a lead today on the car. By tomorrow afternoon, it will be on a ship headed to Shanghai."

"How we know you tell truth?" the Korean said, his voice rising. "Maybe you sell goods to other country. Boss not get proof of shipment by tomorrow, you dead."

"Do you want the U.S. government to know you're procuring nuclear materials from independent sources?" Van Buren tossed back, "Hold tight and everything will be fine. I delivered the three other shipments, didn't I?"

When he heard the dial tone, he yanked the multiline phone out of the wall and hurled it across the room. It struck an original drawing by Leonardo da Vinci. The glass shattered and the frame fell to the floor. The drawing had been given to him by a client who'd purchased three hundred assault rifles. He later learned it had been stolen from a museum in Amsterdam. So no one realized it was an original instead of a print, he'd covered the signature with tape, then made certain it wasn't visible.

He ripped off his jacket and wadded it up in a ball, stuffing it in the trash can. How could his men fail to track down a one-of-a-kind 550 Barchetta Pininfarina Ferrari?

He'd already wired thirty million dollars to his unnumbered bank account in Zurich. Each of the three cars he'd successfully shipped had contained ten pounds of plutonium. One pound of plutonium was the size of a baseball. His mechanic had been ingenious. He'd constructed a lead compartment that contained a half-pound ingot of plutonium in each of its twenty sections. This enclosure went into an aluminum case, which was hermetically sealed and mounted on the modified radiator inside the engine cavity.

He knew North Korea intended to use the material in an attempt to construct a nuclear bomb. It was their backup plan in case they weren't able to get the plutonium from their nuclear reactor, which was closely monitored by the international community. Van Buren believed nuclear weapons were more for leverage than for their explosive capabilities. Even if they built the bomb, he didn't think they would ever use it. On the off chance that they did, he hoped the United States wasn't their intended target. As soon as he made his last shipment and pocketed his remaining ten million, unknown to Eliza, he had made arrangements to relocate her and his children to his seven-thousand-square-foot winter home in the Virgin Islands. No country on earth would nuke the Virgin Islands. The beaches were pristine, and the landscape so lush and beautiful, even terrorists loved it.

After chugging down three cups of coffee, Van Buren glanced at his watch and saw it was almost six. Time to wake up his men and tell them they had twenty-four hours to bring in the Ferrari. He laughed, thinking how easily they'd deceived the Ventura police. Van Buren's source inside the department had informed him that the cops thought the chain of murders had been committed by a serial killer, exactly what he wanted them to believe.

When you brokered arms, you had to be prepared to take down anyone who got in your way. When the car had disappeared en route to the shipyard, the situation had instantly became volatile. They'd already killed nine people in their attempt to find the Ferrari. If not for the Mexican punk who had carjacked the vehicle after the flatbed truck they'd used had broken down in Oxnard, Van Buren would already have his ten mil and the car would be on its way to Shanghai.

Raphael Moreno had killed one of his men and injured Dante Gilbiati. Dante had gone on a hideous killing spree, fearing what Van Buren would do to him when he learned he had allowed someone to steal the Ferrari. Having worked for the mob, Dante had been trained never to leave a witness alive. He had murdered the Hartfield family because Moreno hadn't come out of the house to tell him the Ferrari wasn't there, and when Dante had gone inside, the people had seen his face.

The Koreans had insisted that he remove the GPS system so no one could track their plutonium. Otherwise, the material would already be in the hands of the man he had spoken to in Shanghai. He wouldn't make that mistake again. His men had been instructed to attach a magnetic GPS to the car as soon as they located it.

At that point, Van Buren had no choice but to call in a professional.

Claire Mellinger, the woman he'd met at the Biltmore Hotel, was one of the top female assassins in the world. She killed by means of a lethal injection. She'd never been apprehended. Like Dante, she killed every witness.

Before the hit woman had arrived, Van Buren had personally executed Dante Gilbiati. This was the kind of situation that caused even an arms dealer to have nightmares.

Van Buren did not condone killing children. He had to draw the line somewhere. His greatest mistake had been to underestimate Raphael Moreno. If things had gone down differently, he would have offered the kid a job. Barely twenty, Moreno had outwitted Dante Gilbiati, a hardened criminal, by hiding in the Hartfields' Cadillac and waiting for the police to arrest him. His family had not been as fortunate. Dante decapitated Moreno's disabled mother, then later returned to kill his sister.

He wondered if Moreno had found out where the plutonium was hidden and was attempting to sell it from inside the jail. Could a petty-ass car thief possess connections of that magnitude? Van Buren had placed three men inside the jail to beat the truth out of Moreno and recover the Ferrari. The three men had left the jail in an ambulance.

As soon as Moreno was placed on a bus to prison, Van Buren would have him snatched and brought to him immediately. The Ferrari had been sighted, then disappeared again. The twenty-year-old appeared to be playing cat and mouse with him. Right now, the only game Van Buren was willing to play was target practice.

Chapter 36

Carolyn's voice pulled Moreno back to the present. He had been speaking so low that she'd moved her chair only a few inches away. Many times his words were slurred, almost garbled, so much so that she couldn't make out what he was saying. It was all being recorded on tape by the PD, to be played over and analyzed by scores of law enforcement officers and criminal psychologists.

Moreno could be leading her down a deadly path, toying with her until the right moment came to make his move. He had admitted shooting and killing the driver of the Ferrari. He had taken a life for no other reason than to steal a car. Murder for profit was not an impulsive act.

"I want to hear more about the car, Raphael," she said, "but right now, I need to know who killed your mother and sister."

"Nothin' happened the first week," he said, "most of the time I hung out with my mom at the hospital. The doc fixed the infection. Soon as I knew she was okay, I thought about gettin' outta the business. You know, going straight. Th-the next day . . ."

Carolyn saw his chest rising and falling with emotion. She moved her leg, accidentally brushing up against his knee. She felt a powerful rush, similar to a bolt of electricity. The experience was terrifying. It was as if she were being sucked into his mind. She cursed herself for bringing in the autopsy pictures. Even *she* felt overwhelmed by the grotesque images. They turned Carolyn's thoughts to her father. What her mother had seen that night must have been as if someone had burned horrifying pictures inside her head, pictures that could never be discarded or stored away in a plastic box. Every time Carolyn looked at pictures of head injuries, she thought of her father's bloody death. Now Moreno had to live with it as well. His mother had been decapitated and his sister's skull had been crushed by a hammer.

Moreno seemed to be emitting grief like waves of radiation. He compressed in his seat. Because of his size, Carolyn knew the heavy shackles must hurt. She convinced herself against reason that he'd slipped one of his hands out of the restraints because they were painful. His skin was chafed on his neck and wrists. She wrestled again with the decision to end the interview. She was in too deep, though, and his story was too important.

She didn't prompt him again. She waited until he began speaking on his own.

"I cruised around that night lookin' for cars," Moreno told her, staring at a spot over her head. "I knew something wasn't right as soon as I walked in the door. The lights were still on in the living room. Maria was supposed to turn off the lights before she went to bed every night. I didn't have my shooter anymore. I had to get rid of it, you know, 'cause I didn't want the cops to find it." He drew in a deep breath. "When I opened the front door, I saw my mother on the floor. I thought she might have fallen out of her wheelchair. Then I saw the blood. There was blood everywhere. Oh, Jesus . . . why did he have to kill my mother?"

Carolyn reached out and stroked his hand. "Take your time. We don't have to go over every detail right now. Let's not talk about your mother, okay? Where was your sister?"

"Maria was alive," he said, speaking louder than he had before. "She was tied up in a chair. When I ran to her, a big man grabbed me from behind. He told me he was going to cut Maria's head off, too, if I didn't tell him where the Ferrari was. Then I seen his face and knew he was the guy who'd shot me. You know, the passenger in the Ferrari."

"What happened then?"

"Shit, I didn't know where the car was," Moreno said, his foot tapping on the linoleum. "I brought the car to the chop shop a week before the guy who killed my family showed up. Angel delivered it to the buyer a few hours after he got it. These people wanted that car back bad. And I don't think it was just to drive it or sell it. I think there was something inside it."

Carolyn knew she had to find Neil as soon as she left Moreno. Everything was adding up, and every road led back to the damn Ferrari. "What makes you think there's something valuable inside the car?"

" 'Cause people were willing to kill for it," Moreno told her, shifting in his seat. "No matter how much the thing was worth, it was a car, you know. Look what they did to my mother! And they killed her while Maria watched. The guy did it so I would take him to the car. He didn't want to take a chance that I would trick him or ditch him."

"What do you think was inside it?"

Moreno shrugged. "Don't ask me, 'cause I don't know. The only thing I know 'bout is stealing cars. I don't even know how to fix a car when it breaks down."

Carolyn retrieved the envelope again and pulled out a mug shot of Dante Gilbiati, which Hank had given her. "Is this the man who killed your family?"

"That's him!" he shouted, trying to snatch the photo out of her hands. "That's the fucker who butchered my mother and killed my sister. Where is he? Give me thirty minutes with him and I'll plead guilty to every murder you got. I don't care if they execute me."

"Calm down," Carolyn said, fearful Hank would think he was out of control and terminate the interview. He was probably furious that she was sitting so close to the prisoner again. But he was also monitoring the conversation, and he wouldn't step in unless it was absolutely mandatory. Hank wanted the information as much as she did. "How did you get away from Gilbiati?"

"He left Maria tied up at the house. Told me he'd come back and kill her if I didn't help him get the car back. We went to the shop, but Angel and the rest of the crew had gone home. The man told me not to call Angel because he knew Angel wouldn't tell him what he'd done with the car and he didn't want to tip Angel that they were looking for it. Angel ain't no sweetheart, you know. Take something he wants and he'll kill you and put you in the ground. No telling how many bodies are buried around the shop. Angel tells us not to hurt anyone because he don't want no trouble with the cops, you know. When one of his crew steps out of line, he drops them right on the spot."

"When you say 'they,' Raphael, who are you referring to?"

"How do I know?" he snapped. "These guys weren't local homeys or anything. I've mixed it up with some of the members of La Colonia Chiques."

Carolyn knew the street gang Moreno was describing was a serious menace. The Oxnard police had recently passed an injunction preventing them from congregating in public in a 6.6-mile radius in Colonia, a barrio populated with low-income people, most of them immigrants. Studies had been done which indicated the children in neighborhoods like La Colonia suffered from asthma and obesity because their parents kept them indoors.

Once more, Carolyn fell silent, wanting for Moreno to pick up where he left off. He seemed far more relaxed, and she felt completing the interview shouldn't be a problem.

"The Chiques are mean mothers, man. But these guys . . . they were the worst."

He was rambling. Carolyn redirected him. "Do you know who Dante Gilbiati was working for?"

"I heard him talkin' on the phone to someone. I think his name was Larry. He got more crazier every time he talked to him, slapping me around and yelling that if we didn't find the car, Larry would fucking kill him. He was scared of him, man. And this guy ain't scared of no one. I can take most guys, even guys twice my size. This one I couldn't touch without takin' a bullet or blade."

"Have you ever been in a gang?"

"Not lately," Moreno said, a smile surfacing. "I work alone. Guys in gangs are losers. Gangs are clubs. Thugs spend all their time watching their backs and goin' to funerals. Why I need that shit? I was making good money boosting cars for Angel and I didn't have to watch my back."

The young man in front of her was truly a mixed bag, Carolyn told herself. His clean-cut appearance was marred by his cultivated street demeanor. She wondered how many people he had killed. The way he told it, he hadn't hesitated when he shot the driver of the Ferrari in the face. "What happened at the chop shop?"

"I went through Angel's desk and found the address of the people who bought the Ferrari, a Mr. and Mrs. Rainey." He leaned his head back and his eyes drifted to the ceiling.

"Look at me, Raphael!" Carolyn said, afraid he was going to spot the guns. "We can't stay here all day. Nine people are dead. If we don't find Gilbiati fast, he'll kill a lot more."

He rubbed his eyes, then began speaking again. "We went to these Rainey people's house and found the lady. After her husband bought the Ferrari, man, she saw him driving around with a young chick, so she gets wasted and trades his Ferrari for some paintings. Gilbiati wanted the address of the store, but she said she'd gone to some guy's home. All she remembered was the numbers of the house . . . '1003,' and that the street had the word 'Sea' in it. He roughed her up, then told her he'd come back and kill her if she called the police."

Carolyn blew a strand of hair off her forehead. As cold as it had been when she'd entered the room, her forehead and upper lip were damp with perspiration. Neil had the Ferrari. She had to get it back before Larry and his men killed him. She also knew Hank would have already dispatched a patrol unit to pick up Mrs. Rainey, and talk to her about what had happened with Gilbiati. But Carolyn couldn't conclude the interview yet. The lab had worked up the car and found nothing outside of Moreno's blood. Even if something had been hidden inside the car, she assumed it must be gone by now.

"Gilbiati drives us to 1003 Seaport Avenue," Moreno told her, his eyes narrowing in hatred. "He tells me to break in and boost the car back while he stands watch outside. I know he's gonna kill me and my sister as soon as he gets what he wants 'cause we can ID him." He paused and swallowed. "I crawled through the window, okay? I see a crib with a baby in it, then I see another kid watching cartoons in the other room. I get to the garage without them seeing me. Nothing in there but a white Caddy. What next, I ask myself. I decide if I stay in there long enough, the guy waiting for me might give up and leave."

Moreno's eyes began wandering around the room. He must sense something wasn't right. She had to distract him fast. "Where did you learn to do that? You know, finding a way out of the restraints."

"That's not somethin' you learn, you know," he said, focusing on her face again. "You born that way. It has something to do with the way your bones and muscles work. When I was a kid, people used to tie me up and put me in a suitcase to see if I could escape. My grandfather was able to get out of anything. Some circus people smuggled him out of the country. I made a lot of loot when I was a kid. Once, I had them tie me up with chains, put me in a suitcase, and throw me into the river."

"What happened to the Hartheld family?" Carolyn remembered the gruesome autopsy and crime scene photos. The baby was heartbreaking, but it was the three-year-old girl who'd touched her the most—her beautiful blond hair curled in natural ringlets around her face, skin like a china doll's, her chubby knees, her tiny hands with the pink-painted fingernails, the bloodstained butterfly clips to hold her bangs off her face. She forced the images away, then asked softly, "Did you kill those people, Raphael?"

"No," he shouted, a muscle in his face twitching. "Why would I tell you this stuff if I'd popped them? You still don't believe me, do you? Get the hell outta here. I ain't talkin' to you no more."

"Knock it off," Carolyn said, moving her chair to a safe distance. "Your tough-guy act is bullshit. You can't pull that on me anymore. Whether you realize it or not, you need me as much as I need you. Don't you want to see the man who killed your family brought to justice?"

He fell silent, a sullen expression on his face. "Okay," he said, looking away. "I locked myself in the trunk of the Caddy, deciding I'll wait there till the police showed up. Then I hear gunshots and screaming. Not one . . ." He tapped his finger on the arm of the chair. "*Bang, bang, bang, bang, bang.* Five people in the house, five shots. Christ, he shot a baby. A little baby couldn't ID him. The guy's a psycho, man. He gets off killing people."

"You stayed in the trunk of the Cadillac until the police arrived, right?"

"Shit, yeah," Moreno said. "What else was I supposed to do? If I came out, that Dante guy would have blown me away. My mother was dead. I knew Maria was dead. I only wanted one thing. I wanted to stay alive until I killed him. That's why I let the police arrest me, you know. I needed protection. Now all I need is a way to do what I need to do."

"Why didn't you tell the police the truth when they arrested you? You pleaded guilty to seven counts of second-degree murder. Two other women have now been killed. You might have saved their lives."

"I got to deal with my own shit, man," Moreno said, his

face twisting in anguish. "Do you know what it's like to see your mother like that . . . her head sliced from her body? Her eyes were open when I found her. She was looking right at the bastard when he . . ." His face turned red and the chains began rattling. "He didn't just chop it off, he sliced it like a butcher carving a piece of meat. That's the picture I see when I wake up, when I go to bed. Every damn minute I see it, even when I take a piss. I can't talk, eat, sleep, understand? When people talk to me, it sounds like they're jabbering in a foreign language. The only reason I keep breathing is the chance that I might be able to kill him. Other than that, I don't care. I'm already dead."

Carolyn stood, linking eyes with him. "If we can prove what you just told me," she said, "we may be able to have your conviction overturned. You'll have to plead guilty to killing the driver of the car. That is, if the body surfaces. But that's only one murder term instead of seven. With good time and work time credits, you could conceivably be out in seven years."

"No shit," he said, the muscles in his arms flexing. "Seven years, huh? You think Dante will still be around in seven years?"

Things were winding down. Carolyn was exhausted, but she felt a sense of pride. She had accomplished what seasoned investigators had failed to do, men like Hank Sawyer and Brad Preston, and she had done it without injuring herself or the suspect. Breaking Moreno would add to her reputation. Maybe she would check out the FBI. The job paid a lot more than what she was earning as a probation officer. Out of curiosity, she asked, "Why did you talk to me, Raphael?"

He smiled. "You're my *salir*."

"I'm sorry," she told him. "What does that mean?"

"Come over here and I'll tell you."

Carolyn assumed it meant something like angel or savior. She wasn't afraid of him anymore. If he'd wanted to hurt her, he would have already done it. She walked over and bent down so he could whisper it in her ear.

Hank shoved the microphone away from his face, turning to Mary Stevens. "What the hell is she doing? I ordered her to stay a safe distance away from him. She's practically sitting in his damn lap. Do you know what the word *salir* means?"

Mary shouted, "Ticket out! She's his ticket out!"

Moreno raised his arms near the probation officer's head.

"The restraints are off! Hold your fire!" Hank yelled in panic. "Carolyn's too close. Shit, he's already got her!"

Moreno had Carolyn in a choke hold. Her blouse was ripped open and he had the microphone from the wire positioned near his mouth. "I know you assholes can hear me. If you want your pretty probation officer back alive, get me the hell outta here. I want an unmarked car waiting at the back of the jail in ten minutes."

"I have a shot," one of the marksmen said over the radio.

Moreno jerked his head back, hearing noises on the ceiling. Carolyn grabbed onto his arm and let her body weight fall to the floor, breaking the choke hold.

A single shot was fired. Moreno tumbled backward onto the floor as his blood splattered on the freshly painted white walls.

Chapter 37

Neil stormed out of the restaurant, almost knocking down an elderly couple. He looked back and saw Melody getting up from the table to follow him.

He fumbled in his pocket for the ticket to pick up his car when he looked up and saw the valet had already pulled it up front. Strange, he thought. How did they know when he was going to leave? Then he saw a tall, lanky man, with long dark hair, and wearing a brown leather jacket, yank the valet out of the driver's seat and force him to the ground. The guy must be trying to steal his Ferrari. Acting on impulse, Neil rushed toward the assailant.

To the left of his field of vision, Neil saw a large, blond man in a blue parka a few feet away. "Leo, the woman's got a gun," the man in the parka shouted, raising his right arm and bracing it with his left.

Neil froze, staring at the man's gun as it shifted to a target behind him. When the gun fired, he thought he'd been shot. Throwing himself onto the ground, Neil glanced underneath the car and saw the terrified eyes of the valet peering out at him. Adrenaline coursed through his veins. He heard the car door close. If a man named Leo tried to drive off in the car, the valet would be run over. Maybe Neil, too!

Any minute, Neil expected a rain of bullets to sear their way into his back.

Melody!

She'd been only a few steps behind him as they'd left the restaurant. Another gunshot resonated in his ears. He pushed himself to his feet just as the man in the blue parka was propelled backward, then sank lifeless to the ground. Spotting Melody over the roof of the car, Neil saw her sitting awkwardly, holding her hand over her stomach. Blood was gushing out through her fingers. Her face was contorted in pain, but he was certain he heard her call his name. He dropped to the ground again and crawled over to her, using the Ferrari to provide cover.

"It's okay, baby," Neil said, cradling her head in his arms. "You're going to be all right. Just hang in there until the paramedics get here." Tears stung his eyes. He gritted his teeth and placed his hand over the wound, then stroked her pale blond hair off her forehead. She didn't move or speak, but her eyes were open and fixed on him. "Hold on, Melody," he said. "Once they get you to the hospital, the doctors will fix you up and you'll be fine."

Neil wasn't aware she owned a gun, but he did remember her telling him she had trained to become an FBI agent when she was younger. After what Melody had told him inside the restaurant, he doubted if he would ever truly know her. That is, if she survived.

The exact sequence of events was muddled. Melody must have seen the man in the blue parka pointing a gun at him. If she hadn't fired, the assailant would have shot him.

"I . . . love . . . you," Melody said, her eyes closing and her head falling to one side.

Raphael Moreno was dead.

Elbowing her way through the SWAT team and jail deputies, Carolyn stormed toward Hank, taking him by the arm. "We have to get to the Chart House," she said, her blouse ripped and her clothes splattered with blood. "Neil must be there with the Ferrari. I forgot, I forgot. Melody told me they were going there."

They retrieved their personal items and guns from the lockers on the ground floor of the jail, then raced out to Hank's police unit, leaving Mary behind to handle the aftermath of Carolyn's disastrous interview with Moreno. She had extracted the truth, but her recklessness and pride had cost a man his life. The autopsy photos had pushed him beyond reason. Why had she let him lure her so close? She should never have dropped her guard.

When Carolyn and Hank were en route, he told her to check his gym bag in the backseat for a T-shirt. She removed her torn blouse and pulled a white T-shirt over her head, then slipped on her shoulder holster and weapon. Just then, the dispatcher advised them of a report of shots fired in front of the Chart House restaurant.

"Unit two-twelve, will you be responding?"

"Affirmative, we're two miles away," Hank said, slapping the portable siren on top of his unmarked car.

"Witness said the shooting involves a red Ferrari," the dispatcher continued. "Thought this might be the vehicle you've been looking for. I'll get some units rolling for backup."

"Keep them out of the area until I advise," Hank told her. "Station one," he added, "this is a direct order. Move them into position, but do not, I repeat, do not allow them to approach the restaurant. The same holds true for fire and ambulance."

"Have you lost your mind?" Carolyn yelled over the shrill of the siren, terrified for her brother. "They may have shot Neil. Why would you tell her not to send backup units and the paramedics?" She grabbed the radio and shoved it in his face. "Rescind your order. My brother may be lying there bleeding to death."

"There's more at stake here than your brother," Hank said,

knocking her hand away. "You don't know what we're dealing with." He squealed into the parking area at the Chart House.

Carolyn saw an unknown man with long hair in a brown jacket, seated in the driver's seat of Neil's Ferrari. The valet was crawling toward the front of the restaurant.

"Block the Ferrari, Hank!" Carolyn shouted, whipping her gun out of her shoulder holster and releasing the safety. "Neil could be in it, on the floor."

The detective drove over the curb, smashing into the front section of the red car. Carolyn flung open her door only inches away from Leo Danforth.

Bullets whizzed over Carolyn's head as she leaped out of the car. Other rounds rattled off from multiple positions behind her. She couldn't be sure, but there had to be eight or ten men and at least four cars.

They had driven into an ambush. Because the police car sat higher than the Ferrari, she could see the man had a gun in his right hand. "Police!" she yelled, training her service revolver at Danforth's head. "Drop the gun or I'll shoot."

As if in slow motion, the man turned to her, his eyes dilated and set. As he rotated his shoulders, she could see frame by frame, the black gunmetal emerging from the right side of his body. Her finger floating just above the trigger, Carolyn squeezed her hand and fired. Fragments of his skull drifted toward the window and dashboard. Tears gushed from her eyes as she opened her fingers and the gun tumbled to the ground.

Carolyn stood in shock, her arms limp at her side. Hank entered the passenger side, grunting as he pulled the lifeless man over the console and onto the pavement. He yelled at her, "Get in the car, Carolyn! You're going to get shot."

She heard Hank, but his words didn't register. A bullet ricocheted off the top of the Ferrari. Hank's attention was diverted by another man rushing toward the front of the car. The detective stood and returned fire. "Save yourself and the car," he yelled over his shoulder at Carolyn, dropping the shooter five feet away.

Neil was alive. After she opened the door and entered the Ferrari, she saw him bending over a blond woman on the ground. It had to be Melody Asher. Gunfire came from the green Jaguar and a white Range Rover parked sideways in the street behind her. A tall, black man was crossing the parking lot, with what appeared to be an assault rifle. Her eyes panned in front of her—more cars, more guns, more men.

She became alert, feeling warm liquid seeping into her clothing. She was sitting in the dead man's blood. Slamming the gearshift into reverse, Carolyn saw another armed male snaking his way through the parking lot a few feet from her. Throwing the car into first, she maneuvered around Hank's police unit. She drove back over a curb, scraping the undercarriage, and made a sharp right. In the distance, a wood fence separated the parking lot from the alley. She blasted through it, then sped down the narrow road.

Hearing sirens, she looked in the rearview mirror and saw police cars merging onto the scene. She turned right onto Vista Del Mar, thinking the safest place to go was the police station. To reach the station three miles away, she needed to take the 101 Freeway south. When the entrance to the freeway on Seward Avenue came up, the Range Rover suddenly appeared in the left lane next to her, blocking her from moving over to enter onto the southbound ramp. The Jaguar was directly behind.

A bearded, slender man thrust his upper torso out of the car window and yelled at her. "Pull over," he said, waving a gun. "All I want is the fucking car, lady. Is it worth dying for?"

Carolyn panicked, afraid they were going to run her into the embankment on her right. Then the road opened at the ramp leading to the 101 Freeway north, and she downshifted to second and took the sharp corner at thirty, losing the

Range Rover. She'd never driven a high-performance car like this Ferrari. It required real physical strength. The muscles in her arms were trembling from exertion. Weaving in and out of lanes, she could now see the California coastline approaching on her left.

She glanced at the instrument panel and saw the top speed was two hundred miles per hour. She was certain she could outrun the Jaguar if she pushed the Ferrari to the limit.

As the needle on the speedometer passed the hundred mark, she realized that Hank had been protecting more than her life when he told her to leave. The killers wanted the car, not her. What in God's name could be inside that would be worth all this bloodshed? If it had been a large parcel of narcotics, the lab would have already found it.

"Shit," Carolyn said, realizing she didn't have a phone. She had to advise the police that she was being pursued. Most of the expensive cars had voice-activated phones. People couldn't drive a car this fast and hold a cell phone to their ears. Seeing a row of buttons on the rearview mirror, she started randomly pressing them. A mechanical voice came on and said, "Ready." Checking the rearview mirror, she could see the headlights of the Jaguar fading.

She was about to order the phone to call 911 when she realized it was ringing. She hit the button, hoping it was Hank. "Hank?" she said.

"Ms. Sullivan, I presume," a male voice said, the last syllable deepening. "What exactly are you doing with my car?"

"Who is this?"

"Let's just say I'm a friend, someone who's concerned for your safety."

"Liar," she shot out. "I know there's something valuable inside this thing. I had a long talk with Raphael Moreno. He told me everything. I know you're responsible for killing those innocent people." More lives had now been lost because of this evil man. It had to be the man Moreno called

Larry. "You're never going to get this car back, Larry. I'll destroy it before I let you have it. The game is over."

"Have it your way."

She could hear him breathing heavily. He might sound calm, but he had to be furious that things hadn't turned out the way he'd planned. The men that hadn't died in the shootout would be dead as soon as he got his hands on them.

"You're a foolish woman, Carolyn," Lawrence Van Buren continued. "If something happens to you, who will take care of John and Rebecca? Your daughter is a beautiful young girl. My men picked them up an hour ago. I hope they control themselves. They loved following her over the past few days. Rebecca shouldn't wear such seductive clothing."

"You sick bastard." Her rage was so intense, she almost lost control of the vehicle as she switched lanes to avoid slower traffic. "I'm going to track you down and kill you with my bare hands. Don't you dare touch my children, understand?" Her finger moved to end the call, so she could dial her house and confirm John and Rebecca were safe. Then she hesitated. She felt as if she was back in the classroom at St. Mary's with Sister Catherine giving them their weekly lecture on the temptations of the Devil. He was bluffing, she told herself. Everything he said was more than likely a lie. After Moreno, she knew better than to trust a killer, particularly one this vicious.

His men had made a mess of things. Now he was taking control. Before she forged ahead, however, she reminded herself of the things Moreno had told her. They had somehow managed to find out where he lived and beheaded his mother. She had no choice but to take the voice on the phone seriously. The children were home alone. His men could have followed her from the courthouse. She couldn't end the call, not when she was negotiating for her children's lives. Her vision blurred. The car veered into the other lane.

John and Rebecca might already be dead.

If that was true, she couldn't bear to hear it. They'd murdered Moreno's sister before he reached the Hartfield house. He had been right when he decided the only course of action left was to save himself so he could avenge his mother's and sister's deaths. The picture of Moreno's mother appeared in her mind—her head several inches from her body. What if they beheaded John or Rebecca? She begged God to save her children.

Carolyn forced herself to think rationally. The urge to turn around and rush to her children was overwhelming, but the risks were too high. If she took the wrong action, Rebecca and John would die. What if the man had been lying and they didn't know where she lived? She couldn't take a chance of leading them to her house.

All she could do was keep driving. She may have outrun the man in the Jaguar, but that didn't mean his cohorts wouldn't head her off from a different direction. Her T-shirt was soaked with perspiration. She leaned closer to the windshield, trying to focus farther down the highway. When she didn't see anything, she hit the buttons for the electronic windows and breathed deeply, desperate for fresh air. She was traveling over 120 miles per hour. Heat was rising from the engine into the interior and she could smell the gas fumes. The wind sounded like a hurricane.

Everything was too real.

Carolyn had been in tense situations before and they'd all resolved themselves. Her gut told her this time might be different.

As if he could read her mind, Van Buren said, "The only way you and your children are going to come out of this alive, Carolyn, is if we make a deal. It isn't really necessary to die. I have men coming from Santa Barbara. It won't be long before they intersect you. I know you're approaching Carpinteria."

She wasn't surprised that he knew her location. The car

must be equipped with a GPS system. But if this was true, why had it taken Van Buren so long to find it after it was stolen by Raphael? An image flashed in her mind. When she'd looked down from Hank's police car into the Ferrari, she'd seen the man bending down with something cradled in his left hand. The gun was in his right. He may have been holding some kind of tracking device.

Carolyn began scraping the walls with her fingers, trying to keep her focus on the road at the same time she attempted to disable the GPS device. Not finding anything, she recalled seeing GPS bracelets that were manufactured for young children. If the device was that small, how could she find it without wrecking the car? She couldn't reach under the seat where it had more than likely been tossed. Taking her eyes off the road could prove fatal.

"I'm listening," she told Van Buren, her fingers tightening on the steering wheel.

"I know all about you, Carolyn." He paused for effect. "A probation officer . . . what a miserable job. I bet you work nights and weekends to make what . . . less than a hundred grand a year. That's a fraction of what I'm going to offer you."

Carolyn saw flashing lights behind her. Maybe Hank had been killed and the police mistakenly thought the killer had fled in the Ferrari. She couldn't tell which department the pursuing vehicles were from, as they were too far away. They could be highway patrol officers chasing her for speeding. Should she stop and pull off the road? How could she be certain they wouldn't open fire on her?

"Did you hear me?" the man on the phone prompted her.

"I heard you," Carolyn shot out. "No deal."

"Money isn't everything," he said. "What kind of price tag would you put on your children's lives?"

The most crucial question was if his men had really picked up John and Rebecca. He was shrewd, playing on her emotions to distract her from thinking straight. How could he have known that his people would fail and she would end up fleeing with the Ferrari?

Carolyn tried to assess her options. None of them seemed viable without tragic results. Giving him the car would be suicide. Why would he need to pay her when he could simply kill her? Turning it in to the police might cause him to take the lives of her children. The only way to stop this diabolical maniac was to eliminate the problem—get rid of the car. Maybe that was what Hank was trying to tell her during the shoot-out at the restaurant.

"Two million," Van Buren said. "Bring me the Ferrari and I'll pay you two million in cash. No one will ever have to know. You can move to another state and build a new life for yourself and your children. Put the money in the right investments and you'll never have to work again."

"I'm hanging up the phone."

"I'm remotely detonating an explosive device sixty seconds after you disconnect. As your friend and future business partner, I suggest that you stay on the line."

Carolyn's mind was reeling. What he said couldn't be true! A moment ago he was willing to pay her two million to bring him the car. Blowing it up didn't make sense. She asked herself if the object she'd seen in the man's hand had been a remote detonator. Another bluff, possibly? Folding now would give him the upper hand. She had to maintain her position. "I don't believe you," she said.

"I'm a businessman," Van Buren told her. "For me to conclude my business deal, you must return the car to me immediately. I can't allow it to fall into the wrong hands and I refuse to barter with someone in the sale of my own property."

"So, if you can't have it, no one can," Carolyn said. "Is that what you're saying?"

"We're running out of time," Van Buren said, his voice sparking with tension.

Carolyn took her foot off the accelerator. It was hard to think at this speed. The approaching taillights slowed. The fog had rolled in and she could no longer see what she had thought to be police units behind her, but she knew she couldn't allow anyone to get close. If the man followed through on his threat to detonate a bomb, the officers could be killed. She pressed her back into the seat cushion and gripped the steering wheel with all her might, pressing her foot down on the gas pedal. The needle moved to 140. She felt as if she were in the cockpit of a fighter plane. The car didn't even shimmy. The noise from the powerful engine was deafening.

Carolyn shouted, "If there's really a bomb in here, why didn't the police find it?"

"I need your answer now, Carolyn," Van Buren said, pressuring her.

The rooftops of million-dollar homes rushed by just outside of Santa Barbara. How large a bomb could fit inside a sports car, and how many people could it kill? She didn't know about such things. At the lab, the techs hadn't been looking for explosives. A car bomb didn't fit with the murder of two women by lethal injections. With everything backed up for the holidays, the lab had probably been pushing one car out after the other or simply too busy drooling over the Ferrari to figure out what was inside. "Tell me where you want me to bring the car."

Van Buren told her he would meet her at the Santa Barbara Airport in fifteen minutes. Once Carolyn agreed, he disconnected.

As tears streaked down her cheeks, she pictured her children's faces. Arriving home late the night before, she had gone into Rebecca's room and kissed her on the cheek while she lay sleeping. Heading to John's room, she'd knelt beside the bed and stroked his forehead, whispering that she was sorry they didn't have more time together.

It took her several frantic attempts to get the damn phone

to dial Hank's cell number. Because it was voice activated, she had to modulate her words perfectly or it wouldn't work. Controlling her voice was difficult when she was hysterical. As soon as he picked up, she said. "Get someone over to my house! They say they have my children!"

"Who?" Hank said. "Where are you?"

"Don't talk, just listen. I've been talking to the man Moreno told me about on the built-in phone inside the car—Larry. He said he'll be at the Santa Barbara Airport in fifteen minutes to take possession of the Ferrari. He says his men picked up John and Rebecca. He even called them by their names and said his men had been following them for days."

"Van Buren," Hank exclaimed. "The FBI informed us that Interpol has been tracking an arms dealer named Lawrence Van Buren. They believe he's shipping nuclear material to North Korea inside exotic cars. That's what must be inside the Ferrari."

She shouted, "My kids, Hank! That's all that is important to me right now."

"Hold on," he said. She heard him on the radio informing the dispatcher to send several units to her home. "Done."

"So what he said was true. I'm a rolling bomb," Carolyn said, the reality setting in. "He says he can detonate it remotely. How much damage can it do?"

"I don't know," Hank said, almost as panicked as she was. "I'm not a nuclear physicist. The FBI told us it was possible to make a nuke the size of a briefcase. The engine cavity of the Ferrari is pretty big. I'm sorry I put you in this mess."

"A nuclear bomb!" Carolyn said, horrified.

"I'll have to call in the military," Hank continued. "If you're approaching Santa Barbara, you're not that far from the air force base at Vandenberg. Stay on the line, I'm going to trace the call in case we lose the connection."

"Hang up, Hank," she said, her fear raging. "I want to hear my kid's voices. After you arrest Van Buren, check the coastline close to El Capitan. Also, notify CHP and any other law enforcement agency in the area to keep their distance in case he detonates the bomb."

Before he could say anything else, she disconnected and told the phone to dial her home number. John picked up on the first ring. "Thank God you're okay. Where's your sister?"

"She's over at Lucy's. You sound—"

"Call and have Paul or Isobel walk Rebecca home." Carolyn tried to sound normal. "Lock all the doors and windows and wait for the police. They should be there by the time your sister is back. You're going to have to be strong, honey, not just for yourself, but for your Rebecca. I love you more than anything."

"Mom, please . . . why are you saying these things?"

"I can't explain. I don't have time. Something came up at work. Everything will be fine. I just wanted to call and tell you that I love you."

"I love you, too, Mom."

"Give your sister a hug for me and tell her I love her. I have to say good-bye now, sweetheart."

She sobbed as she reached up and pushed the button to end the call. The worst was over. Her panic subsided; she was resolved. In a strange way, she felt as if her life had been counting down to this moment. She'd heard that a person existed to perform one simple act—to turn right instead of left, preventing a fatal accident, to smile at a deeply depressed person and give them the will to continue living, to place a few dollars into the outstretched hands of a starving beggar.

Carolyn knew the exact spot for the one act she may have been placed on earth to perform. She saw the signs for the Santa Barbara Airport and continued driving. She didn't have long. When Van Buren realized she had failed to make the turn leading to the airport, he would detonate the bomb. In a matter of hours, she'd been responsible for two deaths. First Moreno, then a short time later, she'd shot and killed a stranger. The sights and smells of his death were all around her.

She could feel a substance sticking to the back of her legs, and knew it was his blood. What disturbed her the most was that she had fired instinctively, as if taking a human life was insignificant. Had it truly been self-defense, or had she responded because of what had happened earlier with Moreno? She could have ducked, tried to shoot the gun out of his hand, or aimed at another spot other than his head. Her actions went against everything she believed as a Catholic. Her body shook as she prayed for God's forgiveness, and for the courage she now needed to save lives instead of take them.

Carolyn saw the cliffs up ahead. She believed the bomb could be defused in the salty water, or at least, it might render the detonator useless. If not, the casualties would be minimized.

She had made her decision, said her good-byes. She would fight to survive, but she was ready. The stretch of road she was traveling on was deserted: no cars, no houses, no buildings. Somehow it was as if God had cleared the way to receive her.

Carolyn yanked the steering wheel to the left, gunning the engine and driving across three lanes. A moment later, she was airborne. As soon as the Ferrari cleared the cliffs, she killed the ignition and breathed in the exquisite silence. She felt weightless and free, as if she had sailed straight into the world beyond death.

Before the car made its descent toward the water, Carolyn removed her left hand from the steering wheel and grabbed onto the door handle. Throwing her body weight against the door, she reached with her other hand for her mother's silver cross, clasping it in her palm just as her head slammed into the dashboard.

Chapter 38

Neil was waiting in the emergency room at Methodist Hospital with six other people. He was perplexed that nothing appeared to be wrong with them, outside of a kid with a runny nose. Why would someone take their kid to the emergency room because they had a cold? After the young black woman beside him finally stopped talking on her cell phone, he asked, "I don't mean to be rude. But why are you here?"

"I have a headache," she said, not looking as if she were in any pain.

"Maybe you should stop talking on your cell phone so much," he said. "Either that, or take a couple of aspirin."

A small man dressed in a blue nurse's shirt came out to speak with Neil. "It will take us about ten minutes to complete the tests; then you can see Miss Asher, but only for a short time. You can see her on the fifth floor, where they'll be prepping her for surgery."

The nurse pushed him aside. When Neil turned, he saw a group of hospital personnel rushing toward the electronic doors. Two paramedics were pushing a gurney. A young man was screaming in agony. As they passed, he saw the man's left leg was missing below the knee. What he assumed was the severed limb was packed in ice beside him. Neil collected himself and headed to the cafeteria to get a cup of coffee.

Melody had suffered a gunshot wound to the abdomen. Neil had held her hand in the ambulance, terrified that she wouldn't survive. She'd be going into surgery to remove the bullet, as well as a portion of her damaged intestines, within the hour.

A tall, dark-haired man walked up to him as he was waiting for the elevator. "Are you Neil Sullivan?" Dr. Graham asked, his voice laden with emotion. "You don't know me, but I saw your picture in the newspaper. Detective Sawyer called me. He said you were with my daughter when she was shot. How bad is she?"

"She'll survive," Neil said, thinking the man was a sleazy reporter. "She told me her father was dead. Pretty nasty trick to get a story."

"I'm not a newsman," Dr. Graham told him, his face laced with concern. "I flew in from New York. I was at her house the other night, but I'm not surprised that she didn't tell you."

Neil wasn't certain what to think. The man sounded sincere, though, and Melody had told her share of lies. "I don't know what to believe anymore."

The elevator door opened, and he followed Neil down the corridor to the fifth-floor surgical center. Before they stepped up to the counter at the nurses' station, Dr. Graham took his arm. "It doesn't matter if you believe me, she's my daughter."

A stern-looking female nurse directed them to the last cubicle. Dr. Graham lingered behind as Neil parted the curtains and stepped inside. Melody's eyes were closed, and her face was alarmingly pale. A woman in the bed beside her was moaning.

By all rights, he should be the one about to go under the knife. Melody had fired at the man rushing toward him and taken the bullet that was intended for him. He touched her shoulder. Her eyes blinked opened. "Neil?"

"Yes, it's me," he said, his voice almost a whisper. "How do you feel?"

"With my hands, dummy," she said, then grimaced in pain. "Fuck, I think I'm going to die."

"Don't talk like that," Neil told her, squeezing her hand. "The doctor said you'll be fine. All you have to do is get through the operation."

No matter how tough she talked, the glamorous veneer was gone and she looked childlike and vulnerable. "You saved my life, Melody."

"All I did was react," she told him, running her tongue over her dry lips. "I had a gun, so I used it." She released his hand and turned her head away.

"I care about you."

"Sure you do," she said, rotating back toward him. "I'm not scared of dying. Death may not be that bad. Isn't that what you were looking for the other night?"

Neil was stung by her sharp remarks. "I was wrong, Melody. No one should take his own life."

"Death is death," Melody said, pausing to catch her breath. "You care about me, huh? All I am is a good piece of ass with a fat bank account. That's why you stuck around for so long, isn't it? Then you were banging a schoolteacher behind my back. You were going to dump me and marry her."

Neil's mind was spinning. His love for Laurel had been an illusion. She had slept with a student. She'd also failed to tell him that she was still married. Maybe Laurel had been the piece of ass instead of Melody. He had her all wrong. She took a bullet for him. The wild party girl was just a protective shell that had finally cracked. He bent down and kissed her forehead. "Once you're back on your feet, we'll be together. Think you can handle that?"

"We'll see," Melody said, her eyes closing.

He walked out and sat down in a chair beside Dr. Graham. "You can go in," Neil said, "but I think she's too doped up to talk."

"Thank you," he said, extending his hand. "Michael Graham. I practiced medicine years ago. The doctor let me look at her chart. Abdominal wounds are extremely painful, but I'm fairly certain she'll do well in surgery."

The nurse came in and told Neil he had a phone call. He followed him to the nurses' station. Dr. Graham walked toward Melody.

"This is Detective Mary Stevens," the voice said. "There's been an accident involving your sister."

Standing beside his daughter, Dr. Graham felt tears roll down his cheek. He never imagined how much he needed to have Jessica back in his life, to be a father again, to love again. The recovery was going to be slow and painful. If she allowed him, he would take care of her every step of the way. Time was suspended as he stood there in silence. He'd missed most of her childhood—birthday parties, Christmas mornings, graduation, and watching his little girl blossom into a woman. The years to follow would be their time together as father and daughter. No matter how long they'd been apart, there was nothing now to stand between them.

Dr. Graham got up and went to the bathroom, soaking a washcloth in cold water. He returned, then gently stroked her face. "Jessica, Jessica . . ." he said, "Daddy is here."

Her eyes opened, connecting with his. Although filled with pain, these were the eyes of his beautiful little girl. "How did you—"

"Stay quiet," he said, interrupting her. "Save your energy, you're going to need it for the surgery." He continued to move the moist rag around her face. Her chin moved up as she closed her eyes. He saw a hint of pleasure. "I just wanted to tell you that I'm here to help you, Jessica. I'll never leave you again."

"Thanks, Dad," she said in a whisper.

FBI agents Gray and Tushinsky had contacted Vandenberg Air Force Base and arranged to have a fleet of SH-2G Super Seasprite helicopters on the crash scene within fifteen minutes.

Hank's car screamed down the 101 Freeway heading toward Santa Barbara. He wanted desperately to talk with Carolyn, but there was no way to contact her again, since she hadn't given him enough time to trace her call. Her purse and cell phone were sitting beside him on the seat. When they reached the restaurant, they'd bailed out so fast, she'd left them behind.

Trying to save Carolyn by telling her to take the car was stupid. He knew that the men were after the Ferrari. In the heat of the moment, he'd gotten her out of the line of fire and put her into, as she had called it, a rolling bomb.

The dispatcher's voice blared out of his console, "Unit two-twelve, do you copy?"

"Ten-four."

"CHP reports that a red car was seen catapulting into the ocean just north of Goleta. What's your ETA?"

His hands shook on the microphone. He should have explained to Carolyn that just because the car might have nuclear material in it didn't mean it was explosive. She'd sacrificed herself for what she'd thought would save the lives of innocent people.

"Unit two-twelve, copy?"

"My ETA's twenty."

Through the darkness, he could see the roadblock in the distance. In the sky, four choppers were flying in circles, their large beams of light zigzagging across the cliffs and into the water. The trail of cars came to a stop. His head dropped. The situation was too similar to the death of his brother. Andy had been out drinking and partying with his friends. A thirty-year-old surfer, Andy had skin that looked like leather and he smoked his first joint before breakfast. They'd built a bonfire on the beach. When Andy had left, speeding to show off his new Corvette, his tire had blown, causing him to lose control and drive off a cliff.

Hank had to make certain the military didn't call off the search for Carolyn. Their priority would be to recover the car.

Several men in military uniforms holding M-16s were signaling for the cars to cross to the opposite side of the highway and turn back.

"I'm Detective Hank Sawyer, of the Ventura Police Department," he said, pulling out his badge and draping it over his belt.

"I'm sorry, sir, we were told not to let anyone through, even police officers. We're evacuating the area. Move on, please. It's for your own safety."

Hank's frustrations ripped through his gut. He held back getting out of the car and causing a scene. Taking a deep breath, he told himself the soldier was just doing his job. He reluctantly drove away.

After his brother's death, he had familiarized himself with ocean currents. Andy had been caught in an upwelling. Along California and Oregon, warmer water pulls surf away from shore, then cold water moves up to take its place. These strong, cold currents could move bodies miles from their point of entry. The water pulled them into deeper waters from north to south along the coast. If he was lucky, it would dump Carolyn back onto the shore through underwater canals. In the Ventura area, there were only about three spots to look. The rescue teams from Vandenberg might not know where they were.

What was he going to do now? He couldn't sit back and

leave Carolyn's fate in the hands of strangers. They didn't care about her. They were military—their primary objective was national security. He refused to abandon her, as he had his brother.

"Station two," he said into the microphone, "get in touch with the rescue party from Vandenberg. Tell them to check near Naples Beach. I'm heading there now."

Five miles down, he pulled off to the shoulder and stepped out onto the roadway. Carefully crossing the highway, he reached the cliff leading to the dark ocean. A gust of wind shot up the rocky hillside. He stepped back, realizing the risk he was taking. A fall could kill him.

His last image of Carolyn flashed in his mind. When she had glanced back toward him, he had seen fear and confusion in her eyes. Her beautiful dark hair had been framed inside the backdrop of the red Ferrari as she sped away.

Was she already dead? It was his direct order that set the events in motion. Her children would be motherless. How could he live with himself?

His decision was made.

He couldn't wait for the rescue team to respond. In a situation like this, seconds could save a life. He stretched out his right leg, then planted it on the first of many rocks. He shone his flashlight downward, becoming light-headed. Although he had done everything possible to conquer it, he suffered from vertigo. He had fifty feet of cliffs, rocks, and sand to navigate. Fortunately, he could see an opening. Slowly he moved one foot after another, trying not to look down. Had he lost his mind? In the distance, he heard the whirling blades of a helicopter.

Hearing voices in the street above, he knew that they had found him. Looking up, he saw the flashlights pointing at him. His right foot slipped on the loose gravel. Reaching back, he tried to regain his balance. It was no use. His body slid down the rocks. He went airborne, crashing into the ocean. The waves tossed him around before sucking him toward the deeper water. Trying to find his footing, he discovered his leg was injured. He could see the flickering of the moon as the water lapped over his face. He knew that struggling would only deplete his energy. Gasping for each breath, he let the water take him.

The strong upwelling carried him rapidly down the coast. This was it, he thought, the sins of his life were finally catching up to him. Then his back hit sand. He'd washed into a canal created by a storm drain. The erosion from the runoffs had created a crevasse that led deep into the sea. In high tide, the water was forced toward land. He rolled over to find the beach. He could see the moon lighting up white water as it rushed in. Small sand crabs were digging their way back into the sand with each wave.

Out of the corner of his eye, he saw a piece of metal. Supporting himself with his hand, he reached out with his other and touched what looked like the door of the Ferrari. Once on his knees, he could see something else floating nearby. Shaking his head, he attempted to clear the stinging salt water from his eyes. It was a body. He struggled to stand, limping a few feet over until he reached her.

Carolyn wasn't breathing.

Pain shot down his left leg as he tried to get her to the shore. He struggled in the ebbing shallow tide. Supporting Carolyn's back, he placed his index finger and thumb over her nose as he began ventilating. Endless moments later, water spewed out of her mouth and she began breathing.

"Hang in there, Carolyn, I'm going to get help."

"Don't leave me, Hank," she choked out. "I don't want to die alone."

"Then I'll have to carry you."

He reached down and picked her up, cradling her shoulders and legs in his arms. The FBI's helicopter was flying down the coast directly at them. Walking in the wet unstable sand, his left leg gave way and he fell. The surf washed up and swept Carolyn out of his arms.

"Don't let me go," she yelled, holding on to his hand as the water fought his grip.

The helicopter was directly over them, its light illuminating the stretch of beach. His fingertips no longer had the pressure of Carolyn's hand. She'd slipped back into the sea. Hank crawled toward the water. A wave crashed to the sand, consuming him. He flopped around like a rag doll, until it deposited him back on the beach.

Hank looked up at the barrel of a machine gun. "Stay still, sir."

"I found the driver of the car," Hank yelled, frantic. "S-she was here. The water took her away. You have to find her!"

"Spread out and search for a female body," the officer ordered the group of five men.

Very soon, a voice rang out: "Got her."

Epilogue

Six weeks later

It was a miracle that Carolyn didn't die in the crash. Her movements were still limited. She'd suffered a severe concussion, a broken collarbone, and had fractured her left ankle. Alex Pauldine at CSI told her that the impact damage suggested the Ferrari had slammed into a rocky protrusion halfway down the cliff and flipped in the air. The car entered the ocean tail-first, ripping off the driver's door which Carolyn had managed to open. She never saw the Ferrari once she was in the water. The crash had thrown her away from the wreckage. Fortunately, Carolyn was able to survive by floating with the currents. She would never forget Hank's face as he rescued her.

Carolyn was dressed and waiting for Hank to pick her up and drive her to the office for the first time since that terrible night. Rebecca and John had already left for school. She looked over at the flowers Paul had sent her, picking up the card and reading his note. He'd done everything he possibly could to help her and the kids, but he had secrets. Her personality was built on integrity; she couldn't be with a man who didn't share the same values. Paul hadn't been honest with her about his past. Melody had woken her up to that unfortunate reality.

Carolyn had fulfilled her promise to Rebecca and given Paul another chance. They had gone out to dinner and things had gone well. Two days later, a package containing three CDs from Melody had arrived with more videos of Paul having sex with young women she assumed had been his students.

Their relationship was over.

Carolyn had spent six miserable weeks in a wheelchair. At her next visit, the doctor was going to remove the cast on her foot, and he had told her she should have full use of her left arm and shoulder again.

Hearing a car pull into her driveway, she struggled on her crutches to maneuver the door open. Hank got out of the van and limped toward Carolyn, a broad smile on his face. "Come on, old man," she yelled.

"Who, me?" he said, looking behind him. "I'm not old, just beaten. You ready?"

"Absolutely," Carolyn said with a voice of certainty.

"What's going on with Melody?" he asked once they were on the road. "The man who shot her died a few days ago. I talked to the DA this morning and confirmed they aren't going to file criminal charges against her. If she hadn't moved everything out of her house before we arrived with the search warrant, we might have been able to charge her with illegal electronic surveillance and withholding evidence in a homicide. We have no proof that the footage of the Goodwin murder was made by Melody. I guess she recorded the video she sent you with Paul in it from another computer, or she didn't film the murder. These days, there're cameras everywhere." He stopped and pulled out a toothpick. "At least she did the right thing by her father. You said Neil told you that once she's fully recovered, she's going to fly back to New York and testify in front of the medical board. Maybe the poor guy will get his license back."

Carolyn said, "You haven't heard the latest, then."

"No, I've been tied up on that stabbing case."

"Some of the documents she showed me were forged, Hank. She legally changed her name to Melody Asher, all right, but she didn't have the woman's consent. The New York authorities have reopened the case, but the real Melody Asher hasn't been located. There's no record of her having married and taken up residence in Israel. Scary, huh?"

"She may have killed that girl," Hank said, incredulous. "God, Carolyn, is Neil still seeing her? You've got to knock some sense into his head."

"I'm working on it," Carolyn told him. "Neil's stubborn, Hank."

When Hank parked at the government center, Carolyn's eyes drifted to the windows of the jail. Moreno was dead, but there would be other violent criminals. She wouldn't push her luck next time. It was a strange feeling being back at the building. Things had changed. She had killed a man; she would never be the same. The best way to put things behind her, though, was to get back to work. She could still accomplish some good in this world. She hobbled into Brad's office and took a seat in a chair in front of his desk.

"Welcome back, baby," he said, picking up a large stack of case files. "Ready to get back to work?"

"Do I look ready?"

He laughed. "You look better than when Hank dragged your ass out of the water."

Brad had been a godsend. She didn't know if she could have made it without him. He'd spent many days and nights sitting in a chair next to her hospital bed. What she had to decide was whether he sincerely cared for her or was merely an opportunist. Now that Paul was out of the picture, it had been the perfect time for him to make his move.

"Do you think they'll convict Van Buren?"

"The case seems to be shaping up," Carolyn said, resting the crutches against the adjacent chair. "I spoke to one of the federal prosecutors yesterday to find out when I have to testify. They caught a break. One of Van Buren's men rolled over and agreed to testify against him. They found Dante Gilbiati's body, the one who killed Moreno's family and the

Hartfields, in a grave at the Shady Oaks Cemetery. You know, that old place where the kids used to congregate on Halloween."

Lawrence Van Buren had been arrested by the FBI and charged with treason, one count of first-degree murder as to Dante Gilbiati, and seven counts of conspiracy to commit murder, as well as murder for hire in the deaths of Laurel Goodwin and Suzanne Porter. He was awaiting trial in a federal court.

Brad made a paper airplane and sailed it at her, flashing a playful smile. "When are you going to be able to fool around?"

"You're disgusting," she said, scowling as she plucked the folded paper out of her hair. "All you ever talk about is sex and race cars. We're at work, Brad. If we're going to keep seeing each other, we need to keep a low profile."

"Don't you know when someone is joking? Oh, they said on the news that Interpol arrested that female assassin. What's her name?"

"Claire Mellinger," Carolyn answered, leaning forward. "When did you hear that?"

"On the radio as I drove to work today. Fascinating, really. Seems she's in the advanced stages of multiple sclerosis. They caught her when she showed up for treatment at a clinic in Cannes, France. She has a kid and a husband. They say she can barely walk. How could she have killed anyone if she was in that bad of a condition? Because of the lingerie thing and the motorcycle outfit, we all thought the killer was a man."

"Precisely what she wanted." Carolyn was relieved Mellinger had been apprehended, but elements of the case intrigued her. "Charley Young thinks she was controlling the symptoms of her disease by taking a smaller dose of the same concoction she injected in Laurel Goodwin and Suzanne Porter. Remember, one of the elements found in the two bodies was a drug used to treat MS. Charley said the heroin and cocaine probably helped her to ease the pain and stay alert."

Carolyn's mind turned to thoughts of her mother. As per Marie Sullivan's request, until her death, her father's work in solving the Riemann hypothesis would remain unknown to the academic and scientific community. Carolyn hoped she could get her mother to change her mind before someone else solved it. Overall, though, she didn't think her father had given much thought to winning a Nobel Prize. His satisfaction had been finding the solution to the problem.

She stared at the files on the corner of Brad's desk. "Are you going to assign me all those? If so, I should get right on them."

"Nah," Brad told her. "I'll go light on you for a while. When do you see the doctor again? The past six weeks have been pretty dry. I didn't nurse you all this time for nothing."

"Asshole," Carolyn said, picking up her crutches and heading toward the door.

"That's my girl," Brad said, smiling.

AUTHOR'S NOTE

The past year has given me a wide range of experience. My beautiful mother passed away. A new grandchild was born, precious Elle Laverne. I was remarried. My new husband, Dan, and his delightful daughter, Christina, are now a part of my extended family.

During the time I was writing this novel, I also underwent major surgery on my back. My oldest son, Forrest Blake, set aside his own work to lend a hand to his mother. Without his help, I know I wouldn't have been able to deliver this book on time. I'm now completely healed, and hard at work on my next novel.

I would also like to thank my best friend and physical therapist, Heather Ehrlick, who came to visit me every day in the hospital as well as when I arrived home.

Many thanks to the entire staff at Kensington Books: my fabulous editor and friend, Michaela Hamilton, who always pushes me to go the extra mile; my publisher, Laurie Parkin; and of course, Steve Zacharius and Walter Zacharius. My agent, Arthur Klebanoff, for his efforts to organize and advance my career. My great family: my husband, Dan, who slept in the hospital beside me; Forrest, Jeannie, and Rachel; Hoyt, Barbara, Remy, Taylor, and Elle; Chessly, Jim, Jimmy, and Christian; Christina; Nancy Beth, Amy, and Mike, plus baby to come. To my sisters and brothers: Sharon and Jerry, Linda and John, and Bill and Jean; also my nephews, Nick, Mark, and Ryan.

Turn the page to read an excerpt from Nancy Taylor Rosenberg's next thriller featuring Ventura County probation officer Carolyn Sullivan—

SULLIVAN'S EVIDENCE

Coming from Kensington hardcover in May 2006!

As the sun disappeared and darkness fell, death lurked in the shadows. Outside, the winds were howling, causing the shutters in the cramped living room to rattle.

Eleanor Beckworth headed to the bedroom to change into her nightclothes. Even when she wore her slippers, the cold hardwood floors chafed her feet. She was a petite woman. Her weight had never risen over one hundred and twenty pounds. When she was younger, she had stood almost five feet four inches tall, but now she was barely five feet. Age had not only shriveled her skin, it had compressed her spine.

Eleanor stopped walking, sensing something. The atmosphere in the room felt different. Was it a change in the barometric pressure? Maybe the storm they were predicting for tomorrow was moving in early. She hoped not, as her roof was badly in need of repair and the boiler was acting up again. Reluctantly, she had called her handyman, Mitch, today. She had space heaters, but she knew they weren't always safe, and she was terrified of fire. Maybe Mitch could patch the roof like he'd done the year before.

Eleanor tried to live on the money she received from Social Security, which was barely enough to pay the mortgage and buy groceries. She had twenty thousand in her savings account and a modest amount of equity in her house. She had pulled out most of the money over the years, but she wanted to leave something for her granddaughter when she died.

Glancing at Elizabeth's pictures lined up on the walls in

the hall, she touched her finger to her lip and then pressed it against her granddaughter's face. She'd raised the girl from the age of three after her daughter, Anna, had been killed in a traffic accident. Since she hadn't married the child's father, the young man had left town, never to be heard from again. Eleanor gladly served as Elizabeth's mother.

Elizabeth was such a darling girl, Eleanor thought, but terribly unlucky when it came to men. Her granddaughter had dated one young man for five years, letting him live with her in her apartment. The man had never contributed a dime, worked only a day or two a week, and refused to commit to a permanent relationship. Elizabeth had finally had no choice but to toss the freeloader out. Her little heart had been shattered.

Men living off women, Eleanor thought in disgust. She remembered the days when a man opened your car door, took you out for a nice dinner, and treated you like a lady. They didn't swoop down like vultures on lonely women, use them like prostitutes, and then take off as soon as they got bored or decided there was nothing more they could take.

"Oh, well," she said, entering the bathroom. She hung her clothes on a hook so she could wear them the next day, and quickly stepped into her blue flannel nightgown. Once she had removed her dentures and was bundled up in her bathrobe, Eleanor performed her nightly rituals. She checked to make certain all the doors and windows were locked. She watered the plants on a ledge above the kitchen sink, then poured out the pills she took every night and placed them inside a plastic lid.

Eleanor had always thought her granddaughter would marry and live close by. She glanced at the clock and wondered why she hadn't called yet. They spoke on the phone once a week, and Sunday was her night to call. She rarely phoned Elizabeth, as the girl sometimes talked for hours. Eleanor couldn't afford to run up her bill calling California, where she now lived. Elizabeth must have lost track of time. She was a computer technician and worked out of her home.

When the phone rang, Eleanor rushed over and grabbed it. "Is that you, darling?" she said. "I was worried I wasn't going to hear from you tonight."

"I'm sorry I didn't call you earlier, Mom," her granddaughter said. Since childhood, she had called Eleanor "Mother." "Matt and I had a terrible fight."

"Oh, my," Eleanor said, "I thought your marriage was working out wonderfully."

"So did I," she said, her voice cracking with emotion. "Matt's not the man I thought I married, Mother."

"Dear, dear," Eleanor said, taking a seat on a stool beside the phone, saddened by what she was hearing. "Maybe you've been on your computer too much and not paying him enough attention. A man needs to be doted on, honey. I'm sure you'll work things out. Where's Matt now?"

"I don't know," Elizabeth told her. "He got so angry. I've never seen him that mad. He's been stomping around here all day. About an hour ago, he left without telling me where he was going."

"It might make him even angrier if he hears us talking. What goes on in a marriage should remain between a husband and wife. No man wants people poking around in his private affairs."

"You're right," her granddaughter said, sighing. "I'm sorry I said anything." She paused and then whispered, "I think I hear Matt now. I'll call you next week."

"I love you," Eleanor told her, hating to end the call so abruptly.

"I love you, too, Mom."

Eleanor was asleep when she heard a noise. Glancing at the clock on the table by the bed, she saw that it was a few minutes past five in the morning. She was certain it was the garbage truck, but she decided to check. Putting on her robe and slippers, she made it halfway down the hall when she saw a large dark figure standing in front of her. "Get out of here!" she shrieked, her hand over her chest. "I have a gun. If you don't leave, I'll shoot you."

When she turned to run back to the bedroom to call the police, the person grabbed her by the back of the neck, then released her. She fell face first onto the wood floor. The man was on top of her, his hot breath in her ear. "My purse is in the kitchen," she panted, pain shooting through her left hip. "There's cash . . . take it . . . you can buy drugs with it."

"Drugs, huh?" the man said, wrenching her arms behind her. "I don't need drugs. Killing is a natural high. Are you afraid to die? You should be."

He rolled off her and yanked her to her feet. She sank against his arm, unable to stand. "I think my hip is broken," Eleanor said, moaning. Breaking a hip at her age was worse than a heart attack. If she couldn't care for herself, she would have to go into a nursing home. "I'll never walk again, you evil man," she spat at him. "God is going to strike you dead."

"Really?" he said, grabbing a handful of her hair and pulling her along behind him. "If there was a God, he would have struck me dead already. The things I've done, the things I've gotten away with. Shit, killing an old woman like you is like swatting a fly."

When they reached the bedroom, he picked her up and tossed her on the bed. Eleanor made a frantic move to grab the phone, when the man ripped it from the wall. The phone tumbled to the floor with a loud thud. She saw the awful man wrapping the phone cord around his wrist, and scooted up close to the headboard to get away from him. "Oh no, please!" she pleaded. "Help me! Please have mercy on me!"

He squared off his shoulders and faced her, the seconds ticking off inside her head. Through a crack in the blinds, a beam of light from a passing car struck his face. "You!" Eleanor shouted, her body shaking in terror and outrage. "For the love of heaven, it can't be you!"

The man circled to the side of the bed, leaping on top of the mattress behind her and planting his feet on either side. "Your eyesight is pretty good," he said, wrapping the cord around her neck. "Too good."

He twisted the cord in his hands, watching as it cut into the crinkly skin on Eleanor's neck. Placing his foot on her collar bone, he extended his leg, pushing her toward the foot of the bed until she began to struggle. "Sorry you're not happy to see me," he said. "I'm the last person you'll ever see. Don't blame yourself. I was going to kill you even if you didn't recognize me."

Eleanor tried to scream but she couldn't. There was no air. Her body buckled and her eyes felt as if they were going to burst out of their sockets.

"Just relax, old girl. It'll be over in a few minutes. All you're going to do is take a long nap." The attacker stood, the muscles in his leg shaking from exertion until Eleanor's body became limp and lifeless. He stared down at her, wiping his mouth with the back of his hand. Once he was certain she was dead, he wrapped the cord around the bedpost and tied it into a knot. His victim's head dangled several inches off the pillow.

Jumping off the bed, he tossed the electric blanket over the body, turned on the bedside lamp, and began rummaging through Eleanor Beckworth's drawers and closets.

When You Visit Our Website:
www.kensingtonbooks.com
You Can Save 30% Off The Retail Price
Of Any Book You Purchase!

- **All Your Favorite Kensington Authors**
- **New Releases & Timeless Classics**
- **Overnight Shipping Available**
- **All Major Credit Cards Accepted**

Visit Us Today To Start Saving!
www.kensingtonbooks.com

All Orders Are Subject To Availability.
Shipping and Handling Charges Apply.